PALADIN UNBOUND

Jeffrey Speight

Literary Wanderlust | Denver, Colorado

Published in the United States by Literary Wanderlust LLC Denver, Colorado.

www.LiteraryWanderlust.com

ISBN Print: 978-1-942856-76-4
ISBN Digital: 978-1-942856-86-3

Cover illustration: Ömer Burak Önal
Map illustration: Thomas Rey

Printed in the United States of America

PALADIN UNBOUND
AN ARCHIVES OF EVELIUM TALE

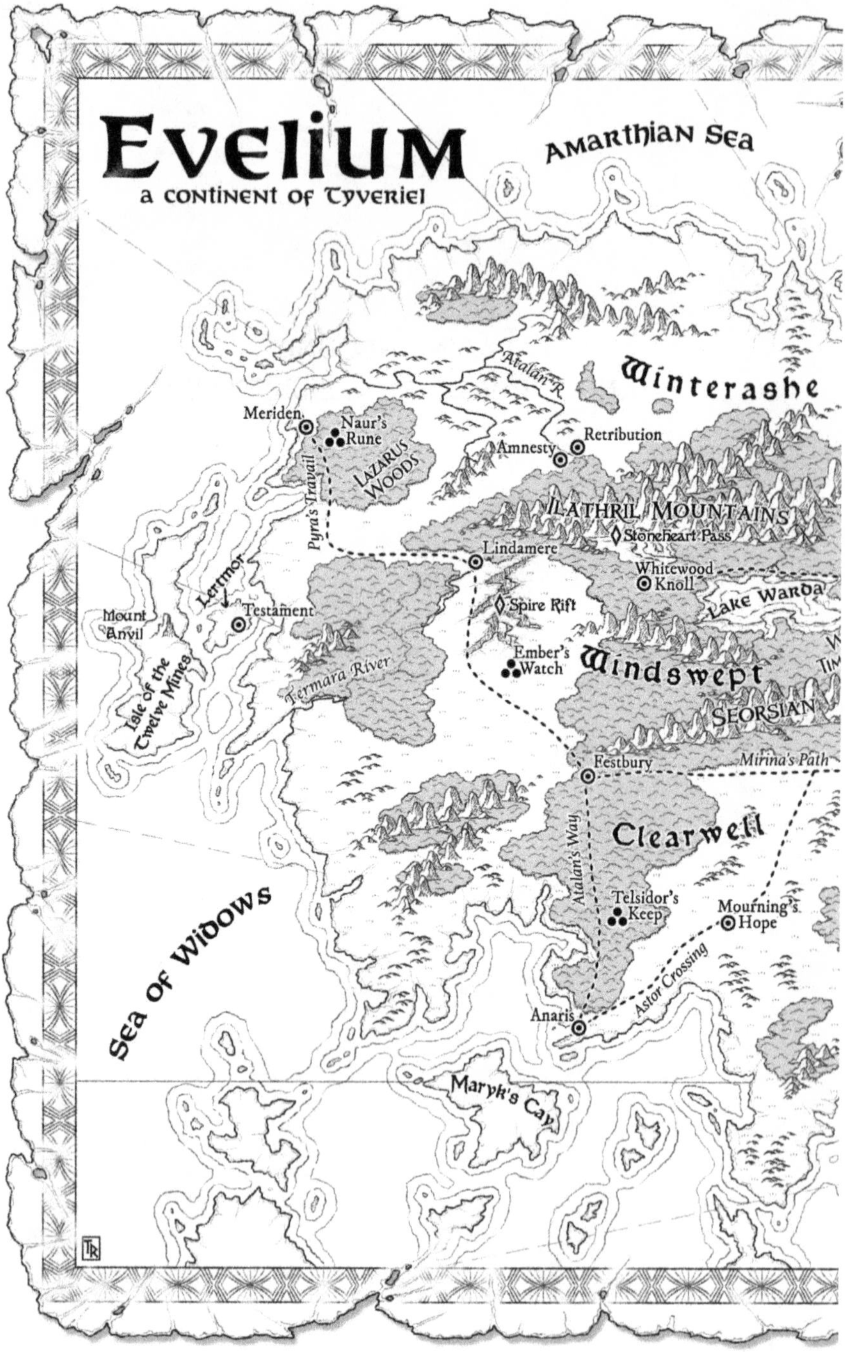
Evelium
a continent of Tyveriel
Amarthian Sea
Winterashe
Atalan R.
Meriden
Naur's Rune
Lazarus Woods
Pyra's Travail
Amnesty
Retribution
Ilathril Mountains
Stoneheart Pass
Lindamere
Whitewood Knoll
Lake Warda
Spire Rift
Ember's Watch
Windswept
Seorsian
Lertmor
Testament
Mount Anvil
Isle of the Twelve Mines
Fermara River
Festbury
Mirina's Path
Clearwell
Atalan's Way
Telsidor's Keep
Mourning's Hope
Astor Crossing
Anaris
Sea of Widows
Maryk's Cay

Oda Norde
The Bite
Nolk
Dun Uk
Ohteira
Goshur Uk
Tribulation
Travesty
Orrat Skag
Requiem
Spara's Trail
Wicked Pass
Morion Swamp
Besik Uk
Vanyareign
Wolfcamp
Wistful
Berlands
Burning Wood
Mountains
Tayrelis
Antiikin
Dire Swamp
Willow's Notch
Englen Penn Way
River Torrent
Farathyr
Triun
Hylara
Gurtharian Ocean

DEDICATION

To Wyatt, Owen, and Henry
Without you I probably would never have started writing this book, but would have finished it a year earlier once I did.

PRΦLΦGUE

...and from the Age of Chaos arose a true King of Men who restored order to Evelium.

—The Gatekeepers' Abridged History of Tyveriel
Vol. 2, Chapter 34 – Unearthed from the Ruins of Meriden, the month of Ocken, 1240 AT

—▲—

The demon-god staggered through the dense woods, his form much diminished, his power drained after a century-long battle. His legions destroyed, he sensed the others hidden in the woods—those he had so fully betrayed were closing in. There was yet one chance at salvation, albeit a despairing one.

Dropping to his knees, he broke the soil, tearing at root and rock—his claws splintering. His amethyst-colored skin was singed and torn, and one of his gnarled horns was broken off at its base. His hunched posture was reminiscent more of a feral beast than an esteemed god of Tyveriel. Stretching his sinuous arms deep into the hole, he closed his vermillion eyes and murmured an incantation in a dying tongue into the rich earth. His failure ensured the language would soon be forgotten in all but the deepest recesses of the realm that should have been his alone.

Within the hole, a red glow emanated from his hands, the ether slipping between his aching claws. As the radiance dissipated, a slab of pure rhodium materialized. Upon the metal slab he had engraved runes in the language of the gods:

From Pragarus I shall return
And all of Evelium shall burn
The blood of twelve thousand souls ensnared
Only the loyal few be spared
I shall ascend to my rightful place
Delivering our world from its fall from Grace
To thee who delivers me from hell
Your eternal thirst, I shall quell

In a frenzy, he buried the tablet and pried a large boulder from the earth beside him, capping his treasure. His inevitable salvation now secured, he stood and pressed on through the lush woods, tree limb after tree limb lashing him as he ran.

"Naur," a woman's voice seethed from the edge of the clearing through which he clambered, "this must end now, brother." Vaila emerged from the shade of the tree line, her graceful form glowing in the early morning sun. Black hair draped flawlessly across the light-blue skin of her shoulders, her gown radiating celestial energy of its own.

She carried a great sword in each hand, their hilts fashioned into angels with outstretched wings extending up the base of the gleaming blades. She strode forward, two more gods—one with a body of stone and the head of a great elk, the other a midnight blue winged-serpent—approaching Naur from behind.

"Vaila, you do not realize how completely you have failed this world," Naur said, holding his fists out before him and summoning a flaming battle ax in each. His brothers behind him dropped into a defensive crouch, but Vaila continued forward, undeterred. "Instead of embracing their flaws and appealing to their strengths, you strive to control the mortal races and sculpt them into something they are not. I wish only to allow them to be themselves and fulfill our promise to them."

"You seek total dominion, Naur," Vaila said. "Don't fool yourself into thinking your actions have come with their best interests at heart, that you fight us out of altruism. You don't care for the mortals. Instead, you would exploit their greatest weakness, so you alone can rule over them for eternity. Your game ends now, brother, but only you can determine how. Whether it be in your death, or your banishment to Pragarus, makes no difference to us."

Her words urged Brinthor and Kemyn forward. Naur glanced back at his brothers and sneered. His lips curling, venom dripped from a mouthful of fangs down his chin. Brinthor and Kemyn dismissed the poisonous warning and closed in on their brother's flank.

Naur spun and embedded both of his axes into Brinthor's lithe form. The great winged serpent screeched in pain. As Brinthor recoiled, Vaila plunged one of her swords into Naur's back, below his right shoulder blade. Without wincing, Naur turned toward Kemyn and readied his next attack. Kemyn stood his ground, his hands glowing red, as though made of magma, flowing into the forms of two stone spikes. Naur tore his axes from Brinthor's body and lunged. Kemyn parried Naur's attack with one of the spikes and thrust the other into Naur's abdomen. Kemyn broke the extremity off within the wound, leaving himself temporarily hobbled.

With this blow, Naur, the God of Fire, fell to his knees and laughed—his lifeblood flowing to the forest floor, withering the flora beneath him. Vaila stepped closer, now looming over him, her form blocking out the sun. He spat at her gown, covering her in blood and black venom before her inner light once again shone through.

"You have won," Naur said, his tone still growling with confrontation. "Do what you will with this failure of yours. Do what you will with me, your scourge."

"End him," Kemyn said. "He deserves worse, but death will rid us of his antics once and for all."

Vaila shook her head.

Kemyn rushed forward and thrust his remaining sharpened hand at Naur's head, but Vaila raised her free hand and froze Kemyn in place, the tip of his weapon inches from dealing a finishing blow.

"No, Kemyn. I cannot allow you to kill him," she said. "Naur, as punishment for your transgressions, your deceit, you shall be bound to Pragarus for all of eternity. There, you shall fester, knowing Tyveriel goes on without you. You shall be forgotten in the annals of history, relegated to the stature of a lesser deity, and then by only the most disparate recesses of the culture that flourishes in your absence."

"Sister," Brinthor hissed, "as always, I appreciate your sense of loyalty and justice, but this time you go too far. An honorable death is more than we owe him, and the cost of binding him to Pragarus is too great."

"I understand the cost all too well. The time has come for us to leave this plane and allow our creation to build its own future. Find its own path. We have wandered these lands since the dawn of time and waged war upon it for the last millennium. Tyveriel needs time to heal. It needs a new beginning. It no longer needs our interference." She paused. "Honestly, I am tired. This war has taken too much from me. We shall recede to the tranquility of Kalmindon and grant this realm its freedom."

Vaila finished speaking and thrust her second sword into Naur's chest, forming an inverted triangle with his other two wounds. She impelled the blade through him to its hilt, Naur's blood drenching the earth. Vaila released her sword and Naur's back arched up toward the heavens in pain, his head bending backward until it touched the ground. The three wounds burned with a pure white light that grew in intensity until climaxing at a level blinding to a mortal's eye.

Beneath Naur, a great portal opened. Within the swirling

vortex appeared the vision of an arid wasteland. He fought the power of the portal, forcing himself onto his hands and knees and peered into the abyss. Accepting his fate, his gaze darted to his sister, whose lips trembled as tears streaked her face. "Worry not, sister," he said, engulfed in the purple aura of the portal. "You only do what you think is right. You always do. Do not weep for me, and remember that, for immortals, even eternity is temporary. We shall see each other again."

▲

The portal collapsed inward upon itself with a blast of energy, taking Naur with it and leaving Vaila, Kemyn, and Brinthor alone in the quiet of the clearing. "Brothers, our war is over," Vaila said, releasing Kemyn from her spell. "We have saved Tyveriel, and now must turn our backs on it and return to Kalmindon." A tear shimmering with the purity of a flawless diamond ran down her face.

Kemyn fell to his knees and glared at Vaila, anger swelling within him. "I choose to remain in Tyveriel," he said, pounding his spear like hand into the ground. "I love this wild land too much to return to the sanctity of the heavens. Kalmindon, in all its perfection, holds no salvation for me."

"I shall stay as well," Brinthor said, a sheepish expression coming over his face.

This was one blow too many, and Vaila cried freely. "Brothers, you know turning away from Kalmindon will strand you on this plane for all of eternity, but with only a remnant of your godly powers. I plead you reconsider and join me in ascension."

"We well know the price of our decision," Kemyn said. He climbed to his feet and pointed his unbroken spike at Vaila, shaking it in contempt. "You are the one who did not consider everything when you opted to spare Naur. Return to your heaven, your precious Kalmindon. We choose the mortal plane."

"If this is your wish, I shall abide by it," Vaila said. "Just know all I did was in my best judgment for us and Tyveriel.

Harbor no ill will against me for my shortcomings. I hope you will miss me as much as I will miss my beloved brothers. Today, I have lost three."

"We shall miss you, Vaila, but this is where our paths diverge. Our best to you, sister," Kemyn said, softening his tone.

Vaila shut her eyes and smoothed her long hair behind her shoulders. She placed her hands together and faded from sight. Their sister having returned to her endless paradise, Kemyn and Brinthor shifted their physical forms. Kemyn assumed the form of a majestic elk, and Brinthor changed into a blue dragon. They looked at one another, Kemyn grunting, no longer able to communicate with his brother. Brinthor raised his head and released an earth-shattering roar. With two thrusts of his great reptilian wings, he lifted off the ground and disappeared into the cloud-filled sky.

Kemyn scratched the earth with his hoof and sniffed at the air. After a moment, he leaped into the forest and disappeared into the wilderness he so loved.

CHAPTER 1

Upon Mount Orys, he declared his dominion over man and beast, alike.

—The Gatekeepers' Abridged History of Tyveriel
Vol. 3, Chapter 5. Discovered in the Private Library of Solana Marwyn, the month of Vasa, 889 AT

—▲—

Candlelit Tavern was a raucous watering hole on its best of nights, and this was not one of those. Umhra the Peacebreaker slouched on a stool too small for his hulking form, fiddling with a blue velvet pouch he wore on his belt, as he watched his five comrades—members of his mercenary crew, the Bloodbound—celebrate their arrival in the City of Anaris. Having traveled from the town of Ohteira with hardly a rest, the Bloodbound was well into their eighth round of Barnswallow's Sowing Moon Ale and had turned to intimidating and insulting the other patrons for drunken entertainment.

Umhra had too much on his mind to partake in such levity. His strong brow furrowed. There would be much competition in securing Lord Espen Morrow's contract—The Bloodbound's reason for the exhausting journey. Morrow's reputation was beyond reproach and could provide the much-needed work his men, who did not share Umhra's strong moral compass, needed. No doubt the odds of success were slim. Several groups of mercenaries had also descended upon the city with similar aspirations of obtaining the contract and each had the distinct advantage of not being half-Orcs.

Leaning forward, his elbows on his knees, a few strands of black hair fell from his unkempt ponytail and dangled in front of his face. He worried his lip around two oversized canine teeth protruding from his lower jaw, and his green-gray fingers ran over the rough surface of his tankard of beer. He surveyed the crowd.

Umhra dropped his head, stared at the floor, and considered how he'd make his case before Lord Morrow. His team marched for nearly a month in pursuit of this opportunity and would, no doubt, be disappointed if all they had to show for their effort was the dried mud that cracked and crumbled from their leathers. The trip had been taxing, the Bloodbound having marched off the main roads to avoid human travelers and the king's guard who might object to a group of armed half-Orcs and delay their arrival.

Umhra kept the bedlam his crew created at a distance, preferring to sit alone. Having spent all of his formative years at the Trinity Temple in Travesty, Umhra was a quiet soul, more comfortable around monks and clerics than this drunken mob.

Despite the distance between him and the fray, his heart raced and his throat closed. Groups of humans, Iminti, and Zeristar, bantered loudly, their spirited conversations spilling over into occasional scuffles as they drank. His men reveled in the chaos, the crowd tolerating the half-Orcs among them—an unusual act—but all the same, Umhra's anxiety swelled.

A man, roughly the size of an eight-year-old human child, danced on a nearby table. His brown tousled hair dripped with sweat, and his once properly-fitted red velvet vest, white linen shirt, and natural leather pants were soaked through and too large on his gaunt frame. He danced with abandon, his ale splashing about the room. Umhra smiled at how reckless and carefree the man jigged. The other patrons gathered around him, forgetting their petty squabbles, and clapped along with the music. The minstrel sped up as if proposing a challenge. Those surrounding the Farestere man roared with approval at the spontaneous entertainment.

"All right, boys," Umhra bellowed, rising from his stool against the wall, "it's time to turn in."

"But Umhra." His lieutenant, Drog the Mancleaver, protested, always the crew's best advocate. "After such a journey, surely you can grant the men a few more moments of levity."

The plea still fresh in Umhra's ears, Thurg the Earsplitter grabbed the Farestere man by the leg and tossed him across the room with a disapproving grunt. The music screeched to a halt and the crowd turned its attention to the half-Orcs. A group of battle-hardened Zeristar, short in stature but broad-shouldered, stood from their seats and stepped over the slight man who lay tangled beneath their table.

"Oy, Orc scum," the foremost of the Zeristar said, scratching his ginger beard with one hand and drawing a silver battle ax over his shoulder with the other. "Is this how you pay us back for letting you stink up our tavern all night?"

Thurg turned to the Zeristar and spit at his feet.

"I think it best we go," Umhra said, sliding past Drog and coming between Thurg and the flushed Zeristar.

Umhra held his arms out, one palm on Thurg's chest, the other facing the Zeristar. "Outside. Now."

Thurg swallowed the rest of his ale and slammed his tankard down on a nearby table. He shoved his way through the crowd, and the rest of the Bloodbound followed.

"He's obviously taken the liberty of one too many tonight," Umhra said, shifting his attention to the Zeristar. "Please accept my apology."

"Anaris has no use of your kind," the Zeristar said. "You'd be well advised to not cross our path again."

Umhra nodded, turned to the barkeep, and tossed him a silver quarter sovereign for his trouble. He followed after his crew, taking a glance over his shoulder at the Zeristar, who had returned to their tankards in celebration.

Umhra threw the door open, a rush of cold air hitting his face, and stepped out into the Anaris night. He found his drunken gang a few doors down. They surrounded a young Evenese woman, her back forced up against the rough wooden façade of the building, her fear-widened eyes darting between the slobbering half-Orcs. Umhra drew his men off with a whistle. The woman ran away down the street in the opposite direction and the Bloodbound trudged toward the camp they'd set up in a patch of woods just outside the city's east gate. The night was cold, despite it being well into the planting season. The crisp air revived Umhra's senses, after the stale, humid warmth of the tavern.

"I'll take first watch," Umhra said, as they walked beneath the arch of the city gate. "You men sleep off that Farestere ale. Drog and I will be heading back into Anaris in the morning to make our case before Lord Morrow. I hope we'll have work shortly." It had been some time since they'd put metal to flesh, and they were all too ready to jump back into the fray. Umhra grimaced, waved them off, and the Bloodbound stumbled about in a drunken effort to ready their camp for the night.

As the men slept, Umhra sat beside the dwindling fire, eating a bit of rabbit leftover from their midday meal. His thoughts wandered to his father—as they often did when he wasn't sure of the path forward. It seemed a lifetime since his father had been slaughtered at the hands of the Tukdari horde that swept through his village all those years ago.

"Sorry to bother you, Umhra," Gori said, taking a seat beside him at the fire, "I was having trouble sleeping, so I figured I might as well keep watch with you."

"Not a bother, Gori. Is there something on your mind that

keeps you up?"

"Nothing specific. My mind just races at times."

"I know that feeling all too well. You are welcome to join me."

"Thank you." Gori warmed his hands. "Were you in the middle of something? You seemed pensive."

"No, I was just thinking about my father."

"You've never spoken of family before. Is he still with us?"

"No, I was four when our village in Orrat Skag was attacked by Tukdari barbarians. My father, Yargol was his name, hid me in the trunk of a dead tree before running out to meet his doom in the form of a goliath's battle-ax. He told me not to make a sound until he returned. I sat, motionless, in the base of this dark tree trunk, listening to the shrill sounds of battle for the first time. I can remember the clang of metal and the sickening crunch of bone. The screams of the stricken and the celebratory chants of the barbarian horde are as fresh in my mind as if their victory were yesterday. The smell of decay, of fire, and burning flesh, are still ripe. As quickly as the barbarians arrived, they left, taking with them the meager amount of wealth and material possessions my Orc clan possessed, as well as every woman they could kidnap, including my mother, Joslin.

"I sat in that tree for days, waiting for my father to come for me, but he never did. Hunger set in and eventually, it drove me from the tree. The worms and centipedes inhabiting its musty, hollow core were not enough to sustain me. I kicked a hole through the rotting wood and was awestruck by the destruction. My village had been razed to the ground and my entire clan slaughtered. Nothing was left but scorched earth and corpses. I found my father's severed head on a pike—a statement to anyone considering reprisal.

"With nothing but the clothes on my back, and the hilt of a broken sword I took from my elder cousin's charred remains, I left Goshur Uk, and made my way west, away from the direction the barbarians traveled. I wandered into areas of Orrat Skag with which I was unfamiliar. The barren landscape, ubiquitous throughout the Orc homeland, offered me little in the way of markers by which I could determine my path. I survived on whatever I was lucky enough to forage and the modicum of dank water the land gave.

"Eventually, I approached the edge of Wicked's Pass. My parents always told me stories about the dangers that resided within that old hemlock forest, and under normal circumstances, I would not have dared enter such a wild place on my own, but the promise of plentiful food and fresh water drove me forward. I traveled by day, unsuccessfully hunting squirrels, rabbits, and birds with a makeshift sling. Before nightfall, I would find an empty burrow or tree trunk and spend the dark hours listening to the sounds of ogres, wolves, and the other wretched creatures that called the forest home.

"One night, under a full moon, an ogre used the burrow in which I was hiding to defecate. As hard as I tried, I could not stay silent and the dumb beast tore into the hole with reckless abandon, sending dirt and feces flying everywhere. I scrambled to escape the ogre's grasp. The beast barreled after me, grabbing me by the ankle and lifting me to its putrid mouth. As it did so, I grabbed the broken hilt and plunged the shard deep into the ogre's neck, severing a major artery. The creature dropped me and clutched its throat. Reeling in pain, the beast took a furious swipe at me, but I rolled just out of reach. With one last howl, the ogre fell to the ground, lifeless.

"I ran. I ran through the night, tripping over brambles and scraping against rocks. By daybreak, I exited the forest and collapsed from exhaustion. It was there that a monk from Travesty happened to stumble across my exhausted body and nursed me back to health in the confines of the temple monastery. He was a loving man by the name of Ivory Lapping, and he raised me as his own child from that day forward."

"That is truly an amazing story," Gori said, his gaze fixed on Umhra. "Did you ever return?"

"No, that life is a distant memory. You men are my family now. There's no need to go back."

Gori nodded. The two men sat together through the first part of the night as a thick fog rolled into the camp. After a few hours, Drog awoke for his shift on watch.

"Glad to see you had some company, Umhra," he said, pouring himself some water from his waterskin.

"Yes, Gori joining me was a pleasant surprise," Umhra said. "But now I must get some sleep." He yawned, patting Gori on the shoulder as he stood. Taking his leave, Umhra went to his bedroll and closed his eyes as Drog threw a log on the fire, sending a plume of embers into the air.

CHAPTER 2

There was little need for faith in the gods, for they had receded and Modig Forene filled the void they left. With mankind's faith split, the magic of old all but disappeared from Tyveriel.

—The Gatekeepers' Abridged History of Tyveriel
Vol. 3, Chapter 2. Discovered at the Private Library of Solana Marwyn, the month of Vasa, 889 AT

—▲—

Umhra arose to the early-morning smell of fox roasting over the roaring fire. He was greeted eagerly by his loyal men, who seemed no worse for wear because of last night's festivities. He brushed the morning dew from his leathers and sat with his men to eat and warm his tired body. As the sun rose through the woods, Umhra stood, still chewing.

"Drog, you and I will head into Anaris for supplies and hopefully some direction regarding Lord Morrow's contract," Umhra said, wiping his face on his sleeve. "He is expected to post his contract today, and I want to be among the first to argue our case for the reward. The rest of you should be prepared to move out at a moment's notice. Weapons readied. Peace made." The men nodded and returned to their breakfasts.

Umhra and Drog gathered their gear and walked back toward Anaris.

"What did you think of that group of Zeristar?" Drog asked as they crossed into the city.

"I didn't take much notice of them, other than to realize they were in no mood for Thurg's antics," Umhra said. "I couldn't allow that to go any further and risk our chance at getting the contract."

"Do you honestly think we have a chance?"

"I don't even know if they will let us into the inner district," Umhra said, hanging his head. "If we can get before Morrow, I'd like to think he would hear us out."

"You give him too much credit, Umhra," Drog said. "I know he's not a Pureblood, but he may as well be with his station. He won't bestow an important contract on the likes of us."

"It's you who don't give us enough credit. We are every bit as capable as any of the other crews here. In fact, I would put us up against any in all of Evelium," Umhra said.

"Yes, but we don't have the right color skin for the job." Drog held out his arms and showed Umhra the olive-green skin that peaked out between his studded bracers and leather cuirass as an unnecessary reminder. "And last I checked, tusks were not a big selling point."

"Maybe you're right, but there are people that can see beyond that. They're just few and far between," Umhra said.

"And they seem to get further between the more money and power they have."

Anaris was waking up. Dew gathered on the thatched rooftops and dripped into puddles at the side of the compacted dirt roads. Dogs lapped at the water and dodged the merchants who shooed them away in preparation to open for business. With broom in hand, a portly shopkeeper threw open the door to his store and performed this ritual with zeal. A particularly disheveled dog spun from the broom's path and crashed into Umhra's strong legs, yelped, and ran off into an adjacent alley.

"Good morning, friend," Umhra said, greeting the shopkeeper.

The white-haired man took a step back. "Good morning, friends. How may I help you fine gentlemen today?" he asked.

"We are travelers looking for honest work. We heard that the Honorable Espen Morrow would require some assistance. Do you know anything about such news?" Umhra asked in as approachable a tone as possible.

"Sorry, friend, I know not of His Lordship's business affairs. I suppose it may have something to do with those that have gone missing over the last few months. But what do I know? I'm a simple man who runs a fine store for outdoorsmen such as yourselves. Can I interest you in a look at my wares?"

Not wanting to be rude, Umhra ducked under the doorway, following the shopkeeper, and entered the tidy little shop while Drog waited outside.

"Gone missing, you say?" Umhra asked.

"Yes, I've only heard rumors and gossip from my customers. I'm best known for my mace craftsmanship, but people come to me for all types of provisions," the man said, encouraging Umhra to handle a fine silver mace. "One of my best pieces yet, if you don't mind me saying."

"I agree," Umhra said, impressed with the quality of work. "Well balanced and absolutely stunning. I have a friend who would very much like this. May I ask how much?"

"Normally, that piece would go for fifty sovereigns, but as a first-time customer, I'm happy to part ways with the mace for forty if you would be so kind as to share your impressions about my work as you travel."

"Most fair," Umhra said, rooting through his money pouch to retrieve the notes.

As he strapped the mace to the side of his satchel, the shopkeeper grasped his arm. Umhra looked up in surprise.

"Friend, be careful what you get yourself into around Anaris. There have been some very strange goings-on around these parts recently. You seem like a good, honest man, and even though we have only known each other for a short time, I would hate to hear of any ill will coming your way," he said, his voice wavering.

Rarely caught off guard, Umhra paused. "Thank you. I appreciate the concern," he said. He placed four ten-sovereign notes on the counter. "And thank you for the mace. I must be on my way."

"Of course. A good day to you."

"And you as well." Umhra excused himself.

Outside, Umhra found Drog waiting near the door of the shop, avoiding eye contact with the passersby that gawked at him as the town awoke. Carts filled with vegetables and other goods rolled past, children played in the street. Umhra placed his hand on Drog's shoulder. "City life isn't so bad, is it?" he asked.

Drog shrugged. "All of this is a bit foreign to me."

The men made their way toward the center of the town, leaving the more mundane stores and homes of the commoner's district behind. Passing through a ring of lush gardens, they entered a district where well-to-do commoners had their homes and businesses.

"Could you ever imagine settling down in a city like this?" Drog asked as they crossed a small stone bridge that spanned the first of two circular canals within the city's walls.

"I'm not sure the city would have us. No matter our reputation or wealth," Umhra said. A woman in a yellow embroidered dress crossed the street in an obvious attempt to avoid them.

Together they walked through the business district, ignoring the disapproving glares and whispers from the wealthy folk in their fine clothes. Approaching another bridge that led to the innermost district of the city, the lord's manor broke into view, its bluestone tower rising above the cluttered horizon.

"Where do you think you are going?" asked a guard in a confrontational tone as Umhra and Drog approached.

"You two surely do not belong here," another guard said.

Crossing their steel pikes to block the path, Umhra sized them up. The men were adorned in shining chain mail armor covered by green tunics with gold lions emblazoned on their chests. Besides the pikes, each man was armed with a shield which matched their tunic, and a finely crafted short sword at their waist. Their helmets were undented, and their boots unsoiled. These men had never seen battle.

Refocusing on his goal, Umhra answered as respectfully as possible. "My guards of Anaris, we come in search of work at the bequest of His Lordship, Espen Morrow. Have you any news?"

Looking down upon the half-Orcs from the apex of the bridge, the first guard replied with a sneer, "I have no news for the likes of you, Orc. I suggest you turn back and relieve your mind of such aspirations as communing with His Lordship."

Now pointing his pike at Umhra, the guard poked at his chest. "Hurry on your way, then."

Drog stepped forward, gripping his ax, but Umhra put his arm out, stopping him.

"As you wish," Umhra said.

Nudging Drog with his elbow, the half-Orcs turned and walked away.

Umhra and Drog found their way back to the Candlelit Tavern, where they ate a small lunch of chicken stew. The tavern was remarkably peaceful when compared to the night before, though unable to rid itself of the smell of stale beer and sweat. Umhra, disgusted with his failure at procuring the contract, hung his head. Seeing Drog's morale fade, he snapped himself out of his self-pity.

"If not this contract, then the next," Umhra said, breaking the silence.

"Of course," Drog said.

"I was hoping we would at least get to make our case before Morrow." Umhra shook his head.

The tavern door swung open, the ring of its chimes

interrupting their conversation. A Farestere man walked in and marched directly to a post in the center of the room. He unfurled a small leaflet and nailed it to the post and left as briskly as he entered.

Umhra walked over to get a closer look. The leaflet was absurdly low for a man of his stature. Trying to crouch down to read the note, he huffed and tore it from the post. As he straightened himself, he read:

By the Will of His Lordship Espen Morrow
Anaris is in need of a hero
Any who deems himself worthy should present his case to the Lord directly
At Town Hall this day at high sun

A smile cracked Umhra's sullen façade. High sun was less than an hour away. Surely there would not be too much competition on such short notice.

"Time to give getting an audience with Lord Morrow another try, mate," he said, sliding the now disheveled paper across the table as he sat down. Drog read and nodded in agreement.

"The note clearly says 'Any,'" Drog said. "Maybe this is the key to getting before Morrow. Should we go back and get the others, and show our true strength?"

"I think it best that just you and I go. After last night, the town knows there are six of us about. No need to attract further attention. Morrow might just appreciate us being tactful in such a manner," Umhra said.

"But, why should we hide our numbers? Are we not to look as strong as possible to win the contract?" Drog asked.

"No," Umhra said, after a moment of contemplation. "If we all go before Lord Morrow and his council, I think we risk scaring them off and we'll only lessen our chances of success. Someday, those of us willing to risk our lives for the meek will be paid the respect we are due regardless of race. Today is not that day."

Drog nodded. "When shall these days end?" He asked.

"Not soon enough."

Reaching across the table and putting his hand on Drog's shoulder, Umhra offered some solace. "Through our actions, not our lineage, do we achieve greatness. Let's go and win this contract and have the Bloodbound be known as great champions of Anaris."

They stood and paid for their meal. Leaving the tavern, Umhra allowed himself to wonder if the guards would let them pass into the central districts of the city. He hoped their possession of the note would be enough to gain them access.

Returning to the inner bridge, Umhra's heart raced in anticipation of once again confronting the guards who had dismissed him earlier. When he did not recognize the two guards now standing watch, he sighed in relief and approached without hesitation.

"Good day gentle guards of Anaris," he greeted the two men who crossed their pikes upon seeing the two half-Orcs approach. "We seek an audience with His Lordship Espen Morrow regarding his charge." Umhra held the paper up for the guards to see. Without making a sound, or even a cursory glance, the guards raised their pikes, and Umhra and Drog passed into the innermost ring of Anaris.

The inner district was truly a sight to behold for two half-Orcs who had spent precious little time in such refined settings. Like the business district, the streets were paved with cobblestones rather than dirt, but here the architecture was more ornate, with slate roofs replacing wood on the large bluestone buildings that were ubiquitous throughout. The people were dressed in aristocratic clothes and greeted each other with pleasantries as they passed on the streets. The shops were bustling and the gardens teemed with exotic plantings from all over Evelium.

Entering the very center of Anaris, the immense town hall and lord's manor became visible. The complex was a collection of large bluestone buildings with spires at each corner, archers keeping watch on the parapets high above. Other guards armed with pikes and short swords patrolled the property on both sides of the eight-foot-high bluestone wall that enclosed it and the lord's manor. With only one entrance at the south, the compound was secure.

"Drog, we have never aimed so high for a contract," Umhra acknowledged. "We will be making our case before Lord Morrow and his wife who is the king's sister, and likely several other members of Anaris's council. We are already at a disadvantage, so we must be convincing that we are a decidedly better alternative to all of the other options."

"I have faith in you Umhra," Drog replied.

CHAPTER 3

Mesorith lay slain, the last of his kind. It was I who tamed these wild lands so that Evelium could once again belong to man.

—Telsidor's Missives
Diary entry dated 8th of Riet, 6 AF. Unearthed from the Ruins of Anaris, month of Emin, 1156 AT

—▲—

Grand Master Evron Alabaster stood upon the pedestal overlooking the large square room that was the inner sanctum of the Brothers of Resurrection. Torches cast the rough-hewn sandstone walls in an uneven light from the pillars upon which they were mounted. The large circular pit at the center of the room lay empty awaiting the contents of several barrels lining the far wall. Everything was in order.

Evron inhaled, breathing in the stale, damp air of the underground sanctum, and gripped the metallic rune on the podium before him in both hands. It glowed red, underlighting him so his fair Evenese skin was colored to match his hooded cloak.

A solitary door, off to his right, ground open—thirty figures in black robes with red inverted crosses on the chest entering the room in a single column and encircling the circular pit. They clasped hands and bowed their hooded heads.

Evron raised his hands in the air. "Brothers, we gather here on this hallowed day to begin the feeding of our portal to Pragarus. Naur has wallowed long enough in its hells and demands that we return him to Tyveriel so he may assume his rightful place as our god-king."

The brothers began to chant, the monotonous chorus echoing through the sanctum.

Evron placed his hands back on either side of Naur's ancient rune. He stared down at its message—engraved in the long since forgotten hieroglyphs of the gods—and smiled. "Please bring forth our first offering to the portal."

Within the circle at the opposite edge of the pit, four men removed the top from a large wooden barrel, exposing the dark liquid within. With the chanting urging them on, the men tipped the barrel toward the pit and spilled its contents upon the dry, stone floor below, releasing a ferrous odor into the room. Evron clasped his hands, putting an end to the chanting.

"Nearly two millennia ago, Naur planted this rune here beneath the Lazarus Woods, pleading for salvation. With this first contribution to the Portal of Pragarus, we have taken an important step to realize our god's prophecy," he said. "Once the blood of twelve thousand souls fills the pit and the Reaping Moon reaches its peak, the portal shall open and Naur will take his rightful place as the uncontested ruler of Evelium and all of Tyveriel." The brothers cheered and Evron raised his hands to quiet them. "Now is not a time of celebration, however, but rather a time to double our efforts, to sharpen our focus, to spread our influence throughout every town in Evelium. Through only our selfless efforts can the world be saved from the decadence of the Forenian Age. Through only our success may it be recast according to Naur's vision."

His words were met with a unified shout of support. Then silence. Then the chant resumed. The Brothers of Resurrection released each other's hands and stepped back from the precipice of the pit. Barrel after barrel arrived at the pit's edge, their tops removed, and sanguineous contents poured within. As the blood covered the floor of the pit in its entirety, evenly spaced vents in the stone floor released air, causing the fluid to bubble as if in a slow, preternatural boil.

"Now go forth, blend in among the masses, and harvest the vital fluids our god requires to end his banishment in the hells of Pragarus. Be careful and let no one know our purpose. By Naur's will."

"By Naur's will," the brothers said in unison.

The sole entrance to the sanctum unlocked with the sound of metal grating against stone revealing the adjoining sanctuary. The brothers filed out of the sanctum, each taking a turn to bow in reverence as they passed the pedestal where the glowing rune sat.

Evron was last to leave the inner sanctum, having remained behind in prayer. After the rest of the group left the sanctuary he walked over and stood in front of a large statue of Naur in the very center of the large, oval room. Evron removed his hood and tied his long blond hair into a single plait. He stared at the demon-god's sinuous form. The gnarled horns, the mouth with fangs bared, the razor-sharp claws on his hands and feet, and the tattered wings were all just as *The Tome of Mystics* had described. Where others saw fear in this image, Evron Alabaster saw beauty and the promise of a new future.

"For generations, we have dedicated ourselves to decoding your rune. Now that we have unlocked the secrets of your return, all has been set in motion. I trust our devotion shall be rewarded. I hope you are proud of the following we have prepared for you." He bowed solemnly, raised his hood, and left the room through another door, which emptied into a large, sparsely-lit tunnel, where a lone chestnut horse waited for him in a side room fashioned into a stable. The ride back to Meriden would take nearly two hours at a healthy trot. Evron did not mind, however, as the trip gave him time to think of all that yet needed to be done to ensure the resurrection of Naur. Everything was in place, but so much still hung in the balance.

He rode through the tunnel his forefathers had labored to construct over the ages, thinking as he did of the efforts the brotherhood made to keep their sanctuary and Naur's Rune hidden from the rest of Evelium. He breathed deeply, cherishing the damp, musty air that hung within the passage, which he had grown to prefer to the fresh air above. Leaving the sanctuary to resume his mundane duties in Meriden always left him feeling hollow. The sanctuary had become his one true home.

At the end of the tunnel, there was another subterranean stable and beyond it a heavy reinforced oak door. He dismounted from his horse and led it into the final empty stall with a pat on its left shoulder. He then walked to the other side of the room, removed his robe, folded it neatly, and placed it in an iron chest along the wall. He walked out of the door, carefully closing it behind him, and emerged in the basement of the Meriden Gatekeepers' lodge.

"Good evening, Grand Master. I trust your return trip was uneventful." A slight, ebony-haired man greeted him from a desk at the center of the room. There was Evenese in his lineage, as witnessed by his angular face and fair skin, but he was not Pureblood.

"Quite, brother. Any news?" Evron poured himself a glass of wine from a decanter sitting at the center of a sturdy rectangular table along the wall to the right of the door through which he'd entered.

"We received word from Master Manteis that he has sent another shipment north," the man said, flashing a proud smile.

"He is most prolific. What a pleasant surprise he has been," Evron praised, swirling the deep-red wine in his glass before savoring his first taste. "See to it I am notified when each shipment arrives. I would like to personally oversee their delivery to the temple."

"As you wish, Grand Master. Will you be joining the others upstairs this evening? Lore Keeper Scarth is expected to be in attendance after supper."

"I suppose I should." Evron sighed. "We cannot have Lore Keeper Scarth getting bored and finding his way to the basement."

"I should think not, Grand Master. With so much at stake, it would be a travesty for him to become aware of what is going on right under his nose." The man scoffed.

"He would find his way to being one of the twelve thousand bloody souls, should he." Evron paused. "With any luck, he may count himself among them, regardless, before this is all over. I do not know if he is as insensible as he lets on, or if he knows better than to interfere in the true business of the Gatekeepers and chooses to continue his involvement in the Order for political favor," Evron said as he ambled to the stairs at the far side of the room.

He paused, took a moment to assure himself that he was presentable. He ran his hands over his hair and inspected his fine embroidered green coat. Satisfied that all was in order, he made his way up to the lodge which was already humming with activity.

The exuberance of the room hit him full on as soon as he entered. Men were gambling, arm wrestling, and boasting about their business ventures over pints of Barnswallow's Sowing Moon Ale. Rays of late afternoon sun filtered through the smoke-filled air from the windows along the western side of the room. Scantily dressed waitresses delivered trays of food and drink about the room, skirting the far-too-common stray hand of the lodge's membership.

Evron waded into the morass, slipping sideways through the crowd, his gaze fixed on the floor.

"Grand Master," a well-dressed Iminti man said, extending his hand, "wonderful seeing you this afternoon. Such a rare occurrence these days. Will you be joining us tonight?"

"I plan to, brother, yes." Evron shook the man's hand. "But I have work to see to if I am going to be able to join tonight's dinner on time. Please excuse me."

"Of course. Tonight, then."

Evron released the man's hand, hurried up the stairs where there was a long hallway lined with private rooms on either side used for business meetings and dalliances alike. At the end of the hall was his office, the door ajar.

Shutting his office door behind him, there was a sense of relief as he sat behind his large mahogany desk. A pile of long-neglected papers lay stacked upon its surface. His focus had been singular for so long, his responsibilities as Grand Master had gone untended in favor of his leadership of the Brotherhood of Resurrection. Turning to the window, he gazed out over Meriden and upon the Lazarus Woods.

"It will not be long now, Evelium. The reign of Naur approaches," he whispered, shutting his eyes for a much-needed rest.

CHAPTER 4

I have convinced the Evenese to welcome all but the least palatable of the lesser races into our new society.

—The Collected Letters of Modig Forene
Letter to Doduf Cepryn dated 21st of Lusta, 2 AF. Unearthed from the Ruins of Vanyareign, month of Ocken, 1301 AT

—▲—

The guards stepped aside, granting Umhra and Drog access to the compound. Umhra paused to straighten his leathers—his left hand coming to rest on the blue pouch on his belt—and then opened the great iron-reinforced oak doors to the main parlor of the town hall. The soft light of flickering candles lit the large, stone room. The heads of fantastic creatures from the far reaches of Evelium were mounted between tapestries that lined the walls. An ornate deer-antler chandelier hung from the raftered ceiling above a large wooden table at the far end of the room.

At the table sat a group of individuals that spoke among themselves in a restrained whisper which echoed unintelligibly throughout the chamber. Awaiting their attention were three distinct parties of a half-dozen or so members, all heavily armed.

Umhra and Drog approached, the temple bells ringing in

the distance, welcoming high sun. Two guards barred the door, closing the meeting off to the outside world behind them.

The reverberation of the final bell still hanging in the air, a guard stepped in front of the table and slammed his pike on the stone floor, calling the chamber's attention to the council members. "I present His Lordship, Espen Morrow, and the noble Council of Anaris."

The four crews stood at attention as a tall, dark-skinned man arose from his seat at the table. He wore a light-blue coat trimmed with gold, buttoned high to his neckline. Upon his head rested a modest gold circlet, identifying him as a member of the Forene family. "Welcome all. I am Espen Morrow, Lord of Anaris. I thank you all for heeding my call to action. Before we begin our conversation regarding the contract I hope to release today, please let me introduce the members of my council.

"To my right, as always, I have the pleasure of introducing my wife and chief counsel, Lady Jenta Avrette, sister of the king," Lord Morrow said, bowing to the beautiful, fair-skinned Evenese woman beside him at the table. She stood, nodded to her company, her long, emerald-green gown flowing. Her blonde hair ran neatly down the length of her back. The entire room bowed in response, holding their genuflection until she retook her seat at the table.

"To Lady Avrette's right is Malthus Nofelt, Provost of the University of Antiquities." Lord Morrow motioned to a human man with porcelain-white skin, dark eyes, and angular features who remained seated, gesturing a small bow toward the crowd. He wore fine, ashen robes identifying him as an academic, one of the most revered professions in Evelium. There was little more precious to the Forene dynasty than the pursuit of intellect, and the proper recording of their historic rise to power and successful rule over the largest kingdom in all of Tyveriel.

"Next to Professor Nofelt is His Holiness, Balris Silentread, Anaris's High Priest," Lord Morrow said.

Balris surveyed the room as he was introduced until his gaze landed on Umhra. Balris's stare was transfixed as though he were seeing a ghost. His sapphire cloak hung loosely on his thin frame. He was a Pureblood and hardly showed his age of three hundred years, with a head of dark hair and barely an age-line to be seen. He stood, and bowed to those gathered, all the while keeping his gaze trained on Umhra and Drog.

"Beside His Holiness is Taleyn Cerryg, our Chief Constable."

A stern-looking Zeristar, with a deep scar on his neck that rose above the high collar of his green tunic, nodded to the room with a grunt. His auburn hair was drawn back into an intricate braid and he wore a thick beard that was impeccably groomed. He looked down upon the room over a crooked nose, a stern frown chiseled on his face.

"To my immediate left is Anaris's Treasury Secretary, Valin Bukalo."

A dark-complexioned man with a tall, athletic build and dressed in a fine purple silk suit stood and took a grandiose bow.

"And last, but by no means least, we have Nathaniel Barnswallow, head of the Merchants' Guild, Brewmaster of Barnswallow's Ales, and proprietor of The Barnswallow's Nest," Lord Morrow said, concluding his introductions.

Nathaniel Barnswallow was the Farestere man they had seen earlier that day posting the note at the Candlelit Tavern. He stood in his chair. "Good day, my fine champions," he said, holding his arms out wide to the groups gathered before the council. "We are most privileged to be in your company." He gave a deep bow and returned to his seat.

The introductions concluded, Balris Silentread stood and approached Lord Morrow. He cupped his hand over his mouth and whispered in Lord Morrow's ear. Lord Morrow nodded and turned his attention back to the mercenaries.

"We thank you all for coming, in many cases, from a great distance at our request," Lord Morrow said. "Your fealty shall be noted and shared with King Arving at once. Despite our intentions of extending a private audience with this council to all that responded to our call, some unexpected news has presented itself which has brought our decision to the fore. At Lord Silentread's request, we have decided that Sir Umhra the Peacebreaker and his group, the Bloodbound, shall be rewarded the contract. I bid the rest of you well."

"Lord Morrow," a strapping man in drab leathers with crossed scimitars on his back, interjected, stepping forward from one of the mercenary groups, "I must object. How can you trust the safety of Anaris to a band of Orcs? And on what basis?"

Lord Morrow's glare darted to the man. "On the basis that doing so pleases the Council of Anaris. It sounds as though you question my judgment."

"Not at all, Lord Morrow." The man recoiled. "My apologies for the outburst. I was just taken aback at the haste of the decision against my fine group's employ. We didn't even have the opportunity to make our case before the council."

"I understand your frustration, but the decision has been rendered. Thank you for your time."

The other three parties made their way out of Town Hall, complaining to each other under their breath. Umhra's mind raced, amazed at what just happened. He turned to Drog, questioning the events, at which Drog merely shrugged and flashed a diminutive smile at the outcome.

"Sir Peacebreaker," Lord Morrow beckoned, breaking the silence, "please join us at the table so that we may proceed with the business at hand."

Lord Morrow sat beside his wife and gestured toward a large dark-wood chair with a supple green cushion directly across the table. Nathaniel Barnswallow welcomed Drog to join him at the end of the table.

"Thank you, Lord Morrow. Members of the council," Umhra said, taking his seat. "Drog and I appreciate your vote of confidence in our group to fulfill your contract, and we're ready to begin presently. I must say, however, that I'm curious as to how you arrived at your decision so quickly."

"Lord Silentread said he knew of you, and that you and your organization were beyond reproach. When a man as esteemed as Lord Silentread speaks in such terms, I tend to listen," Lord Morrow said.

Umhra looked over to Balris Silentread who flashed a friendly, but unfamiliar smile.

"Sir Peacebreaker, Anaris is seemingly under attack," Lord Morrow said, wasting no time.

Espen Morrow did not come off as one prone to exaggeration, but Umhra had a hard time understanding what exactly he meant. Having been in the area for nearly two days, he had not witnessed as much as a mild disturbance, other than those caused by his own party.

"Over the last few months, several citizens of and visitors to Anaris including Lord Barnswallow's younger brother, Nicholas, have gone missing along Ember's Way, just north of the city limits. We are afraid the disappearances are the work of an agent of Vred Ulest, if this name has meaning to you."

"It does, Your Lordship. We've spent some time in Winterashe and are familiar with his claim to the throne. But what would an agent of Ulest's be doing south of the Ilathril Mountains? Would that not be an infraction upon the Treaty of the Fracture?"

"Yes, it would," Lord Morrow said, "May I also assume you are aware the Treaty of the Fracture has been strictly enforced for two generations of the Forene dynasty and any such breach would ensure civil war?"

"I understand, my lord."

"Delightful," Lord Morrow said. "I was afraid the severity of this situation would be lost upon you. At the very least, Sir Peacebreaker, we need to understand what is going on along Ember's Way. Ideally, however, you and the Bloodbound would rid us of this problem, with prejudice."

"I assure you we are up to any challenge we find in those woods. That is if you should so please." Umhra paused and waited on the council's formal decision. Lord Morrow turned to each member of the council, each of whom nodded.

Lord Morrow stood and placed his hands on the table. "Let the record show that the Council of Anaris has entered into an official contract with Sir Umhra the Peacebreaker stating the council will pay five thousand sovereigns to Sir Peacebreaker, to be divided among his party as he sees fit, in exchange for the investigation and elimination of the previously described threat to the fair City of Anaris. Payment shall be remitted in the form of a ten percent advance for expenses and ninety percent upon satisfactory completion of the contract." Lord Morrow turned to Umhra and motioned him to rise. As Umhra stood, Lord Morrow extended his hand. Umhra welcomed the gesture, and the men shook hands in agreement of the terms.

Treasurer Bukalo approached and handed Umhra a green velvet billfold. "Five hundred sovereign notes for your expenses, Sir Peacebreaker. Good luck."

Umhra accepted the billfold and placed it in his satchel. "Thank you, Lord Bukalo," he said. "If it pleases the council, I would like to take our leave and get started immediately. My men are ready and waiting for my return."

"By all means," Lord Morrow said. Drog stood and joined Umhra before the council. They bowed and turned toward the door.

Nearing the door, Balris Silentread caught up to them from behind. "Sir Peacebreaker, may I trouble you for a moment?" he asked. Umhra motioned for Drog to give him and the priest a moment to themselves. "Sorry to bother you," Balris said. "You are from Travesty, are you not?"

Umhra's throat tightened, butterflies fluttering in his stomach. "Not originally, Your Holiness, but I did live in Travesty for many years during my childhood and adolescence. That was a long time ago, however. Is that somehow our connection?"

"A long time ago for you maybe, but what is twenty years in a life of three hundred? You were only four when Ivory brought you to the rectory. He raised you well, it seems. And against many of the other priests' better judgment, if I recall. Possibly, you have taken a different path than the one he prepared you so carefully for, but likely the exact path he expected. A path less fraught with persecution."

Umhra's eyes narrowed and he chose his words carefully. "I followed his final wishes explicitly. Being a half-Orc in this land is quite hard enough, I assure you. He ultimately didn't feel the need to add outlawed warrior of the gods to my burden."

"Indeed. He was a great man and among my best of friends. I was saddened to hear of his passing."

"None more than me," Umhra said, hanging his head. "He was as much a father to me as my own, and I can never repay him for his kindness. Not in this life, or the next." Umhra paused. "But Your Holiness, I must insist this revelation stays between us. A long time has passed since I was last involved with the church, and I intend to keep that part of my life protected and out of sight."

Balris stepped closer and grasped him at each shoulder. "Son, life takes us all in our own direction, but I can see that you never left the church. It might take you some time to find your way home, but you will." Umhra stiffened. "Just remember, when you feel as though you have lost everything, your faith will always be there for you."

"Thank you, Your Holiness. I must be on my way." Umhra stepped away from the priest's embrace and threw open the heavy oaken door.

The bright afternoon sun was blinding for a moment, but there was Drog, waiting for him, loyal as always. Umhra took a moment to calm himself.

"Everything okay?" Drog asked.

"Yes," Umhra said, "That was all just a bit much."

"Indeed."

The men maneuvered through the crowded streets and made their way toward camp. "Five thousand sovereigns?" Drog asked when they had a little room to talk. "What's out there that they would offer so much in compensation to the likes of us?"

"They either have far too much money, or they don't expect they will be paying out the rest of the contract," Umhra said. "We need to proceed with the utmost caution. Not only could the mission itself be perilous, but I have no intention of news getting back to King Ulest that we had any involvement in this if the activity along Ember's Way is connected to him as the council suggested. I have no interest in drawing the ire of him or King Arving in their standoff over the throne."

Drog nodded. The rest of the way back to their camp, the men silently prepared themselves as best they could for what lay ahead. As shocked as he was they won the contract, Umhra was even more excited to report back to his men they had and would set off at once on a new adventure.

They left Anaris behind. The rest of the Bloodbound had broken down the camp and were ready to head out by the time Umhra had arrived and Drog returned. "Men, gather around," Umhra said as he approached. "Drog and I return from Anaris with news. Lord Espen Morrow has awarded us a contract worth five thousand sovereigns."

"Bound by blood, bound to spill it," the men cheered, hoisting their weapons into the air.

"No doubt any contract worth so large a sum will prove most treacherous, but I believe we are up to any challenge before us. As I understand it, some people have gone missing north of Anaris. We are to travel Ember's Way in search of those responsible, free the taken if they are still alive, and exact justice on the perpetrators. This is a most delicate situation and we are to proceed with the utmost discretion. No unnecessary risks. May the gods be with us. We leave now."

Again, the men cheered, but this time more reminiscently of an Orc war cry that carried through the woods. Anyone within earshot would have rightfully been shaken.

The Bloodbound lined up single file, Umhra walking the

line to inspect his soldiers. He approached Gori, paused, and then grabbed the fine silver mace from the side of his satchel. He thrust the weapon into Gori's chest. "May your enemies fall at your feet."

Gori took the mace and admired it, his disfigured face, the left half of his jaw having been torn apart by the mace of a Tukdari fighter a decade ago, greeting him in its reflective surface. "I shall bring you glory through its work. This is a most generous gift."

"Much deserved," Umhra replied, "you've worked hard over the last year, and your loyalty is to be commended."

Continuing down the line, Umhra completed his inspection of the formation. What they lacked in numbers, they made up for in tenacity. Umhra nodded to Drog who thrust his ax forward and proceeded to lead the party out of camp toward Ember's Way.

CHAPTER 5

The Waystones were forgotten and all, but one, lost to time.
—The Gatekeepers' Abridged History of Tyveriel

Vol. 2, Chapter 2. Unearthed from the Ruins of Meriden, the month of Ocken, 1240 AT

—▲—

The Bloodbound made their way northwest along Anaris Path, passing several small farms that provided a variety of local crops and meats to the town. Farmers worked the fields and tended to their herds. At the intersection of Anaris Path and Ember's Way, the party arrived at Pell's orchard.

"Gentlemen," called a delicate voice from beyond the stone wall that marked the Pell's property, "give me a moment, if you will."

Umhra halted the party as a tall, thin Evenese man appeared from behind an iron gate adorned with a script letter P. He wiped muddied hands on a worn leather apron that covered otherwise gentile clothing and flashed a broad, welcoming smile. He swept his salt and pepper hair away from his face and wiped his glasses with a handkerchief he retrieved from beneath his apron.

"Are you the men that Lord Morrow has chosen to rid Anaris of this terrible pestilence?"

"We are, my lord. Who may I ask are you to show such interest?" Umhra asked.

"Oh, of course, sorry. I am Lord Xavier Pell, owner of this property and counsel to Lord Morrow."

"Our pleasure, Lord Pell. I am Umhra the Peacebreaker. Is there anything you can tell us about what has been happening along Ember's Way north of town?" Umhra grimaced, regretting the question, and his inability to have avoided the encounter in the first place. He was not sure if Pell could be trusted but having lived in the area so long and having a reputation to uphold, he could prove useful.

"I should say so," Pell said. "Will you men join me for a cup of tea? I will be happy to tell you all that I know."

"It would be our pleasure," Umhra said, "but I fear we don't have much time."

"I will have a rush put on it. Please come."

Pell opened the iron gate, entered the property, and held it open for Umhra and the Bloodbound. The other side of the stone wall was a vision of beauty. Gardens abound on both sides of the gravel path that led to an ancient stone home of immense size.

"My family claimed this property over one thousand years ago and built this home from the stones tilled from the orchard's fields," Pell said with pride. "My great-great-grandfather, may he be among the gods, started all of this with two apple seeds he won in a battle of wits with the wizard Aldresor just after the Great Kingdom was conceived by Modig Forene. He planted those seeds on this very plot, and the rest, as they say, is history. I am the fifth-generation owner of the property, doing my best to keep my forefather's legacy alive. I'm sure you've heard our fabled tale."

"Indeed, Lord Pell," Umhra said, hiding his ignorance of the Pell family's past. "Maybe there will be a time, when less hangs in the balance, when we may return and enjoy a story from the scion of such great history himself. For now, I think it best we remain focused on the threat at hand."

"Of course," Pell said, approaching the oversized red-hued wood door of the home. "Please, come." He opened the door and waved the Bloodbound into his home.

The inside of the home was every bit as impressive as the property was outside. The foyer was warm and inviting. Under a great vaulted ceiling, oil sconces lit the room. Bear-hide rugs softened the floor and paintings of Pell's orchard covered the walls. A young woman entered the room from a door to the left.

"Lord Pell, may I be of help to you and your guests?" she asked, her voice wavering.

"I assure you, there is no need for you to be nervous, my dear," Pell said. "My friends are here on behalf of Lord Morrow, and will join me for a cup of tea and maybe some tarts if they are fresh."

"Of course, my lord. I hardly remember a time when the tarts were not fresh. Shall I serve you in the greenhouse?"

Lord Pell nodded and the young woman curtsied, first to Pell and then to his guests before she hurried back through the door from which she appeared.

"Please excuse her nervousness. She is a local girl, without much worldly experience. I assure you she is as sweet as Elandril's Honey and means no offense." Pell smiled. "Please, follow me."

Pell exited the foyer through an arched doorway at the far side. The men followed and entered a huge parlor. Pell turned a small brass wheel on the wall and numerous oil sconces and four large chandeliers alight in concert, filling the room with an inviting glow. Drog gasped.

"My father designed this marvel," Pell said. "The wheel is attached by rod and cog to each sconce. When the wheel is turned, each is lit in near unison. I, myself, am still struck a wonder by it from time to time."

He proceeded through the room, past comfortable sitting areas, card and game tables, and a bar stocked with ales, wines, and liquors from all over Evelium. The men followed, mouths agape, passing oil paintings of each of the masters of Pell's orchard, culminating in a recent commission of Xavier himself.

Lord Pell continued out of the room through a glass door and led them into the greenhouse. This room had glass walls on three sides and a glass ceiling. Slightly more humid and notably warmer than the rest of the house, there was a large banquet table carved from a single ash tree and stained to match the gray stone floor. Beyond the table were stands of apple seedlings and other garden plants growing in direct sunlight.

"Please, take a seat, my friends." Lord Pell gestured toward the table as he took a seat at its head.

The young woman that greeted them in the foyer swept into the room and set the table with exquisite Evenese glass and silverware. From her tray, she also presented a fragrant pot of tea and a plate of apple tarts. After filling each cup and placing a tart on each plate, she clasped her hands and stood behind Pell's left shoulder. "The tea is from Festbury, the apple tarts made fresh from the cellared fruit of last season's harvest. Shall you require anything further, my lord?"

"I do not expect so, my dear. Thank you." Pell dismissed her with a wave of his hand and addressed the table as she closed the door.

"Please enjoy the tea and pay special attention to the tarts. They are from a family recipe that showcases the best the orchard has to offer. Enough of my blustering, we have business to attend to, as I know you are in a hurry."

Umhra sat forward in his seat in anticipation of Lord Pell's story, the rest of his party devouring the first of their tarts and slurping their tea.

"It is no secret that people, including poor Nicholas Barnswallow, have gone missing along Ember's Way. Several abandoned carts and roaming horses have been discovered over the past several months. There is no telling as to an accurate number of the taken, but the disappearances began four months ago close to the ruins of Telsidor's Keep." Pell paused.

"I'm not familiar with Telsidor's Keep," Umhra said. "Can you tell us about this place?"

"I'll admit to being a bit of an amateur historian when it comes to Anaris and its surroundings," Pell said. "Before the founding of the Forene dynasty, Artemis Telsidor was a well-known adventurer throughout Evelium. I'm sure you have heard the name. He is credited with having slain the Black Dragon, Mesorith, allowing the Zeristar to return to Mount Anvil and develop the Twelve Mines. Being such a prolific adventurer, Telsidor obtained untold treasures over his years. He built a secret keep for his treasure deep in the woods approximately a day's journey on foot, north of Anaris. After his death on Shent, the keep was found and overrun by goblins and other terrible things that used to roam these parts. Since then the keep has been explored and looted countless times. All that is left now is the broken yett, its crumbling walls, and whatever inhabits the cavernous undercrofts below. Do you think there could be some involvement with the keep and the goings-on up that way?"

"To make numerous persons disappear, whatever or whoever is responsible must be operating from some fairly large and protected location. It's possible Telsidor's Keep could be ideal. Do you know of a way to efficiently locate the keep?" Umhra asked.

"Along Ember's Way, a day's travel north of Anaris you will see a black rock foreign to this region of Evelium on the right-hand side of the road about three feet into the brush. It is told Telsidor placed this stone himself, having procured it from an island in the Sea of Widows. Turn east at this rock and walk for another few miles and you shall arrive at a clearing. The entrance to the keep resides at the far end of this clearing."

"Thank you, Lord Pell. You've been a great help to our cause and Anaris," Umhra said.

"The least I can do, Sir Peacebreaker. Please finish your tea and tarts before you get on your way. I fear it will be some time until you can partake of such pleasantries again."

The men sat for another few minutes enjoying their food, then Umhra stood from his chair. "The tarts were a wonderful treat, Lord Pell, but it's best we get going if we are to make progress before sundown. Thank you for welcoming us into your home, and for sharing your knowledge with us. We hope we have an opportunity to enjoy your company again at some point. Possibly after a successful conclusion to our quest."

"You are most welcome, Sir Peacebreaker. May the gods shine upon you along your journey. I shall see you to the gate."

Lord Pell stood, shook Umhra's hand, and bowed to the others around the table. The men stood and bowed in return. Pell then took them back through the parlor and foyer and escorted them to the gate through which they had entered his property.

"Good fortune to you, our heroes of Anaris. Travel safe," he shouted, closing the gate and pausing to watch the Bloodbound make its way north on Ember's Way until out of sight.

CHAPTER 6

I have come to an agreement with the leaders of the Kormaic faith that, in exchange for their fealty, the church be recognized as the one true religion of Evelium.
—The Collected Letters of Modig Forene

Letter to Admiral Kellan Essl dated 1st of Jai, 7 AF. Unearthed from the Ruins of Vanyareign, month of Ocken, 1301 AT

—▲—

The setting sun glistened through the trees as the Bloodbound set up camp in a clearing they found a short distance from Ember's Way. They had not made much progress since leaving Pell's orchard as evening approached and they were wary to travel at night until they understood the nature of what they were up against.

"I'll set the tripwire," Xig the Boarkicker said, taking a coil of metal wire from his satchel. "You two mind takin' a piss to mark the territory?"

"Watch your boots," Bat replied, shoving Gori aside and stepping up to a tree to relieve himself. Gori laughed and followed suit nearby.

Thurg built a modest fire and prepared a dinner of rabbit and fiddleheads while Umhra and Drog sat beside him planning tomorrow's travels.

"I have a feeling Telsidor's Keep and the disappearances are connected," Umhra said, tossing a small stick into the fire. "I'm not sure how, but our priority is finding the stone Pell spoke of and exploring those ruins."

"The keep is the only lead we have at the moment," Drog said. "Sounds like as good a plan as any."

The men ate dinner together and discussed the plan for the following day. All were in agreement with Umhra and Drog's suspicions that Telsidor's Keep was somehow intertwined with the fates of the missing. There was an excitement around the camp. Anticipation. As the Sowing Moon rose over the tree line and into a starlit sky, the fire was put out and Xig took watch while the others turned in.

Xig hailed from an Orcish settlement on the Island of Lertmor off the western coast of Evelium near the Isle of the Twelve Mines. His was a very different upbringing than the Orcish that hailed from Orrat Skag. Orcs on Lertmor were among the first to integrate themselves into Evenese culture. Vastly outnumbered by all other races in the western territories of Evelium, Orcs adapted to local norms to better fit in. As such, they were just another member of the diverse society of Western Evelium and were, for the most part, accepted by others in this region, unlike in many other parts of the vast land.

Xig's village was one of the more unassuming on Lertmor. His father was a mason and his mother a maid for the wealthy Ravensong family in Testament, the largest village on the tiny island. As a child, he would often accompany his mother to work and was usually allowed to play with the children of the house for which she cared. Over the years, he became friends with the boy who went by the name Lucius. When the boys were twelve, they were playing in the woods and found a boar piglet trapped in a hunting snare. The two friends decided to free the young animal. Lucius held the piglet carefully while Xig loosened the snare from around its left hind leg. As Lucius stood holding the piglet, its mother charged out of the nearby brush straight for him. Surprised, Lucius did not have time to react, but Xig instinctively kicked the boar as it ran past him. His kick rang true and knocked the boar off course, just grazing Lucius who was knocked to his back with a gash in his thigh. The piglet, now free, ran off with its mother into the woods. Xig tied off the wound, lifted Lucius onto his back, and carried him home to his mother.

Ever grateful for Xig's heroic action, the Ravensongs treated Xig as one of their own. A few years later Lucius was accepted to the military academy on the mainland in Lindamere, and Lord Ravensong saw to Xig being accepted as well. Neither returned to Lertmor. Lucius was killed during their first campaign after training by a swarm of goblins. Xig was there, but he was unable to save Lucius. Xig eventually met Bat, who encouraged him to join the Bloodbound and travel Evelium with his own kind—with those who would understand and respect him. He agreed, and now they trusted each other with their lives. Even now, the rest slept peacefully knowing Xig was looking out for them.

▲

It was late into the night when Thurg awoke. He looked to the moon and shook his head. "Overslept again." He rubbed his eyes and looked around the camp.

"Xig?" he whispered, as not to disturb the others. There was no reply. Thurg threw off his blanket and rose from his bedroll. The fire was little more than fading coals, a small pile of wood unused beside it. He walked the perimeter of the camp, peering out into the dark woods, and then rushed to Umhra's side.

"Umhra." Thurg jostled his leader awake, "Xig is missing."

Umhra sat, his eyes wide. "What do you mean, missing?"

"He never woke me for my shift on watch. When I awoke on my own, he was gone. The tripwire is still intact, but he is nowhere within the perimeter."

There was a strict protocol about not leaving the safety of

the camp's perimeter once it was set and Xig was never one to disobey orders.

"Let's wake the others and sweep the area," Umhra said. "Maybe we'll be able to track him or at the very least get a sense of what happened."

Umhra and Thurg stirred the others awake and they searched the surrounding woods for any sign of Xig.

"Do you think he deserted?" Gori asked as he returned to camp.

"No," Umhra said. "I've known Xig for many years. He would never desert us. Besides, he would have left tracks if he simply walked away."

"Surely if he were attacked, he would have alerted us, or we would have been woken by the struggle," Drog said.

"Unless whatever took him swept down from the sky and he didn't have advanced notice," Gori said, looking up to the heavens as the sun breached the horizon and shown through the trees into the clearing. The rest craned their necks. Thurg shuddered.

"We'll wait for him until we are through with breakfast. If he doesn't return on his own by then, he either doesn't want to or can't," Umhra said, his voice wavering.

"Do you think this has something to do with the disappearances farther north?" Thurg asked.

"I'm not certain." Umhra frowned. "If there is a connection, this would be the closest abduction to Anaris, which could mean the city is at risk. We will carry on with our plan to root out whatever is behind this before they get more brazen."

The group ate slowly, taking turns pacing the perimeter of the camp as if Xig would come walking out of the woods and greet them as though nothing had happened. They had no such luck. Finishing their simple meal of bacon and biscuits, they packed up camp.

Umhra called them to attention. "Time to move out. Today we find the black rock and then, Telsidor's Keep. After last night, this mission has become much more important. Going forward, we rotate teams of two for everything. Nobody wanders off, not even to take a piss." Umhra nodded to Drog, who led the team back to Ember's Way.

They walked, not a word between them for several hours until a cart approached from the north. Pulled by a modest, feeble looking mule, the wooden wheels creaked and rattled over the numerous potholes and bumps in the weather-worn road. Approaching the Bloodbound, the driver hauled on the reins, the mule came to a halt.

"Greetings," the elderly Farestere man said. He wore a purple velvet waistcoat and brown leather pants. His white hair flowed in the breeze and he wore round tortoiseshell glasses that magnified his eyes to a most absurd size. "Nice to see someone along Ember's Way on this fine day. The ride from Festbury has been a lonely one."

Umhra approached the cart. "Friend, this road is not safe. Have you not heard?"

The cart was laden with cured meat wrapped in waxed paper; the smell was nearly overwhelming. "Of course, I've heard about the goings-on along Ember's Way, if you get my meaning. I might live in a hole, but not under a rock. Well, technically I do live under a rock, but metaphorically speaking, if you will. I need to make my monthly delivery to Anaris and no silliness like we are talking about is going to stop me from conducting my business."

Umhra cocked an eyebrow. "Pardon me. My men and I have taken an interest in the disappearances along Ember's Way. May I ask what you've heard up in Festbury regarding the matter?"

The little man leaned back in his seat and pulled an ornate wooden pipe from his waistcoat pocket. He took his time packing it with tobacco and then struck a match on the side of the cart and lit the pipe. "Well, we in Festbury normally don't take notice of the affairs of Evelium in its broader sense. I'm one of the few that leave the town even when times are peaceful. Most just keep to themselves and mind their business, if you get my meaning. There have been whispers over pints of ale, however, about what has been happening along the road to Anaris. My wife was quite near a fit when I told her I was making my usual trip south this month, but I already missed last month's delivery, and I have a reputation to maintain and customers to provide for. Regardless, I'm sure I'll be sleeping in the study when I get back if you get my meaning. Alas, I'm not sure anything I've heard would be of use to you, I'm afraid."

"Please," Umhra said, "share what you can. Every little bit of information we gather can help us. Even the most mundane."

The man blew a smoke ring into the sky. "All right, then. We hadn't taken notice of any wrongdoings or oddities until we heard that Nicholas Barnswallow had gone missing. Everyone in these parts knows Nicholas, and not only because his brother Nathaniel is the brewmaster of Barnswallow's Ales. I know down in Anaris they prefer the Sowing Moon variety, but in Festbury we usually enjoy Reaping Moon. A much fuller taste in my opinion, but not over-hopped.

"Nicholas is also known to be a bit of an eccentric fellow. He lived in the woods for a year talking only to the animals to best a troll that wandered those parts, causing troubles. A Farestere besting a troll, quite unheard of, yes. That Nicholas sure is special though, and at the end of that year, the troll was never seen or heard from again. Nicholas would never tell the story of what happened. Many others would be boasting until it was untenable.

"But Nicholas's disappearance got our attention in Festbury. He's a bit of a hero to us tiny folk. We started asking questions of any visitors who passed through Festbury, of which there are not many, mind you. Those of us who travel between Festbury and Anaris started paying attention to more than our pipes along the road if you get my meaning." The man paused to draw on his pipe.

"And, what was the result of these questions and increased

vigilance?" asked Umhra, his tone flecked with impatience.

"As I said earlier, not much of what I know would be useful to you. I will say, about a half-day north of here the woods are unseasonably cold and quiet for a stretch, which is never a good sign. If you are heading up that way, please be careful. I don't give off the aura of anything of much importance, but you men practically glow with bravado. Now, I must be on my way. I have a delivery time to meet and I intend to do just that. I wish you luck and bid you farewell until our paths cross again." The man tucked his pipe between his teeth and snapped the reins. His mule begrudgingly lurched the cart into motion.

"Thank you, and safe travels," Umhra said. The Farestere man raised his hand in the air in acknowledgment and continued toward Anaris. Umhra turned to his men. "Well, that was paying a lot for a little. We march on."

CHAPTER 7

The crater's impact left a scar upon Orrat Skag. From then on, the land could barely sustain life.
—The Gatekeepers' Abridged History of Tyveriel

Vol. 1, Chapter 3. Unearthed from the Ruins of Meriden, the month of Anar, 1217 AT

—▲—

Umhra led his men onward for hours, not encountering another soul but for the occasional squirrel or bird. As the Farestere man had warned, the forest in this area was eerily cold and still. Bat peered over the wall of an abandoned wagon along the side of the road as they passed.

"The black rock should be somewhere in this area," Umhra said, interrupting the solemnity of the march. "Keep your eyes open."

Their pace slowed as they combed the east side of the road to locate the exotic black rock Xavier Pell told them about. The better part of a mile later, Gori grabbed his bow and nocked a large black arrow. The group paused, hands on their weapons as he fixed his aim on something in the woods. The bow creaked in anticipation under the strain of his draw. Gori loosed the arrow which whistled into the woods, striking true to his aim, and prompting a scream from his quarry.

Out of the woods burst four men dressed from head to toe in black. One hobbled behind the others, with Gori's arrow jutting from its left shoulder. Their eyes were garnet red, their glow intensifying as they rushed into battle.

Gori drew his mace but was caught by a glaive thrust forward by one of the bandits. The blade sliced into Gori's side as he spun to avoid a mortal blow. He fell in the process and rolled onto his back with his assailant raising the glaive over his head, preparing to run him through.

Umhra rushed over to protect the now prone Gori and drove his sword into his assailant's torso just beneath his right armpit, causing the glaive to fall to the earth. Tearing the sword free, a spray of gore was released from the wound. The man fell to his knees and then face-first onto the dirt path.

The two remaining unharmed men focused their attention on Drog who split off to the right, trying to angle around them. They lunged at him with their glaives, but he deftly parried both aside with the broad side of his ax.

Thurg and Bat attacked the distracted men from behind. Bat buried his ax in the side of one as he spun around to defend himself. The other man ducked under Thurg's longsword and jumped on him, dropping his glaive, and brandishing two daggers. He thrust the blades at Thurg's neck and face, Thurg covering his face with his arms in self-defense. Drog jumped on the man's back and wrested him from Thurg, threw him to the ground. The man scrambled backward, Drog stepped over him and removed his head with a swing of his ax.

The man Bat had injured swung his glaive in despair. Bat dodged just out of the weapon's reach. The man's momentum carried him forward, and Bat crashed his ax down upon his head, splitting his skull in two straight down to his chin. He kicked the body from his ax's grip and turned toward the last of them.

The final man, Gori's arrow still lodged in his shoulder,

dropped his weapon and surveyed the half-Orcs who had deftly felled his comrades.

"Who are you?" Umhra demanded with a growl. "What is your involvement in the disappearances in these parts?"

The man remained silent, and removed the mask from his face, exposing onyx-colored skin, streaked with irregular white lines. As the sun hit his face, the white lines slowly turned red like his eyes. Further intensifying, small beams of light started to show from within.

"Run," Umhra yelled.

The Bloodbound scattered into the woods on either side of the path. As they dove for cover, the man exploded. In succession, each of the bodies of their dispatched foes, followed suit, leaving four impassable craters on Ember's Way. The sound of the explosions echoed in the woods, and the smell of charred flesh pervaded the air.

Drog rolled from Thurg, who he had dove upon to protect. A cloud of blood and dirt slowly settled to the ground, as the men regathered on the road.

Umhra extended his hand and helped Gori to his feet. "Nice spot, mate," he said. "If they got the jump on us, no telling the damage."

"What were they?" Gori asked, dusting himself off.

"I've never come across anything like them," Umhra said. "I once read about such creatures in the archives at the temple in Travesty. I believe they were Dokktari. A race of men from Wethryn. Not of this world, but rather from a barren plane of chaos."

"How would such creatures get to Evelium?" Bat asked as he inspected one of the craters.

"The few texts I've read say they are attracted by evil and will jump planes of existence to further its bidding. What their presence tells me is we are in the right place. I'm certain we will find what we are looking for in the keep. How is everyone? Thurg?"

Bat and Drog tended to Thurg who had several puncture wounds and gashes on his face and neck.

"I am fine," Thurg said, shoving them away. "Only my pride is hurt."

Shaken but undeterred, the Bloodbound returned to their search for the black rock. It was only a few moments later when Bat discovered the stone, about one hundred feet north from where their skirmish with the Dokktari occurred.

"Over here, Umhra. This must be the rock that Pell spoke of," he said.

Umhra approached and knelt by the rock and brushed some dirt from its surface. It was obvious, even to Umhra's untrained eye, this was not a rock native to Evelium. Unlike those in the surrounding area, the stone looked as though it was made of black glass. The rock had sharp, irregular edges, and was translucent despite its dark color, producing a haunting glow from within.

"Obsidian," Umhra said. "Like from the great crater in the homeland."

"It is said that such a rock can hold the souls of men," Thurg said, covering his mouth with both hands.

Each of the Bloodbound took a turn to admire the beautiful rock and touch it as if doing so would imbue some kind of power or luck. "We march east into the woods from here. The remnants of Telsidor's Keep should be a few miles directly ahead. The keep holds the answers to our contract, and hopefully to Xig's disappearance as well." Umhra stood and led his men into the woods.

There was no obvious path, making the three-mile journey an arduous task. Umhra walked with purpose while Gori and Thurg lagged and nursed their wounds. Drog bound up alongside Umhra. "What if this keep is overrun with those things?" he asked, his tone marked with concern.

"Well, the good news is, I believe they only explode when exposed to daylight. They will be much less dangerous in the depths of the keep," Umhra said. "As for strategy, do you remember the catacombs at Tribulation?"

"Of course. How could I forget all of those spiders?" Drog shuddered.

"Then you'll remember we defeated those spiders even though we were vastly outnumbered, and we succeeded because we drew them into the narrow passages where we could take turns fighting them one or two at a time. I suspect this keep will have similar areas we can use to our advantage. Hopefully, the Dokktari will be the worst we run into within the keep."

Dusk was setting in when the Bloodbound arrived at what used to be the clearing Xavier Pell spoke of. The lea was now quite overgrown, partially obscuring their view of the ruins on its far side. They did not dare step foot out into the relative openness of the clearing itself. Instead, they slowly navigated their way around the perimeter until they arrived at a better vantage point from which to observe the former yett of Telsidor's Keep. The rusted iron gate had long been pried from its hinges and discarded amongst the piles of rubble and crumbling walls. Vines grew over the rather unimpressive stone façade.

"It's hard to believe the labyrinthian structure Pell described is down there as modest as these ruins are," Drog whispered.

The Bloodbound crouched behind a large rock at the edge of the clearing as the sky grew dark. Everything was quiet. After several hours of inactivity, their confidence grew.

"There doesn't seem to be anything in the way of patrols," Bat said. "Should we go in? I want to find Xig and I fear we are running out of time."

Umhra nodded. "It's time," he said. "No torches."

CHAPTER 8

I have heard that the Dark Father's embrace grants eternal life to the worthy.
—Telsidor's Missives

Diary entry dated 26th of Bracken, 45 AF. Unearthed from the Ruins of Anaris, month of Emin, 1156 AT

—▲—

Under a moonlit sky, the men crept to the yawning entrance of Telsidor's Keep. Among the crumbling ruins within the yett was a single stone tower shorn in half by time and neglect. Beneath an ornate archway at the center of the tower, stairs fell away from them into darkness. Umhra entered and edged down the first stairs, giving his eyes time to adjust to the diminishing light. Gori, Thurg, Bat, and Drog followed their leader into the unknown.

Umhra kept one hand on his sword and another on the wall of the staircase. The stones grew colder and damper as they descended the stairs, which curved in a gentle arc. Umhra crossed the apex of the arc, the darkness giving way to faint light. Continuing down the stairs, a long, torchlit hallway became visible. Umhra held his fist in the air and his men halted their progress. Seeing no obvious danger, Umhra walked down a few more stairs. The hallway was clear, but the presence of two torches, freshly lit, was proof someone was inhabiting the keep's depths. Umhra crept along the hallway. A third of the way along its length, he stepped over an old pressure plate embedded in the floor. Safe on the other side, he waved his men down. Drog, who had begun keeping a map, detailed the long passageway on a piece of parchment.

The men inched their way down the hallway, careful to avoid several other pressure plates spaced at regular intervals. They passed the second torch which cast a glow revealing an iron door at the hallway's end. The door was halfway open and the lock mechanism had been pried from it. The men stopped as Umhra peeked through the opening.

The door opened into a large room that spanned left for at least sixty feet and was supported by two dozen pillars connected by stone archways. Four large candelabras hung from the ceiling and shed a soft light across the room. On the far side of the room stood two more Dokktari, dressed like those the Bloodbound had encountered in the woods, but with their faces exposed. They stood guard on either side of a door. The Dokktari engaged in an animated conversation in a language unfamiliar to Umhra.

Umhra backed away from the door. "There are two more Dokktari at the far corner of the room. They seem distracted enough with each other for us to set an ambush. Gori and Bat, sneak in and hold your position behind the pillars to the left. Thurg and Drog, do the same on the right. Once you are in position, I am going to make myself known to them and try to draw them to me. When they pass you, take them out from behind as swiftly and quietly as possible."

"Should we keep one alive for interrogation?" Drog asked.

"No," Umhra said, "I fear they would be of little value and I don't want to risk them alerting anything else further within the keep."

"Very well," Drog said, "let's keep this clean, boys."

Gori and Bat slipped into the room and backed up against the two nearest pillars to the left of the door. Drog and Thurg followed suit on the right. Once they were readied, Umhra stood in the doorway, casting a clumsy shadow into the room. His silhouette attracted the Dokktaris' attention and, abandoning their post at the door, they strode toward him with glaives at the ready.

"Stupid fool," one of the Dokktari called across the room, his speech awkward and broken. "You die in this place."

Umhra was silent. He drew his blade and took a brazen step into the room. The Dokktari couldn't resist his brash taunt and hurried their pace toward the lone intruder. A toothy smile cracked across each of their faces.

Umhra stood his ground and took a defensive stance, the Dokktari baring down on him. When they crossed beyond the last row of pillars, the Dokktari reared their glaives high overhead preparing to strike Umhra in a coordinated assault. Gori and Thurg emerged from the shadows and thrust their swords into the Dokktaris' backs. The blades burst through their chests, blood showering Umhra.

The glaives fell from the Dokktaris' hands. Drog managed to catch one, but the second fell just out of Bat's outstretched hand and rattled against the rough stone footing. He grimaced at the clatter.

"A little payback," Thurg said, tore his sword clear.

"Okay," Umhra said, "let's put these two in the corner where the shadows are deepest. Hopefully, they will go undiscovered."

The group propped the bodies in the corner, leaving a trail of garnet-colored blood across the floor. They placed the glaives beside the bodies in the darkness and turned toward the door the Dokktari had been guarding. The door was identical to the one through which they had entered, but was shut.

"What's our next move?" Drog asked while inspecting the heavy iron door.

"We continue forward and take what comes our way,"

Umhra said. "If anyone has any reservations, speak now."

Not one of them wavered.

"In that case, I'll open the door. Fan out about ten feet behind me. If anything comes through, we back up into the hallway across the room and fight them there."

The Bloodbound stepped back into the flickering light of the candelabras behind them.

Umhra grasped the handle of the door and shouldered it ajar until it clicked to lock in place. He peered through the opening to a narrow staircase leading down one hundred feet to a lengthy bridge which extended to a brightly lit doorway several hundred feet beyond. With no danger in sight, he opened the door the rest of the way, a geared mechanism in the floor clicking every fifteen degrees. He waved his men on and they began their way down the staircase. After a half-minute, the door slammed shut behind them.

Thurg ran back up the stairs and pulled, but the door would not give. They were locked in Telsidor's Keep. The din of the shuttered door rang through the chamber. Umhra peered into the shrouded abyss below the bridge, where the floor undulated from the disturbance.

At that moment, with the only option being to endeavor onward toward a still obscure enemy, Umhra's confidence was uncharacteristically shaken. He was overcome by the sense that, for the first time, he had taken on a challenge possibly too great. With retreat no longer plausible, he shifted his thinking from achieving victory to minimizing their losses.

Winded, Thurg caught up with the group who was approaching the bridge. "No going back now," he said.

Umhra turned to the group. "There may be no easy way out of this keep, and it's still unclear what dangers we face ahead, but I will do everything in my power to get us through this together. We must work smarter and more effectively than we ever have before." He was walking a fine line between despair and foolhardiness, neither trait he had ever held in high regard.

"Let's press on and meet whatever stands in our way with valor." Gori slammed his mace against his armored chest.

The rest agreed and the group crossed the bridge. Umhra did not call their attention to depths below, but several times while they traversed the narrow path, the ground writhed far beneath them, shifting toward them as if aware of their proximity.

The Bloodbound crept to the end of the bridge where Umhra halted, the doorway he had seen from atop the staircase marking the way forward. The screech of large, rusted gears turning emanating from the walls before him, he turned to face his crew. To a deafening rumble, the bridge collapsed with Bat and Thurg still standing on its edge. Gori spun and dove back for them, his chain mail shirt scraping against the damp stone as he slid toward the burgeoning chasm. Drog grabbed his torso, stopped him from going over the edge.

Gori grasped into the darkness, found purchase with Thurg's right hand, and held fast. Umhra dove to the shorn edge of the bridge and reached for Bat. Grabbing hold of Bat's fingertips, Umhra looked into Bat's eyes which were wide with terror. He felt Bat's fingers slip from his hand and watched as he fell out of sight.

Rocks fell to the floor far below with a resounding crash, followed by silence. Umhra laid on his stomach, staring into the plume of dust billowing from below, still feeling the scratches of Bat's nails on his palm. Drog came to his side and helped Gori hoist Thurg over the edge of the abutment to safety.

"Bat!" Umhra shouted into the pit hoping for a reply.

Silence. Then some shuffling below accompanied by the sound of rocks shifting. Finally, an echo from below. "My legs are pinned by the rocks," Bat said.

"I'm coming down for you," Umhra said. He clutched a small blue pouch he kept lashed to his belt, ran his fingers over the edges of the object within, and shook his head. Instead, he unwound the rope lashed to the front of his satchel and tied it to a sturdy rock once part of the bridge's façade. He put his feet at the edge of the stonework and leaned backward, testing his footing.

"Wait," Bat said, his voice desperate. "There's something else down here."

They could hear the sound of Bat drawing his ax to defend himself. Then he screamed. Umhra motioned to rappel down to him, but Drog caught his arm.

"No Umhra. It's too late," Drog said, hauling Umhra back onto solid ground as he motioned down into the pit, where the dust had settled enough for them to witness Bat overcome by a horde of undead. Bat lashed out with his ax at the horde, eviscerating those at the fore, and sending them to the ground. A second wave of undead stumbled over still writhing bodies and Bat swung again. This time his ax lodged in the spine of one of the undead. Unable to pry his weapon free, and with others encroaching, he released the ax and drew a dagger from his belt. He plunged the blade into the head of another with what little leverage he could with his legs pinned beneath the rocks, the blow penetrating the zombie's skull as it bit at his chest. Bat's shoulders were grabbed from behind, one of the living dead tearing into his neck with rotting teeth. The other creatures joined in, and Bat's screams echoed through the chamber as his leathers were ripped from his body and his flesh devoured.

The four remaining members of the Bloodbound collapsed to the cold stone floor. Now down two men and with no means to exit the keep the way from which they had entered, hope was fleeting.

"What–in the name of Kalmindon–is going on in this place?" Drog asked.

"I wish I knew, but it is among the evilest of places I have ever seen," Gori said.

"Yes, and we four are going to do away with whatever lurks ahead," Umhra said. He pounded the stone with his fist. "Even if it's the last thing we do in the mortal plane. And we burn that pit before we leave this place. I don't care how, but the undead must be incinerated." He forced himself to his feet and offered Thurg a hand. Drog and Gori both took one last look into the pit and then followed as Umhra turned to face the glow of the doorway that led deeper into the keep.

Crossing the rune-covered threshold, they entered another hallway that was more brightly lit than the first, with oil lamps lining the right wall every ten feet. The walls were smeared with blood. The smell of death strong and only increased as they neared the open door at the end of the hallway.

Peering into the next room, Umhra gasped. On the wall farthest from him, hung the disemboweled body of Xig, flayed open with utmost precision. He must have suffered greatly. The walls were decorated with similarly dressed corpses, likely some of the missing from Ember's Way. Several of the corpses still writhed despite life having long since left them. From the ceiling hung several blackened iron cages dripping with decay, the floor stained beneath them.

There were three doors along the far wall, only the middle of which was open. Umhra directed Drog to check the closed door on the left and Thurg and Gori, the one on the right. Both were locked. As Umhra walked through the middle door into a short hallway, the door slammed shut behind him, separating him from his men.

Umhra strained against the locked door. It would not budge. He could hear other doors grind open, and what sounded like an army of Dokktari troops rushing into the room on the other side. He bashed the lock mechanism with the pommel of his sword, but could not dent its hardened form. On the other side, the familiar sounds of battle rang in his ears as though he was stuck in the tree trunk back in Goshur Uk. Helpless. "Drog," he screamed, crashing against the door. Something struck him from behind, and the back of his skull burned. He fell backward. Two Dokktari stood over him, one with a wooden staff in his hand. Everything went black.

▲

Drog, Gori, and Thurg were outnumbered twenty to one, as Dokktari poured into the room. Drog was overwhelmed by a dozen Dokktari, each thrusting their carefully honed glaives through his armor, severing his body mid-torso. Outnumbered as they were, Gori and Thurg were backed out of the room and down the hallway through which they entered. Knowing doom was at hand, Gori removed the oil lamps from the wall, as Thurg did his best to hold the Dokktari at bay. Returning to the room with the fallen bridge, Gori threw one of the lamps to the ground at the egress of the hallway, causing a fierce fire that gave him and Thurg a fleeting moment.

"Thurg, my brother, it has been the greatest honor of my life to fight at your side. Now take these lamps and leap with me into the afterlife. May Kalmindon be graced by your presence," Gori said.

Thurg took two lamps and the men turned toward the pit. "May the gods have favor on you, my friend. The honor has been mine."

They ran toward the pit, leaped, and crashed into the undead horde below. Their lamps burst into flame, ignited the decrepit corpses in an inferno. Gori and Thurg laid together, their bodies were broken.

Thurg screamed, the fire intensifying around them.

"Brother, be strong." Gori grabbed his hand. "You are not alone." The fire engulfed them. Both men shut their eyes, surrendered.

CHAPTER 9

The other continents grew to view Evelium as the cultural center of Tyveriel.
—The Gatekeepers' Abridged History of Tyveriel.

Vol. 3, Chapter 15 – Discovered in the Private Library of Solana Marwyn, the month of Vasa, 889 AT

—▲—

Umhra's head ached. His eyes fluttered open, his hands bound behind his back. He was on his knees, forehead to the cold stone floor, as if genuflecting. He sat up, the room a blur.

"Good, you are awake," said a measured voice from directly across the room. Umhra struggled to focus. "To be honest, I never thought your little band of Orcs would have come as close as you did. You seemed like such a simple group."

Umhra shook his head to clear his mind. Two large oil lamps stood on either side of an ornate red rug adorned with a black flame pattern covering the unforgiving stone floor. Four stone steps came into focus. They led up to another matching red rug upon which sat a throne. The chair's frame was made entirely of bones. Upon the throne sat a tall figure dressed in a dark red robe with black flames embroidered upon the sleeves. Umhra remained silent.

He looked about the room, the haze clearing. They seemed alone. Sounds of muffled revelry carried from the other side of an iron door behind him. He tested his bindings.

"Look at me," said the man in front of him, his tone forceful.

Umhra obliged. The man removed his hood and leaned forward, hands on his knees.

"Malthus Nofelt." Umhra's jaw dropped.

"Poor Sir Peacebreaker, I have been known by so many names over the ages. During my mortal life, I went by Artemis Telsidor. I have used many other aliases since—each to suit a purpose. Malthus Nofelt is just one of them. My true name is Manteis the Immortal." Nofelt let out an instinctual hiss, baring two sharp fangs for Umhra to see, as if for proof of his greatness.

"Why?" asked Umhra. He swallowed down his fear.

The vampire stood from his throne and walked to the back corner of the room to a cage similar to the ones from the room where Xig's body had been displayed. In the cage, a small man was sitting with his legs dangling limply from the cage, his forehead supporting his weakened body against the iron bars. The vampire observed his prize, lifting his face by the chin between his fingers. The man's red tangle of hair clung to his face in a cold sweat. The remnants of a green waistcoat, a linen shirt, and brown leather pants were tattered and twisted around his frail body. The man resisted the vampire's touch. There was still life in him.

"I suppose no harm can come from entertaining one so close to death," Manteis said, releasing the caged man from his grasp. "Your question is one of great import, Sir Peacebreaker. Why am I disguising myself among the people of Anaris? Why have my long-perpetrated abductions now become evident to the simple-minded? Why have I amassed an army of Dokktari to do my bidding? Why have I kept you alive while I have disposed of your friends? As your dying wish, I will answer these questions so you may go to the next life with peace of mind." He turned to

Umhra and flashed a grim smile.

Manteis ambled toward Umhra, admiring a ruby ring on the pinky of his own pale, bony hand. "Have you heard of the Brothers of Resurrection, Sir Peacebreaker?"

Umhra shook his head.

Manteis sighed. "I should not expect that any one of your, shall we say, diminutive stature would have. The brotherhood is an organization whose roots go back to Meriden during the War of Rescission. I first learned about them during my mortal life as I explored the depths of Evelium. This was, of course, before Modig Forene declared his dominion over this land. When Evelium was still a wild and fascinating place. But I digress, and into politics of all things. I have watched the brotherhood grow up over the years to the point where it now infiltrates every city, town, and village in all of Evelium. Its power has become unquestionable and the time has come for it to release Evelium from the bondage of the Forenian age and return our land to prior glory." The vampire turned and walked back up the stairs and stood with his back facing Umhra.

Umhra struggled to free himself from his bindings. "There is no need for you to struggle, My Hero of Anaris," Manteis said, mocking Umhra without turning to face him. "I will free you from your restraints. You are no threat to me and will not live out the hour."

The rope around Umhra's wrists unwound and fell to the floor. Umhra righted himself and knelt back on his heels.

"Please continue, my lord. How will this Brothers of Resurrection bring King Shale Arving and all of Evelium to their knees? I must admit your story sounds far-fetched."

"The details of how the brotherhood will free us, well, that is to say, me, are not to be shared. I will, however, indulge you in saying the God of Fire, Naur, will take his destined seat as ruler of the mortal plane soon enough. My role is but a minor one in this great event in history. I am simply to raze Anaris to the ground and kill the king's sister, Jenta Avrette, and her insipid husband, Espen Morrow. I shall take quite a bit of pleasure in it, I assure you, when the time is right. As to why you are graced by my presence and conversation? This is simple. Unlike your friends, you are covered in the stench of morality and rightness. I needed to see to it personally that you were properly broken before you met your end. The others were but pawns in our game."

Umhra searched the small blue pouch at his waist which he had not opened in years. He retrieved a small platinum pyramid-shaped icon and put it on the floor in front of his knees. He whispered.

"Yes, pray to your gods. You have most definitely outstayed your welcome, Sir Peacebreaker. I have important work to do and you shall be my sustenance for the day. Please do not be prolonged with your prayers, I will only give you another moment of my time," the vampire said, his hubris palpable. Victory was within his grasp.

Umhra's whispers grew in strength. He spoke in a celestial tongue not common to man, or Orc, or vampire. He prayed in the very language of the gods. The prayers nearing a shout, the vampire turned, eyes wide, jaw slack. From his spine, platinum plates grew around Umhra's body, one plate giving way to the next until the entirety of his form was covered in radiant armor.

The gaps of the armor now shone with a vibrant blue light. By the time he lifted his head to look upon the vampire, he had been transformed. He glowed with a luminance that made the creature of darkness recoil. Manteis hissed at Umhra and rushed to the edge of the steps. Umhra held his hand up, palm facing his advancing foe, and froze him in place.

"How could this be?" The vampire struggled. "A Paladin? But there has not been a Paladin in Evelium in over eight hundred years," he said, his body frozen in place on the platform above where Umhra still knelt. "Sir Peacebreaker, it would seem we are on the same side of this battle—you are a heretic from a bygone age and I am a defiled creature of chaos. You have hidden yourself well, and rightfully so. A Paladin may be reviled by society as much as I if we exposed ourselves to the scales of justice."

Undeterred, the light from Umhra's body grew with his chant. The door flew open, Dokktari from the room next to them drawn by disturbance. Umhra finished asking his god for forgiveness, and for the strength to end the evil he faced. A blinding light burst forth from his body as though he were a star at the end of its life, emitted one last nod to the universe as a supernova. The empyrean light incinerated Manteis, burning his image into the gnarled back of the bone-framed throne in front of which he had stood, the ring on his finger clattered to the ground. Behind him, the Dokktari burst into flame, one after the other exploding as the immense release of power swept over them, tearing a hole in the wall.

The flash dissipated and Umhra fell to the ground, much of his vital energy spent. He writhed on the ground, grasping for his platinum pyramid, a totem to a faith he long ago left behind. His eyes rolled back in his head and he fumbled the icon in his fingertips, casting it across the floor. As he struggled, his mind wandered back to Ivory Lapping, to his adoptive father and the monk who trained him to become a Paladin.

"Umhra, there will be a time for you to reveal your powers," Ivory said, sitting with his adopted half-Orc son in the basement of the Trinity Temple. His face was soft and kind. His brown hair, which he kept short, was thinning. "Until that time reveals itself to you, keep your true nature and abilities hidden. You will find no sympathy from the Forenes if they discover what you are. The church long ago traded its right to train warriors of the gods for the safety provided by the Forene dynasty and recognition as the true religion of Evelium. I have foreseen a time, however, when all of the military might in Tyveriel will not be able to save us. You will be our only chance for salvation."

"Sir Peacebreaker?" a voice interrupted his dream. "Please

do wake up, Sir Peacebreaker. I am afraid your work is not done yet."

The small man in the cage was now standing, wild-eyed as if the adrenaline of what he just witnessed willed him back to life. He pointed to the smoldering doorway where a group of five Dokktari not destroyed by Umhra's burning daylight, rushed into the room. The first into the room raised his glaive over his head and slashed it down upon Umhra. Umhra rolled out of the way toward the steps leading to the Manteis's throne. From his knees, he grabbed one of the large oil lamps standing on either side of the throne and threw it toward the Dokktari who was set aflame and screamed. His wild flailing held the others at bay long enough for Umhra to get back to his feet.

"Your sword and shield are here beneath my cage," said the young Farestere man as he rattled the bars keeping him imprisoned.

Umhra ran to the corner and grabbed his sword and shield—blue smoke wafting off his form—as the other four Dokktari gained entrance to the room. At his touch, the sword and shield took on the same brilliance of his newfound armor and glowed with the same blue light he radiated within. He spun his sword in his left hand and looked to the gods. At that moment, it was as if the very sun shone down upon his form. He met the Dokktari in the center of the room, taking one's head off with an effortless swipe of his blade. He spun, plunged his sword into the chest of another. The two remaining Dokktari jumped back to regain their composure. They then leaped in unison toward Umhra. One Dokktari glaive scraped against Umhra's shield, the handle shattering under the force of the deflection. The other found a gap in Umhra's armor at his left shoulder. Umhra recoiled and then spun around, tore himself free of the glaive's blade. Blood poured down his gleaming chest plate from the gaping wound.

With a returning slash, Umhra took the Dokktari's legs clean from his body. The unarmed fourth made for the exit, but Umhra thrust his sword through the Dokktari's chest. The imminent threat vanquished, Umhra tore his blade free and turned toward the cage.

"There will undoubtedly be more," said the Farestere.

"Then how do we get out of here?" Umhra asked approaching the cage, his wound burning under his armor. With a swing of his sword, he cut the lock and opened the door.

"I'm afraid I may be too weak to travel quickly," said the Farestere, "but there is a hidden exit along the far wall which can be opened by pulling the largest bone in the back of the vampire's throne."

Umhra threw his shield over his back to free a hand and helped the weakened man to the ground. Umhra could now plainly see the puncture wounds upon his neck and wrists, the pallid tone of his skin. The Farestere's legs buckled, but then he found a modicum of strength. Umhra was exhausted. "We will continue at whatever pace you can muster," he said.

"My name is Nicholas," the Farestere man said. He hobbled over and picked up the ruby ring from a pile of ash on the floor. "Happy to have this back. And, I'm sure you'll be needing this?" He took a few more labored steps and picked up Umhra's icon. He turned and offered it on an open palm, blue vapor enveloping his hand.

"Yes, thank you." Umhra took the pyramid and returned it to the pouch on his belt.

"If you pull on the femur at the apex of the throne's back, a door will open along that wall," Nicholas said.

Umhra wrenched the bone backward. A section of the wall along the far side of the room recessed with a low rumble and slid open exposing a narrow, unlit hallway.

"Barnswallow?" Umhra questioned.

"Indeed." Nicholas Barnswallow, one of the missing, flashed a shallow grin.

"Your brother and the Farestere of Festbury have been very worried for you."

"As well they should have been. If not for you, I have no

doubt the vampire would have had his way with me in short order. I had very little left to give."

Umhra took a small oil lamp from the wall. Blood was still running from the wound within his armor and dripped on the floor. He held the lamp out against the darkness of the tunnel, his sword at the ready.

Cobwebs danced as a steady breeze tugged at the hallway's natural stone walls. Sword in hand, Umhra depressed a large lever on the wall to his right and the wall slid back into place, cutting them off from the throne room.

The battered men labored along the hallway which pitched upwards for miles. Under normal circumstances, Umhra would have marveled at the undertaking it must have been to build the keep and all its facets. At the present, however, his only concern was survival.

After several hours, they approached a staircase leading up to an iron door above. At the foot of the stairs, Umhra fell to one knee.

"You need rest," Nicholas said.

"I'll rest when I see you to safety." Umhra placed a hand on the floor to steady himself.

"At least let me check your wound."

Umhra grimaced, lifting his arm to expose his damaged armor and the gash the Dokktari's glaive had left in his side.

Nicholas gasped. "By the gods, you are gravely injured. We must get to Anaris at once."

Nicholas tore a strip of linen from the bottom of his tattered shirt and packed it within Umhra's armor against the wound. "Hopefully, this will help staunch the bleeding a bit." He offered Umhra a hand, helped him to his feet, and they ascended the stairs. The door was locked, a rusted chain wrapped through its handles.

"Stand back." Umhra readied his sword. Nicholas backed down the staircase as Umhra struggled to hoist his sword overhead. Putting what energy he had left behind his weapon, he broke the chain. Umhra put his weight against the door which gave way much more effortlessly than he had expected.

The door swung open and the men found themselves behind a small waterfall. The rush of the cascade pounded the smooth stone of a small plateau, sending a cool mist into the air. Taking a deep breath, they gained a second wind and worked their way down a stone path along the side of the fall and out into the surrounding woods. Resting for a brief moment, the men drank from the cold stream below the fall.

"Ember's Way must be over there." Nicholas pointed to the west. The sun had not yet risen. Unsure as to the day, they got back on their feet and limped onward, following Nicholas's direction.

They trudged for the better part of an hour and exited the woods at a familiar stretch of Ember's Way. Farther south than Telsidor's Keep, Umhra recognized this place. It was close to where the Bloodbound camped the night Xig disappeared.

They clambered from the brush at the side of the road and onto Ember's Way, turning south toward Anaris. Umhra collapsed face down in the dirt path, his blood soaking the packed earth. Nicholas spun, rushed to his savior's side. He grabbed Umhra's armor by the collar of his breastplate and strained to get him to the side of the road. He was too weak and Umhra far too large and weighed down with armor.

▲

Nicholas struggled with Umhra's dead weight. A snarl greeted him from over his shoulder. He turned to see two very large wolf-like creatures emerge from the edge of the woods. They sniffed at the air and growled at the obstruction between them and an easy meal.

Nicholas grabbed Umhra's sword—which would have been a challenge even at full strength—but was unable to lift it in his weakened condition. The dire wolves' eyes glowed red as they circled and chattered back and forth to one another. Nicholas searched Umhra for anything that he could use as a weapon. Concealed at his waist, he found a dagger. With shaking hands, Nicholas pointed the blade at the dire wolves.

"You two better move on, you cannot have this one," he said in the dire wolves' language.

"The little one is quite special," said one dire wolf to the other as they separated to flank Nicholas. "I believe I will eat him first."

"Then I get more of the big one. Getting through his armor is going to take a bit of work," the other said.

"I'm warning you," Nicholas said.

"He's the size of a child," one dire wolf said. "Does he believe us to be dullards?"

"And the dagger is laughable," the other said, her hackles up.

The dire wolves crouched, preparing to attack, when two arrows flew out of the darkness, each hitting a target with a direct blow to the chest. The beasts roared and turned in the direction of the attack. Two more arrows hit the dire wolves, each through their right eye. Both collapsed to the ground, dead.

A hooded man approached from the wood's edge. "Nicholas Barnswallow is that you?" he asked from afar. Throwing back the hood of his brown cloak, he revealed an eternally young face—a gift from his Iminti heritage—but with softer features than the Evenese. His left cheek was marred by a scar running from just beneath his eye to the crest of his jaw. His dark hair and tan skin strongly contrasted his sky-blue eyes. He ran to Nicholas's side, secured his bow over one shoulder.

"Laudin," Nicholas said, wrapping his arms around the man. "My friend here saved my life and now he needs me to return the favor." Nicholas gestured to Umhra who lay unconscious on the ground. "Can you help me get him back to Anaris? I believe His Holiness may be able to help him as I am too weak in my current state."

"Of course, my friend. As I see you more clearly, it's obvious that you may need some tending to as well," Laudin said then whistled loudly. A beautiful buckskin horse trotted up the road. The stallion's toned frame twitched as he approached the group, his black legs stomping anxiously into the dirt. Laudin held out his hand and the horse pressed his muzzle into it and settled down. "Let's get him up on Ansel. Are you strong enough to ride?"

"With your help, I should be able to manage," Nicholas said.

Laudin knelt at Umhra's side and rolled him over onto his back. Umhra's now dimming blue glow shimmered with an erratic pulse from within his platinum armor. "He is a Paladin?" Laudin asked, running a hand through his hair.

"Yes. I was as astonished as you. I'll tell you my full tale when time is less pressing, but I assure you, he saved me from a great vampire and an army of Dokktari with a blast of divine light. The fiends were incinerated upon the spell's touch. It was one of the most amazing things I have ever witnessed in all of my adventures," Nicholas said.

"This must be kept quiet." Laudin stood. Umhra's armor vanished in a cloud of blue ether. "We must hurry. He's fading." Laudin lifted Umhra to his feet and then up onto the back of his steed. "I can't begin to fathom how he even exists. To my knowledge, there hasn't been a Paladin in Evelium since the onset of the Age of Forene. The sun is on the verge of rising. We must get him to the temple at Anaris before we call attention to ourselves." Laudin lifted Nicholas onto Ansel's saddle before mounting the horse himself. "Ansel, go." The horse jumped to a start and hit his full stride in moments.

CHAPTER 10

The gods have left us to fend for ourselves. Despair has spread throughout the land.
—The Tome of Mystics

Unknown Origin. Unearthed from the Ruins of Oda Norde, month of Bracken, 1320 AT

—▲—

Nicholas and Laudin raced for Anaris while Umhra draped limply over the saddle between them. The horse galloped against the rising sun. Passing Pell's orchard, they careened through Anaris's north gate, paying no notice to the two guards who instinctively gave chase. They went, in full haste, directly to the temple and threw open the door.

A monk sat at the temple's altar in meditation but jumped to his feet at the clamber.

"We need His Holiness immediately. This man's life depends on it," Laudin said, laying Umhra on a pew toward the rear of the nave.

The monk stared wide-eyed at the scene. "Now," Laudin said, taking an aggressive step toward the monk. The monk turned toward the east transept, but the temple door swung open again. The two guards from the north gate burst into the room.

"Oy! Who do you all think you are to rush past the gate without identifying yourselves and disrupt the peace in Trinity Temple? We will have you in irons for this behavior, you bastards," one of the guards said.

"I assure you that will not be necessary," said Balris Silentread, entering the sanctuary from the east transept. "I do apologize for my friends alarming you, but they are here on official church business at my request. They were asked not to waste any time and took my request quite literally, I am afraid. And please refrain from using such language in a house of the gods."

"Of course, my highest apologies, Your Holiness," replied one of the guards. "It will not happen again. We shall take our leave."

Balris rushed over to where Umhra lay on a stone pew. "Sir Peacebreaker." The body lay lifeless. "What tragedy has befallen him? Never mind. Quick, carry him to my private quarters. We need to remove his leathers before I can tell if there is anything I can do. Brother Kaleb," he said, turning to the monk who was still standing slack-jawed. "Please help carry Sir Peacebreaker, will you?"

The monk snapped to attention and helped Laudin carry Umhra back through the door at the east transept, following Balris and Nicholas who hurried out of the sanctuary. The private quarters of the temple clergy were serene. A short hallway lined with three stained-glass windows illuminated by the early-morning light. Another monk, portly and bald, sat on a stone bench reading an ancient tome. Upon seeing the frantic group enter the hallway, he rushed to the far doorway and swung the heavy oak door open for them. Balris led them through an empty sitting room and up a stone staircase, coming to a windowless hallway lined with doors. The last door led them into his private quarters.

"There. On the bed. Place him gently and remove his leathers and undergarments," Balris said as he filled a small bedside basin with water from a pitcher resting on his dark wooden dresser.

He prayed over the water as Laudin and Brother Kaleb placed Umhra on the bed. Nicholas jumped up on the bed at Umhra's side and began dismantling the straps of the leather armor covering his chest. He wrenched the cuirass from Umhra's body and pulled his thin linen shirt off over his head. Laudin and Kaleb each took a leg and removed his boots and pants. It took them a moment, but they managed to strip him of the rest of his leathers and undergarments and cover him with a fine linen sheet.

Laudin placed Umhra's clothing alongside his sword and shield in the corner of the room. As he did, Umhra's icon fell out of the small velvet bag where Umhra had kept it hidden for so long. He picked the icon up off the floor and inspected the small pyramid.

"Your Holiness, his totem is made of platinum," he said. "I've never seen such a thing. Never knew any existed."

"Are you certain?" Brother Kaleb asked, coming over to look for himself. "Yes, definitely platinum. Not in all my years. Am I mistaken, Your Holiness, to say that he is a Paladin? I thought—"

"You thought right, Brother Kaleb," Balris said, "And yes, my son, Sir Peacebreaker is a Paladin. The only of his kind to my knowledge. Please keep his secret between us in this room. I would hate to put Umhra or the church in harm's way."

"Yes, of course, Your Holiness."

"Laudin, please put the icon on the nightstand. Its proximity may help in the healing process," Balris said.

Balris carried the basin to the bedside and washed Umhra's wound. Radiating from the laceration was a deep purple bruise with tendrils extending out across Umhra's shoulder and chest. "As I feared, whatever weapon caused this injury was poisoned. I must act fast if he is to be saved."

With one hand, Balris grabbed the silver medallion that

hung around his neck, placing his other hand upon the wound. He closed his eyes and prayed aloud. His speech became more forceful, and a warm glow emanated from Umhra's wound as the poisonous discoloration withdrew. The light grew until those in the room were forced to avert their gaze. Balris held his hands in place, keeping the light focused within the wound, and completed his prayer. The light dimmed. He backed away from Umhra, revealing little more than a scar where the open gash was just moments ago.

Balris checked Umhra's pulse. "I suspect he will remain unconscious for some time, but I believe we acted in time to save his life. Brother Kaleb, thank you for your help. You may go about your day, but please no word of this to anyone. As for you, Nicholas Barnswallow, I am glad to see that you are alive, although I believe you are quite anemic, and in need of some attention yourself. You and Laudin will stay here at the temple until Sir Peacebreaker is well. Tonight, I request you both join me and a few trusted associates over dinner to recount your story. I know Lord Morrow will be interested in Umhra's return."

"Most agreeable, Your Holiness," Nicholas said, his voice hoarse.

"Are you certain that's necessary, Your Holiness?" Laudin frowned. "I'm in fine health, and you have my word that I will not speak of this unless under your direction."

"I know you will feel stifled by the request, Laudin, but I think it best until Lord Morrow is informed and comfortable with the path forward. I promise to make your sequester as enjoyable as possible, including free access to the courtyard."

"As you wish, Your Holiness."

"Let me show you each to private rooms." Balris stood and opened the door, guiding Laudin and Nicholas into the hallway. "Laudin, please make yourself comfortable in the second room on the left. Let me know if you should want anything. And thank you for your efforts on behalf of all that is good and right today.

I am sure this will not be the last time the gods will call upon you as their implement." Balris gave a deep and sincere bow in Laudin's direction.

"Think nothing of it, Your Holiness. You may call upon me as you deem necessary." Laudin returned the bow and saw his way to the room Balris had offered.

"Nicholas, my child, please." Balris opened the door to the adjacent room and ushered Nicholas inside. Nicholas went straight to the bed and collapsed. Balris filled a washbasin with water and placed it on the bedside table. "Take your rest, and clean up," he said. "But before I leave you in peace, let me heal your wounds." Balris once again clasped his silver hexagram medallion and placed his other hand upon Nicholas's forehead and prayed. The puncture wounds on his neck and wrists burned with a supernatural heat.

After a moment, Balris opened his eyes. "That should get you on your way to a full recovery, but there is no substitute for rest and nourishment. I shall have a page call for you at supper time."

Nicholas looked up at Balris, welcoming the warm flood of renewed energy. "He's extraordinarily powerful, Balris. I owe him my life."

"I know, Nicholas. But I believe once you get to know him you will realize that you don't owe him anything at all," Balris said. "Get some rest and tell us your story at supper. For now, I want only for you to concern yourself with your own well-being. I will have some food sent to you and Laudin post haste. You must be famished."

"I hadn't noticed until just now, but indeed I am." Nicholas's stomach growled. "Thank you, Balris." Tears welled in his eyes. Balris embraced him for a moment and then left Nicholas to get some rest.

CHAPTER 11

The dragons are feared most of all, but it is the Blights who threaten mankind's very existence.
—The Collected Letters of Modig Forene

Letter to Artemis Telsidor dated 12th of Mela, 996 AC.
Unearthed from the Ruins of Vanyareign, month of Ocken, 1301 AT

—▲—

Laudin shuddered at the click of the door latch, then bound across the room and threw open the window. He sat upon the ledge and welcomed the cool spring breeze on his face, the warm sun taking over when it ebbed. He peered out over the temple grounds. For the foreseeable future, the hedges forming the property's perimeter might as well have been the fortified walls of the Wretch, this room, his cell.

He took a deep breath, rummaged through his worn canvas satchel, and retrieved a piece of parchment and writing charcoal. He scribed an encoded message, written in a tongue no longer spoken in Evelium, and then curled the note into a tidy roll and made a shrill call out into the air.

He scanned the woods abutting the northern wall of Anaris, of which his room offered a view. Moments later, a harrier darted from the edge of the woods, climbed over the city wall, and the hedgerow of the temple compound, itself. The raptor's gaze fixed on Laudin as it ascended to his third-story window. Laudin held out his arm and the bird took hold and folded its wings. Laudin showed the hawk inside his room and let him perch on the back of a chair. He tossed the bird a welcomed scrap of meat from his bag.

"As always, thank you for answering my call, Taivaron." The bird spread its wings wide before refolding them and hopped back and forth on the back of the chair. "I need you to deliver a message for me to each of the Barrow's Pact." He placed the rolled parchment in a small vial attached to the harrier's right leg.

"I'm afraid your journey will be taxing, my friend. The last I heard from Shadow, he was familiarizing himself with settlements in the east. You may want to try Willow's Notch. Gromley has returned, for what reason I cannot pretend to understand, to his people at the Twelve Mines, and Naivara... well...she could be anywhere. She set off months ago to begin her Gold Suffusion."

Laudin stroked Taivaron's back and the bird bobbed its head up and down in acknowledgment of his request. He then offered the bird his forearm. Taivaron hopped on and Laudin released him out the window.

"Make haste," he said aloud to himself as Taivaron flew north out over Anaris and disappeared over the woods. "There's no telling what befalls us."

▲

Leaving Nicholas to his rest, Balris returned to his room where Umhra lay, stable but yet unconscious. Balris closed the door behind him and dragged the chair from his desk over beside the bed. He sighed.

"I don't know what to make of you, Sir Peacebreaker. I am unsure whether to now consider Ivory as a fool or a genius. I cannot fathom what made him think training you as a warrior of the gods was a good idea and yet, something is tugging at my soul telling me you have been sent to us with a purpose."

He leaned over, placing his right hand on Umhra's forehead, his left gripping his medallion. He closed his eyes and healed Umhra for the second time. Upon completing the ritual, Balris stood and walked over to his desk. Taking out a pen and parchment, he wrote a brief note.

A private dinner at the temple tonight.

Peacebreaker has returned.

While he wrote, Umhra's icon pulsed on the bedside table. Faint and irregular at first, the light grew in intensity and consistency. Umhra awakened.

"I cannot keep you hidden." Balris folded his letter and sealed it closed. "I must call on Espen and Jenta and have you share your story with them. We must have faith they will know what's best."

"I agree," Umhra said, his voice dry and weak.

Balris turned to the Paladin sitting up in bed. He smiled and rushed over to Umhra, who strained to get to his feet.

"Rest, Sir Peacebreaker," he said, supporting Umhra's arm. "You have been through a tremendous ordeal."

"Thank you for your concern and your aid," Umhra said, ignoring Balris's request. "There is much to be told, Your Holiness. Send your letter, I am prepared to meet my fate head-on."

"I thought that would be your position. I shall send my letter and return to you shortly. There is more I can do to fortify you yet." He smiled, walked to the door. "It is good to have you back among us," he said and left the room.

CHAPTER 12

With Aldresor's riddle solved, the seeds of a great family fortune were sown.
—The Gatekeepers' Abridged History of Tyveriel

Vol. 3, Chapter 11. Discovered in the Private Library of Solana Marwyn, the month of Vasa, 889 AT

—▲—

Dinner that evening was a quiet affair, not held in the main banquet hall of the temple, but rather in a private dining room reserved for Balris and his guests. When Nicholas and Laudin entered the room, Lord Espen Morrow and Lady Jenta Avrette were standing before a large circular table speaking with an anxious Nathaniel Barnswallow. Nathaniel ran to his younger brother, hugged him firmly, and then held him back, gripping him by the shoulders.

"No worse for the wear, I must say, Nicholas. You had us all worried sick," Nathaniel said, inspecting Nicholas with a discerning eye.

"All thanks to Balris, I assure you. You wouldn't have been so happy to see my condition this morning. And I'm afraid my mental state has not yet settled," Nicholas said. "Please, meet my friend Laudin. He saved Sir Peacebreaker and me from the fate of being devoured by two dire wolves this morning just before sunrise. Laudin, my brother, Nathaniel."

Nathaniel turned to Laudin and took his hand in both of his. "I'm eternally grateful for your heroic deed. I hope you will consider me the best of friends and call on me for whatever you see fit. There is nothing in this world more precious to me than my little brother." Nathaniel choked up. "I'm sorry. I suppose seeing Nicholas returned safely is a bit overwhelming."

"Think nothing of it, Nathaniel. I was lucky to pick up their trail when I did," Laudin said.

Espen escorted Jenta over to the men.

"Oh, how rude of me," said Nathaniel. "My apologies, Your Lordship, for not introducing you and Lady Avrette."

Lady Avrette smiled at Nathaniel. "No apologies necessary, my dear friend. I am quite pleased to see Nicholas has returned safely."

Lady Avrette extended her hand to Nicholas, who bowed. Lord Morrow turned to Laudin. "I am Espen Morrow, Lord of Anaris. Our thanks to you for returning our Nicholas and Sir Peacebreaker to us. You are forever welcome in our fine city."

Lord Morrow gestured to the table. "Please let's all be seated. Maybe you can share with us a little about yourself while we wait for Balris and Sir Peacebreaker to join us."

Laudin bowed to Espen and Jenta, and they each took a seat at the table.

"Sir Peacebreaker will be joining us? He is awake then?" Nicholas asked, his face lighting up at the notion.

"Yes," Lord Morrow said. "It will take some time for him to mend fully, but Balris has given him an excellent prognosis."

"Excellent news," Nicholas said. "I'm so looking forward to getting to know him better. Without him, Nathaniel, I would never have returned from Telsidor's Keep."

"Laudin," Lady Avrette said, "please tell us a little about yourself. It's not often we get to meet a true ranger."

Laudin turned his focus from the door to Lord Morrow's

beautiful wife. Her pale-green eyes waiting for him to speak.

"I assure you Lady Avrette, my story, as I'm able to tell it, isn't of much interest," Laudin said. "I was raised in Farathyr, the son of a general in the king's army. My parents were very traditional in my upbringing, but I was anything but traditional in my needs. From a young age, the wild called to me. I would adventure for extended periods, exploring the vast wilderness of our land. I learned to commune with the animals, I trained in archery, sword work, and the natural magic of Fara, and when I had convinced myself of my capabilities, I set off on my own to see what Evelium had in store for me."

"Most fascinating," Lord Morrow said. "You must share with us some of your adventures when we have the time."

Laudin nodded as the door opened and Balris entered the room followed by Umhra. Those seated at the table stood and greeted their host and the guest of honor.

Nicholas ran over and took Umhra by the hand. "You look much better, Sir Peacebreaker. I'm delighted to see you up and about," he said sincerely.

"Thank you, Nicholas. My thanks also for your help in getting us out of the keep and back to Anaris. Please, call me Umhra."

Nicholas led Umhra over to the table and showed him a seat next to Nathaniel, who greeted him enthusiastically. Balris sat between Umhra and Lord Morrow. All of the parties were in attendance and the dinner convened.

Other than a few scrapes and contusions, Umhra looked vibrant as Nicholas imagined a great Paladin would. Balris had taken the liberty of ordering some clothing Umhra would find acceptable. Tonight, he wore natural leather pants with matching boots and a green linen shirt. His black hair was tied back in a neat ponytail.

"I had the pleasure of getting to know Umhra a little today, and I must say he is a most remarkable man, with a most remarkable story for us tonight," Balris said. "I do want to remind all of you, however, he has been through a harrowing experience from which he is still recovering. Let's not stress him any more than need be and even then, only after we eat."

Balris rang a small bell on the table. A door opened and in paraded a cadre of servers, each with a platter piled high with food. The platters were placed in the middle of the table and the servers left as quickly as they entered. With the room now to themselves, everyone turned to the bounty before them. Umhra nudged the food about his plate, his gaze fixed on the knife he wielded in his meal's destruction. Sweat beaded on Umhra's forehead, and he shifted uncomfortably in his seat. When he pushed his plate away, having barely touched his food, Balris sat back in his chair and looked at him with sympathetic eyes.

"I know our guests will have many questions for you tonight, Umhra, but here you are among friends. Maybe you could begin by telling us exactly what happened on your quest to Telsidor's Keep."

Umhra took a small sip of water and cleared his throat. Easing his chair away from the table, he leaned forward toward the group as if he were preparing to tell a great secret.

The room hung on Umhra's every word as he recounted the Bloodbound's journey to Telsidor's Keep and horrors they confronted within. He told of Malthus Nofelt's betrayal as the vampire Manteis and of the Brothers of Resurrection and what little he knew of their plan.

"How did you live to tell of such an encounter?" Lord Morrow asked, sitting back in his chair and arching an eyebrow.

Umhra looked to Balris, and then down at the table, his hand moving to the pouch on his belt.

"Go on, Umhra, your secret is safe among these people."

"I reached into the pouch in which I've kept my icon hidden for so many years, having not used it since my adoptive father died." Umhra produced his icon and placed the small pyramid in the center of the table for all to see. "It was he who trained me in the ways of the Paladin."

"Paladin?" Lord Morrow stood from his chair. "How can

this be? The king must know at once."

"Espen. Do we not owe Sir Peacebreaker more than such a base response?" Lady Avrette said with a calm but forceful tone. "My brother shall know of this in due time, but I intend to hear our hero out."

Lady Avrette's gaze turned toward the icon from which blue ether danced into the air. "Umhra, is your icon platinum?"

"Yes, my lady. It is."

"I am unaware of anyone accomplishing such a Suffusion in Evelium or beyond. At least since the War of Rescission when Mystics still walked among us. This is an accomplishment most rare, especially at such a young age."

Umhra ignored the comment and continued his story. "I prayed to Vaila. Manteis found this amusing at first until I showed my divine power, at which point he became quite concerned. As he lunged toward me, I protected myself from the undead and then released a force of daylight through the keep, incinerating Manteis instantly and destroying many of his Dokktari minions in the process. At that point I lost consciousness, my power drained, having not used my abilities in so long. The next thing I remember is Nicholas calling my name to wake me. Nicholas, would you mind telling the rest?"

"It would be my pleasure, Umhra," Nicholas said, standing in his chair and leaning forward, his hands on the table. He told of their subsequent escape from Telsidor's Keep. The room was still for a moment, as those around the table contemplated the story.

Finally, Nathaniel broke the silence. "A truly amazing tale," he said. "Laudin, how was it you were there to assist?"

The ranger placed his goblet on the table. "When I heard Nicholas had gone missing, I was in Festbury visiting with the Farestere, as I do when I travel through these parts. We were all quite upset about the news, so I set out, working my way from Festbury down to Anaris, hoping to find some information on what had happened. By the time I picked up his trail, I realized

I was behind the dire wolves in tracking a bleeding man or woman. When I caught up with the beasts, they had engaged Nicholas and Umhra and I took them out from afar."

Espen returned to his seat, sat back, and rubbed his chin. "Sir Peacebreaker, I apologize for my earlier outburst, but I feel as though we must inform the king. It sounds as though this conspiracy is much larger than we initially thought. If there is, in fact, truth to the words of Malthus, or Artemis, or Manteis, the fate of Evelium hangs in the balance. The problem I see is if we were infiltrated here in Anaris, and if this Brothers of Resurrection has been successful elsewhere as purported, we have no idea whom to trust outside of this very room. As this is the case, the king will not be able to enlist his army to rid Evelium of this scourge. We must take a more thoughtful, precise approach." Lord Morrow's face twisted, he rubbed his forehead.

"Your Lordship," Laudin said, "upon getting Umhra and Nicholas safely back to the temple, I took the liberty of sending for help from my most trusted allies. Together we make up a band we refer to as the Barrow's Pact. My suggestion is we meet with them and the king in secret, and if the king pleases, we will make our way to Meriden along with Umhra and Nicholas and discover the truth behind this brotherhood and put an end to their great aspirations of overthrowing the king."

Lord Morrow considered the offer. After a moment, he turned to Balris. "What say you, Balris. Can such a scheme succeed?"

Balris looked at Laudin as he replied to the question. "Lord Morrow, there is no doubt Laudin is trustworthy. I would put my own life in his hands. I know of the allies he speaks of, and they have been quite instrumental on behalf of good on several occasions. I think this might be our best option, but we will succeed only if Umhra and Nicholas join this group with unbridled investment and only when they are completely healed of their afflictions." Balris then turned and placed his hand on Umhra's shoulder. "Umhra, shall such an arrangement be acceptable to you?"

"I do not doubt in my heart I can be great allies with Laudin and Nicholas, and anyone either of them see fit, but as soon as I'm well, I have unfinished business to attend to before I'll be able to consider my path forward." Umhra frowned, tears welled up in his eyes. "I left five of the best men I have ever known in Telsidor's Keep. I intend to return to the keep, clear the undercroft of any evil remaining, and retrieve the bodies of my friends so they may have a hero's passage into the afterlife."

"My companions should arrive in Anaris by the time you are well. Let us come with you to Telsidor's Keep and help in this most worthy of efforts. We'll see to the return of your friends and they shall be celebrated as the selfless heroes you knew them to be in life," Laudin said. The others around the table nodded. "Our participation will also give you some insight into the nature and abilities of the Barrow's Pact."

"I accept your gracious offer, Laudin," Umhra said. "I have much progress to make before I will be ready for any such mission. For tonight, I bid you all peace and well-being. I shall adjourn to my room."

The party stood in unison. They each took their turn bidding Umhra good night and the great warrior hobbled out of the dining room and back to his quarters.

As the door closed behind him, Lord Morrow turned to his wife. "Jenta, my dear, how will the king receive the news of a Paladin surfacing in his kingdom? I fear he holds fast to the norms of his forefathers. And one of Orcish blood, no less."

"I had been considering Shale's response all the while Umhra spoke. He might take the news harshly if we send word in advance, but if he were to meet Umhra face to face at our recommendation, I hardly see how he cannot see what I do. Umhra is truly a hero," Lady Avrette said.

"Very well. I shall send word only that a party from Anaris is coming to his court at our request. We say no more and let Umhra and the Barrow's Pact speak for themselves."

CHAPTER 13

Spara was at the edge of the clearing that day. She saw it all and was left blind as payment for her curiosity.
—The Tome of Mystics

Unknown Origin. Unearthed from the Ruins of Oda Norde, month of Bracken, 1320 AT

—▲—

A young Ryzarin sat at a worn gaming table holding his cards casually, one arm draped over the back of his chair. The candlelight flickered, revealing the age and state of disrepair of the Nightcrawler. Located in the village of Willow's Notch, the Nightcrawler rightfully claimed to be the oldest and, by reputation, the seediest tavern in all of Evelium. With his cards clutched in his left hand, the graphite-skinned Ryzarin peered, unaffected, at his counterparties.

Around the table sat two particularly bedraggled human men and a Farestere who reeked of whisky. The Farestere blinked, stared at his cards, adjusted the distance at which he held his hand. The Ryzarin assessed his quarry, and then shoved the unkempt pile of notes and coins sitting in front of him on the table into the pot. His lilac eyes twitched subtly. One of the human men raised an eyebrow, shoved what currency he had left to the center of the table, and called the Ryzarin's bluff. The other two followed suit.

The first of the two human men stroked his graying beard and shared his hand. “Full house, eagles over bards,” he said and puffed out his chest.

The second threw his cards on the table face down. “Bah. Two pair. The wife is gonna have my head.”

A grin spread across the Farestere’s face. “Four wyrmlings. Read ’em and weep.” He flipped his cards over, each bearing the depiction of a juvenile white dragon. The Farestere hiccupped.

No sooner had the Farestere’s cards hit the table, the Ryzarin revealed his rouse, weeks in the making, by throwing four black dragons face up on the table. “It’s been a pleasure, gentlemen, but I think our game has arrived at its inevitable conclusion,” he said, dragging the pot toward him with outstretched arms.

“Barra Argith, I will have your head for this,” said the bearded man, his face reddening. He stood from his chair and drew a tarnished silver blade from his scabbard. With his other hand, he flipped the table to its side, sending the uncollected coins scattering across the dusty, wide-planked floor, and the few remaining notes fluttering into the air. The other two players and a few other men who had been slumped over drunk at the bar, dove for the coins sent clattering under the adjacent tables.

The bar erupted into chaos, one man throwing a haymaker at another who went for the same sovereign notes. The Farestere man fell over a Zeristar and crawled for coins on the floor. Avoiding the ensuing brawl, the Ryzarin swept through the mayhem, plucking a few fluttering notes out of the air, and slipping out the door into the cool of the night. He lifted his black hood over his telltale white hair and all but vanished into the darkness.

“Where to next?” He wondered aloud with a smile, turning the corner into a dark alleyway.

He had been wandering Evelium since he was cast out of his Ryzarin colony located deep below the Ilathril Mountains. He left his given name, Barra Argith, behind except for circumstances where he needed a respectable sounding alias when seeking refuge or some advantage on a mark. He preferred the name Shadow, the translation of his given Ryzarin name to Evenese.

He passed beneath a canopy of alder trees lining the narrow dirt path to the Weary Monk and recognized the familiar call of Laudin's harrier, Taivaron. The bird swooped out of the night sky and perched on a low alder branch just before him along the path.

"Hello, my friend. How exciting to see you." Shadow greeted the bird. He held up his arm and Taivaron drifted down from his perch. Shadow noticed the vial on the harrier's yellow shin. "I see you bear news from Laudin. It's been some time since I've seen him or the rest of the Barrow's Pact." He sighed.

Shadow untied the note from Taivaron's leg and placed the hawk on his shoulder. He unfurled the parchment and read the coded message within:

Come to Anaris immediately.

Evelium's sovereignty is at stake.

Laudin

"It seems my conflict has been resolved. I leave for Anaris tonight. Taivaron, Gromley is next on the list. You must go to him at once." He re-secured the note to Taivaron's shin. "Fly safely, friend. Thank you for your efforts. I shall see you again soon, I suspect." He transferred Taivaron back to his arm and thrust him into the sky. As quickly as he appeared, the harrier disappeared into the ebony night.

Shadow continued on his way to the Weary Monk which was dark but for a solitary light offering its honey glow through the innkeeper's window. The modest wood building creaked in the evening breeze, its shutters rattling with each gust. Shadow opened the front door and peered inside. Rish must have fallen asleep reading again. Shadow stepped into the darkened foyer and rushed to the stairs.

"Shadow, is that you lad?" a voice asked from the innkeeper's quarters.

Shadow stopped, one hand on the banister. “Sure is, Rish. What can I do for you?”

The door to Rish’s room creaked open, and a kind-looking man, portly, and in his later years, joined him in the foyer. He wore plain clothes and spectacles that sat slightly askew on his nose. His feet were bare and he held a tattered book under his arm. “It’s just I haven’t seen you for the better part of the month, and I hate broaching the matter, but you are quite behind on your room payments.” He stretched his arms and yawned.

“Of course, Rish. Sorry about that. Always slips my mind, what with being so busy looking for work. How much do I owe you?”

“Let’s just call it ten sovereigns and we’re even.”

“You’re too kind, Rish,” Shadow said. “No wonder the place looks so distressed. I know I owe you at least twice as much. You really shouldn’t be so forgiving.”

“Money isn’t everything, lad.”

“Have you looked around lately, Rish?” Shadow said, handing the man twenty-five sovereigns from a small black pouch on his hip. “Money is *everything*. I had a good night, keep the little extra for your troubles. Consider it interest.”

“Most kind, Shadow. Maybe I’ll fix the leak in the roof you’ve been going on about.”

“I gave up on that dream a couple of months ago, Rish.” Shadow laughed. “Besides, no need on my account. I’m taking my leave tonight. Won’t be back for some time, I suspect.”

“Sorry to hear that. It’s been a pleasure having you about. Except for hounding you about the rent, that is. Where are you off to?”

“Not sure.” The lies flowed far too easily. “There is so much I still haven’t seen.”

“Ah. To be young and unattached. I remember the days fondly,” Rish said, a far-off look in his eyes. “Well, I’ll let you be on your way then. May the gods be with you, young man, and thank you for settling up before you left."

"You as well, Rish."

Shadow bound up the stairs two at a time, leaving Rish alone in the foyer. He entered the room in which he had stayed for the last several months. While he had grown fond of Willow's Notch, he did not regret his hastened departure.

Shadow crouched beside the low-set bed which clung to the wall opposite the doorway, nearly spanning its entirety. He slid a black satchel from deep beneath the wooden frame. Then from his belt, he drew a silver dagger and carved an S on the wall behind the bedside table. With utter detachment, he left the little room and descended the stairs. The foyer was now empty, the light from Rish's room snuffed out.

Shadow continued his way outside and around the back of the inn. The path was narrow and lined with a tangle of lavender which filled the early-morning air with a mild, pleasant fragrance. Behind the inn were a modest yard and a small stable where a few horses, most well past their prime, were kept. One stood out from the rest. This was Shadow's steed, Ramoth, who grew restless upon his master's return.

The midnight-black horse greeted Shadow with a nicker, scratched his hoof at the stall door. "We have a long ride ahead of us, boy." Shadow opened the stall door and patted the horse on his muscular neck. He led Ramoth out of the stable and into the yard. Ramoth shook his mane and snorted. Shadow saddled, then mounted the horse and cracked his reins. Ramoth leaped forward into a gallop and the two rode west out of town, hugging the edge of the Dire Swamp where the will o' wisps drifted through the air hoping an errant soul would come their way. As day broke with a thick fog hanging over the rolling foothills of the Seorsian Mountains, the pair rose out of the lowlands and rode for Anaris.

CHAPTER 14

The two swords were forged in Antiikin. One was given to Modig Forene and the other claimed by Telsidor from its ruins.
—The Gatekeepers' Abridged History of Tyveriel

Vol. 2, Chapter 37 – Unearthed from the Ruins of Meriden, the month of Ocken, 1240 AT

—▲—

Gromley Strongforge, a cleric in the Zeristar clan of the Twelve Mines, sat at a large banquet table, fiddling with the gold amulet he wore around his neck out of boredom. The amulet was in the shape of an eight-pointed star, signifying his order's commitment to maintaining the bond between the Zeristar's prominent families. He was broad-shouldered and short of stature—which was customary of the Zeristar—but his black hair worn short and full beard, braided neatly, identified him as a man of the cloth. Unlike the other clerics of his order, however, Gromley detested life within the mountains, much preferring the expanse of the surface.

He had not been out of the halls of Mount Anvil for months and ached for adventure. As his uncle, Fardrom, lord of the Western Zeristar, addressed the clan for the second consecutive hour, Gromley had an urge for fresh air. Throwing his chair back from the table, he excused himself, and left the banquet hall, cutting between the immense pillars to hasten his escape.

Navigating the stone hallways and staircases of his childhood, he made his way to an expansive balcony positioned above two immense iron doors that served as the main entrance to the Zeristar stronghold. He placed both hands on the balcony rail, inhaled deeply, and surveyed the Isle of the Twelve Mines. His view extended eastward to the Straight of Mesorith which separated the island from Lertmor and, farther beyond, mainland Evelium. Peering into the distance, he noticed a bird of prey approaching from the southwest, its form unique from the seagulls complaining overhead despite their obvious domination of the skies. He waited on the bird, which dropped from its glide path on a high air current and dove with purpose in his direction.

The bird descended rapidly on its approach. Gromley recognized the raptor as Taivaron and a broad smile cracked his austere expression. "My wonderful Taivaron," he called out to the bird, holding his robed arm as high as he could.

Taivaron landed on his arm, panting with exhaustion, revealing the great distance he had traveled in locating the next member of the Barrow's Pact on his list. "Why've you traveled so far to visit me, my friend? Shall we see?" Gromley took the note from the heaving bird's shin and read.

"We must leave immediately," Gromley said. "Taivaron, you will stay by my side until you are rested from your arduous journey. I am afraid as soon as you are able, you must fly to find Naivara. You would know better than I, but I suspect she will be found deep in the Wistful Timberlands. Last I heard, she was preparing for her Gold Suffusion." Gromley put the bird on his shoulder and made for his room to gather some necessities.

Returning to the depths of the mountain stronghold, Fardrom was waiting for Gromley in the great stone hall. "Did you think I would not know what your departure from my address of the clan would mean?" he asked as Gromley approached, pointing at the raptor perched on his nephew's shoulder. "What might seem like an innocent, if not un-Zeristar, act of stepping out for some fresh air, always holds a deeper meaning for a cleric. Now I see you with the ranger's harrier on your shoulder and I know you are off on another expedition."

"Uncle, you know I love our people, and all I do is on behalf of the Zeristar. Laudin does not call upon me for trivial matters and, as such, I heed his call when it arrives. For him to send Taivaron from Anaris, and even farther I suppose, speaks to the import of the matter at hand. I mean to set sail for Anaris this afternoon and I do not expect to return until the expedition has met its end."

"I know there is no talking you out of this, nephew. You are every bit as stubborn as your father, may his soul have found peace at the side of Orys. Ever since you were a child, you were prone to wandering off and getting yourself into trouble. I see no reason for you to stop now. If this matter is of such urgency as you claim it to be, I bid you safe travels and will pray for your success. You are the last of our family's bloodline. Your loyalties do not belong only to the ranger, but to your family and forefathers as well. Remember that."

"Uncle, I am a Strongforge cleric, not a Cepryn. My father saw to that when he bequeathed me to the Order. There are no Cepryns left but you."

"You are his son, Gromley, whether you have taken the Strongforge name or not. You will always be a Cepryn first in my eyes. I wish you saw it in the same light."

Fardrom turned and made his way back to the great hall where the clan elders were still in session. Gromley stroked his beard, considering his uncle's words, and turned toward his quarters.

He entered the room through a heavy, iron-reinforced, wood door, and placed Taivaron on the high back of a chair in the corner next to his bed. Kneeling on one knee, he hauled a chest from underneath the bed; the heavy container scraping across the stone floor. He opened the chest and removed an ornate silver war hammer, engraved with an image of the Anvil Stronghold on both sides, and two throwing axes. The hammer was given to him by his father, Thelrik Cepryn, just before Gromley traveled to mainland Evelium for the first time. It had belonged to his family for generations and was Gromley's most prized possession. He gripped the sturdy shaft, which set his heart racing. He admired the weapon for a moment, and then retrieved a leather pack from the chest and placed them on the bed.

He went to an armoire at the far side of the dimly lit room. The doors groaned as he opened them for the first time in over a year, revealing a shield with the same mountain scene embossed in gold, a set of chain mail armor, and a deep orange cloak with gold adornments. He took pride in the weight of the armor as he took each piece from the cabinet.

Taking meticulous care while he dressed, he finished his metamorphosis by throwing the cloak around his shoulders and tying it across his chest. He secured his shield over his back and grabbed the pack, his hammer, and the axes. He then waived Taivaron over. The great bird flew over and landed on the Zeristar's broad shoulder, gripping onto the thick orange fabric of the cloak to steady himself. Gromley gave one more glance around the room, and then walked out and closed the door.

He traversed the endless labyrinth that was the stronghold, coming to a small secondary exit—little used by the clan—to leave without causing a disturbance. He'd leave the explanation of his sudden departure to his uncle, knowing his unforgiving clan would not understand his compulsion to get involved in the happenings of the topsiders on the mainland. A Zeristar's place, after all, is in his mountain.

He forced a large, rusted lever from left to right, and the locking mechanism of the door released. Gromley walked out into the warm sun of the late spring afternoon. He closed the door behind him, tugging at it to make certain it was locked, and he made his way down a narrow stone staircase carved out of the bottom of the mountain leading to the wharf at the Bay of Tailings. When he arrived at the wharf, the gulls he found so annoying earlier, now called him to the open water with their cries. He breathed in the salty air and let it fill him with the essence of the mystery awaiting.

The wharf hummed with chaotic activity. It served as the center of commerce between Anvil and the mainland. The Zeristar miners traded their coal, gold, diamonds, and other jewels, and miscellaneous discoveries from deep within the Twelve Mines for basic commodities such as grains, cured meats, textiles, and any other goods in short supply. As such, the wharf was a vibrant site teeming with diversity.

Gromley passed a group of Iminti seamen and walked the length of the central pier. "Wharfinger," he said, "I will be taking the Hammertoss out for a jaunt and need provisions for a month to be on the safe side. Can you arrange that for me, mate?"

The wharfinger finished yelling at a young Zeristar who had dropped a crate of cabbages as he unloaded a ship from Meriden. "Another fantastic adventure, Gromley?" he laughed. "I'll have the Hammertoss ready to sail within the hour."

Gromley continued to the last slip on the central pier where the Hammertoss was moored. "Thank you, mate," he said over his shoulder to the wharfinger who dismissed him with a careless wave of his hand and returned to berating the wharf hand who scrambled on hand and knee to gather the scattered produce.

Gromley approached the Hammertoss, a spring in his step. It was a small, but sturdy vessel of classic Zeristar design, with a high figurehead depicting a Zeristar warrior holding a war hammer with both hands back over his head as if prepared to throw the weapon at an enemy. The single sail was a deep orange, matching Gromley's cloak, and the vessel had a small cabin below the deck for storage and refuge from inclement weather. Gromley bounded aboard, placing Taivaron on the boom, and put his belongings in a small chest immediately in front of the tiller at which he would steer beneath the stars.

He peered out over the open water as two wharf hands arrived and loaded the cabin with provisions, including a barrel of fresh water, food for at least a month, and miscellaneous gear Gromley might need for such a long journey at sea. Gromley threw each of the wharf hands a half-sovereign piece for their efforts and finished making his final preparations to set sail. He took one last look at Mount Anvil in the distance and untied his moorings, setting the boat adrift. He rowed into open water until the sail caught the wind and lurched the Hammertoss forward. Gromley was on his way to Anaris, to Laudin, and the rest of the Barrow's Pact.

CHAPTER 15

How is one to contend with an ally that has grown too strong? The strength of the Paladins could be society's undoing.
—The Collected Letters of Modig Forene

Letter to Admiral Kellan Essl dated 22nd of Vasa, 7 AF. Unearthed from the Ruins of Vanyareign, month of Ocken, 1301 AT

—▲—

A pack of wolves enjoyed a midday nap amongst the tall grasses of a sun-drenched clearing surrounded by a thick, ominous woods. At the epicenter of the pack, sleeping without concern, was the alpha female, her thick tail shading her eyes. She was somewhat larger than the rest of her pack and had a red tinge to her coat that made her stand out from the sea of gray she napped amidst.

The pack's restful slumber was interrupted by the unwanted chatter of a bird in the trees at the perimeter of the clearing. The alpha female opened an eye in a half-hearted attempt to identify the annoyance. At that moment, a sleek gray blur strafed the pack before lifting back up into the trees on the other side of the clearing. The she-wolf's green eyes met with those of

Taivaron. She stood, stretched her front legs, and then her back, and gave a wide-mouthed yawn. She trotted over to the harrier and polymorphed into her Reshinta form. The rest of the pack returned to its nap, undisturbed by the change.

Naivara Marabyth was strikingly beautiful by conventional standards, although she was not considered so by her tribe. As such, there was no place for her among the fair-haired Reshinta.

Setting off at the age of sixteen, she found her calling among the wild creatures of Evelium and those that protected them. Welcomed just as she was, she vowed never to return to her people and what she deemed to be their petty, superficial customs. Instead, she communed with the people of the forest and learned their ways and those of their god, Tayre.

Naivara's long, flowing, red hair cascaded over a plain silver circlet and framed her pale face. She wore an olive-green leather vest covered in ornate etchings, yellow pants, and olive-green boots that rose above her knees. In her hand, she held a gnarled quarterstaff fashioned from the branch of a yew tree. Her vibrant green eyes welcomed Taivaron. "Come to me, Taivaron. Let me see what gifts you carry," she said. Taivaron dropped down from the tree and perched on the knob at the top of her quarterstaff. Naivara gently removed Laudin's note from the harrier's yellow shin. She read the note.

"I knew when I saw you, all was not right," she said. "Why is it that you never come to me with good news?" The harrier tilted his owl-like face and chirped a few times. "I will need just a few days to complete my Suffusion and then, if you are agreeable, I will fly with you back to Anaris."

Taivaron hopped off of the quarterstaff and flew back over to a low-hanging branch nearby.

"All right then, back to work."

Naivara retreated to the center of the wolf pack and sat back on her heels. From her satchel, she removed a plain gold circlet, similar to that of the silver one she wore across her forehead. She'd had it fashioned for her by a jeweler in Festbury when she was there last with Laudin. Gently, she placed the gold circlet on a smooth oval stone in front of her and closed her eyes in meditation.

For a long while, she sat, staring at the circlet, the forest around her quiet and still. She prayed to her chosen deity—Tayre, the God of Forests. Through the night and into the next day, she meditated on the circlet, connecting with the band as if they were one. As the sun climbed to a peak over the clearing in which she sat, the forest closed in around her, blocking out the sky.

The circlet and the stone upon which it sat pulsed, as if under an invisible force. The pressure built, and the stone transmuted into liquid form, taking on a similar visage to that of a large ball of mercury. Naivara's reflection, distorted by the rounded surface of the transformed stone, was met by the image of a being not of the material world.

The god's face was jagged and wild, his skin resembling the bark of an ancient aspen tree. Within two of the diamond-shaped lenticels covering his face, were small forest green eyes. Three branch-like horns protruded from Tayre's head. He had no other facial features—no nose or mouth. He was the definition of primordial life.

"Naivara," he said. His voice rumbled like thunder. "For your faith and devotion. For your deeds in my name, I come to you."

"Thank you. I am humbled. I present to you my gold circlet for Suffusion, should you deem me fit."

"Gold is reserved for but a few of my devotees. You are a jewel among them and I grant this request with pleasure. Tell me, child, what gift have you prepared for me?"

"This pack of wolves. I have been with them for many a month and have taught them your ways. They have seen the light of Tayre in the darkness of this forest and have agreed to devote themselves to you."

"These creatures, so wild and noble, are a worthy offering.

I shall watch over them and see them thrive. Your Suffusion is granted."

"Thank you. I shall not disappoint you."

Tayre's image faded from the smooth surface of the transmuted stone. Naivara maintained her focus, the circlet levitating over the stone and spinning slowly. From its smooth, gold surface grew small tines until it resembled a delicate, unending branch of a tree. The circlet returned to the rock and the rock reassumed its natural form. The forest retreated, the sky cleared.

Two days had passed since Taivaron's arrival, and Naivara completed her Suffusion. She removed the silver circlet, her hair flowing wildly in its absence, and tucked it into her satchel. She leaned forward and picked up her new circlet, placed it upon her head, and smiled. The circlet shrank subtlety for a perfect fit. She stood and turned to her pack.

"I must leave you for a while," she said. "I have enjoyed our time together and hope to return to you again in the future, should fate allow. Tayre will look over you now, have no fear." Several of the wolves paced to Naivara's side and nuzzled her at the hip. She took a moment to pat each of them, said her goodbyes. Then, she closed her eyes, whispered a few words in her druidic tongue, and polymorphed into a female harrier. With a few powerful thrusts of her wings, she met Taivaron on the branch where he waited for her patiently. The two birds chirped back and forth for a moment and then lifted off into the southern sky.

CHAPTER 16

The Zeristar retook the Isle of the Twelve Mines and triumphantly returned to their stronghold within Mount Anvil.
—The Gatekeepers' Abridged History of Tyveriel

Vol. 2, Chapter 42 – Unearthed from the Ruins of Meriden, the month of Ocken, 1240 AT

—▲—

More than a month had passed since Taivaron left in search of the rest of the Barrow's Pact. In that time, and with Balris's help, Umhra and Nicholas had healed quite thoroughly. Umhra trained and studied tirelessly as he prepared for his return to Telsidor's Keep. To pass the time, Nicholas had immersed himself in his music, prolifically writing song after song on his lute. Laudin seemed the least settled of all, spending much of the day watching the horizon from the vantage of the temple's central spire, where the view was unhindered for as far as the eye could see.

The ranger was anxious. Anxious for the convergence of the Barrow's Pact. Anxious to finish his sequester at the temple and begin a new and dangerous adventure. Each day as the sun set in the west, he would brood for a moment over having to spend another night behind lock and key.

That changed one clear afternoon when Laudin set his spyglass on a ship approaching Anaris from the southwest. The vessel was of Zeristar design and boasted a burnt-orange sail.

Anxiety turned to excitement, and Laudin descended from the spire to report the good news to Nicholas, Umhra, and Balris. In the courtyard, Nicholas was performing a new song for Balris under a pear tree while Umhra trained in the midday sun. Laudin called to his friends. "A Zeristar ship approaches from the southwest. It's Gromley's ship, the Hammertoss. I expect he could be here as early as tomorrow at high sun."

Nicholas stopped mid-song, his lute still ringing the last note he struck.

"That's fantastic news," Balris said. "I'll let Lord Morrow know that we may begin our final preparations. Hopefully, the others aren't too far behind. Nicholas, the song is truly uplifting. I'm sure the rest is equally so. Perhaps you'll play it for us all when we need it most." With that, Balris excused himself and returned to the temple.

Laudin walked over to Umhra, who had stopped his exercises. "Umhra, if Gromley is this close, then Shadow is already on his way and Taivaron must have located Naivara by now. The Barrow's Pact is converging upon Anaris. We will see to it that you meet your goal at Telsidor's Keep. That I promise. Then we'll set off and tell the king your story and explain the imperative at hand."

"Please, tell me about your friends. I should like to know more about them before they arrive," Umhra said.

The two men sat under the pear tree with Nicholas. Umhra wiped his sweating brow. Laudin wasted no time in telling his new friends about the great allies who would arrive shortly.

"Gromley Strongforge and I met one night at the Speckled Pony up in Requiem ten years ago. He'd recently left the Isle of the Twelve Mines for the first time. He was in search of adventure. He'd spoken to a local jewel merchant in town who told him a fanciful story of a great treasure supposedly buried amongst the dead in a group of barrows outside of town. Gromley had told the merchant he had a partner and that the three could go to the barrows and find the treasure together for an even split. Not having the partner he had promised, Gromley was looking for someone to accompany him on the expedition to find this treasure along with the merchant," Laudin said.

"Hearing this, I thought if I didn't help this naïve Zeristar, he would surely end up dead. After an hour or so of discussion, I agreed to go along for an even third of our findings. Frankly, I never thought we'd find anything, and I would have gone just for the experience, but I figured that the poor fellow was in over his head and could be taught a lesson while not being taken advantage of or harmed by this supposed jewel merchant.

"The next morning, we met early and visited with the third member of our party. This 'jewel merchant' was a young Ryzarin, and as suspicious and untrustworthy a character as I'd ever met. While his charms worked on the unsuspecting Gromley, I saw through his charade immediately. Expecting the worst of this Ryzarin, who called himself Barra Argith, we set off in search of the barrows and the lost treasure.

"It was a three-day hike out of Requiem over the exposed plains of Windswept before we would arrive at the burial mounds. On the first night, the jewel merchant offered to take the first watch. Not trusting him, but also not seeing the likelihood of him attempting any subterfuge until we located the treasure, I agreed, but only feigned sleep as to monitor his behavior. To my surprise, he was vigilant in his protection of our small camp and spent most of the time sharpening his daggers while patrolling the perimeter. He woke me in a timely fashion and seemed to fall asleep quickly when I relieved him of duty, although I do believe that I noticed him watching me as the night wore on."

Nicholas, having heard this story more than once before, tuned his lute and smiled at Umhra, who was captivated by Laudin's tale.

"On the second day, we encountered a goblin camp just north of Spara's Watch. We were able to evade them initially, but a small scouting contingency caught our scent and managed to track us down. Outnumbered twenty to one when the entire camp arrived, Gromley and Barra proved themselves most useful in this first battle of ours. Gromley wielded his war hammer with skill and Barra swept lithely through the enemy, dropping one after the other with a dagger in each hand. Ultimately, there were too many of them, and we were surrounded. Just as they closed in on us, a herd of buffalo stampeded over a nearby ridge and ran directly into the goblin horde, eliminating at least half of their number as they raced past us. The tide had turned, and we were able to negotiate victory with only a few remaining goblins retreating to live another day.

"The buffalo herd settled only a short distance from us near one of their fallen. With a goblin spear stuck in its side, the beast took its last breath. As it exhaled for the last time, the buffalo transformed into a beautiful Reshinta woman with red flowing hair. Where her buffalo form died, she sat injured, but quite alive. I must admit, I was quite taken aback the first time Naivara Marabyth's welcoming green eyes met mine," Laudin said.

"Gromley rushed to the young woman's side. He convinced her to let him lay his hands upon her, despite her initial protest. He exposed an amulet kept tucked beneath his armor and placed his free hand upon the wound. A honeyed glow grew from beneath his hand as he prayed to his god. In an instant, Naivara was healed. My newfound friend was more than he initially let on, as well.

"After a brief rest, Naivara explained to us that she'd been in the area protecting this herd of buffalo from the goblin horde which had been making its way through the region, decimating the population for meat, hide, and horn, and trading the ample excesses they were harvesting to Orcs and Ryzarin in exchange for weapons they could use in their raids on peaceful villages throughout their territory. When she saw how distracted they were with us and how we were fighting valiantly, but sure to lose nonetheless, she opportunistically led the stampede right into the heart of the tribe to inflict mass casualties on their highest ranks.

"That night we camped together, surrounded by the buffalo herd, whom Naivara suggested were very grateful for our assistance in ridding them of the goblin scourge. Sitting around our fire, I stated quite plainly I would go no further on our quest until everyone revealed their true nature and intentions.

"Gromley revealed he was a cleric of the Order of Anar from the Twelve Mines and he'd left his home in the depths of Mount Anvil seeking adventure and comradery from those outside his very controlled Zeristar upbringing. Barra's true nature had been exposed during the battle against the goblins. The truth poured out of him like the Greater Falls into the River Torrent. He told us his story of being cast out by his Ryzarin clan as a youngling, only twenty-four seasons old by the Ryzarin calendar, for once venturing up to the surface because he wanted to see what the sun looked like. Tainted as a topsider, he was not welcome to return and had been on his own ever since. He wandered Evelium, struggling to subsist for some time until he started utilizing his innate skills in persuasion, thievery, and deception to survive. Such a path necessitated him to live as a nomad, moving between villages and cities, looking for any way to make ends meet. After hearing about a great treasure buried in the depths of the Barrows of Amari, he put a team together to locate and retrieve the riches. His deception was purely employed because he feared his true story wouldn't be viewed as believable. His ruse laid bare, he asked us to call him by his chosen name, Shadow which is his Ryzarin name translated to Evenese.

"Satisfied with their explanations, I thanked them both and asked Naivara if she would care to join us for an even split of the riches. At first, Shadow protested my offer, but he quickly saw the value of having someone with Naivara's skill set join our cause and conceded to split the profits four ways. Naivara, mostly out for entertainment I believe, agreed to join us and so, the Barrow's Pact was formed."

Laudin stopped, considering his story complete.

"Well?" asked Umhra. "What of the barrows and the treasure?"

"That's a story for another time," Laudin said, smirking. "What needs to be known at the moment is the Barrow's Pact survived that first adventure...and several more since."

"Fair enough. Though, you must promise to finish the story. Maybe after we return from Meriden, having put the Brothers of Resurrection behind us," Umhra said.

"Agreed. For now, let's focus on the task at hand."

Laudin stood. "I think I'll run to the watchtower and check in on how Gromley progresses."

"Lovely story, ranger. But I dare not call this arrangement discrete," a familiar voice said from over his shoulder.

Laudin turned to see a hooded figure dressed entirely in black. What little was exposed of his ashen skin glistened in the bright sun, revealing how out of place he was. Cunning lilac eyes examined his companions.

"Shadow, my friend. How wonderful it is to see you. I spotted Gromley's ship earlier today but had no idea you were already so near." Laudin put his right hand on Shadow's shoulder.

"Would you expect to spot me coming, like that clambering Zeristar?" Shadow laughed.

"Please, come," Laudin said, turning back toward Nicholas and Umhra. "You, of course, remember Nicholas. And this is our new friend, Umhra. Gentlemen, this is Shadow of whom I told you."

"A pleasure to see you again, Shadow." Nicholas stood and took a playful bow.

"The pleasure is all mine, Nicholas. You look well."

"Time heals all wounds, I suppose," Nicholas said.

Umhra rose, extended his hand. "An honor. Laudin speaks most highly of you, and I find him to be a man of great sincerity. Anyone he sees as worthy can count on my sword."

Shadow nodded and shook Umhra's hand. "I'll remember that. Nice to meet you."

"Come Shadow, we have much to discuss. It's been too long," Laudin said, leading Shadow across the courtyard and into the temple. They climbed the spiraling staircase to the spire's peak and sat, keeping watch on Gromley's ship, the salted breeze crystalizing on their cloaks.

"A bit serious, your new friend. No?" Shadow asked as they both looked out over the Sea of Widows.

"Perhaps," Laudin said, "but then again, I know of no other Paladins to compare him to."

Shadow pivoted his head toward Laudin, his eyes wide. "A Paladin? What trouble have you invited us into now?"

"Yes, and a powerful one, it seems. He has attained his Platinum Suffusion. Helping him in his quest to save Evelium from the return of Naur is bound to be quite a remarkable experience," Laudin said.

Shadow buried his face in his hands. "I should have stayed a common thief."

"Why? When you are an exceptional one."

▲

The following evening, the sun low on the horizon, Laudin stood on a wide wooden pier at the westernmost end of Anaris Harbor. The water lapped gently against the rock-strewn shore behind him, as the Hammertoss, with its orange sail, approached the dock.

Manning the tiller, Gromley guided the boat toward shore and lowered the sail. As the Hammertoss approached the mooring, Gromley threw a rope to his friend. Laudin tied the rope around a piling. Upon securing a second rope at the aft of the boat, Gromley leaped ashore and bear-hugged Laudin.

His beard was crusted with salt. "After nearly a month at sea, I am certain to be most pungent. You must excuse me, but I cannot contain my excitement to see you, dear Laudin, and to be away from Mount Anvil on another adventure. After I bathe, you must tell me all about why you called me here, as Taivaron's message was most vague," he said, giving Laudin a stiff shove in the arm.

"Absolutely, Gromley. I'm happy to explain everything... after a bath."

Laudin jumped aboard the Hammertoss and gathered Gromley's personal effects. He had forgotten how heavy the Zeristar hammer and shield were. He passed them over the side of the boat to their owner and effortlessly leaped over the port side rail of the Hammertoss carrying the rest of Gromley's belongings to rejoin him on the pier.

"Gromley, my friend, it's a great pleasure to see you again," Laudin said, putting his free arm around the Zeristar. "Possibly this time, I can convince you to stay with us, where you belong, and not return to the Twelve Mines. I'm sure once you learn of the mission at hand, you'll be most intrigued. For now, let's get you to the temple and cleaned up a spot."

▲

Gromley reappeared for dinner and he was impeccably groomed, with his long black beard woven into a complex braid. He wore a fine orange velvet coat over a white shirt and royal blue pants tucked into high leather boots, his gold amulet prominently displayed around his neck. The rest of the group was waiting in Balris's private dining room.

Gromley strode directly to Shadow, grabbing him upon both arms firmly. "How've you been, you shifty bastard?" he greeted the Ryzarin with a bellowing laugh.

Shaking his head, Shadow put his arm around Gromley's neck and head-locked him for a moment. "It's nice to see that some things never change, you irritating mountain dweller.

Please meet our new friends," he said, gesturing to the table where Umhra sat.

"Well, word to the gods, what do we have here? A platinum Paladin?" he asked, inspecting Umhra and able to see his divine nature where others could not. "Brother, I would wager you are the only of your kind. I am humbled to have the opportunity to meet you."

Umhra stood. "How am I so obvious to you?" he asked, shaking Gromley's hand.

"One of the benefits of my studies is that of true sight," Gromley said. "Pleased to meet you, Umhra is it?"

"Yes, and you must be Gromley. Laudin has told me great things about you."

"And he's told me so little about you," Gromley said. "Oh Laudin, you never cease to amaze me. What other surprises you must have in store." He held Umhra's hand in both of his.

The hearty Zeristar then introduced himself to Balris, thanking him for his hospitality, and walked over to the Barnswallow brothers. "I assure you I am among your biggest fans," he said to Nathaniel. "Your ales are most resplendent, Lord Barnswallow."

"Thank you, Sir Strongforge," Nathaniel said. "It's a pleasure to meet you, my brother has shared with me many stories of your adventures."

Gromley turned to Nicholas. "You look wonderful, young Nicholas," he said, grabbing Nicholas's hand. His brow furrowed, his smile faded. "I sense, however, all has not been well for you recently. I am glad to see you have recovered."

"Thank you, Gromley," Nicholas said. "It's nice to see you as well. Congratulations on your Gold Suffusion. Most impressive."

"Well, there is little else to do as a cleric of the Twelve Mines. My people are so unfortunately secluded these days," he said, taking a seat at the table and casually commandeering a large platter of roast pork.

The night was cool, and a quiet breeze played with the

candlelight about the room through open windows as the men dined. Laudin implored Umhra to once again tell his story so both Shadow and Gromley could hear his tale. "I suspect this conversation will go on well into the night, as Gromley is bound to have a lot of questions for you Umhra. Please, start when you are ready."

Umhra sat forward at the table and wet his throat with a sip of ale when Taivaron burst into the room through an agape window behind him and landed directly on the high back of Laudin's chair. A moment later, a second harrier, this one a female, flew into the dining room, circled the table once, and then transformed into her Reshinta form.

"Now *that* is an entrance." Gromley laughed, raising his tankard into the air with a splash.

The final member of the Barrow's Pact had arrived. Naivara smiled, and the candlelight intensified about the room. "Sorry for the bravado, but flight was the most expeditious means of travel," she said.

Laudin lit up in her presence. "Naivara, welcome to Anaris. Thank you for heeding my call." He stood and bowed deeply in a grand gesture of admiration.

She rushed over and embraced him, her arms locking around this back. "Wonderful to see you Laudin, and you, Gromley, Shadow." She walked around the table greeting her friends. "Nicholas and Nathaniel, a pleasure." She tussled Nicholas's hair as she passed. Nathaniel kissed her hand. "And who are our new friends?"

Balris stood and bowed. "Lady Naivara, I am Balris Silentread, head priest of this temple. This is Umhra the Peacebreaker, the very reason for your summoning to these parts. Umhra was just about to begin telling Gromley and Shadow his story and about the quest awaiting you, should you have it. Please, have a seat and partake of anything you wish."

Naivara looked at Umhra, tilting her head as she sat next to Laudin across the table. She stared into his eyes as if she were reading his soul. Umhra shifted in his chair under her gaze.

"My pleasure, Lady Naivara," he said, fumbling his words.

She nodded but did not break eye contact. For the next hour, Umhra retold his story of Telsidor's Keep, the vampire Manteis, and the impending doom if Naur was to be successfully returned to Tyveriel by the Brothers of Resurrection.

"It occurs to me, the first thing we must do is return to this keep and ensure the vampire's lair is secure and doesn't pose any further threat to the people of Anaris," Gromley said. "Then we must make our way to Meriden and cut off the head of the snake to make certain Naur cannot materialize in our plane. Should he step foot in Evelium, we shall all be ruined."

Umhra turned to Gromley. "We are of like mind, Sir Strongforge. I also intend to return with the bodies of my lost friends if possible, so they may be given a proper burial when the time is right."

Gromley nodded. "Umhra, if I may address you as a friend, please call me Gromley. I assure you the Barrow's Pact is up to this challenge and shall be at your side, faithfully, until we succeed or death takes us. Are we in agreement?" he asked, looking at Laudin, Shadow, and Naivara. Each answered his question with a nod. "Our decision has been made. When do we leave for the keep?"

Balris, who had been quietly listening to the conversation, leaned forward to the table. "I shall arrange for horses and a cart and we can depart the day after tomorrow if all shall be ready by then."

"You will be joining us?" Umhra asked.

"I will. Lord Morrow has asked I go as far as your audience with the king."

"That's welcome news," Umhra said, a rare smile cracking his austere expression for a moment.

The party was in agreement and spent the rest of the night celebrating the reunion of the Barrow's Pact, and the new friendships they would forge in battle.

CHAPTER 17

What a mistake it was to fight on behalf of order.
Chaos is far more beautiful.
—Telsidor's Missives

Diary entry dated 5th of Prien, 47 AF. Unearthed from the Ruins of Anaris, month of Emin, 1156 AT

—▲—

The horses nipped at each other and stomped the cobblestone arcade as the party prepared to leave the temple's grounds. Ansel, Laudin's buckskin, and Ramoth, Shadow's barb, were amongst the group and fed off the rising trepidation within their respective masters. The party was busy loading gear and provisions into a wooden wagon led by two large chestnut draft horses.

"Gromley, Naivara, Shadow, Umhra, and I will be on horseback," Laudin said. "Balris, Nicholas, and Nathaniel will take the wagon. We are going to enter the keep through the hidden door behind the waterfall through which Umhra and Nicholas escaped. I'm confident I can track their path back to the door. Balris and Nathaniel will stay with the cart and horses while the rest of us enter Telsidor's Keep, clear it of any remaining evil, and recover the remains of Bat, Drog, Gori,

Thurg, and Xig. We will return with whatever we can manage. If multiple trips are required, so be it."

Umhra was quiet, pensive. He paced about the staging area, his gaze to the ground, and mounted a dapple-gray steed named Splinter, recommended for him by Balris. The rest of the party did the same, following Laudin's lead, and made their way out of the courtyard and beyond the walls of Anaris.

The party passed Pell's orchard when Umhra slowed Splinter and lagged behind. The hour was too early for even Xavier Pell to be out amongst his beloved apple trees, but Umhra's gaze locked on the front gate nonetheless.

Laudin dropped back letting the rest of the party trot unnoticed to Ember's Way. "Everything all right, Umhra?"

"None of this is right." Umhra paused. "Sorry. Pell's orchard is the last place the Bloodbound was truly all together as a team. Within two days of leaving this place, all the people that mattered most to me in the world were destroyed."

"I can't pretend to understand what you are going through. I haven't suffered such loss, myself. What I can tell you, is we will do right by your friends and have your back to the bitter end."

"Thank you. Chasing down the Brothers of Resurrection and putting an end to their plot somehow seems less daunting than this ride back to the keep."

Laudin smiled, pat Umhra on the shoulder. "Then let's get this over with." He cracked his reins.

Picking up speed but being careful not to leave the cart too far behind, they rode until arriving at the location where Umhra and Nicholas exited the forest, hunted by the dire wolves. The carcasses of the two beasts had been dragged to the side of the road and were now hidden amongst the tall grass. Someone had seemingly skinned the creatures, and now a cast of vultures was picking at the remnants of rotting flesh clinging to their skeletal remains.

Waiting for the wagon to arrive, Laudin spoke to the other riders. "We will make our way into the woods there," he said, pointing to a narrow break in the undergrowth of the forest. "We should be able to find the river easily enough and follow it upstream to the waterfall. From there, we follow Umhra's lead as he and Nicholas are the only ones among us with any knowledge of this dark place."

The wagon caught up, and Nicholas hopped out to join the others. Balris and Nathaniel steered the cart onto a suitable embankment a little farther up the road and collected the other horses. "May the gods watch over you all with a careful eye," Balris offered as he returned to the cart with Nathaniel. Clutching the silver triangle around his neck, he whispered a few words, and they vanished from sight.

The party waded into the dense woods, Taivaron hopping from tree to tree overhead. A half-hour passed and the sound of running water greeted them directly to the north. Traversing the forest along a deer path, they found the river which was surging wildly, despite being only fifteen feet in width. They turned upstream, used the riverbed to hasten their progress. Laudin and Naivara dashed effortlessly, but the rest struggled to maintain their footing on the slippery rocks lining the shore. The rocks grew larger as the band continued upstream until they eventually formed a series of cascades, at the top of which was the waterfall behind which hid the secondary door to Telsidor's Keep.

Umhra strode to the front of the group. He climbed the stone path and led the others behind the fall, the cool spray of water reviving his senses. There, still open, was the iron door of the keep, untouched since Umhra and Nicholas had escaped from its cavernous depths.

Nicholas shuddered, took a step back from the doorway. Umhra drew his sword and placed his fist over his chest so that the blade pointed to the heavens. "I'm ready," he said, and then gave a nod to Nicholas.

"I am too," Nicholas said. He stepped forward to Umhra's side.

Gromley grabbed a small, smoke-gray globe from his satchel, held it out in front of him, and let it go. The sphere floated in place and set aglow, casting away the shroud of darkness, and revealing the long hallway before them.

Along the floor of the hallway was a trail of coagulated blood. Umhra led them back to whatever untold evil remained in Telsidor's Keep. The hallway descended for some time before eventually leveling out toward its end. On the right side of the stone wall was the lever, covered in blood, Umhra had used to close the secret door to Manteis's chamber when he and Nicholas had fled.

Umhra paused and turned to the rest of the group. "Once the lever is thrown," he whispered, "this section of the wall will slide away, opening a doorway to the vampire's throne room. There is no telling what kind of monsters, or in what numbers, are on the other side. I believe I destroyed a goodly portion of the Dokktari within the keep, and hopefully, the others fled once their master was killed, but there were also undead in this place. At the time, they were largely isolated to a vast pit, but they may now be roaming the dark rooms within, so stay vigilant. Are we ready to proceed?"

Everyone except Nicholas nodded. Umhra walked over to the young Farestere and knelt. "Nicholas, I saved you from this dastardly place once before. I have no intention of letting any harm come to you now or in the future. Stay close, and I shall see you back with your brother in short order. I promise."

With a deep breath, Nicholas said, "I am ready, Umhra. Open the door, so we can get this over with."

Laudin took a position in front of the part of the stone wall that Umhra said would slide away, becoming the doorway. He drew his bow and affixed his aim upon the entrance, the groan of the beautifully carved risers straining under the pressure of the bowstring the only sound in the hallway. Laudin nodded to Umhra, who pulled on the lever. The great stone wall lurched toward the party, uncomfortably narrowing the hallway for a moment, and then slid with a loud grinding sound out of the way, exposing the throne room before them.

The sight that welcomed them was abhorrent. The bodies of five Dokktari were still strewn about the room where Umhra had slain them. One beheaded, another with both legs severed from its body, a third charred by the doorway, the final two, run through by his blade. The cadavers now swollen with bloat, the stench was overwhelming.

"Paladin indeed," Gromley said, stepping into the throne room and past the shadow of Manteis the Immortal burned into the back of the bone chair. The wall on the far side of the room was sundered by the blast from the spell Umhra had cast and the subsequent Dokktari explosions. "You made an impressive mess here, Umhra."

Everything was quiet. Shadow searched the corpses, covering his nose and mouth with his arm, but found little more than a few quarter-sovereigns and some random trinkets which had likely been taken as trophies from the Dokktaris' prior victims.

Laudin and Umhra crept over to the former doorway leading out from the throne room and peered into the adjoining room, avoiding the rubble. Two rows of ornately carved stone tables suggested the room was originally used as a banquet hall, most likely for Telsidor and his friends, ages ago. There were half-eaten corpses scattered about and dried blood strewn across the tables, walls, and floor. Six iron cages hung from the ceiling, still dripping with the fluids of decomposing bodies.

They stepped into the room. Several of the bodies within writhed upon their approach. Laudin slung his bow over his shoulder and drew his scimitar, the runes etched on its blade glowing green in the presence of the undead. He uttered a light, airy whistle, and Gromley, Shadow, and Naivara appeared in the doorway to his rear. Several of the undead were getting to their feet, while others dragged what remained of their bodies across the stone floor, leaving a trail of gore in their wake.

The Barrow's Pact fanned out around Umhra with Laudin

at the fore. Nicholas joined the party as Laudin took the head of the first of the undead with a quick swipe of his sword. Gromley stepped up to a second on the group's left and crushed its head with his war hammer, sending a burst of putrid blood across the room.

The party pressed into the room, clearing it of undead as they proceeded. Reaching the other end of the room, a doorway led to a short, narrow hallway, the walls smeared with blood. At the end of this hallway, Umhra recognized the closed door as the one which cut him off from the rest of the Bloodbound. He ran down the hallway and wrestled furiously with the door. It still would not give way. As if he could still hear his friends on the other side, he applied all of his strength to the door, but to no avail.

"Umhra," Nicholas said, running to the door. He grabbed the Paladin's arm.

Umhra shook his head, fell to his knees, and stared with tears in his eyes at Nicholas. "This is where I got separated from my men and was taken before Manteis. I can remember the sound of the battle on the other side of this door. Being here, I realize how unprepared I am for what we're about to see."

Nicholas leaned in toward Umhra. "Do you not yet realize, Umhra, you're the only one who can deliver Evelium from Naur's clutches? By rights, there should be no Paladins in this land to save us from such darkness but there is. There have been no records of anyone attaining a Platinum Suffusion, even in the name of a lesser god, since the Age of Grace, but here you are with your icon you have kept hidden for so long. I see quite clearly that without you, all hope was lost before we even knew what we were fighting against. Can you not?"

"And I kept my icon hidden. I kept it hidden when my men needed me most. How could I be such a weak fool?"

"You had no idea what you were confronting. After living your life in the shadows, how were you to know this was the occasion that would require you to reveal your true self? But now, you are awake. For that, we are all grateful, as there is work to be done if we are to save Evelium."

Umhra got to his feet. "You are a truly special young man, Nicholas," he said, doing his best to suppress the tears. "Let's continue onward."

The rest of the party entered the hallway and approached the men. Shadow walked past them directly to the door and inspected it closely. "There must be a trigger mechanism for this door somewhere. Spread out and search for a lever or pressure plate."

The group scoured the hallway, high and low, but no such trigger was found. While the rest searched, Laudin slipped into the prior room. "I think I found what we're looking for," he said after a few moments.

Umhra and Shadow doubled back into the room and analyzed the apparatus. "This could be the mechanism," Shadow said, looking at a raised stone along the wall that had a small gap along all four sides. "Clear the others out of the hallway just in case I'm wrong, but I believe this will open the door when depressed."

Laudin and Umhra made their way back into the hallway. "Let's all back away for a moment so Shadow can try to open this door. We aren't sure if the trigger we found will activate some other mechanism. Remain vigilant. If the door opens, there is no telling what may come through," Umhra said.

The group reconvened in the dining hall and stood affixed on Shadow. Umhra positioned himself against the opposite side of the doorway so he could maintain a vantage on the hallway and the door at its end.

The door clicked open, one notch at a time. "This next room is where I was separated from my men. They fought a large number of Dokktari at this point. I expect we will start finding their remains but am wary there could still be Dokktari or undead lurking about. Also, the eviscerated body of Xig was prominently displayed on the first wall. I cannot pretend this is going to be a pleasant experience for any of us," Umhra said as the door continued to click open. The only thing that poured through was the stench of death, mixed with the choking odor of smoke.

With a loud final click, the door was agape. Umhra led the party into the hallway and was first to look into the next room. A horrible sight, indeed. Several dismembered Dokktari corpses lay strewn across the floor, dried blood was everywhere. A glance to his left confirmed Xig still hung in his place along with several other corpses. The remains in the cages hanging from the ceiling were desiccated.

Umhra darted across the room to Drog's body. Severed in half, there was a horrific expression frozen on his face. "Bound by blood," Umhra said, hanging his head for a moment as he knelt beside his fallen comrade.

The rest of the party entered the room, covering their faces with their sleeves. Gromley and Shadow checked the other two doorways. Both led to descending staircases. The men stood at the ready in front of each.

"Laudin," Umhra said, removing several large waxed canvas tarps from his pack, "I am going to pack Drog and Xig away. Would you mind helping, if you can, and have the others stand watch?"

"Of course," Laudin said. Naivara and Nicholas kept watch at the final doorway, while Umhra and Laudin placed the pieces of Drog's body in the center of the first waxed tarp. Umhra folded the tarp around the body and bound it with a length of rope from his pack. The outside of the tarp was inscribed with white paint that read, *Drog the Mancleaver, Hero of Anaris.*

Umhra shifted his attention over to Xig and placed a tarp on the floor beneath him. He paused for a moment, staring at Xig's body so crassly displayed on the wall—shook his head. He then dragged a wooden pedestal over from the nearby blood-stained altar at which these terrible mutilations were committed.

Xig was bound to the wall by five ropes looped through

large iron eyelets. Umhra pulled his dagger from his belt and first cut the rope at Xig's feet, and then at each wrist. Umhra then stepped up on the pedestal and cut the rope from around Xig's neck. As the rope around his chest was frayed and then severed, Xig's body fell onto Umhra's shoulder. It was lighter than he had expected. Xig was a large man in life, but his body was merely a dried shell.

As Umhra turned from the wall, Laudin grabbed Xig's feet and the two men laid him on the waxed tarp. Umhra again folded and tied the tarp so *Xig the Boarkicker, Hero of Anaris* was prominent in its display.

When he was finished, Umhra turned to address the others. "I don't know where those two doors lead, as they were locked when I was last in this room," he said, pointing to the doors Gromley and Shadow were guarding. "This door leads to the room where the bridge collapsed into the pit filled with undead." He pointed to the door on the other side of the room. "At least one of my men is down in the pit, but there is no telling how many of those foul creatures await us there. How shall we proceed?"

"I say we clear these stairwells first and wherever they lead, as we know the bridge is down in the other room, and likely little threat can come from the pit until we descend into it," Shadow said.

"That makes sense. Should we split up, or take one stairwell at a time?" Gromley asked.

"No. I will place a tripwire at this doorway and then we will take yours first," Shadow said. From his bag, he took a length of fine wire and a bell. He strung the wire in front of the doorway about a foot off the ground and gingerly tied the bell to one end. "That should alert us to anything coming up from this stairwell while we explore the other," he said.

CHAPTER 18

The storm having past, we drove the blights back into the Wistful Timberlands.
—The Collected Letters of Modig Forene

Letter to Englen Penn dated 7th of Emin, 998 AC. Unearthed from the Ruins of Vanyareign, month of Ocken, 1301 AT

—▲—

Umhra and the rest of the party positioned themselves behind Gromley, the glow of his orb lighting the way. The staircase curled down to the left, ending in a short hallway with an ornate iron door at its end. Illuminated by the orb, Umhra made out an image engraved on the door's face. There was a platinum inlay, depicting the culmination of a battle in which a solitary warrior stood triumphantly upon the remains of an immense dragon, its nostrils still smoking. The warrior's sword stuck into the beast's head at the temple, the dragon lay lifeless in the shallow water below the cliffs of Mount Anvil.

"This must be a rendering of Telsidor's victory over the dragon Mesorith," Nicholas said.

"A great moment in history, indeed," Gromley said. "It was Telsidor's triumph that freed my people from the rule of Mesorith and allowed for the founding of the Twelve Mines beneath Anvil. The legend goes, Telsidor leaped from the cliffs and plunged his sword into Mesorith's head just before the dragon took flight from its lair to lay ruin to his fleet. To think such a great man like Telsidor ended up being such an odiferous monstrosity."

With the head of his war hammer, Gromley nudged the door open. The orb drifted forward, revealing a large oval room, its walls lined with ancient tapestries, each depicting one of Telsidor's conquests. At the very center of the room was a stone sarcophagus etched with intertwined Evenese symbols. On the lid were the words *Manteis the Immortal*. Beneath each tapestry resided a large chest, each made of silver and identical to the next.

Gromley and Umhra walked over to the sarcophagus and inspected the symbols. Knowing Manteis had been destroyed did not make removing the lid any easier. After a pause, they shimmied the heavy stone lid perpendicular to the base, revealing a black satin lining. Otherwise, the tomb was empty, as suspected. Shadow walked the perimeter of the room taking particular note of the chests. Laudin and Naivara walked the room admiring the tapestries and attempting to decipher Telsidor's story.

"These seem to be a detailed history of the vampire's entire life," Naivara said, speaking for the first time since entering the keep. "His mortal life starting at the first on the left, his transformation into a vampire in the middle, directly behind the sarcophagus, and his exploits since on the right of the room."

She and Laudin stood before the central tapestry which showed an ancient and wretched creature hunched over the limp body of Telsidor, his sword cast to the floor in a room of white stone. Looming above them was Manteis arisen having taken his vampiric form. It would have been a beautiful piece of artwork if not for its macabre depictions.

"If all of these chests are nearly as bountiful as this one, we will be among the richest in Evelium," Shadow said.

Shadow knelt before the chest under the final tapestry which depicted the god Naur anointing Manteis in a pool of blood as he sat on the throne of Shale Arving. Shadow held up his hands, his fists full of gold and miscellaneous jewels.

Gromley walked over to the next chest and opened it carefully. It was also filled with wealth. The party took turns opening the containers and marveling at their contents, temporarily overcome with avarice. Umhra paid no mind to the gold and jewels the others boasted of finding in their respective chests. Instead, he walked over to the first chest which sat below a tapestry of Telsidor posed over a frost giant in what was presumably Oda Norde. Telsidor held his longsword overhead, the sword gleaming in the sunlight. Umhra knelt on one knee and opened the chest. Unlike the others in the room, this chest had a singular item resting in its belly.

The longsword from the tapestry was even more beautiful in reality. It shone as though polished yesterday. The sword's perfectly tapered blade and ornate gold and silver handle were like none Umhra had ever seen. On its hilt, the name *Forsetae* was etched.

Gromley approached and peered over Umhra's shoulder. "It cannot be. The almighty Forsetae," he said. "This is the very sword used to destroyed Mesorith and so many other foul beings at Telsidor's hand. The blade was forged in an alloy known only to the clerics of Antiikin. It is said Forsetae will never lose its edge and is imbued with divine properties by those who forged it."

Umhra grabbed the sword and lifted it from the chest. In his hand, the weapon glowed red, and then turned purple, and then blue. A searing heat entered his hand, rose through his arm, and flooded his body.

An unfamiliar hand. A cold voice resonated within Umhra's mind. *A worthy hand. Introduce yourself, hero.*

I am Umhra the Peacebreaker. I am the last known Paladin of Evelium, and I seek to save our land from impending destruction.

And you would have me be your tool in this endeavor? the voice asked.

Not my tool, my partner. Umhra thought.

I have been held by evil for too long. I have forgotten my duty, my code.

The evil that corrupted you is gone. I slew the vampire Manteis. Let me remind you of your true nature, as envisioned by your creators.

You know of my history? Forsetae asked.

Not intimately, no. All I know is you were created by Evenese clerics, and somehow found your way into the hands of Telsidor. That you were at his side through his historic victories, when he was turned into a vampire, and likely for the many atrocities he committed since, through no choice or fault of your own. Umhra said.

You cannot fathom my transgressions at his hand. Forsetae's voice wavered.

Let me help you leave such darkness behind. To reclaim your rightful place in the light.

I can sense your conviction, your sincerity. I am agreeable to this arrangement. I shall bind myself to you, Umhra the Peacebreaker, in the name of all that is good. Forsetae said.

And I to you, great Forsetae. You have my word. Umhra thought.

"This sword is strong," Umhra said to his friends in the room. "I've never experienced such a weapon."

The rest of the party gathered around Umhra and Gromley.

"It is meant to be yours," Gromley said. "Forsetae's powers can be harnessed only by the pure of heart and its blade meant only to be used against evil. Forsetae translates into Evenese from the ancient dialects as 'Judge.' It has chosen you, Umhra."

"It has said as much," Umhra said. "It has been corrupted, but I believe I can restore it."

The rest of the party was now staring at him, confused.

"The sword spoke to you?" Shadow asked.

"Yes. I am as surprised as you. Forsetae agreed to bind itself to me in exchange for my efforts in its restoration."

"Outside of Umhra claiming Forsetae as his own, we leave the rest of the treasure here for now. We will inform Balris of its existence and have it split equitably between the families of those who went missing at the hands of Manteis. Anything he and the Council of Anaris see fit for us to have will suffice. Does anyone dispute this?" Laudin asked.

Shadow raised his hand. The rest looked at him, frowned. His shoulders dropped. "Fine, we give the treasure to the families of the fallen." He said, dropping what he was holding back into a chest and closing the lid.

"Shadow, what about the gems you put in your satchel?" Laudin asked.

Shadow rolled his eyes and slid his hand into the black bag he wore slung across his chest beneath his cloak. He retrieved a handful of miscellaneous gems and returned them as well.

"All right, enough time here. Back to what we came for," Laudin said.

He led the party out of the crypt. Umhra took one more look at the tapestries and placed Forsetae diagonally between the handles of his shield, the heat receding from his hand. The party ascended the staircase, returning to the room above. Shadow deconstructed his tripwire and placed the materials back in his bag. The group then proceeded down the second staircase.

The staircase led to an empty room with two iron grate doors along the right wall. The grate doors allowed access into the pit, which still smoldered from a great fire.

Umhra surveyed the carnage Gori and Thurg had created. All but a few of the undead had met their demise in the blaze. "I would guess from the sight of things Gori and Thurg may have met their end in this pit. I already know what remains of Bat is down here. If I am right, this room would account for all of my men. I will enter the pit and try to identify them amongst the myriad of charred remains. I assume they would be located to the right of the room where the bridge collapsed. If anyone would rather hold back, I completely understand."

"Please, Umhra. Don't consider any of us faint of heart or in the least bit not committed to your efforts here and going forward," Naivara said. "I'm sure we all agree we shall enter the room together and help you find Gori, Thurg, and Bat."

Gromley lifted his hammer over his head and smashed the padlock clean off the door. The noise reverberated off the walls of the pit and caught the attention of the few undead that remained inside. The undead staggered to the gate, grasped in vain through the bars at the living. Umhra, Laudin, and Shadow made light work of them, skewering them on their swords and daggers from behind the relative safety of the iron gate. Forcing the bodies out of the way, the group worked its way into the pit and around the tangled mass of charred remains.

Umhra searched the pit—fervent despite choking in the smoke. Across the room, beneath a pile of twisted corpses, a silver glint caught his attention. He waded through the sea of decrepit bodies and debris and found Gori's remains clutching the mace Umhra had given him before leaving Anaris. Beside him were Thurg, and Bat, their bodies broken, burned, and partially devoured. The scene was too much for Umhra to take. He instinctively retrieved his icon and prayed. Not only did he pray for the souls of his fallen friends, but also to quell the rage he felt rising inside. Gromley approached and knelt next to Umhra, and joined him in prayer, while the rest stood solemnly, paying their respects.

After a long moment, Umhra grabbed the remaining three waxed tarps from his pack and Gromley helped him spread them across the stone floor. With what little free room there was, Umhra wrapped Gori and Thurg in their respective tarps, careful to place the mace upon Gori's chest, and bound them with rope. Then he turned to Bat, whose lower half was still pinned below the rubble of the collapsed bridge.

"Would you help me free him?"

"Of course, Umhra," Gromley said.

Gromley, Laudin, and Shadow helped Umhra hoist the large stone fragment from atop Bat's body, and Naivara and Nicholas dragged him free. They let the slab drop with a crash, sending a cloud of ash into the air.

Umhra wrapped his friend's body in the tarp labeled *Bat the Firespitter, Hero of Anaris*. Now, with all of the Bloodbound accounted for, and Telsidor's Keep cleansed of any threat to the people of Anaris, Umhra had kept his promise, and could now turn his attention to the insurmountable existential threat that loomed over all of Tyveriel. He stood and hoisted Bat's body over his shoulder.

"There's no need for that, Umhra. You have done your part, now let me do mine," Naivara said. She waved everyone off a few steps with her hands and closed her eyes. Her gold circlet—untarnished amidst the death and destruction—generated diffuse wisps of green smoke. The smoke intensified and she transformed into a brawny grizzly bear. When the transformation was complete, she waved her head up and down and grunted. Gromley, Umhra, Laudin, and Shadow placed the wrapped tarps on her back.

With a snort, she left the pit and ascended the staircase, barely fitting between its walls. Umhra shrugged to Laudin, raising an eyebrow. Laudin gestured toward the stairs, and the men followed the great bear. The group collected Xig and Drog and returned to the throne room. Passing Manteis's throne of bones one more time, they left by way of the passage they'd entered, closing the stone door behind them.

Naivara lumbered down the long hallway, squeezed through the final doorway, and out from behind the waterfall. They all welcomed the fresh air after hours spent in the acrid atmosphere of Telsidor's Keep. They continued, following Naivara's lead, back toward Ember's Way. Dusk was upon them when they returned to Balris and Nathaniel, who were still hidden along the side of the road. As they emerged from the undergrowth, their friends and horses reappeared and Nathaniel ran to them.

"Most happy to see all of you have returned safely. Especially you, brother," Nathaniel said, hugging Nicholas.

"Thank you," Nicholas said. "There is much to talk about on the trip back to Anaris."

Balris stepped down from the wagon and greeted the rest of the group. "I see you accomplished your primary objective, Umhra. I had no doubt you would," he said, shaking Umhra's hand. "And I see you have found yourself a new sword."

The men loaded the canvas tarps into the back of the wagon. "Thank you, Balris. This was most important to me. The keep is clear of evil, and there are numerous bodies to gather and return to their families. I fear most are in terrible shape, unfortunately. Identification will be challenging in many cases, and impossible in others. There is also a large treasure in Manteis's crypt. That is where I located the sword, Forsetae. We agreed the treasure should be divided fairly between the families of those who suffered at the hands of the vampire," Umhra said.

"That is very generous of you all, but under Evelium law, the treasure belongs to you and the Barrow's Pact," Balris said.

"Yes," Laudin said, joining the conversation, "and as such, we have decided you and Lord Morrow shall decide how to split the treasure, as it is far more than we should ever need."

"I wouldn't go as far as to presume it is far more than *we* should ever need," Shadow said, inciting a laugh from the rest of the party.

Naivara returned to her normal form. "All the wealth in the world wouldn't be enough for you, Shadow."

"You know me too well, Naivara. I admit it, proudly."

"Once we are on our way to Vanyareign, I will have Lord Morrow dispatch his most loyal and honest men to the keep and clear out the remains and return with the treasure to the temple where it can safely be appraised, divided, and distributed according to your wishes and Lord Morrow's discretion," Balris said.

With the wagon loaded, the party mounted their horses and began their trip back to Anaris. The hour was late by the time they returned to the temple. The party was exhausted from the day's travails. Once Balris arranged for some of the clergy to unload the cart and attend to the bodies of Drog, Gori, Thurg, Bat, and Xig, the group trudged into the temple for a late dinner and much-needed rest.

▲

Umhra returned to his room, moonlight streaming through the lone window. He lit the oil lamp on the bedside table. He slipped the strap of his satchel over his head and dropped the laden bag to the ground. With a sigh, he palmed the hair from his face.

He unbuckled his sword belt and fell into bed, his legs aching. A glint caught his eye from the corner of the room where his shield lay askew against the wall. He labored from the bed and trudged over, grabbing Forsetae's hilt. A reposeful warmth ran up his arm and flooded his body.

Ah. Hero Peacebreaker. You call on me.

Yes.

What do you require? I sense no immediate threat.

I wish to know you better. What can you tell me about your past?

An odd request, but I see no harm in it. In life, I was known as Odug Mysien, Stalwart of the Order of Ninniach.

A Paladin.

Yes, like yourself. I sense your connection to Kalmindon. Your conflict as well.

How did you come to be bound to this weapon?

The clerics of Antiikin forged this weapon as a harbinger of justice. They were in need of a soul worthy of such a charge. I promised myself to them, and upon my death, I became Forsetae—the Judge.

In your time, Paladins were revered? Umhra asked.

As warriors of the gods, we held a certain station in society, yes.

Today, being a Paladin is punishable by death. It is considered treason against the king and heresy in the eyes of the faith.

Ah. The reason you hide your true nature. It is not the Paladin's fate to lurk in the shadows in the name of his own welfare, but to be a beacon of light in the darkness when there is no hope, despite the cost. You can only hide for so long.

I am but one. The last of our kind. How am I supposed to save Tyveriel from reckoning?

One Paladin on the battlefield can change the course of history. You must have the resolve to come forth and become the beacon of light Tyveriel needs.

Umhra nodded, turning the sword over in his hand, inspecting its superior craftsmanship. He then put the tip of the blade to the floor and held it between his knees. He drew his sword from its scabbard, leaned it against the side of the bed, and sheathed Forsetae in its place. He slid both weapons beneath his bed and wrenched off his boots.

CHAPTER 19

There are worse things living beneath the Ilathril than the Ryzarin. This I don't say lightly.
—Telsidor's Missives

Diary entry dated 19th of Anar, 990 AC. Unearthed from the Ruins of Anaris, month of Emin, 1156 AT

—▲—

Early the next morning, the Barrow's Pact met with Umhra and Nicholas over a breakfast of farm-fresh eggs and apple pastries from Pell's orchard to discuss the next phase of their mission. "I think it best we formalize our commitment to one another," Gromley said, shoveling a fried egg into his mouth. "Umhra and Nicholas, what do you say to officially joining the Barrow's Pact?"

"Of course," Nicholas said without hesitation.

Umhra paused for a moment. He had not considered committing to another group so soon after losing his own. He leaned back in his chair and looked at each of his party mates around the table. "I would be honored," he said with sincerity. They had more than proven themselves in the keep, and surely, he would need their help if he was to thwart Naur's resurrection. After this was all over, he could reassess his future.

"So be it," Gromley said.

"We are chosen family now," Naivara said, welcoming Nicholas and Umhra to the group. "The strongest bond there is."

Balris and Lord Morrow entered the room and joined them at the table.

"I have made arrangements for you all to travel to Vanyareign and meet with the king to explain the happenings at Telsidor's Keep and the need to address matters going forward with the utmost discretion," Lord Morrow said. "There is a trade caravan scheduled to leave for the capital in two days. I have arranged for your party to be included as a security detail. This will provide you with cover for your passage into Vanyareign. Once you arrive, you will meet the king and his most trusted guard, a young man by the name of Talus Jochen. You shall inform them of your findings here in Anaris and gain the king's support for your mission to Meriden.

"I have only a moment, but I wanted to address you all face to face," Lord Morrow said. "Balris has informed me of your success in your second visit to the keep. I am most appreciative you were able to rid us of this scourge. Anaris is forever in your debt. I have also been made aware of the sizable wealth the vampire Manteis was in possession of in his crypt. Your honesty and willingness to share the treasure are most admired. I shall see the bodies of our people recovered and the treasure escorted safely to the temple to be accounted for and divided up as to your wishes. Finally, Balris and I will see to arrangements for your friends, Umhra. They shall be written into the history books and remembered as our greatest heroes."

"Thank you, Lord Morrow," Umhra said, still surprised his former band of half-Orc misfits had been received with respect by the elite of Anaris, despite so many times being marginalized by the city's commoners, and those across Evelium.

As quickly as he arrived, Lord Morrow took his leave. Umhra leaned back in his chair. "Balris, are you certain you want to come with us?" he asked. "I know Lord Morrow wants you there, but I cannot promise you a safe return. That goes for each of you—you keep company with a Paladin, a traitor to king and country, and heretic to your church.

"Of course, I am certain, Umhra," Balris said. "And I intend on seeing this through to Meriden as well. I plainly see now what Ivory saw so many years ago. Evelium needs a savior. One of the old guard from a bygone age, if we are to succeed in stopping the resurrection of Naur. I believe I speak for everyone in this room when I say, if our assistance helps in getting you even a modicum closer to that goal, we will be at your side every step of the way."

"No one in this party will waiver, Umhra. One way or another, we will be there with you at the end of this," Laudin said.

Umhra nodded and stood from the table. "There is much to do in preparation for our journey. I shall get started with my part at once."

He left the room, making his way out to the fresh air of the courtyard he'd grown quite fond of in his stay on temple grounds, and removed Forsetae from its sheath. He inspected the blade.

"Umhra, may I have a moment?"

Umhra looked up from the blade, his gaze meeting Nicholas's smiling face. "Of course, Nicholas, what's on your mind?"

"Well, it struck me I hadn't properly thanked you for saving me from Manteis."

"You've thanked me hundreds of times, Nicholas. There is no need."

"No. What I mean is, we Farestere believe when someone does you a good deed, you show your appreciation with a gift. Now, there is no way for me to give you a gift that comes anywhere close to repaying you for what you did for me, so I did my best."

Nicholas produced a platinum chain from his vest pocket. It was a sturdy but elegant chain mail weave with a pyramid-shaped cage hanging from its center. "I don't see any reason for you to hide your icon anymore. You should be proud of who you are."

Umhra took the chain, allowing the cage to dangle, empty, from his hand. He walked over to a bench in the shade of the pear tree he favored and sat. "I don't know what to say. I'm not sure anyone has ever paid me such kindness."

Nicholas sat next to him. "I wanted you to know how much you mean to me. No matter our reception in Vanyareign, or the outcome of our mission, you will always be my hero."

"I think it's you, that will always be mine." Umhra smiled, put an arm around Nicholas's narrow shoulders, and held his chain up to the sun.

▲

Umhra paused at the door, his open palm on its rough surface, his mind racing. He had no idea what to expect in the adjacent room where the bodies of the Bloodbound were being prepared for burial by the temple's grave cleric. He forced a swallow and sighed.

"You may enter," a cool, steady voice said from within the room.

The door gave way with ease—swung wide—exposing Umhra to the scene within faster than he had expected. On five tables dispersed throughout the sun-filled room, lay the bodies of his lost brothers covered in plum-colored shrouds. Shelves lined the left wall, the myriad containers upon them open and filling the air with the strong scent of herbs. Standing at the head of the farthest table was a figure cloaked in dark brown robes, their face obscured by an oversized hood.

"His Holiness told me to expect you," the grave cleric said. "I have finished preparing the bodies according to the writ. Their souls may now pass into the gardens of Kalmindon."

"Thank you," Umhra said, coming to the side of the first table and peeling back the shroud, revealing Thurg's charred remains. They had been painted ochre and packed with herbs and other aromatics. Umhra hung his head.

"Their deaths weigh on you as though you are responsible," the grave cleric said.

"Yes."

"A foolish notion," the grave cleric said. "And an arrogant one at that."

Umhra glared at the robed figure, caught off guard by their harsh remarks.

"You do not hold sway over life and death," the grave cleric said. "At least not yet. Your responsibility is to honor their lives and what they meant to you. All else is folly."

Umhra nodded. "Would you mind if I had a moment alone?"

"Not at all." The grave cleric folded their hands. "But first, join me in prayer so they may better know your presence."

Umhra folded his hands and closed his eyes, blue ether escaped from the pouch on his belt where he kept his icon.

"Lost to this world, but found unto the grace of Kalmindon, hear us. For though you walk the tranquil gardens, there is one here that mourns you and seeks solace. He comes to you with a pure heart but a clouded mind. Heal him."

Umhra opened his eyes to see the grave cleric unfold their hands and leave the room. He pulled a dagger from his belt and ran its blade across his palm—squeezed his fist tight. Sheathing his dagger, Umhra drew Thurg's shroud down to his waist. Umhra placed his palm onto Thurg's chest, leaving behind a bloodied print.

"Bound by blood," Umhra said.

He covered Thurg with the shroud and repeated his ritual with each of his fallen friends. Finished with his goodbyes, he stood at the center of the room surrounded by death. "I won't let you boys down again. I promise."

▲

Two days passed faster than anyone in the group wished. Nicholas spent the time with Nathaniel. Balris and Umhra rehearsed their message to the king. Laudin and Naivara were inseparable as they lazed around the temple grounds, keeping to themselves. Shadow and Gromley caught up with one another over a deck of cards, being careful not to get caught gambling on the sacred grounds of the temple.

Inevitably, the morning arrived when they were to meet up with the trade caravan as it prepared for the long journey to Vanyareign. Just within the east gate, a group of merchants was loading their wares into a dozen wagons, each led by two draft horses. Umhra smiled coming upon Xavier Pell who doted over two carts of fresh and dried apples which were a prized part of the shipment to the capital.

"Lord Pell, it's wonderful to see you again," Umhra said, approaching Xavier's cart.

"Sir Peacebreaker. The pleasure is mine. Lord Morrow mentioned you would be overseeing our shipment to Vanyareign as our security detail. I found this news most comforting. He was quite evasive when I enquired about your visit to Telsidor's Keep, however. Tell me, did you fare well?"

"Without going into too much detail, we were successful, but at great cost," Umhra said. "Ember's Way has been secured and all shall return to normal. I respectfully ask for your discretion with this information, as Lord Morrow would like to make an announcement to the general public when the time is right and I would hate to have his moment stolen."

"Of course, my good man. Let me be the first to thank you for your efforts on Anaris's behalf," Xavier said. "Please convey my gratitude to your friends as well. Will they be joining you on this trip? Hopefully, when we return, you can visit me. I should like to spend more time with each of them, as they were pleasant when you visited the orchard."

"Unfortunately, they will not be joining the convoy to Vanyareign. I have joined another group of exceptional warriors who will ensure your safety and that of your goods. I've learned to trust them with my life. Surely that says enough to have you trust them with your apples," Umhra said.

"Surely, indeed," Lord Pell said with a chuckle. "I'm sure my apples will be quite safe. I bid you well, Sir Peacebreaker. May the gods keep watch over you."

"Thank you, Lord Pell. May they have favor on you and yours as well."

Lord Pell returned to his work and Umhra walked the length of the caravan. The twelve carts were teeming with trade items from a variety of merchants in the Anaris area. Beyond Lord Pell's apples, there were cured meats, textiles, weapons, furniture, and whale oil. No wonder a security detail was necessary.

At the front of the caravan, two soldiers stood beside a wagon which had already been provisioned. Two junior soldiers manned the wagon, awaiting their orders. Unlike the green worn by the guards of Anaris, these men wore sky-blue tunics trimmed in silver, each with a large silver eagle on their chests. One was tall, with a strong build, and a pleasant face. The other, who outranked the first based on the epaulets on his left shoulder, was smaller in stature, with narrow, piercing eyes and dark features.

"Fine soldiers of the king," Umhra said as he approached, "how are you today?"

"We'll be much better once these damned merchants finish fussing about, and we can get on the road. It would be nice to make more than a few hours of progress today," the senior soldier said loud enough for everyone to hear. "Who may I ask is inquiring?"

"My name is Umhra the Peacebreaker. I'm part of the

security detail Lord Morrow requested to be sent along with this caravan to Vanyareign. I understand the roads we'll be traveling can be less than hospitable at times. Can you share some of your expectations, as I'm still acquainting myself with the region around the capital?"

"Orc security...what will Lord Morrow think of next?" the senior soldier asked, avoiding eye contact.

The junior soldier stepped in. "I'm Corporal Penarin and this is Company Major Shelling. We don't expect too much trouble along the way, as we travel this trade route regularly with little more issue than the normal wildlife, or the occasional band of brigands. Regardless, your group's presence will be appreciated, no doubt. We are on a tight schedule if we are to meet our deadline, which the major is intent on. If all goes according to plan, we should pass Antiikin by day and at pace, eliminating any risk it may pose. After passing the ruins, we'll head north on Englen Penn Way, which will lead us directly into the capital."

"Thank you," Umhra said. "My group and I are at your service for the duration of the trip. Please let us know if you require anything."

Corporal Penarin nodded with a shallow smile, while Major Shelling turned his attention back to the merchants, shooing them off so the caravan could prepare to depart. Mounting their indistinguishable bannered chestnut horses at the very front to the procession, the soldiers rode the length of the caravan one last time on each side and then departed Anaris's east gate. Each of the wagons, manned by two drivers, lurched to a start, their wood and iron wheels creaking into motion.

Umhra met up with the Barrow's Pact at the last cart, which was being driven by Balris and Nicholas. Laudin handed Umhra the reins to Splinter, and they were on their way. Leaving the city, a gentle, salt-filled breeze met them from the south. Looking to his right, Umhra caught sight of the small, makeshift camp, where the Bloodbound had spent its first two nights in

Anaris. Once again reminded of his loss, he hung his head in grief as he put Anaris behind him and set out for Vanyareign.

Turning northward onto Astor Crossing, the small forest surrounding Anaris on three sides gave way to beautiful rolling meadows, blanketed with wildflowers, and speckled with the occasional random poplar or dogwood. The brackish air permeating their experience in Anaris soon gave way to the sweetness of the Shining Meadows. Spider webs still glistened with the morning dew, while small songbirds darted from one side of the road to the other in dutiful pursuit of their breakfasts. Umhra inhaled deeply and settled into his saddle. Taking their cover seriously, the security detail took turns patrolling the length of the caravan as it plodded north. Hardly anything broke the peacefulness of the day, but for the occasional wolf wandering through the meadows in search of a hare.

"Mind if I stretch my legs?" Naivara asked Laudin, the sun rising high overhead.

"By all means," Laudin said.

Naivara handed her reins to Umhra and hopped down from her horse. Obscuring herself from the rest of the caravan behind Balris's wagon, she transformed into a fox and bounded out into the fields with wild abandon. Disappearing for moments at a time only to spring out amidst a patch of wildflowers, she was in her element. Naivara was not made to delve into the dark places of Evelium, but rather revel in the splendor of its open, happy ones. A pleasant trip through the bucolic fields, the men kept one eye on the caravan and the other on Naivara as she frolicked.

By late afternoon, fences began staking their claim to the land, and the wildness of the meadows ceded their natural beauty to the monochromatic grass fields of pasture. Naivara rejoined her group, brambles in her hair, and took again to horseback. Nicholas, who had been writing furiously since leaving Anaris, tuned his lute and sang.

Under bright of sun and gentle breeze
She became a fox with utmost ease
Through meadow shining as we road
She jumped and danced and ran and glowed
A beauty only known in myth
The lovely Naivara Marabyth

Naivara blushed. “Nicholas, thank you.”

“Rarely so easy a subject,” Nicholas said. “You should try writing a song about Umhra.” The entire party laughed, Umhra included.

The road meandered around a particularly large sycamore, and the village of Mourning’s Hope came into view. A modest village, Mourning’s Hope spanned both sides of Astor Crossing and ran three rows of buildings deep on either side.

Diverting from the main road, the caravan negotiated a narrow alley between the Bleating Lamb, where they would spend the night and Lady Claret’s House of Treasures. Once beyond the buildings, the alley opened into a small grass field, partially covered by a wooden roof extending off the back of the Bleating Lamb. The wagons positioned themselves as close together as possible, first filling up the covered area and then stretching across the field along the back of the weathered wooden inn.

Without a word, Major Shelling disappeared into the inn, with Corporal Penarin jumping down from the helm of their wagon, brushing himself off in a cloud of dust, and approaching Umhra.

“I’m sure you’ll be fine out here for the night watching after the cargo?” he asked.

“Think nothing of it, Corporal,” Umhra said, “We are quite accustomed to such arrangements.”

“Very well then. I will have food and drink sent out to you. Until tomorrow, Sir Peacebreaker.”

“Until tomorrow, Corporal.”

The sun slipped behind the buildings of Mourning's Hope, the sky turning a fiery orange. Laudin, who was setting a small fire in the center of the makeshift camp that Gromley and Shadow constructed, looked up and studied the western sky for a moment.

"It looks like we're in for some weather tomorrow or the next. That sky is a warning if I've ever seen one."

Balris and Nicholas turned to the west and nodded. The rest of the party kept to their current business without so much as a glance upward. Umhra, Shadow, and Gromley tended to the horses, while Naivara sat in an undisturbed section of the field meditating, her hands extended, brushing the top of the tall grass and murmuring a druidic mantra.

▲

As morning broke, the group awoke to the crow of a rooster. Umhra, who had fallen asleep leaning against a wheel of one of the merchant wagons, cleared his bleary eyes. A red morning sky backlit Laudin who was squatting over the fire, prodding it back to life with a stick. Naivara sat not too far away from him, once again deep in meditation. Balris, Gromley, and Nicholas stirred in their bedrolls, as Shadow slipped around the corner from points unknown.

Umhra stood and walked over to Laudin who greeted him with a kind smile. "I have a feeling the rest of this trip is going to be more eventful than our first day," Umhra said with a tone of concern.

"Agreed," Laudin said. "We still have six days travel to the capital, with little between us and the king but the plains of Clearwell until we near the Wistful Timberlands. For the rest of the journey, we travel through dense forest, to be broken only by the occasional hamlet, until we near the outskirts of the capital. Both the plains and the timberlands can be precarious."

The door to the Bleating Lamb swung open and Corporal Penarin emerged, squinting as the low-hanging sun hit his weary eyes. He approached Umhra and Laudin, releasing a gaping yawn.

"Sir Peacebreaker," the Corporal said, completing his yawn, "the major has requested the caravan be prepared to depart, as he is nearly finished with his breakfast. Could you please prepare the wagons so they are aligned facing the north end of the field?"

"We'll set to it immediately," Umhra said, extending his hand to greet the Corporal.

"Most excellent," Penarin replied with a salute, leaving Umhra's hand awkwardly unmet. The Corporal returned to the inn.

▲

"And who is responsible for this job when there is no extra security detail accompanying these trade convoys?" Shadow asked. "No doubt the lazy soldiers and merchants that ate and slept comfortably indoors last night." He muscled a particularly stubborn pair of horses out from under the canopy.

"Speaking of sleep," Gromley said, stretching a stiff back, "where did you slink off to last night?"

"Nowhere," Shadow said. "I was just restless and took a long walk."

Gromley raised an eyebrow and shook his head. "You are a moth to the flame, Shadow. I will never understand why you are compelled to seek trouble out when so much of it finds you without any effort."

Shadow laughed. "A safe life is hardly one worth living, I suppose."

Together, they made light of the work, so by the time Major Shelling stepped into the yard, the caravan was ready to depart. "Splendid," he said to the party, "I'll be sure to let Lord Morrow know of your fine work."

The merchants emerged from the Bleating Lamb in small groups. Rubbing their eyes and stretching as they hit the crisp early-morning air. They climbed aboard their respective wagons and slouched in their seats awaiting Major Shelling's orders.

"All have been accounted for, sir," Corporal Penarin said to the major as he finished his inspection of the convoy and took his seat.

"Thank you, Corporal," the major said. He turned to face forward and raised his hand high into the air. At the rear of the line, Umhra was the last to take his mount upon Splinter. Major Shelling thrust his hand forward, directing the caravan into motion, Umhra urging Splinter forward with a nudge from his heels. From the open skies of the field behind the Bleating Lamb, the narrow alley between the inn and Bella's Finery was claustrophobic, with barely enough leeway for the carts to pass. Emerging from the alley, the caravan thundered back onto Astor Crossing.

CHAPTER 20

Civilization was nearly lost to the War of Rescission. By its end, only remnants of humanity remained.
—The Gatekeepers' Abridged History of Tyveriel

Vol. 1, Chapter 47 – Unearthed from the Ruins of Meriden, the month of Anar, 1217 AT

—▲—

The caravan continued onward throughout the day, the open vistas of Clearwell giving way to the untamed wildness of the Wistful Timberlands. Here the road sloped upwards, rising into the foothills of the Seorsian Mountains and toward the choking darkness of the forest.

Turning onto Mirina's Path, the caravan headed east, the weather Laudin predicted the evening they spent in Mourning's Hope darkening the sky and obscuring the peaks of the mountain range to the north. What began as a tempered rain, soon broke free into an unbridled deluge. The caravan's progress slowed as water rushed down from the mountains, washing over the road, rendering entire sections impassable without great care and effort. More than once, the wagons slid toward the edge of the road under the force of the flooding, their horses straining in the mud, hooves clambering wildly to keep them from toppling down the adjacent hillsides.

Major Shelling halted the caravan in an area that seemed at least level and sound and sent word back through the train to have Umhra ride up for a word. Umhra road the length of the caravan toward Major Shelling's cart, merchants fighting the wind and rain to secure waxed tarps to protect their goods.

"Major, you called for me?" Umhra said over the storm.

"Yes, Sir Peacebreaker. We are going to have to stop here for the night. I am afraid if we carry on, we will only make things worse on ourselves. I do not want to risk losing a wagon or worse."

"I would tend to agree, Major. Why, exactly, did you need me for this? If you don't mind me asking plainly."

"Because resting here means that tomorrow night at this time, if all goes well, we will be passing Antiikin. We will be forced to travel through the night and the entirety of the next day to reach Tayrelis. I will need you and your comrades in arms to be at your best if we are going to pass Antiikin by the light of the moon," Major Shelling said.

"Not to question your judgment, Major, but why not camp short of Antiikin tomorrow night and then pass it by day?"

"Sir Peacebreaker, I have orders requiring this caravan be in Tayrelis by morning in two days, and I intend to meet my deadline," Shelling said, his tone stern.

"Understood. We'll do our part."

With a nod, Major Shelling dismissed Umhra and ordered the carts to position themselves for the night. Umhra nudged Splinter back to inform Balris and the others of the major's plan. While he disagreed with Shelling concerning the strategy, he admired his sense of duty.

The wagons were angled two-by-two with the horses tethered together at the front. As each successive pair wedged itself into place behind its predecessor, the soldiers and merchants crept under the tarps covering their wares and turned in for a restless night's sleep. The storm raged on throughout the night as Umhra kept watch, insisting his friends get some semblance of rest. He sat on Splinter in the pouring rain for hours on end, guarding those he promised to protect, with only his leather cloak protecting him from the storm.

With every flash of lightning, the darkness parted for a fleeting moment. Umhra used every opportunity the lightning provided to peer into his surroundings as far as each flash made possible. A vibrant streak of blue crossed the sky and revealed the figure of a woman standing amidst the storm down the path a short distance ahead.

He dropped down from his saddle, drawing his sword and leaving the caravan behind. Plodding through the mud, he drew close, the rain itself coalescing to manifest her image.

"My champion," the apparition said against the driving rain, her form shimmering despite the lack of light.

Sheath me, you fool, Forsetae warned. *You are in the presence of the god, Vaila.*

Umhra returned the blade to its scabbard. "Vaila?" he asked.

"Let the others shoulder your burden," Vaila said, her voice fading in and out, "there is much for you to see."

"What do you mean?" Umhra asked.

"There is much for you to see, my champion. Rest."

As she finished talking, the storm abruptly broke, her form collapsing to the ground with a splash and the clouds clearing to reveal the waning moon. All was quiet but for the rushing of water slaloming down through the foothills in rivulets to the plains below.

Umhra returned to his post and for the rest of the night wondered what Vaila had meant. Only when the meadowlarks welcomed the bright morning sun rising over the eastern horizon, did people start to emerge from under their tarps. Laudin and Naivara were among the first to greet the new day, followed by

Major Shelling and Corporal Penarin, who rooted about stirring the rest of the caravan. As soon as the caravan was in motion, Umhra took his leave, handing his reins to Laudin who tied them to the horn of his saddle, and climbing from Splinter onto the wagon Balris and Nicholas were manning. Without a word, he slipped under the tarp and folded his hands behind his head, exhaling, exhausted from his long vigil.

▲

Umhra rubbed his eyes and threw the tarp aside. Crawling up to the front of the cart, he found Balris clutching the reins, Nicholas sitting beside him enjoying an apple.

"Balris, may we speak for a moment?" Umhra asked, wiping his brow with his sleeve.

"Of course, Umhra, I always have time for you." Balris's friendly tone was as sincere as Umhra could ever remember being spoken to before.

"I just had a dream. A vision, I think," Umhra said in a whisper to ensure that Balris and Nicholas alone were in earshot.

"What did you see?" Balris asked as Nicholas stared at the Paladin, eyes wide with anticipation.

"It was the night of the Reaping Moon. There was a temple, hidden deep within an old forest. Within the temple, there was a cult. I can only assume this was the Brothers of Resurrection Manteis mentioned when he so foolishly told me of their plan. The cult possessed an ancient rune cast in pure rhodium. Upon a large altar before the rune, was a deep pit filled with blood. A group of robed brothers surrounded the pit. They held hands and prayed together. Their leader walked from behind the podium that held the rune and slit a brother's throat. His blood met with that within the pit, completing their ritual and opening a swirling portal to a hellish plane. In the distance, I could see a large demon-like figure approached with the intent of entering Evelium."

"If what you saw was, in fact, a vision, I am afraid the

Brothers of Resurrection have made considerable progress with their plan to return Naur to power. I hope only that the king considers our plea and grants us passage to Meriden. There has not been an envoy sanctioned to travel north of the Ilathril into Winterashe at the behest of the king for many years." Balris frowned.

"Yes, while I very much admire Lady Avrette and Lord Morrow, at times, I wish we hadn't needed to involve them and go through formal channels. It's served only to slow us down, as we could be well on our way to Meriden right now. I'll go to Meriden despite what the king says, Balris. Nobody will stand in my way," Umhra said.

"I understand your concern, Umhra, but I assure you Lady Avrette and Lord Morrow have our success at heart. They believe wholeheartedly we are Evelium's best chance. Lord Morrow's endorsement, and more importantly that of Lady Avrette, will bear great weight with the king. When politics are involved, however, I am afraid there are no certainties."

Umhra nodded, understanding Balris's position, and climbed toward the back of the cart where Laudin was riding, Splinter in tow. Laudin trotted over and handed him Splinter's reins. His brow furrowed, Umhra climbed upon Splinter's back, Taivaron hopping from the horn of his saddle to Laudin's shoulder.

"Everything okay?" Laudin asked.

"I feel as though we are wasting precious time."

"The king will understand and see us on our way to Meriden. He has to."

"I wish I shared your sense of optimism," Umhra said.

"And, I understand your trepidation. You have the most at risk."

▲

Late in the afternoon, the caravan crested a ridge with the sun at its back and the ruins of Antiikin took over the horizon. While many of the spires making up the center of this ancient city had long since crumbled, others still rose high into the sky, their polished jade façades still reflecting the sun as they had in the days of their construction. The merchants chattered nervously at their sight. The guards were solemn and quiet.

"We're camping here for the night, no?" asked a merchant, his cart teeming with handcrafted furniture.

"Nay," Major Shelling said. "We lost too much time as a result of the storm. We will continue on through the night."

"Have you lost your faculties, Major Shelling?" another merchant asked. "That's Antiikin."

"I know quite well what *that* is," Major Shelling said, turning to glare at the merchant. "And I assure you my faculties are fully intact. We will continue on through the night."

With a red sun falling below the foothills behind them, lightning cracked across the sky over the ancient city despite the storm having passed. The sky darkened quickly, and night enveloped the travelers. The growing unease intensified amongst the group.

"I want minimal use of light," Shelling said, his voice gravelly, wavering.

The night wore on, and everyone remained silent, their watchful eyes peering as far into the darkness as this late hour would allow. The occasional glow of the merchant's oil lamps might as well have been a series of beacons against the ebony sky. If there was anything in Antiikin casting a gaze on the horizons, they would no doubt be noticed.

Mirina's Path narrowed at a tight turn marking the point closest in proximity to the ruins. As the caravan negotiated the turn, there was a sudden burst of green light from one of the great spires. The light arced up into the night sky and then plummeted back to ground level where it proceeded to streak toward the caravan at an alarming speed. No fewer than a dozen others just like it followed in close pursuit.

"We are under attack. Circle the wagons and arm yourselves

as best you can," Major Shelling said, drawing his silver short sword from its scabbard. "Sir Peacebreaker. Take defensive positions and prepare for battle."

Umhra unsheathed Forsetae and began riding full stride toward the front of the caravan.

Confront them and let me do your bidding. They will know my blade, Forsetae said.

Umhra turned off the road and raced out into the fields toward Antiikin. Laudin and Gromley followed after him, while Naivara and Shadow remained back with the caravan.

When Umhra was far enough from the caravan to ensure its safety, he reined Splinter in, forcing the horse to come to an abrupt halt, throwing divots of dirt and grass into the air. He positioned himself directly in the path of the first streaking light.

As the light bore down on him, Umhra was able to make out the ethereal shape of an ancient king. The crown the king wore was distinctly Evenese, a style predating the Forene dynasty. The spirit of the king raced at Umhra, followed by a ghost army. The king's sword was drawn and pointing directly at him, his decrepit face twisted with rage. Umhra jumped down from Splinter, and removed his icon from its pouch, clutching it by the chain Nicholas had given him in Anaris. He placed the chain around his neck and closed his eyes, a divine blue light intensifying from the icon which hung at his sternum. His platinum armor appeared and grew out from the icon, surrounding his entire form in blue ether.

Umhra opened his eyes, the apparition within striking distance. Both swung their swords, meeting together with a clash of metal on metal, sending a shockwave out around them. Umhra thrust forward and threw the ghost king backward. The spirits behind the king slowed and then stopped behind him as he held his sword high.

"Ancient spirits of Antiikin, we mean you no ill will. We are but weary travelers on our way across Evelium. Please let us go in peace, and we shall leave you in yours," Umhra said, breaking the silence between them.

"Weary travelers, you say?" the ghost king said as the other spirits encircled the three men, Laudin and Gromley putting their backs to Umhra's in a defensive stance. "In our time, weary travelers did not carry with them the great Forsetae. How did you come to possess this most prized of Pureblood weapons, mongrel?"

"The sword had fallen into the hands of a vampire. Having dispatched the evil fiend, I claimed Forsetae as my own in exchange for its restoration. It's in safer hands now than any time in the last thousand years," Umhra said.

"In the safe hands of an Orc?" The king scoffed.

"No, in the safe hands of a Paladin," Umhra said, embracing his destiny. "This weapon was forged to do good. I could feel its strength the moment I first grasped it in my hand. Forsetae possesses power well beyond its blade."

"That blade was stolen from the halls of Antiikin ages ago, and I shall see it returned to its rightful place. To its rightful owners. You will not leave this field with our sword in your possession. If you leave this field at all," the king said, flourishing his sword.

The preternatural king's glow intensified with his rage. He approached Umhra, sword readied. Umhra held his ground, defiant. Laudin and Gromley flanked him, facing the whirring spirit warriors who had increased their cadence in anticipation of an attack.

"I implore you, great king of Antiikin," Umhra said. "Give me time. I will convince you of my worth, as I have done with this sword. If I fall short of Forsetae's expectations, I will return it to you myself. The very fate of Evelium is at stake, and we need every advantage we can gather. You've been without your hallowed blade for so long already, and all the while it sat in the hands of Telsidor, the vampire Manteis. Surely you won't miss it terribly for a few seasons longer. You have my word, if

I should survive, I will return to you and relinquish Forsetae to your ancient halls."

"You claim to have smitten Telsidor? This immortal Manteis?"

"I did. His destruction is how I came into the great Forsetae's possession. I intend to right his wrongs and set Evelium on a path avoiding certain destruction. He was in league with those who intend to return Naur to our fine land so he may remake it to his liking. Was it not he that razed your fine city? I'm sure you would agree with me this would be most unpalatable."

Silence ruled for a long moment. The king, his eyes narrowed, stared at Umhra. With all his might, Umhra forced himself to maintain eye contact with the ethereal monarch. The rest of the apparitions continued to circle but slowed their pace, weapons still at the ready. Finally, the king spoke.

"You are no Pureblood, but I can sense your honesty and valor. Forsetae glows pure in your hand, so it seems the weapon agrees, corrupted though it may be. We shall let your party pass with the promise you shall come to Antiikin after your mission and return Forsetae to its rightful place among our relics. I, King Eleazar of Antiikin, shall judge your worth at that time."

"You're most fair, King Eleazar," Umhra said, bowing in respect. "I shall keep my word and see you again."

"Then on your way, Paladin. I have nothing to do but wait."

King Eleazar turned to face Antiikin and faded from sight, sending a glowing green mist into the night sky. His warriors followed suit, leaving Umhra, Laudin, and Gromley alone in the field. The night seemed darker than ever with their preternatural light gone. Umhra sheathed Forsetae and faced Gromley and Laudin.

"That sure was entertaining," Gromley said in jest.

The three men shared a brief sigh of relief as they climbed back upon their horses. Umhra took one more look at Antiikin as his platinum armor retreated plate by plate, beginning at his chest. He spurred Splinter back toward Mirina's Path, tucking his icon within his leathers. The members of the caravan were silent and wide-eyed as the men returned.

"What was that Sir Peacebreaker?" asked Major Shelling.

"I was able to reason with them," Umhra said, not stopping to acknowledge the major.

"Reason with them? And what about the glowing armor?" Major Shelling pressed further.

"Parlor tricks, Major."

"Reason and parlor tricks against an army of ghosts," Major Shelling said, his jaw going slack.

"We are free to go, Major. That's what you and these merchants wanted if I'm not mistaken. I've delivered you safe passage. I dare say we might not be so lucky should we linger," Umhra said as Splinter trotted to the back of the caravan.

"Very well, but we will finish this conversation, Sir Peacebreaker," Major Shelling said.

"As you wish, Major."

Umhra fell in line next to the final wagon and an excited Nicholas. The merchants whispered to one another, trying to ascertain what strange magic they had just witnessed. The Barrow's Pact gathered around Umhra as Major Shelling ordered the caravan forward toward Tayrelis. The carts rumbled away from Antiikin. Umhra took a long look over his shoulder and then turned his gaze to the path ahead.

CHAPTER 21

I tracked the elk for days. My arrows were true, but they shattered upon his hide.
-Telsidor's Missives

Diary entry dated 15th of Vasa, 978 AC. Unearthed from the Ruins of Anaris, month of Emin, 1156 AT

—▲—

By the next morning, the caravan entered the city of Tayrelis and turned due north onto Englen Penn Way. A large city, Tayrelis thrived off the relentless growth of the Wistful Timberlands. Weaving along Englen Penn Way, the great River Torrent flowed from the Ilathril Mountains, around Vanyareign, and down to Hylara, a major port city. The entirety of the length of the road was paved in cobblestone and graced with large stone bridges where the river coursed below. Those areas in proximity to civilization were well maintained, including torchlights at regular intervals, which improved travel conditions materially.

Nearing the river, the greens of the foliage along the road grew deeper relative to those of the grasslands and foothills of Clearwell. Tayrelis was a town that got up early. The sawmills were heaving logs out of the river at daybreak, the shouting of the log drivers waking the city with the reliability of the most adamant rooster.

The caravan rumbled along the outer ring of the city. They passed neighborhoods crowded with small wooden homes and modest shops. Umhra smiled, watching the children run up to the passing convoy.

Naivara pointed to the center of the city, still a good distance from the road the caravan traveled, where an enormous marble statue of Tayre, the God of Forests, looked out over the city named in his honor to the wild forest to the west. Three great branch-like horns protruded from the sides and the back of the statues head. The effigy's face bore jagged, wild features, and the marble was carved with such meticulous care to give the textured effect of wood.

"He walked the great forests of Evelium for thousands of years before the War of Rescission." She leaned over to Umhra. "My people, those who adopted me, were very close to him and were left as stewards to his forests. Some say he still finds his way to the deepest, darkest, most wild parts of Evelium and just sits, perfectly unnoticeable to man or beast. The likeness of the statue is a little off, however. He has made himself known to me during my Suffusions, but I would love to see him in the real world someday." She smiled at the notion.

Umhra nodded, throwing one more glance at the immense statue of the living tree god as they left Tayrelis behind them.

Just outside of Tayrelis, they crossed over the River Torrent, taking them out of Clearwell and into Windswept. The activity along the road increased. Soldiers patrolled the populated areas of Windswept with regularity and with increasing frequency as one neared Vanyareign. Merchants and other travelers passed regularly as well, returning from the capital or points farther north still. The proximity of the capital was palpable.

Major Shelling continued to drive the caravan onward without rest. Their speed increased on the solid footing of the cobblestone road, and the merchants did not seem to mind the exhausting pace, with their journey so close to an end.

"You all right?" Shadow asked Umhra. "You're looking a little pale."

"I'll be fine. Just a little nervous about going before the king tomorrow. I keep practicing what I'm going to say to convince him to allow us passage to Meriden instead of having me executed."

"How's that going?"

"So far, not well. I have no idea what to expect."

"Well, you won't be alone. I just hope we don't have to fight our way out of the castle to get you to Meriden."

"I should hope our audience with him doesn't come to such an end. With any luck, he will share his sister's pragmatism."

"We can only hope," Shadow said. "You'll find the words when it matters."

Umhra nodded, returned to ruminating on the possible outcomes of his conversation with the king. Traveling into the heart of Windswept without rest, the day dragged on, the customary chatter of merchants and guards, alike, falling into a weary silence. As the sun set on their second day without sleep, the dark gray towers of Castle Forene pierced the heavens to the north. Rising over another ridge, the city of Vanyareign became visible extending from the base of Mount Orys upon which the castle sat. A long, spiraling road rose out of the east side of the city, joining it with the castle high above.

From the apex of the ridge, Umhra observed the capital, to which this was his first visit. He was awestruck not only by its size but more so by how fortified Castle Forene was by both natural and structural means. High on Mount Orys, and with but one road leading to the castle, the only means by which to gain access to the king were through the city, or by air. The castle was as inconvenient from a provisioning standpoint as it was unmatched defensively.

The castle's sheer outer battlement rose out of the face of Mount Orys, with no obvious footing at its base. The emerald-green conical spires of the towers of the inner battlement alone were visible behind the outer wall's cover. Each tower of the outer battlement, of which there were eight in all, was armed with a large ballista, and evenly segmented by numerous arrow loops.

A vast birch forest blocked them from the city. Beyond the woods, the River Torrent split in two, creating a natural moat around Vanyareign. Immediately adjacent to both branches of the river on either shoreline and within the floodplain between them, were several large farming complexes.

Dropping down from the ridge, the caravan entered the Burning Wood, which got its name from the uniform undergrowth of red fern. The stark contrast of the white-scarred bark of the birch trees and vibrant red of the ground cover was nothing short of breathtaking. Once again, Naivara couldn't resist herself. Dismounting, she polymorphed into a white wolf and took the liberty of a run through the ferns, weaving between the thin trunks of the birch trees.

"She certainly grows on you." Umhra nudged Laudin.

"You think this is fun. Wait until you see her in battle. You will fall in love too," Laudin said.

"I sure hope not. It would be awkward for me to steal her from you." Umhra said with a laugh. "Thank you for all that you've done so far, and for all I suspect you are yet to do. This has all been such a tempest. Having lost everyone I held dear in my life. To be accepted by others so quickly has been a pleasant surprise."

"It's certainly not because of your charming personality," Laudin said. Umhra laughed under his breath.

"But seriously, it's my pleasure to support you in this mission, and my duty to Evelium to see this through," Laudin said.

"For me, this goes beyond duty, Laudin. While duty drives me to save Evelium and deliver from destruction even those who would refer to me as a mongrel or heretic, I don't throw myself at the mouth of hell for Evelium's salvation, but my own. Since the day my village was slaughtered as I sat pissing myself in the trunk of a dead tree, I've been hiding. Hiding my true nature, hiding my power. All these years traveling the countryside, being paid a paltry sum to draw the blood of others, I've been running away from my destiny. It's time for me to find out who I really am...what my limits are...who I'm meant to be. It's time for me to run toward life and embrace what it holds in store for me."

"Self-discovery is an admiral pursuit," Laudin said. "You owe yourself no less."

Umhra nodded as they exited the woods, Naivara rejoining the party and taking her natural form once again. Passing several farms, the caravan crossed Bastion Bridge and entered Vanyareign through the expansive south gate.

The capital city was unlike anything Umhra had ever seen before. He marveled at its sheer enormity and the frantic pace of life that buzzed around them as soon as they crossed under the gate's portcullis.

Vanyareign was a complex grid of interweaving neighborhoods intersected by major thoroughfares dividing the city into districts. Diversity abounded, with seemingly all walks of life bustling in the streets, running businesses, and interacting with one another. Human, Evenese, Iminti, Zeristar, Farestere, and even the occasional Orcish commingled in a manner which was unlike the smaller cities and towns he had visited.

The streets were crowded with tents and stands where the lesser merchants hocked their wares. This made navigating the caravan increasingly difficult as it progressed. At the very heart of the great city, all of the major roads converged at the Grand Bazaar, a large rectangular park filled with yet more street vendors, picturesque seating areas, and walking trails welcoming those in need of a respite from the stresses of city life.

Taking the Grand Concourse around the park, and leaving Englen Penn Way behind, the caravan continued to the Osprey

District in the northeast of the city where they found a large, heavily guarded military complex. Upon arrival, they were greeted by a thin human man dressed in fine silk robes with slicked-back hair. He was followed by a small group of soldiers who stood at attention and saluted Major Shelling and Corporal Penarin as they climbed down from their horses and conferred with the gentlemen they accompanied.

"Yes, yes. This looks like a wonderful delivery of goods from Anaris. Major Shelling, you have excelled as usual," the lithe man said, extending his hand to Major Shelling.

"Thank you, my lord. Serving you has been an honor, as always," Major Shelling said, accepting the handshake. "We met with little obstruction, other than a terrible storm nearly washing out Mirina's Path the other night and a brief delay near Antiikin."

The men turned and walked past the still saluting guards. After Corporal Penarin passed, the guards fell in line behind him and the group entered the barracks within the facility through a heavily reinforced oak door.

"Is that it?" asked Shadow.

"I shall find out," Balris said, walking toward the barracks. He entered the building and was gone for several moments before returning.

"We are free to go. Our job is complete," he said, returning to the group. "Shall we head into the city? Our audience with King Arving is not until tomorrow morning."

"I suppose so," Laudin said, his tone showing annoyance at their unceremonious dismissal.

As the Barrow's Pact made its way toward the gate of the military complex, Umhra walked over to Xavier Pell, who was gathering his personal effects from his cart.

"My good Lord Pell. Please be careful on your return to Anaris. Don't let anyone talk you into passing Antiikin after nightfall. It's not safe. I hope when my calling has been fulfilled, I can come and visit you at the orchard and hear more of your tales of Anaris's history."

"I would certainly enjoy your company, Sir Peacebreaker. May the gods have favor on you and your journey," Pell said, putting his hands on Umhra's arms. "I must say, what you referred to as parlor tricks outside of Antiikin gave me hope for your success and our future. I look forward to hearing about your triumphant return."

Splinter in tow, Umhra ran after the rest of his group before they were lost to him amongst the frenzy of Vanyareign. The group walked through the busy city streets, enjoying some of the local delicacies and stopping at several vendors to inspect their goods. Umhra kept a comfortable distance but gave the party their moment to relax.

"I took the liberty of sending a courier in advance of our trip to secure lodging accommodations at the Marwyn Homestead," Balris said as they walked. "I am sure you will all find the amenities quite to your liking."

"That's a bit much for this crew, Balris. No?" Shadow asked.

"You are familiar with the homestead, Shadow?" Balris asked.

"Quite. When I lived here several years ago, I worked with an organization known as the Hands of Time. A local thieves' guild whose existence is widely disputed within the capital. We frequented the lounge at the Marwyn Homestead where drunk, rich patrons made for easy marks. Ah, the memories."

Balris shook his head. "I suppose you might be right, Shadow, but I figured we could all use some good rest while we are here. Who knows when we will see such comforts again?"

"In that case, I'll try to behave myself," Shadow said with a wink.

Eventually, the group found themselves in the Grand Bazaar. They weaved their way through the morass of street merchants, performers, and busy citizens and visitors, and finally arrived at the Marwyn Homestead at the southwestern edge of the bazaar.

Made of elegant brownstone construction, the Marwyn

Homestead was the height of fine dining and lodging in all of Evelium. The property took up an entire city block just off the southwest corner of the Grand Bazaar, and the homestead itself was the largest private structure in the city. Umhra hesitated as they neared the front steps leading up to the large double stained-glass doors.

"I'm not sure about this," he said.

Balris turned to Umhra. "You will be fine, Umhra. We will check into our rooms, freshen up, and change into our fine clothing. We can meet for dinner in the main dining room at sunset."

Shadow rushed up the stairs with childlike enthusiasm, obviously excited by all the potential exploits the evening held. As Umhra approached the homestead, the doors swung open, each held by a doorman. The porter, a tall, thin Evenese Pureblood, greeted the party with a deep, cartoonish bow. The porter was wearing purple satin pants with a matching coat, buttoned to his neck. A single silver medallion hung low across his chest and depicted the Marwyn family crest, consisting of grapevines encircling two soaring doves. His red hair was kept short on the sides and back but danced wildly atop his head.

"The Marwyn Homestead welcomes your return, Lord Balris Silentread of Anaris," the porter said. "We most look forward to your stay and that of your companions. You look most...weary from your travels." He looked down upon them from the top stair. "Your rooms are ready for you as I am sure you would like to clean yourselves up before your dinner reservation which is being held for you at sunset, as per the request in your letter."

"Thank you. My friends and I look forward to a stay unmatched throughout the land," Balris said.

With a grandiose gesture, sweeping his right hand through the doorway, the porter implored the party to enter. Having experienced the Marwyn Homestead before, Balris and Shadow led the way. Nicholas, Gromley, Laudin, and Naivara followed, their eyes wide, jaws agape. Finally, Umhra entered, feeling quite out of place among such refinement.

"Oh, it's amazing, Balris," said Naivara.

"Yes, my dear, truly special," Balris said, glancing over his shoulder with a smile.

The main parlor of the inn had dark wood paneling from floor to ceiling. Fine handwoven rugs graced the floor in an unending display of color. Fresh flowers sat on a large pedestal table in the center of the room, the arrangement stretching up toward the ceiling which loomed fifty feet above. All of the windows were stained glass, matching the doors at the main entrance, the most ornate of which was a large round domed window in the center of the ceiling. Around it, four large crystal chandeliers hung, casting soft candlelight across the room.

There were several private seating areas dispersed throughout the room and a large formal dining room with a lavish entrance off to the right. The dining room was presently filled with patrons filling themselves on a late lunch.

The party walked to the back of the room, passing several smaller rooms on their left and were greeted by a thin Evenese man who sat behind an elegant desk stationed between two staircases leading up to long balconies running the length of either side of the room.

"Yes, yes. Balris, my friend. How excellent to see you again. Thank you for returning to my fine home," said Hurston Marwyn, looking up from his ledger of expected guests. His spectacles dangled precariously at the end of his nose. His stark white hair was worn slicked back with oil, and he wore a finely embroidered navy blue silk suit. The jacket was perfectly tailored and a single button held the front flaps together over a saffron high-collared shirt.

"Always an honor, Lord Marwyn. Please let me introduce you to my friends. This is Shadow Argith, Gromley Strongforge, Nicholas Barnswallow, Naivara Marabyth, Laudin of Farathyr, and Umhra the Peacebreaker," Balris said formally.

Lord Marwyn examined his pending guests with a discerning

eye. He was quiet for a few moments as he tapped his quill thoughtfully on the edge of his desk.

"You, Sir Argith, have been a guest here before. Several years ago, if I recall. You seemed to enjoy yourself at the time, I hope you do once more," Lord Marwyn said.

"I'm sure I will, my lord," Shadow replied with a nod.

"Sir Barnswallow, I know your brother well. Nathaniel is well respected throughout the kingdom, and we are proud to serve several of his fermentations here at the Marwyn Homestead. It is a pleasure to make your acquaintance," Lord Marwyn said.

"Thank you, my lord. I look forward to my stay," Nicholas said.

"I cannot say I know the rest of you, but a lady as fair as Lady Marabyth is always welcome, and I assume you other lads clean up well enough." Lord Marwyn laughed. "Any friend of Balris's is a friend of mine. Welcome to the Marwyn Homestead."

"Thank you, my lord," Gromley, Laudin, and Umhra said in unison.

He passed six gemstones, each a different color, across the desk to Balris. "You are all on the second floor. Up the stairs behind me to my left, halfway along the balcony and down the central hallway. I look forward to seeing you all at dinner. I hope to get to know each of you a little better. Would you care for me to show you the way to your rooms?" He leaned back in his chair and folded his arms across his chest.

"Thank you, Hurston, I am sure we shall find our way just fine," Balris said, placing his right hand over his heart.

"Very well. I look forward to seeing you all this evening."

Lord Marwyn returned to his ledger, and Balris started up the stairs. Several fine oil paintings graced the stairway wall ascending to the second floor. Shadow stopped to admire one of a young lady dressed in a sheer white gown. She stood in the middle of a stand of birch trees, surrounded by red fern. On the frame beneath the painting, there was a small metal plaque that said *Lady of the Burning Wood by Dramien Colm.* The girl's hair was a deep chestnut brown and her eyes darker still. There was a certain melancholy to her gaze.

"An original Colm," he whispered to Naivara.

"A what?" Naivara asked.

"This piece of art is an original Dramien Colm. I knew the young woman in the painting when I lived here."

Naivara looked the painting over. "She looks sad."

"I suppose she does. She wasn't when we were together. Regardless, the artistry is unparalleled, you must agree."

Naivara shrugged. "If you say so, Shadow. I'm not knowledgeable of such things. You might as well be speaking to me in a foreign language." She continued up the stairs. After lingering on the painting for a moment, Shadow followed.

Once on the landing, Balris led them across the balcony which overlooked the main parlor on three sides of the second floor. Guarded by an ornate mahogany railing, the balcony was lined with several matching cream-colored rugs, each decorated with delicate foxglove—the official flower of Vanyareign—at each corner. Along the left and right sides of the balcony, there were three hallways each, all leading to guest rooms. Balris turned down the second as Lord Marwyn had instructed and stopped at the second door on the left. The door had a small glass sign at its center. On the sign was painted in near-perfect penmanship, "Sir Nicholas Barnswallow."

"I suppose I shall take my leave for now. Until dinner, then," said Nicholas, receiving an emerald from Balris. The stone perfectly matched a small green metallic recess in the door below the knob. Nicholas fit the stone into the recess and the door unlatched and popped ajar. Nicholas popped the jewel out, entered the room, and closed the door.

The rest followed suit, one by one as Balris made his way down the hallway, passing out the appropriate gem for each of the rooms. At the end of the hallway, Balris gave Umhra a gem for the room next to his. "Until dinner, then," Balris said.

"Yes," Umhra said. "Rest peacefully." Balris entered his room, leaving Umhra alone in the hallway.

CHAPTER 22

Madness overcame her. She insisted the Gray Queen was coming.
—The Tome of Mystics

Unknown Origin. Unearthed from the Ruins of Oda Norde, month of Bracken, 1320 AT

—▲—

Evening arrived and the dining room at the Marwyn Homestead was set into a frenzy. Patrons from high society within Vanyareign and visitors from all of Evelium descended to partake of the cuisine prepared by the homestead's master chef. Umhra and Gromley, who were prompt as always, waited in the center of the parlor for the rest of their party.

"This is so awkward," Umhra whispered, watching a woman arrive wearing a fanciful gown, a myriad of refined gentlemen dressed in well-tailored suits swooning.

"I assure you, I'm feeling quite out of place, myself." Gromley gazed at the floor.

Umhra brushed his olive leathers and smoothed his hair with his hands.

Laudin, Naivara, and Nicholas were the next to arrive. Nicholas was charming in a fine gray vest and red pants. He wore a matching red ascot loosely tied around his neck. Laudin, while less conventional in his attire, managed to fit in quite nicely with the growing crowd in a pair of tan leather pants, a white linen shirt, and a blue vest he acquired while in Anaris.

It was Naivara who stood out, even among the most sophisticated of women at the homestead. She wore her red hair pulled back by braids that began at her temples and converged at the nape of her neck. A fine ribbon of gold was woven through her hair and bound the hairstyle together at her midback. Her dress was a delicate sheer emerald color with an open back and her bare arms were adorned with gold bracelets that wound around her wrists and up past her forearms. Several men were caught gawking at the young Reshinta by their jealous wives.

"By the heavens," said Gromley, as she greeted him and Umhra in the center of the parlor, "You are quite breathtaking this evening, Lady Marabyth."

"Thank you, Gromley. You look quite dashing, yourself." She smiled.

Balris and Shadow joined the group. Balris in a long midnight blue coat, green ascot, and gray pants, and Shadow in a suit of black leather, his white hair slicked back. With the party now together, they made their way to the main dining room, weaving between the many couples awaiting their reservation time while enjoying an aperitif with friends.

They neared the dining room, the porter approached to greet them.

"Lord Marwyn awaits you at his reserved table," he said, gesturing toward a large round table at the back of the dining room between two large stained-glass windows.

Beside the gaunt figure of Hurston Marwyn, was his wife, Noemia, who wore a fuchsia velvet dress, her long blond hair draped over each shoulder, and a large sapphire pendant resting just above her chest. Her fair Evenese skin was flawless in the soft ambiance of the dining room.

Noticing the party's approach, Hurston stood and edged his

wife's chair back from the table. He offered his arm and helped her rise to meet his guests. "Noemia, you remember Lord Balris Silentread, High Priest of the Trinity Temple in Anaris."

"Of course, dear. It's lovely to see you again, Lord Balris," Noemia said.

"The pleasure is all mine, Lady Marwyn," Balris said with a slight bow of his head.

"And these, my love, are Balris's trusted companions and our honored guests," Lord Morrow continued.

Lady Marwyn curtsied to the rest of the party, each of whom returned the pleasantry in kind. Guiding his wife back to her seat, Hurston returned to his own.

"Please, join us for dinner," he said. "Balris, we have much catching up to do."

"The pleasure would be ours," Balris said, taking a seat next to Hurston.

The rest of the party took their seats, with Noemia requesting Naivara to join her at the table. As soon as they were settled, the house sommelier approached the table and presented Hurston with a bottle of fourth vintage Revelry Red from the Revyl Family Vineyard on Shent. This was, indeed, a rare vintage from the finest known vineyard in Tyveriel. The thin Iminti sommelier hovered over the table, awaiting Hurston's approval.

Hurston took his time, swirling the wine about his mouth. "Splendid," he said, turning his attention from the bottle to his guests. "I believe you all will find this wine truly remarkable."

"No doubt, Hurston," Balris said. "Thank you again for your hospitality."

"Think nothing of it, Balris. You and any person you call friend are always welcome in my home." Hurston placed his hand on Balris's shoulder.

As the sommelier carefully poured the wine, a human waiter dressed from head to toe in red velvet tucked up to the table.

"Tonight, we have the pleasure of offering a salad of hand-picked wild field greens from the Shining Meadows, graced with delicate slices of Pell apples, toasted pine nuts from the heights of the Seorsian range, and an aged vinegar dressing from the Revyl Family Vineyard on Shent. For our main course, we pleasure you with roast quail, wild-caught from the plains of Clearwell, served over wild rice from the headwaters of the River Torrent. Finally, for dessert, you will enjoy the unrivaled confections of Vanyareign's own Laurine Bestwig." Concluding his presentation, the waiter took a deep bow and backed away from the table.

"Overselling it much?" Shadow leaned over and whispered to Umhra who was sitting rigidly at his side. "Relax, mate, this is an experience to be enjoyed. There is enough time for anxiety at court with the king tomorrow."

Umhra hadn't even considered that he would, in twelve hours, be addressing King Arving and his most trusted inner circle. His heartbeat quickened, and his stomach turned in anticipation. His throat tightening, he clambered from the table.

"Please excuse me for a moment," he said, his mouth dry, his brow damp.

He turned from the table and made his way through the crowded parlor and out the front door. The cool evening wind hit his face, sending a brief shiver down his spine. He shook off the chill and stepped down the stairs and into the street, searching for a quiet place where he could remove himself from the hum of the city. Walking around the side of the Marwyn Homestead, he found a small courtyard with a stone statue of a young boy holding a shield in one hand and thrusting a seemingly toy sword up into the air. Umhra sat on a bench amidst the flowered yard, took a deep breath, and allowed the fragrance of the cool evening air to fill his senses. He retrieved his icon from its pouch and turned it between his fingers.

"I never asked for this," he whispered, turning the icon over in his hand.

For a moment, all was quiet. Then, the eyes of the statue glowed blue and Vaila spoke, invading Umhra's mind.

One who is chosen has no need to ask. Your path was decided the moment you were conceived. I was in need of a champion, and you were a most obvious choice.

"So, all of this...Everything I have been through hasn't been of my own free will, but rather of your bidding?"

Not my bidding, my child. You have wandered from the path on your own accord. You returned on your own accord. We are inextricably bound to one another for all time. Did I forsake you when you hid from me? When you denounced me? Or was I there for you when the vampire sought your end?

"You were there for me. You've always been there for me. I understand that. I've always felt your presence, regardless of how hard I tried not to. Vaila, what lies ahead? Will we succeed?" Umhra asked, looking around to assure himself nobody could hear him talking aloud to himself. Surely, he would end up incarcerated if the wrong ears should pry.

The fates are yet to be sealed. There are too many variables at play, and my powers limited without vantage in Pragarus. Naur's strength grows. His following grows, and ours continues to weaken. I am afraid that you and your companions are Evelium's only chance at survival. If you fail, Naur will return and we shall have to destroy all that lives and start anew.

"Can you not intervene? Can you, and the other gods, not stop Naur from ravaging our world?"

The Rescission precludes me from interfering with life in the material world. We shall not break our promise to allow the world to be an imperfect place. If Naur finds his way back, such is the destiny of our greatest experiment. You will need to be my beacon.

Umhra leaned forward and put his head in his hands.

"I shall be true. I shall see this through to the end. No matter the cost. I ask but one thing in return. Should I survive, may you grant me peace of mind?"

Peace of mind is not mine to give, but for you to take. Your very life is a contradiction, a tangled web. Your half-blood anatomy—the offspring of an Orc chieftain and his war-claimed Tukdari bride—doomed you from the start. My champion, you were made to be broken. Where I admit to having interceded in your life was in guiding the monk, a man of pure intentions, to save you from certain death and teach you how to commune with me. Oh, how your base nature resisted the path of a Paladin. For him to bestow upon you the name Peacebreaker was most fitting. Even with your training complete, you left my church and hid me away in favor of surrounding yourself with the savage and unclean. Still, you have found no home. This is not my doing, but of your own free will. I am sorry that it took such loss to renew our bond—that only in the face of great peril you have chosen to discover who you really are and what you are capable of. Nonetheless, I have been waiting for this day. When you finally accept your destiny, you will find the peace of mind you seek.

"The path before me is obscured," Umhra said. "Will you continue to make yourself known to me?"

No. I have already interfered too much, and at great expense. What I may share, that you should find soothing, is my brothers, Kemyn and Brinthor, still walk Evelium. Kemyn has assumed the form of an elk stag and Brinthor that of a blue dragon. Should they make themselves visible to you on your travels, you will know you are progressing toward your goal. For they will be drawn to my light within you, Vaila said.

The eyes of the statue faded, and Umhra was overcome by a sense of calm. He stood and took in a deep breath of fresh air, and then sighed. He left the courtyard and returned to the dining room at the Marwyn Homestead.

"Everything all right, Umhra?" Balris asked when he rejoined the table.

"Yes, thank you for asking. I had simply forgotten something," Umhra said.

Not paying much notice to the matter, the dinner continued. The party ate and drank late into the night. Never had they enjoyed such a wonderful dinner. The Marwyn Homestead had indeed exceeded its lofty reputation.

Just after midnight Lord Marwyn stood from the table. “I think the time has come for us to turn in for the night,” he said, helping Noemia from her seat. “It has been a pleasure dining with you all, but the hour is late and I have an early start. Please, stay as long as you like.”

Balris stood, took Hurston’s hand. “The pleasure has been ours I assure you. Thank you both for the exquisite dinner and engaging conversation. I believe we all grow weary as well and are ready to turn in.”

“Yes,” Naivara said. “Noemia, it’s been wonderful getting to know you tonight.”

“You as well, my dear. I hope you enjoy your time in the capital.”

“No doubt we will. Thank you.”

“Then we bid you good night,” Lord Marwyn said. He and Noemia made their way out of the dining room. The rest of the party, sated and tired, returned to their rooms for a full night’s sleep.

CHAPTER 23

There is no more a majestic sight than a legion of Paladins poised for battle.
—The Collected Letters of Modig Forene

Letter to Her Holiness Tahira Rhys dated 10th of Lusta, 2 AF. Unearthed from the Ruins of Vanyareign, month of Ocken, 1301 AT

—▲—

Umhra and Nicholas sat on the front steps of the Marwyn Homestead when Laudin returned from his early-morning walk.

"Beautiful morning, Laudin," Nicholas said, looking up from his notebook. "Did you enjoy your walk?"

"Indeed. There is something about the solitude of nature early in the morning that has always called to me."

"I'd hardly call this nature," Nicholas said.

Taivaron hopped from Laudin's shoulder to the newel of the banister against which Umhra leaned. "When the city is quiet like this morning, it's a close second." Laudin smiled. "Besides, any day on this fine land is worth celebrating."

"Agreed. I had no idea you were such an optimist," Nicholas said with a chuckle.

"Don't confuse gratitude with optimism, my friend." Laudin winked. He turned to Umhra who wore his base leathers, the platinum chain Nicholas gave him showing at the edges of his collar. He was quiet, solemn—his brow furrowed as he considered the day ahead. "Someone means business.."

"If all goes well when we meet with King Arving, we'll be sworn to contract," Umhra said. "That contract shall steer us in the direct path of extreme peril. While I don't doubt your resolve, and I much appreciate our alliance, I must ask one more time whether any of you would choose a less harrowing future for yourselves. I wouldn't think any less of anyone who should."

"The way I see it," Shadow chimed in, guarding his eyes against a low-hanging sun as he exited the Marwyn Homestead with the rest of the party on his heels, "if we don't succeed in stopping the Brothers of Resurrection, there's no point in living. Therefore, we might as well die trying."

"Agreed, and well said," Gromley said.

Looking around and seeing that everyone agreed, Umhra continued. "All right then. We shall go to the king, get permission to travel to Meriden, and rid us of any threat the brotherhood poses."

"Very well," Balris said. "Follow me to Castle Forene."

The party made their way back toward the center of the great city and through the Grand Bazaar. They approached the north gate, were halted by two of the king's Eagle Guard who stood watch at the entrance to King's Walk, the path leading up to Castle Forene. One, a man with dark features, the other a woman with a deep scar across her neck. They were dressed in traditional sky-blue tunics over gleaming plate armor.

"Do you all have official business at the castle today?" the male guard asked of Balris, who led the party.

"We do, my good man. Here is our official invite," Balris said, proffering a sealed parchment from his satchel and handing it to the guard.

"Very well. Give me a moment to verify with our records

and you should be on your way," the guard said, taking the note from Balris and heading over to a small building on the east side of the gate.

When he returned with the parchment in hand, its seal had been broken.

"All seems to be in order," the guard said, handing the document back to Balris. "The court is expecting you. Have a fine day."

"You as well," Balris said, taking the parchment.

The party walked through the large white stone arch, leaving Vanyareign behind. Several peasants on mule-drawn carts sat on the other side, waiting to take a fare up to the castle. Noticing one particularly young boy, maybe twelve at most, Balris called him over.

"Young man," he said. The boy snapped to attention.

"Yessir?" the boy asked.

"Would you be so kind as to usher us to the castle gate?" Balris looked up the road toward Castle Forene.

"Of, course, sir," the boy said.

"Let us be on our way. We have important business to tend to."

"Right away, sir. Please, climb aboard." The boy waved for Balris and the party to join him on his well-worn cart.

Balris sat up front next to the boy, while the rest of the group climbed into the back, sitting shoulder to shoulder on the two bench seats the cart had been outfitted with. When everyone was in their place, the boy snapped the reins. The mule did not budge. Again, he snapped the reins, and the mule looked over its shoulder in disdain.

"C'mon now. Let's get up to the castle for these fine folks," the boy said.

With a third snap of the reins, the mule begrudgingly set into motion. The ride was smooth, despite the poor condition of the cart. They crossed the eastern branch of the River Torrent, and wound around Mount Orys, ascending toward the castle. The gray stone lightened in color as they rose and the jagged terrain of the mountain's base smoothed into the immense outer walls of the castle compound. The trip up Mount Orys took just shy of a half-hour, the cart coming to a halt under the main castle gate. Balris turned and handed the boy two sovereign notes.

"My lord, this is far too generous. I can work all day and not make this much money."

"But you should not have to," Balris said. "Consider today a good day and get something nice your family needs."

"I'll be sure to, sir. It's been a pleasure meeting you," the boy said.

"And you as well," Balris said, stepping down onto the cobblestone.

He turned to face the immense portcullis of Castle Forene, the true enormity of the castle making itself known. The gray façade stretched up into the sky, the green conical spires partially hidden by cloud cover high above. Two more of the king's Eagle Guard marched forth through the portcullis to greet the party.

"Sir Balris Silentread?" asked one of the guards, his blue tunic meeting the persistent breeze of the elevation.

"Yes, and these are my associates," Balris said.

"Excellent, the sovereign awaits you," the guard said with a wave, inviting the party into the castle's bailey.

Balris and the rest of the group followed the guards through the bailey. The courtyard was manicured with meticulous precision, a large open lawn of vibrant green grass interrupted only by a solitary bristlecone pine tree—the oldest tree in all of Evelium—on a stone platform in the center. The tree, which had witnessed the War of Rescission thousands of years earlier, was a gnarled shell of its former self but continued to bear a few pinecones each year, marking the onset of the spring festival season of the Sowing Moon.

At the far side of the bailey beyond the ancient tree, were two enormous doors made of gold. The guard led the party to the doors and they opened with a resonant sound of metal scraping on stone.

The room on the other side of the doors was dimly lit, with no exterior windows, and only the soft glow of several candelabras marking the center hallway. The great room of gray stone was lined with sturdy gilded pillars on each side and stretched on to another set of gold doors ahead. Between the pillars were marble busts of the great figures of Evelium's history. Each of Evelium's great kings and other leaders of note was present, culminating in a bust of Modig Forene himself directly in front of the gold doors.

"Follow my lead," Balris said. "There is an etiquette to be followed before entering the king's court."

Near the end of the room, the two guards stepped to the side of Forene's bust and stood at attention, waiting for the group to act. Balris stepped in front of the bust and genuflected on one knee.

While looking down at the ground he said, "Father of Evelium, in your honor, I approach the king's court, and to his command, I promise myself." He then rose and stepped away from the bust and waited beside the guards. One at a time, the others followed suit, and when they were all in a line beside the bust, the guards proceeded to the great doors.

They knocked, the sound of their gauntlets hitting the doors echoed throughout the chamber. The doors opened, revealing four more guards, each gripping a thick golden rope with a knotted end, who pulled from the other side. By contrast, the room within was well lit, casting a bright light upon their expectant faces.

The hallway continued, but in the natural light of the amply windowed room, the detail of exquisite terrazzo floors became evident. In twelve-foot squares, the intricate tile work depicted scenes from the Forene family's historic reign over Evelium. At the entrance to the room, the first such scene showed Modig Forene himself, standing atop Mount Orys, his sword buried deep in the rock, declaring the site of his castle, and the center of his new kingdom.

Standing at the foot of the first picture, the party looked forward past five more such scenes and upon the Raptor's Throne of the House of Forene. The throne, made entirely of gold, was in the shape of a huge eagle with wings that wrapped around the sides to protect the king. The eagle's great head reared up into the sky in a call of victory, while its talons grasped the bodies of a dire wolf and blight, depicting Modig Forene's victory over the untamed wild of Evelium.

Upon a green velvet cushion sat King Shale Arving, awaiting his guests. On the right side of the room, halfway between the entrance and the throne was a large stone table with a green and gold runner. Around the table sat several advisors, all wearing matching yellow doublets, identifying them as members of the Elders Syndicate. They were quibbling, as politicians do, about the most trivial matters confronting the capital and the kingdom. Directly behind the king, offset to the right, was a young man in studded leather armor and a blue tunic, similar to those of the guards, except there was a great eagle's head emblazoned upon the chest instead of the full eagle form on the standard guard tunics. He was tall, and muscular, with long, blond hair, and a trimmed beard.

"May I present Lord Balris Silentread and associates," the guard who led them into the room said, stepping to the side.

"Come, friends of my sister," King Arving said. "Please, stand before your king and inform me of the quest my sister says is of such crucial import to the safety of our land."

The party approached the king on his throne. As they did, the Elders Syndicate excused themselves through a doorway at the back of the throne room. The king waited patiently as the group approached, a kind and inquisitive look on his face. His deep brown hair was held back by a simple gold circlet crown that crossed his forehead and he wore a deep blue set of robes lined with gold embroidery.

"My lord," Balris said, "I am Balris Silentread, High Priest of the Kormaic Temple of Anaris. With me are Sir Umhra the Peacebreaker, Nicholas Barnswallow, Gromley Strongforge of the Twelve Mines, Shadow Argith, Lady Naivara Marabyth, and Laudin of Farathyr. We come to you at the bequest of Lord Espen Morrow and your sister, Lady Jenta Avrette, to discuss a terrible occurrence in Anaris that shed light on a much larger and nefarious conspiracy against your rule and the very survival of Evelium."

"Please, go on. Tell me your story." King Arving leaned forward with a straight back and his hands on his knees.

"Umhra, please," Balris said.

"Good morning, Your Highness." Umhra bowed. "While working under Lord Morrow's employ, I discovered that a secret society based in Meriden, known as the Brothers of Resurrection, is preparing to overthrow your rule by calling the god, Naur, to Evelium through some lost ritual. They have purportedly infiltrated all of the major towns and cities throughout the kingdom, waiting for the right moment to launch their offensive and claim Evelium in the name of the God of Fire. We would like your permission to go forth to Meriden, dismantle this cult, and in so doing, save our fair land from an eternity under Naur's dominion."

The king's face dropped. "Tell me, Sir Peacebreaker. Why, other than you having the support of my sister, should I send you on my behalf into Winterashe to dispatch this cult?"

"My lord, I am a Paladin. The only of my kind, to my knowledge," Umhra said, well knowing this revelation exposed him to charges of heresy and treason. King Arving sat back in his throne, his eyes fixed on Umhra. After a moment, he shifted his gaze toward Balris.

"Your Holiness, can you explain this to me? Is it not your understanding the Kormaic Ministry elected, by its own free will, to end the training of Paladins in favor of the protection and position provided by the House of Forene?" the king asked rhetorically.

"Yes, my lord. You speak of the Kormaic Writ. I assure you, Umhra was not formally trained by the church, but rather by an individual monk within the clergy who had a certain understanding of events yet to come and saw fit to secretly train Umhra in the lost ways of the Paladin. A monk who was a dear friend, and whom I always knew to make decisions based on what was in the best interest of the people of Evelium and the king he loved so well. I would humbly request the king not take any offense, as I assure you there was none intended," Balris said.

King Arving turned back to Umhra. "Show me."

"My lord?" Umhra asked.

"Prove to me you are a Paladin as you say, Sir Peacebreaker."

Umhra freed his icon from within his leathers and let is show plainly. He closed his eyes and whispered a prayer to Vaila. His armor materialized around him in an intricate weave of platinum plate. From within, a blue light grew until wisps of smoke curled off of his form. King Arving gasped. "Platinum... Sir Peacebreaker, I am sure you are well aware the news you deliver is punishable by your own death. Yet, you stand before me in a spirit of honesty and integrity which I find most worthy of respect. While I may not find comfort in even my sister keeping your existence from me until this moment, I understand the reason behind me being kept in the dark and the apparent severity of our current situation. My first impulse is to send the full military force at my disposal into Meriden to end this threat, but I have vowed to operate within the agreement set forth by the Fracture and so cannot. As such, I shall grant you passage to Meriden to complete your mission, but only with a most trusted delegate from the Raptor's Grasp at your side."

The Raptor's Grasp was a special forces division of the Royal Army of Evelium that carried out the king's most delicate and secretive military orders. With no official ranks, one was able to join the Raptor's Grasp only by special invite of the king after showing valor beyond compare in the name of Evelium. Their numbers unknown, they were unmarked unless within the castle walls where their safety was ensured.

"We fully understand your position and are strengthened by your trust. We, of course, welcome your delegate as a brother in arms," Umhra said.

The young, fair-haired man standing behind the throne approached and whispered to the king. King Arving acknowledged him with a deep, contemplative nod.

"Let me introduce Talus Jochen." King Arving gestured toward the man. "He is my choice to join you on your journey. I am certain you will not find a more capable fighter in all of Evelium. Talus has raised a concern he feels deserves priority over Meriden, however. Talus, please speak."

"Thank you, my lord," he said with a bow, his voice deep and strong. "It occurs to me, if what you say is true, and a great threat looms over our fair kingdom, we must first root out the arm of this Brothers of Resurrection which has infiltrated Vanyareign and ensure the safety of the king before traveling to Meriden. Should we leave this loose end, and are successful in Meriden, the villains assigned to assassinate the king will surely take their chance. As you know, this would end the Forene bloodline. I see no victory in such an outcome."

"Agreed," said Umhra. "Do you have any thoughts on where to start?"

"Unfortunately, no. The perpetrator could be anyone, and we surely don't want to enlighten the Brothers of Resurrection that we're aware of their plans. It's one thing to discover such a fiend in a town the size of Anaris, but I'm afraid this will prove much more complicated an effort in the capital. Any news notifying them of part of their network meeting their demise would surely lessen our chances in Meriden," Talus said.

"I may have an idea," Shadow said, stepping forward.

"Please. Sir Argith, was it?" King Arving asked.

"Yes, Your Highness. When I lived in Vanyareign several years ago, I was a member of the Hands of Time," Shadow said.

"What is the meaning of this?" King Arving asked, turning to Balris in shock. "A High Priest of the Kormaic faith fraternizing with Paladins and thieves? Who else do you shepherd before my court? Are there any witches or demons among you?"

"Please, my lord. Shadow's path has not been straight, but he has found his way to a life of honor. I trust him with my life, and your own sister saw fit to send him here, well knowing his history. As with Umhra, he comes in the spirit of honesty, and with the desire to see done what is best for your kingdom."

"Very well, I will hear him out, but my faith in your band of misfits is being tested," the king said.

Shadow cleared his throat. "If anyone would know about an underground network plotting to send Evelium into eternal chaos, it would be the Hands of Time. And more specifically, Moric Tilk. If I were to contact Moric, he might share this information with me."

"You mean to tell me that you're going to contact the head of the Hands of Time, a man who isn't even confirmed to exist, and seek his aid in a matter of utmost delicacy such as this?" asked Talus.

"First, I assure you he exists, as he was my teacher, and I was his protégé. Second, it's in his best interest to put an end to this matter as well. Chaos is bad for business, and all Moric cares about is his business. I would not suggest contacting him if I didn't believe it might aid our cause. Unless, of course, someone else has a better idea," Shadow said.

"Let me see your tattoo," Talus said, his face stern.

Shadow bunched up his left sleeve and held his forearm out for Talus and King Arving to see. In the middle of the forearm, just above the wrist, there was a small tattoo of a clock held in the palms of two skeletal hands.

"Hearing no other course of action, I agree to let Sir Argith contact Moric Tilk and attempt to ascertain whether or not he knows anything regarding the Brothers of Resurrection, or who their representative within Vanyareign may be. You have two days, and Talus will accompany you," the king said.

"At a distance, I hope. Your soldier here doesn't exactly look like he belongs in such circles," Shadow said.

"At a distance," King Arving said. "You are dismissed until two days then. I now consider us in contract, and I wish you luck."

"Please then, follow me," Talus said. He bowed deeply to King Arving and turned toward a door at the back of the throne room. Each taking their turn to give a respectful bow toward the king, one by one they followed Talus through the doorway.

CHAPTER 24

The Keep became a necessity. Over the years, I had amassed countless enemies and wealth.
—Telsidor's Missives

Diary entry dated 20th of Mela, 27 AF. Unearthed from the Ruins of Anaris, month of Emin, 1156 AT

—▲—

"Come to my quarters. We can discuss our plan while I gather my things," Talus said, leading the party down a long stone-walled interior hallway. Coming to a flight of stairs at the end of the hall, Talus ascended them two at a time with ease. The rest followed as quickly and quietly as they could, Nicholas with some effort.

At the top of the spiraling stairs, they came to another hallway, lined with doors. Halfway down the corridor, Talus opened a door on the right and welcomed the group into his private quarters. The room was sparse, with nothing on the stone walls except for a map of Evelium hung slightly askew on the wall to the right. The first room had a small round meeting table with four chairs, and a small cupboard in the corner. The room to the rear was a simple bedroom with only a modest bed and footlocker in view.

"Do you have a plan as to how you'll contact Moric Tilk?" Talus asked Shadow as he closed the door behind them.

"I know exactly how to contact Moric. That won't be the difficult part."

"Are you not on good terms?" Talus asked.

"Our terms are on a fine footing, I assure you. The problem will be getting Moric to talk without scaring him off or having to explain my interest in the Brothers of Resurrection." Shadow's tone was terse.

"Where can we find him?" Laudin asked.

"The Hands of Time uses a small tavern in the Lark District called the Griffon's Respite as a front," Shadow said. "On an evening like tonight the tavern should be quite busy with patrons, so I see no harm in all of us going as long as we don't enter together as a group. I think it best you, Naivara, and Balris arrive first and get a table for dinner. Talus, Umhra, Nicholas, and Gromley can post up at the bar and order a few ales. I'll arrive separately and seek an audience with Moric."

Talus walked into his bedroom and unbuckled the brown leather belt holding his tunic in place. He took off his tunic and folded it at the foot of his bed along with the coiled belt. He then opened the footlocker and removed a satchel, a crossbow and quiver of bolts, and a longsword. The sword was an especially fine weapon, the blade engraved with ancient runes that pulsed with a green light in response to Talus's grasp. The sword's gold hilt was cast so the wings of an eagle enveloped the base of the blade. A blue sapphire was embedded in the pommel.

"That is a truly special sword," Umhra said.

"Yes, this is Aquila, the very blade favored by Modig Forene when he claimed dominion over Evelium. Given to me by King Arving. I'm the first from outside the Forenian bloodline to wield the weapon," Talus said, holding the blade out for Umhra to inspect. "I'm certain, however, it's no more special than yours." He nodded toward Forsetae, which Umhra now wore on his hip.

Umhra presented the blade to Talus. "This is Forsetae,

forged by the Evenese clerics of Antiikin," he said.

"Remind me to have you tell me the story of how you came into such a unique sword's possession some time," Talus said, admiring the blade.

"Gladly," Umhra said, giving Talus a moment with the weapon, then returning Forsetae to its scabbard.

"Assuming you're able to gain access to Moric, how do you plan on extracting the information we need?" Talus asked, rising from his footlocker and turning his attention back to Shadow.

"That, I haven't figured out. I expect he'll be somewhat guarded, having not seen me in years. He still owes me a favor, however, so I think he'll talk if we wipe the slate clean," Shadow said. "Moric doesn't like being indebted to others."

"Understood. Let's make our way into the city. We can divide there until we see one another at the Griffon's Respite in the late afternoon," Talus said.

They left the room, Talus being sure to grab his dark green cloak that hung behind the door, and made their way back down the hallway. They descended the staircase, past the landing and doorway to the king's court, and continued into the castle's depths by the flicker of torchlight. Winding down the spiraling stairs, they reached an armory.

"Through that door is the stable," Talus said. "From there we can exit the castle into the western courtyard where we can easily hire a cart to take us into the city. We can find a quiet place and stage our approach to the Griffon's Respite."

"May I suggest we return to the Marwyn Homestead?" Balris asked. "We are welcome there and will not be bothered."

"It's all the same to me," Talus said.

The stables were meticulously maintained. The stalls were painted a rich forest green, offsetting the gray stone walls. Each stall had a copper sign hanging on its door, marked with the name of the horse housed within. The windows along the three exterior walls provided a surprising amount of natural light, allowing the many stable hands to hurry about without the aid of torch or lantern this time of day. At the far end of the straw-covered cobblestone aisle between the stalls was a portly man shoeing a blue roan stallion. The horse's black mane and tail were in stark contrast to its light blue-gray body. It tussled about anxiously while the man applied a shoe to his front left hoof.

"That is Maelstrom," Talus said as they neared the horse, "my steed." He walked over to the horse and patted the broad side of his neck. The horse snorted in response. "I'll be back for you soon, boy. We have a long journey ahead of us."

"Aye, Master Talus. I'll have him at the ready for you, sir," the stable master said.

"Thank you. Most appreciated."

Leaving the horse's side and opening the large, metal-studded wood door at the far end of the room, he led the group past two more castle guards and out into a courtyard on the western side of the castle. A gravel path, lined with fragrant honeysuckle, led to the front of the castle where several carts were lined up waiting on those in need of transport back down into Vanyareign. The boy who guided the party up to the castle two hours earlier was waiting patiently in the middle of the line. Seeing Balris, his face lit up, and he jumped down from his cart.

"Most pleased to see you again, my lord. May I be of assistance?" the boy asked.

"Why yes, you may, lad. Would you be so kind as to give us a ride back down into the city?" Balris smiled.

"Of course, sir. Are you ready at present?"

"Yes. Thank you."

The boy led Balris and the rest over to his cart. After ensuring that everyone was comfortably aboard, he climbed up to his seat and nudged his mule, who, after a few prods, towed the cart out of the line and turned toward King's Walk. The path seemed steeper on the descent than it had earlier in the day on their approach. The cart rattled from side to side as the boy tugged at the reins to keep his animal at a somewhat comfortable pace for his passengers.

"Can you keep an important secret?" Balris asked, leaning closer to the boy so he alone could hear.

"I should think so, my lord," the boy said.

"Excellent," Balris said. "I wanted you to know we will be heading off on a very dangerous mission on behalf of the king himself, and I felt I should thank you for the important role you played in our day."

"You're most welcome, my lord. I'm afraid my role could've been filled by anyone at the base of the mount. That being said, I'm happy you chose me and wish you much luck on your adventure," the boy said.

"Possibly, it could have been filled by anyone, my boy, but the gods favored you. I do not believe in chance." Balris patted him on the shoulder.

The boy smiled broadly at the thought he was somehow an integral part of a great mission by order of King Shale Arving. This was an honor a peasant boy rarely had the luxury of even contemplating.

"Where will I be taking you then, my lord?" the boy asked with a sense of purpose.

"To the Marwyn Homestead, my lad. A safe delivery will be considered the fulfillment of your quest."

"Right away, my lord." The boy snapped the reins.

Re-entering the city through the north gate, the boy steered his old cart through the northwestern neighborhoods of Vanyareign, which had a very different feel than the other parts of the city the party had experienced. Graced by fine homes with private courtyards surrounded by stone walls or iron fences, with sections of upscale shops and other businesses interspersed between them, there was a refinement unmatched in the city other than by the Marwyn Homestead.

"I thought you all might appreciate a trip through the Kestrel District on our way to the Marwyn Homestead. This route is quite pleasant and won't delay us at all. Normally I wouldn't be allowed in these neighborhoods, but with my present company,

I don't see there would be a problem," the boy said, looking over his shoulder.

"Thank you," Nicholas said. "A most beautiful section of your fine city."

"Someday, I would like to own one of these houses," the boy said, staring longingly at a large stone home as they passed.

Nearing the southernmost point of the Kestrel District, the street broadened in preparation for its terminus at the Grand Bazaar. The boisterous bazaar met the group with a frenzy of activity. The boy turned the cart westward, and then south around the immense park and into the Trogon District. He guided the cart over to the side of the road at the front steps of the Marwyn Homestead and hopped down from his seat and helped his passengers down.

"It's been a pleasure serving you today. I wish you well in your future endeavors." He bowed to his patrons.

"My lad, the pleasure has been ours. We thank you for your assistance," Balris said, handing the boy several more sovereign notes. "To help with buying that house of yours up in Kestrel District." He smiled.

"Thank you, my lord. You've been most kind. I promise to make good use of this extraordinary gift," the boy said. He then climbed back up on his cart and snapped the reins. Guiding the cart out into the street, he was quickly obscured by the city traffic.

Approaching the stairs, the front door opened, and the porter stepped out onto the landing. "Welcome back, Lord Silentread, and friends." He bowed.

"Good day," Balris said to the porter. "We will be staying only for a short while. We have a meeting this evening we must prepare for. Would there, by chance, be a small room we could use in privacy until we depart?"

"Of course, my lord. The library is at your disposal. The second room on the left of the parlor."

The group followed Balris into the Marwyn Homestead once

more. They walked through the parlor and entered the library as the porter had instructed. The room was constructed of dark wood paneling, with four high-backed chairs with side tables, and a leather couch arranged throughout the room. In one corner, there was a desk and chair complete with parchment, ink, and quill. Bookshelves stretched from floor to ceiling along two of the walls, filled with tomes from across Evelium and the lesser continents. A fire crackled in a polished hearth of carved stone depicting an image of classic Evenese-style ships crossing the Sea of Widows.

"I like the way you travel," Talus said as he nosed around the volumes along the near wall.

"I do not expect our journey to be quite so comfortable going forward. I am personal friends with Lord Marwyn and saw no fault in enjoying the accommodations before heading into the unknown," Balris said, his tone uncharacteristically sharp.

"No offense implied," Talus said, "I've never been within the Marwyn Homestead and find it quite striking."

Shadow interrupted, leaning against the high back of the couch. "I'm asking you all now to trust me and give me the space I need to speak with Moric. I'm not sure how he is going to take my unexpected arrival, nor the questions I'll pose. I'll need to think on my feet without distraction. This isn't going to work if you continue to act like a soldier." His gaze met Talus's with conviction. "You're going to have to think like a thief if you're to blend in and not ruin our chances at getting Moric to speak freely."

"You worry about yourself and getting the needed information from Moric. Let me worry about meeting your lofty expectations," Talus said, pointing at Shadow.

"You both better get past this vainglorious posturing and focus on the mission at hand. Greater things hang in the balance that your egos," Gromley said, taking a seat beside the fire and leaning his war hammer against the wall.

Both men acknowledged Gromley's position with a nod of

their heads. "If I'm to understand, Gromley, Nicholas, Umhra, and I will set up at the bar," Talus said, shifting the focus back to the task at hand. "Separately, Lady Naivara, Laudin, and Balris will arrive and take a table for dinner. Finally, you'll arrive, and seek an audience with Moric, and we just see what happens."

"Correct," Shadow said. "I have no way of telling what my reception is going to be. Therefore, I have no way of telling what course of action will be required of me until then. The important thing is that none of you let on we know one another unless necessary."

"If that's the best we can do, then so be it," Talus said, "You're the only one who knows Moric, and I see no other way."

"We leave in an hour. We can walk together until we get into the Lark District, but from there we go our separate ways," Shadow said, walking over and putting his hand on Gromley's shoulder. "Let's just hope Moric decides against killing me at first sight. Until then, we go to our rooms and prepare."

CHAPTER 25

There remain rifts between the planes. They are no longer common as they were in the Age of Grace, but they exist nonetheless.
—The Tome of Mystics

Unknown Origin. Unearthed from the Ruins of Oda Norde, month of Bracken, 1320 AT

—▲—

The sun warmed Shadow's face as it fell behind the outer walls of Vanyareign. The group proceeded south toward the Lark District in the direction of the Griffon's Respite. Shadow led the way, as he was familiar with these streets, and took a hastened pace in anticipation of his potential rendezvous with Moric Tilk and his former comrades in the Hands of Time. He had long since left behind his days of common thievery, and butterflies fluttered in his stomach at the prospect of returning to his old haunt. He welcomed the familiar adrenaline high he always got when involved in something truly deceitful and dangerous.

They entered the Lark District, the streets becoming narrow and the buildings humble, especially when compared to those in the Kestrel District. A myriad of tenements rose high enough to see over the wall and out onto the west branch of the River

Torrent. Here the group separated as to approach the Griffon's Respite at their own times and from their own directions. Shadow slipped around a corner into an alleyway between two buildings, vanishing from plain sight. The others split and took their agreed-upon paths to the tavern.

When Shadow approached the center of the district an hour later, he smiled as he passed the quaint shop of Sidro the Tobacconist. Walking beneath the store's awning, a navy blue sign farther down the street caught his eye. The worn black lettering, weathered from years of exposure said *Griffon's Respite*. His throat tightened.

He opened the heavy wooden door and entered the familiar dingy interior, the reminiscent smell of sawdust and stale beer filling his senses. A half-dozen steps led down and opened up into the tavern's main barroom. The rough-hewn tables scattered about the room were just now filling up, as locals from the district who frequented the establishment finished their work day and sought solace in the company of others. Dust drifted in the sunlight that streamed into the room from the small, street-level windows lining the top of its northern and westerly walls.

The bartender, a heavy-set human man with tousled brown hair and friendly mutton chops, leaned against the bar polishing a glass with his dishrag, engaged in conversation with a young, well-built man in brown studded leathers. Accompanied by a half-Orc, a Zeristar, and a Farestere, the five men laughed boisterously while enjoying a pint of Barnswallow's Angry Ogre Ale, its over-hopped formulation disarming their senses.

Beyond the bar, there were several tables arranged where people sat eating supper. At one of the tables sat Naivara, Laudin, and Balris, their conversation drowned out by the din of the room, a bottle of wine half spent between them. A young lady, a peasant by the weathering of her face beyond her years, approached them, and placed several plates of food about the table. She wiped her hands on the front of her simple blue dress, which was stained with food from a long, weary shift, and hurried over to another table that grew restless in her absence.

Shadow approached the bar on the right side and casually held up his hand to get the barkeep's attention. Turning to welcome his new patron, the barkeep smiled broadly, exposing his half-filled set of yellowed teeth. "Well, what do you know?" he said, sliding over to Shadow. "Shadow Argith, it's been many a long year. What brings you back to the Griffon's Respite?" His tone was welcoming.

"Hey there, Myrph. Good to see you, friend. I'd like to visit the Edge." Shadow whispered leaning over the bar and putting a firm hand on Myrph's shoulder.

Myrph took a step back, a serious expression coming over his face. "Are you sure that's a good idea, mate? He was pretty upset when you left, and you know he holds onto these things."

"Aye, I know. To be honest, I've missed him terribly. To be very honest, I have little choice in the matter. I'm here on important business," Shadow said, his expression stoic.

"Well, if you insist." Myrph paused. "Disston is around back. He can lead you to the Edge."

"Thanks, mate. Hope to see you in a bit. Maybe we can catch up some," Shadow said.

"I'd like that," Myrph said.

Shadow turned and made his way toward a door at the back of the bar.

"Shadow," Myrph said. Shadow stopped in his tracks. "Ampeleia is gone, mate. She took her own life shortly after you left. I'm telling you so you don't go asking about her in front of the boss."

Shadow's head sunk. "Thanks, Myrph." He continued to the door, a hollowness filling his soul.

He swallowed his sorrow, nudged the door ajar, and poked his head into the adjoining room. "The barkeep told me to come back here and talk to some asshole named Disston," he said, making eye contact with the middle-aged man sitting on a chair tilted against a door on the other side of the storeroom. His blond hair was grimy and his face unshaven for the better part of a week.

"Well, shit," the man said, "the prodigal son has returned. Things are looking up. Until now, this day was shaking up to be pretty damn boring."

"Good to see you too, Disston," Shadow said, entering the room and extending his hand.

Standing from the chair, Disston grasped Shadow's hand. "The years have been kind to you, friend. Have you traveled as far as you hoped when you left us?"

"And then some," Shadow said. "Is Moric here?"

"If you want him to be. I'm not certain I would if I were you, though." Disston cocked an eyebrow.

"I need to see him. Regardless of the reception," Shadow said.

"Follow me then, mate." Disston turned to the door and tossed his chair aside. Opening the door, he revealed a torchlit staircase leading below the bar. He entered the doorway and descended the stairs. Shadow hesitated for a moment. Then followed.

The air cooled with each step. Shadow's senses flooded with recollections. The dampness in the air, the unevenness of the torchlight. Then, the violin. Reaching the base of the stairs, they walked a long hallway with an iron door at the end. Disston held up his hand, motioning for Shadow to stop. Complying, Shadow gave Disston a wide berth.

Disston tapped on the door. A moment later, the tap was returned from the other side. Disston tapped again. This time the response was one of sliding locks and the turning of a large gear. The door sprung open a few inches and sat, ajar, until Disston muscled it open.

The music got louder, no longer dulled by the closed door. A beautiful melancholy song bounced off the stone walls around them, drawing them closer. Disston urged Shadow forward with a tilt of his head. Shadow stood tall and walked into the room.

Inside, two guards sat, one on either side of the door, their crossbows were drawn and ready. A third man, an Iminti with dark features, counted a stack of sovereign notes at a round stone table on the right side of the room. In front of him, there was a doorway to another room. Shadow slowly edged into the doorway and waited.

The violinist continued playing, facing the far-right corner of the room, his back to the doorway. His hair gray with age, he wore burgundy leathers, and a dagger affixed to either hip at his belt. His tall frame waved back and forth passionately as his bow caressed the strings of his instrument. Holding a final note, his head sunk and the instrument dropped from his chin. He carefully placed the violin and bow on a narrow table against the wall.

"I wrote that after she passed," he said, his shoulders dropping.

"I was deeply sorry to hear of your loss, Moric. Ampeleia was a very special young woman," Shadow said, bowing his head in respect. "I had no idea she was gone until I saw Myrph just moments ago. Otherwise, I would've come to you sooner to express my deepest sympathies."

"It is probably best that you did not know, Shadow. I am afraid that Redemption would have pierced your heart if you had," Moric said, gripping the handle of the dagger on his right hip.

"And I would have allowed you justice," Shadow said, hanging his head in repentance. "I never meant for her to get hurt. Or you, for that matter."

"I know, child, but you were warned to leave her alone," Moric said, his tone growing cold. "She looked at you in a way no man is good enough to deserve. I told you then, she was too fragile a creature to fall in love. You, at the time, were young and insular, and ultimately, she was claimed by her grief. I do not question your love, but your judgment."

Moric turned with a speed almost supernatural and let his

dagger fly at Shadow's chest. Shadow drew his own and parried the blade aside. Hitting the wall to Shadow's left with a crash, the blade clattered across the floor, and then returned to Moric's hand as if it had never been thrown.

"You are faster than when you left us," Moric said.

"And you have not slowed a bit," Shadow said, knowing he got lucky, but not wanting to show his former teacher he had been shaken.

"Why, may I ask, do you return to me now?" Moric asked, sheathing his blade. "I knew you would one day stand before me again, but with a new purpose."

"Moric, if I may speak plainly, Evelium is in trouble," Shadow said. "I thought you might be able to provide some information that would help me in putting an end to the existential threat."

Moric walked across the room, toward Shadow, his dark eyes expressionless. Shadow could tell as he approached that the years since they were last together weighed heavily upon his former master.

"And why would I do that?" Moric asked, a shallow smile coming across his face.

"Because existential threats are not good for business, Moric. If Evelium collapses, the Hands of Time collapses. Symbiosis, you used to call it. I wouldn't come to you without advance notice and ask a favor if the matter wasn't of the utmost importance. You know me too well to think I would trouble you with trivial matters," Shadow said, attempting to disarm Moric with his words.

"Walk with me," Moric said, slipping past Shadow, and into the room through which Shadow had entered. Shadow turned and followed Moric past the table where the Iminti man was still counting his money. Moric activated a stone plate on the wall behind the table and, with a guttural scrape, the wall recessed and slid open, exposing a tunnel sloping downward at a shallow angle.

He stepped inside the tunnel. Shadow followed as he had so

many times before.

"There are no ears but our own here," Moric said, the door rumbling closed behind them and releasing a small plume of dust into the air. "Now, what is so important that you have returned to me?"

"Moric, what I'm about to tell you is of utmost sensitivity. The king himself has entrusted me and a few friends with this directive. As I mentioned, it's of an enormity that puts all of Evelium at risk. From you, I request only a modicum of information, which I suspect you possess."

"Go on." Moric waved his hand in permission.

"There is a cult in Meriden with the aim of returning Naur to the material plane so he may ravage Evelium and sit upon the Raptor's Throne. This cult has infiltrated even the disparate regions of the kingdom and, we suspect, the very continent. They are abducting victims and exsanguinating them for some rite necessary to give rise to this reckoning. My question for you is simple. Have you noticed any such activity in Vanyareign, and who is involved?" Shadow looked at Moric expectantly.

Moric ran his hands through his hair, draping his long bangs behind his ears. "I could always tell when you were lying, Shadow. I can tell now you speak with sincerity and genuine concern. I can never forgive you for what you took from me in your youth, but I can rise above my loss, and the pain your return causes me, and land on the side of virtue. You are looking for Varina the Decayer, the ancient witch of Morion Swamp. We have been aware of her coven's activities for some time now, but stayed out of her way, as she stays out of ours. We had no idea that they were part of a greater cause, I assure you. They have a band of Dokktari aiding them. That is all I know. If that is what you came here for, then I bid you leave me in peace."

Moric continued down the tunnel leaving Shadow standing alone, looking after him, somewhat surprised by his candidness. "Thank you, Moric. You have always been the father I never had. I shall pray to the gods until my final day that you forgive me."

Without sound or gesture, Moric walked beyond Shadow's field of vision, the echo of his footsteps fading away.

▲

Disston and the other men were awaiting Shadow's return. "You get what you need?" Disston asked as Shadow reentered the room.

"Yes," Shadow said.

"Then you're lucky you didn't get what you deserve," Disston said. "He'll never be the same."

"Mistakes were made. I regret the ramifications of those mistakes to my core. I can't turn back time," Shadow said.

"I suppose not. You and your friends have ten minutes to clear out upstairs. I wouldn't consider returning if I were you." Disston's tone was cold.

"Understood. I'll see my way out. It was nice seeing you, Disston."

One of the men beside Disston turned to the door and slid two large deadbolts aside. Throwing a lever on the wall, a set of gears and chains rattled. The door once again jumped open. Shadow muscled it the rest of the way open and left the Hands of Time behind for a second time. He made his way back out into the bar where his friends awaited him. Without making contact, he swept up the staircase and out into the cool evening air. His head was spinning, his stomach in his throat, his heart broken.

Gromley was the first to find him outside squatting at the corner, hyperventilating. "Shadow, everything all right? You look like you've seen a ghost."

"I did, Gromley," Shadow said. A tear streaked down his face.

Gromley put his hand on Shadow's shoulder. "If all goes well, there will be a time to break down when this is over. For now, you take what pain you are feeling, whatever its source, and you bury it inside you and make it your focus. I promise I will be there for you when the time comes. Now get up before the others get out here. Especially that Talus. You wouldn't want to let him see you this vulnerable. Did you get to Moric?"

"Yes. I got what we need. The road ahead is daunting," Shadow said, standing. "Thank you, I needed that."

"I'm always here to call you a wuss when necessary." Gromley smiled, giving Shadow a stern pat on the back.

The others trickled out of the bar, Umhra being the last to rejoin the group as he waited to make sure the rest were safely outside.

"Shadow has what we need. I suggest we not speak of this in the open. We should head back to the Marwyn Homestead and decide upon our next course of action," Gromley said.

The others agreed and, together, they headed northwest through the bustling streets. The knowledge of what lied ahead weighed upon Shadow, driving him toward the privacy of the Marwyn Homestead where he would be able to unburden himself. The others followed, barely speaking along the way, their gate close to a jog to keep pace with Shadow.

▲

The parlor and dining room of the establishment were overflowing when they arrived. Lord Marwyn, was caught in conversation with a graceful Evenese woman on one of the sofas near the entry. Seeing the group enter, he begged her pardon and approached.

"I hope all is well, Balris?" he asked, sensing a purpose to their gate. "Will you be joining us for dinner tonight?

"All is well, Hurston," Balris said. "Unfortunately, our business requires us to forego dinner tonight. In fact, we may be leaving presently, or at the latest, in the morning."

"Well, I shall be sorry to see you all go. I have so enjoyed having you all here at my home. Such a refreshing change from the disingenuous formality of our regular patrons," he whispered with a wink.

"We thank you again for your efforts. An unparalleled

experience as usual," Balris said.

"I shall stand in your way no longer. May the gods shine upon each of you." Lord Marwyn bowed to his guests and returned to his seat on the couch and his conversation with the Evenese woman.

The group made their way upstairs and gathered in Balris's room. As Umhra closed the door behind them, Shadow turned to the group, unable to keep his secret any longer. "There's a witch, Varina the Decayer. She and her coven live in the Morion Swamp, just north of Vanyareign. They have a band of Dokktari helping them with the abductions. That's all Moric shared."

"That's plenty," Laudin said. "Get the horses. Tonight, we ride to the Morion Swamp and hunt a witch."

"I'll return to the castle immediately, get Maelstrom, and meet you at the north gate. I know this swamp, and how to get there. It's a dark place, just off Spara's Trail. No one dares enter. We must use caution when approaching this hag," Talus said, as he made for the door.

"Good. We'll meet you there in an hour," Laudin said.

Talus rushed out of the room, leaving the door agape. The rest followed, gathering the few belongings they had left in their rooms and regrouping at the top of the stairs. Walking back down toward the crowd below, Shadow paused for a moment in front of *Lady of the Burning Wood,* the Dramien Colm painting he had admired when they first arrived at the Marwyn Homestead. He ever so gently touched the young lady, painted so carefully on the canvas. "I am sorry, my love," he said. "I'm sorry I wasn't there for you when you needed me most."

Making their way through the crowd and out into the streets, the party rushed to the rear of the homestead where Lord Marwyn's private stables housed their horses, including two Balris had secured for Nicholas and himself. Being careful not to attract attention, they road slowly through the city streets, preparing for the conflict before them. Arching around the Grand Bazaar, they turned toward the north gate. They arrived early and waited for Talus to join them. The night air was crisp, more so than normal for the season.

CHAPTER 26

Forene's armies spread throughout the land. They brought with them the promise of protection for those that swore their loyalty.
—The Gatekeepers' Abridged History of Tyveriel

Vol. 3, Chapter 4 – Discovered in the Private Library of Solana Marwyn, the month of Vasa, 889 AT

—▲—

Spara's Trail weaved along the eastern banks of the River Torrent, north to the Ilathril Mountains. Other than Requiem, a border town four days' ride north of Vanyareign, and Lindamere, far to the west, there was little in the northern expanses of Windswept but for the scattered ruins of the Mystics. Unlike Englen Penn Way south of the capital, the roads to the north were poorly lit after a couple of hours ride and rarely patrolled beyond the lights. Wild country. They rode on through the night.

The road gradually descended away from Mount Orys, and the river slowed and widened as it fought the gradient to the southeast. The flooded plains on either side made possible the conditions for the Morion Swamp to flourish. Tupelo, black willow, and cypress trees overtook the highland species as they approached a sharp westerly turn in both the river and the road.

"This is where we enter the swamp," Talus said, the sun flirting with the horizon. "From here, we must continue on foot."

"Gather the horses over there," Umhra said, motioning to a stand of young trees just off the side of the road. "They will be comfortable there. Balris, would you mind?"

"Not at all," Balris said.

The horses were tied to the thin red trunks without protest. With the party entering the swamp, Balris closed his eyes and grasped his icon. Under his breath, he muttered an indiscernible phrase. From the icon within his hand, an energy grew in concert with a circle of white arcane light beneath the horses. Along its circumference, points intensified, and then connected forming the shape of an eye within. The horses faded from eyesight and earshot. Satisfied, Umhra trudged into the swamp, his associates in tow.

The early-morning light, which was just beginning to burn off a foreboding fog that held in the air, was quickly snuffed out under the dense canopy of cypress and tupelo. The landscape was rugged and sporadically graced by ancient willows, the girth of which exceeded that of most common homes. Travel was slow, with the mud holding onto their every step and increasingly bubbling with a sulfurous release. Large water snakes slipped gracefully through the duckweed-covered waterways that pooled between the mounds of sodden earth.

For hours they slogged on, surveying the landscape for signs of the Morion Coven. Laudin sent Taivaron up into the canopy and walked ahead, effortlessly maneuvering over the muddy earth searching for any detail that could unveil Varina the Decayer's locale. Suddenly, he dashed off course, heading east toward the heart of the swamp. When Umhra and the others caught up, he was kneeling next to a small pile of stones.

"This way," Laudin whispered. "Be prepared for anything."

From the trees ahead hung innumerable twines, each displaying the skeletal remains of a small animal or a small icon hand-fashioned from twisted twigs. Stakes protruded from the swamp water, each boasting a skull. There was seemingly no preference for the type of victim, with man and beast equally represented.

Gromley instinctually grasped the talisman he wore around his neck in dedication to Orys. He gasped. "This is truly a place of evil magic."

"Indeed," Umhra said, moving up toward the front of the group and unsheathing Forsetae. "An overt warning."

Blue smoke wafted from the blade as he walked into the morass of totems, ducking under those that hung low as not to disturb them. Gromley joined him, the totems hanging more than a foot above his head. They pressed onward, their friends directly behind them, following the wicked path through the swamp. The path led them to an immensely large black willow tree, devoid of life, but adorned with as many icons as it once undoubtedly had leaves. As they neared, torches lit of their own accord around the great tree's perimeter revealing an opening in its side.

They crept up to the opening in the tree. Umhra peered inside. "A staircase heading beneath the swamp," he said, turning to Balris for affirmation of their next step.

"They know we are here," Balris said. "That much is obvious. We might as well go inside directly."

Umhra nodded and led the party into the tree. The interior of the willow smelled of decay, the stale air warmer than expected. Uncountable masses of spiders scattered underfoot. The group descended deep under the swamp, as the staircase, constructed haphazardly of stone and earth, spiraled downward, coming to light one torch at a time as they progressed. Deeper still they delved until the staircase gave way to a short tunnel terminating at a door made of gnarled tree branches. A soft glow emanated from within the room on the other side.

The door slowly creaked open as the group approached.

"Come in," a raspy voice said from within. "There is no need for caution. You are already dead." The words were met with stifled laughter.

"Why do you always tell them?" another voice asked. "You ruin the surprise."

"They deserve to know what the fates have in store for them, surely," the first voice said.

Umhra threw the door open and entered the room, the rest of the party on his heels. Five hags stood at one of several chest-high tables upon which the body of a young woman lay. Pale and lifeless, her hands and ankles were bound to the stone slab which was stained with the deep crimson of dried blood. Beneath the table was an iron trough, gathering a viscous fluid still dripping lazily from above.

"This is most unholy!" Balris said. The witches laughed.

"You have come into our home, and are offended by what you witness? What the priest finds most unpalatable, to us, is that of beauty. These lives are given, so new life may be breathed into our land. So our ways will no longer be scorned and our beliefs no longer marginalized. As you can see, position determines perspective," the one Umhra assumed was Varina the Decayer said.

Looking away from the table and to the witches for the first time, Umhra was greeted by the crooked, toothy grins of his hosts. Each of the decrepit creatures had thin, stringy hair that hung down to their waists. Their robes were soiled and tattered, their skin pallid and scarred with ritualistic carvings. Their glares met, two of the hags vanished from sight, while two others closed their eyes, and began chanting under their breath. Varina the Decayer stood motionless, observing the intruders as one would the pieces of a chessboard in determining their next move.

Weapons at the ready, Umhra and Gromley charged toward Varina and the other visible witches. The two witches who had vanished suddenly reappeared directly behind Balris and Naivara. The witches sunk their wicked nails deep into their victims' necks and whispered into their ears.

"*Etara shatari mah.*" A pulse of pain followed, and the blood vessels in Balris's and Naivara's necks blackened.

Shadow threw a dagger, and it sunk deep into the back of the hag gripping Naivara. She howled in pain, a second dagger plunging into her side. Both daggers disappeared and returned to Shadow's hands. Naivara spun, her steps unsteady, but the hag again vanished.

Laudin drew his scimitar and struck out at the witch holding Balris, the sword burying itself within her shoulder, partially cleaving her arm from her body, and releasing a spray of lifeblood and gore. She released Balris, grasping her wounded shoulder. Balris fell to the floor. Nicholas ran to his side.

Umhra and Gromley rushed the table, Umhra heading straight for Varina the Decayer and Gromley for one of the other hags. They bore down upon the witches who each released a purple beam of energy from their hands. Both men deflected the assault with their shields and continued their pursuit. Gromley swung his war hammer, connecting with the hag's chest—her brittle bones cracking on impact—and sending her flying back against the rear wall of the room. She crashed to the floor, gasping for air.

Umhra swung Forsetae at Varina and took her right arm clean from her body. The witch hissed and released a shock of electrical energy into the Paladin's torso.

"You cannot destroy us," she said leaning in, while the energy flowed through his body. "All you will do is release us from this plane and return us to our own. We shall return, and when we do, we will come for you."

"I welcome you to try," Umhra said, shrugging off the pain and taking another stroke at Varina. Forsetae cut deep across her abdomen, sending a sickly red ichor spraying across the room. The witch doubled over, clutching the gash.

The other two witches reappeared, striking out at Talus and Naivara. This time Naivara was prepared, ducking beneath the witch's grasp, a sharpened fingernail clipping a lock of hair. Spinning, Naivara whispered a few words in Reshinta and thrust her hands out toward the hag's chest. A sphere of radiant light grew in the space between her hands and then shot forward, blasting a hole directly through her enemy. The witch staggered backward for a moment, her eyes wide with shock. The hole in her chest cavity glowed with embers from the charge that ran her through. Finally, she dropped to her knees, and fell, lifeless, to the floor.

Talus anticipated the hag behind him as well, and before she could strike, spun with Aquila at the ready, slicing a gouge in her neck. The witch grabbed her throat and tried to scream, but no sound escaped. Instead, the witch's malodorous lifeblood seeped from the wound and she too tumbled to the floor.

Gromley met with the last of the Morion Coven, whose eyes were still shut in meditation. He swung his hammer toward her, the weapon passing through her image, which fluxed, revealing her rouse. The witch appeared behind the cleric and touched him on the back of his neck with one of her gnarled fingers. Gromley collapsed to the ground, defenseless against her evil caress.

"Your god cannot protect you here, Cleric," she whispered triumphantly as he fell.

Seeing the decrepit creature standing over his friend, Shadow threw his daggers into the hag's back. She howled in pain, grabbing in vain for the blades that punctured her blackened heart. As she fumbled about in agony, Talus walked over to her, and with one thrust of Aquila, ran her through. The life fading from her body, the daggers returned to Shadow's hand, and Talus cast her aside.

Umhra stood over Varina the Decayer who clutched her wound, Forsetae bathed in her blood. Glaring at the Paladin and knowing her fate was sealed, she thrust her remaining claw forward in one last attempt to make her power felt in the material plane. A mote of purple energy burgeoning in her hand,

Umhra swung his sword with prejudice and took her head from her body.

An eerie silence fell upon the room. Gromley stirred and sat up groggily, the hag's spell fading with her lifeforce. Nicholas sat with Balris's head resting in his lap.

"Gromley, over here, please. Balris needs you." The cleric snapped to attention and staggered over to Nicholas's side. He grabbed the talisman around his neck with one hand and placed his other upon Balris's forehead. A white light emanated from the talisman and flowed from his hands into Balris. For a brief moment, there was no response, but then, with a cough, Balris returned to consciousness.

"I apologize," he said, sitting upright with Nicholas's assistance. "She was upon me before I could react. I will be more aware going forward."

"She could have gotten to any of us," Talus said, extending a hand, and helping Balris to his feet. "Now, what of the Dokktari? Should they not be here?"

Laudin made his way to Naivara, who was still bleeding from her neck. He inspected the wounds gently, and then reached into a small pouch on his belt and packed the gashes with agrimony salve to help stop the flow of blood.

"That was too close," he whispered in her ear.

She smiled and held his hand in hers. "I can hold my own, Laudin. You love too deeply."

"I know you can, and I know I do," he said, returning the smile, "I don't expect either will change anytime soon."

"I suspect the Dokktari are out hunting for the next cadre of sacrifices," Shadow said. "As they are wont to travel by daylight, they could return at any moment. We should scour this lair for any insight into the Brothers of Resurrection and their plan while we wait. If they don't return within the hour, they likely caught wind of us and retreated to the safety of their fae realm."

"Agreed," Talus said. "Be careful what you touch, though. Lairs as these are fraught with dangers. There's no telling what foul magic the coven has hidden here."

The party spread out about the large room, investigating as they advanced. There were no records, no correspondence at all. Nicholas found a small basket filled with glass vials, each containing a swirling purple and green liquid within. Otherwise, there was little of interest or value. Umhra cut the leather straps binding the naked body of the young woman to one of the tables. Her ashen skin was covered in runes carved by hand into her flesh.

"Gather close," said Balris, "Someone is coming." The team heeded his request and they vanished from sight. Laudin drew his bow and nocked an arrow, affixing his aim on the doorway across the room. They waited silently, as the clambering of an unknown party grew.

The Dokktari struggled with another young woman, bound at the wrists and gagged. Her dark skin glistened with sweat, the bottom of the light-blue linen nightgown she wore soiled from the trip through the swamp. Her captors, their obsidian-colored skin a close match to their dark leather clothes, took turns forcing her forward by the bindings that bit into her wrists and whipping at her with a cat o' nine tails. They were too distracted by the young woman and her relentless resistance to notice the witches strewn about the floor.

An arrow materialized out of thin air and penetrated a yellow eye of the Dokktari closest to the girl. A crossbow bolt followed, piercing the temple of another. In reaction to two comrades falling, a third Dokktari dispelled Balris's incantation, as the girl, who was now unrestrained, made for the corner of the room in an attempt to hide. As the party became visible, Naivara and Umhra both released rays of light, causing the two rear Dokktari to explode, taking out a large section of the entry wall of the room. The great tree overhead shifted, having its support cast asunder, rubble cascading to the floor.

The remaining three Dokktari backed up, dropping their glaives.

"Wait." One threw his hands up in surrender. "We have no quarrel. We will return home and leave you be. We only work for witches, we are not allies. We share not their desires." His Evenese broken and ineloquent.

Balris held his hand up, insisting the party halt the attack. "You three leave here now, and never come back. If we see any of your kind in the capital or any other city of Evelium, I will not restrain my friends from ending you all. Go, before my patience wanes."

The remaining Dokktaris backed out of the room and left without a trace. Naivara ran over to the young woman who was cowering in the corner. She removed the gag from her mouth and the bonds from her wrists. "You're safe now, they can't harm you anymore," she said, trying to calm the distraught girl.

The girl smeared her sweat-soaked hair away from her face, tears streaming down her cheeks. "Who are you? What were they?" she asked, pointing toward the remaining Dokktari bodies on the ground.

"We are friends. They were not," Naivara said honestly. "What's your name, and where are you from?

"Alessa. Alessa Elmont. I live in Vanyareign with my parents in the Kestrel District. Can you take me home?" the girl asked, glaring wide-eyed at the lifeless arm of the other girl on the table above her.

"Of course, my dear," Naivara said, "Let's be on our way. I'll give you a ride back to our horses." The girl looked at Naivara, tilted her head. Naivara closed her eyes and whispered to herself. At the end of her incantation, she shifted shapes into that of an elk. The beast leaned down to Alessa, who was awestruck and nuzzled her to her feet.

Umhra wrapped the body of the other young woman with a waxed tarp from his bag and followed the rest out of the lair. Talus, who had gathered the head of Varina the Decayer in a sack as proof of her demise, led the party back through the swamp in the direction of their horses.

Naivara, in her elk form, had little trouble with the terrain, even with the extra weight of Alessa on her back. As she walked, a great elk stag appeared not far from her in the swamp. The beast had an aura that shunned the darkness of this defiled land. Umhra stopped the party, halting Shadow with a firm hand upon his chest, and placed the wrapped corpse he carried on the ground.

"Kemyn," he said to the creature.

The animal tilted its head and approached the group. The party stood beside Umhra, their gazes darting between each other and the massive beast. Laudin helped Alessa down from Naivara's back. She startled at his touch but accepted the assistance upon seeing his disarming smile. Naivara resumed her natural form.

"Your sister said you would make yourself known to me if I was on the right path," Umhra said.

The bull drew closer, his radiance growing with every step. When he was less than a few feet away, he stopped and looked the group over. He took one step closer, singling Umhra out, and scraped his hoof at the marshy ground before him several times. His efforts revealed a small irregularly shaped nugget of a silvery-white metal. Umhra knelt and picked the acorn-sized deposit from the earth. He brushed it against his satchel and looked up into Kemyn's eyes.

"Thank you." He bowed his head and stared at his gift.

The elk snorted and shook his head. He then turned and bounded off into the swamp and out of sight.

"Rhodium," Shadow said, leaning over Umhra's shoulder.

"What did we just witness?" Talus asked, surveying the swamp around them.

"We were just in the presence of one of the Great Creators," Naivara said. "And he bestowed upon Umhra the first quantity of metal required for ascension."

"Ascension?" Talus asked. "That is but a myth. There is no record of anyone attaining Suffusion beyond platinum since the Mystics. I grant that even Platinum Suffusions are an extraordinary rarity going as far back as the Age of Grace."

"Just because there is no record, does not mean the gods would not favor Umhra in this manner," Balris said. "How else can you explain what we just experienced?"

"I can't," Talus said, "but you all take an enormous leap of faith."

Umhra stood, still looking at the metal in his palm. "Vaila spoke to me the other night. She said Kemyn and Brinthor would appear to me if we were progressing in the right direction. This is a good omen. I hesitate to take it as anything more than such. Let's get back to Vanyareign, there is much to be done."

At the edge of the swamp, the sky brightened, welcoming the party's return. The mud encasing their boots dried to a gray crust and crumbled away as Balris released his incantation on the horses. The party untethered their mounts and prepared for the ride back to the capital. The ride would have been enjoyable, as the day was nearly perfect, if not for the weight of what lied ahead. The apparent employ of Varina the Decayer by the Brothers of Resurrection was a testament to the brotherhood's far-reaching power and influence throughout Evelium. The road forward would no doubt prove every bit as treacherous as the group could anticipate.

CHAPTER 27

A war ensued between the Orcs of the east and the Barbarians that were forced out of Evelium by Forene's Edict of Unity.
—The Gatekeepers' Abridged History of Tyveriel

Vol. 3, Chapter 7 – Discovered in the Private Library of Solana Marwyn, the month of Vasa, 889 AT

—▲—

Talus led the ride back to Vanyareign, the group making their way to Castle Forene. Upon their arrival, he guided them to the stables where he rode through the large doorway, past four castle guards who stood watch over the entrance. Jumping from Maelstrom, and tossing the reins to a stableman, he ran for the stairway leading up to the king's throne room. The rest rushed after him, laboring to keep up as Talus was driven by a depth of loyalty with which they were unfamiliar.

Two guards posted at the rear entrance of the throne room snapped to attention as Talus approached. "Is the king at his throne?" Talus asked.

"No, sir, not at the moment," the guard on the left, a tall, thin man of no more than twenty years of age, said. "Shall we send for him?"

"Yes. Let him know I have returned, and I and the Barrow's

Pact are waiting for him in the throne room. I will see to having the room cleared so we may have privacy for this conversation," Talus said.

"Very well, sir. Consider it done," the young guard said dutifully.

The other guard opened the door, letting the party into the throne room one at a time. Alessa walked nervously at Naivara's side, her eyes wide with wonder as she entered the king's throne room.

Inside, the Elders Syndicate was in session, arguing furiously, as was often the case. "My elders," Talus said, interrupting them, "we require a moment of privacy with King Arving. I respectfully request you take your recess early today."

The elders turned from their discussion and stared in unison at Talus. One of their ranks, a Zeristar man with a neatly groomed red beard streaked with white, stood back from the table around which the syndicate was gathered. "That sounds like a splendid idea, Sir Jochen," he said. "The conversation was getting a bit drawn out."

An Iminti woman, with deep wrinkles and silver hair, attempted to rebut, but the Zeristar man silenced her, throwing up his hand.

"Thank you, my lord." Talus bowed in sincere respect to the man. "I appreciate your support in the matter."

The Zeristar nodded in return, and then shuffled his chair neatly under the table and made for the exit. The others followed reluctantly, griping to one another regarding the unfinished nature of the conversation in which they had been immersed. As the last of the Elders Syndicate left through the doorway to the right of the throne, all was silent in the expansive room. Talus walked to a hutch on the far side of the room and returned with a silver platter. He placed the platter in the center of the table around which the Elders Syndicate had been gathered, lifted Varina the Decayer's head from his sack, and placed it prominently upon the platter. Alessa gasped in horror, burying her face in Naivara's cloak.

"Umhra, would you mind placing the corpse over by that door?" Talus asked unaffected, pointing to the same door through which the Elders Syndicate had exited. "I will make sure she is identified and returned to her kin."

"Of course," Umhra said, complying with the request.

Naivara wrapped her arm around Alessa. "We're all friends here, Alessa. The king's people will see you back to your family. This is all just a minor formality."

A door to the left of the throne opened and two guards entered the room, followed by King Shale Arving. Naivara gently held Alessa back, placing both hands firmly on the girl's shoulders and giving her a look of encouragement. Alessa wiped the tears from her eyes and stood as tall as she could, facing the king.

Shale Arving was dressed in fine scarlet robes, trimmed in gold. Talus led the party in genuflection as the king approached them after dismissing the guards who accompanied his entrance. "Please rise, and tell me of your exploits," King Arving said, crossing the room to them, "And who, may I ask, is your new companion?" He nodded toward Alessa, who averted her gaze to the floor.

"Your Majesty, my king," Talus said, "through Shadow's connection with Moric Tilk, we were able to ascertain that Varina the Decayer was working in the interests of the Brothers of Resurrection. We rescued this young lady from a group of Dokktari who worked for the witch's coven. Before we talk further, may we call to have her safely returned to her family?"

"Of course." King Arving approached Alessa. "My dear, I am so sorry for your tribulations at the hands of these fiends. Please call on my court for anything you or your family need as recompense for your suffering." The king held her hand, walked her to his throne, and rang a small gold bell kept at its side.

The two guards again opened the door through which the king had entered, allowing a short, rotund man egress into the room. Balding and bespectacled, the man rushed to the king's side. "Sire," he said with a stammer, "how may I be of assistance?"

"Please have this young lady escorted to the baths, so she may be properly returned to her family," King Arving said, "Please treat her with the utmost care. She has been through a traumatic experience."

"As you wish, sire," the man said, "Please, my dear, follow me."

Alessa turned and looked back at Naivara, tears welling in her eyes.

"Everything will be all right. You are safe now," Naivara said, coming to take Alessa's hands in hers. "You will be back with your parents in a matter of hours."

Alessa nodded, released Naivara from her grasp, and followed the man out of the throne room, the guards closing the door behind them.

"Varina the Decayer, you say?" the king returned to the matter at hand.

Talus stepped aside revealing the severed head of the hag, sitting slightly askew on the silver platter. King Arving walked over to the head of Varina the Decayer and looked upon it, rubbed his chin. "Any idea who the other girl was?" he asked.

"I'm afraid not," Talus said. "By the looks of the coven's lair, there were, no doubt, many others who met the same end. Likely either consumed by the hags or disposed of in the swamp. With your permission, I shall have the Raptor's Grasp look into the identity of the young lady and try to return her body to her family so she may be properly interred."

"Of course," King Arving said, "and, make certain they are invited to the court once they are located."

"As you wish, my lord." Talus nodded.

The king walked over to his throne and sat, placing his head in his hands. Looking up after a moment of reflection, he surveyed the group. They met his gaze expectantly. "You together shall travel to Meriden, and rid Evelium of the Brothers of Resurrection. You must do this with the utmost discretion, not attracting any attention from my cousin and his soldiers once you enter Winterashe. If you are discovered by them, you have no affiliation with my court, and you shall be disavowed, as this is a direct violation of the Fracture. Are we in agreement?"

"Yes, Your Majesty," Umhra said on behalf of the group. "We mean to see this through to the very end."

"Very well. Should you succeed, there will be no statues honoring your efforts. No parades around the Grand Bazaar. Should you fail, there will be no ceremonies mourning your loss. No effort to recover your remains. Upon your triumphant return, there shall be a sizable reward from the treasury, however, and my sincere gratitude. This is the least I can do to recognize the risk you are about to take on the behalf of our fair kingdom. Now, be on your way. May the gods look down upon you in favor," King Arving said.

The party bowed, and Talus led them out of the throne room. "Return to the stables and wait for me there. I'm going to find one of my men upstairs and have the Raptor's Grasp identify our anonymous young lady and return her to those with whom she belongs."

"Very well," Gromley said, "we shall have the horses readied. Are we to head for Requiem, or do we remain in Windswept for as long as possible?"

"I suggest we start west and stay in Windswept as long as our progress isn't slowed," Talus said. "The less time we spend in Winterashe, the better."

"Agreed," Balris said. "We shall meet you in the stables presently."

"Then we are in agreement." Talus nodded and ran up the stairs while the others descending to the stables.

When they entered the stables, their horses had been brushed, stalled, and were enjoying a fine blend of fresh alfalfa, clover, and lolium.

"Will you be taking them right back out?" asked the stablemaster as they approached. "They haven't had much of a rest."

"Unfortunately, yes. Talus will be joining us as well. We need the horses readied immediately," Balris said.

"Very well, but please don't drive them too hard if you don't have to," the stablemaster said. "Give us but a few moments."

"Thank you," Balris said.

The man nodded, turned, and called to the stablemen to begin preparing the horses for an immediate departure. The stable was thrust into a state of activity. By the time Talus entered the room, Maelstrom was saddled and waiting for him, Umhra's hands on his reins. The members of the party mounted their respective horses, and once again left Castle Forene.

Staying to the Vanyareign Loop, which encircled the capital outside its walls, the party passed several large farming complexes along the interior of the River Torrent's delta. Crossing the bridge just outside of the west gate, they left the capital behind, the homesteads outside the city walls becoming smaller and farther apart as they proceeded, until they disappeared entirely.

CHAPTER 28

With the south now claimed, I fear that the north shall never be fully integrated.
—The Collected Letters of Modig Forene

Letter to Prakten Modig dated 18th of Prien, 4 AF. Unearthed from the Ruins of Vanyareign, month of Ocken, 1301 AT

—▲—

The trail was at times narrow and overgrown, lacking the regular attention of roads near the capital or farther south in Clearwell. The Ilathril Mountains loomed to the north, visible only at the occasional break in the dense canopy. Sunlight dappled the ground beneath Splinter as Umhra rode alongside Laudin.

Talus had led the way out of Vanyareign but now dropped back, taking an unexpected interest in the rest of the party, and particularly in Shadow.

"Where do you hail from?" he asked, his approach awkward, easing up beside Shadow, the path widening.

"Not far from here. At least as the crow flies. I was born and raised in the Ryzarin colony of Balaern, deep below the Ilathril. I left there many years ago and haven't had a steady home since. I spent some time in Vanyareign, as you know, but time in Winterashe as well. Most recently, I was living in Willow's Notch, but I answered Laudin's call and rode to Anaris, where this all began," Shadow said, "Yourself?"

"Originally, Tayrelis. My parents entrusted me to the king's court when I was seven. They couldn't afford to keep me and my two younger sisters after my father was injured in the lumber yards and could no longer work. Queen Lisbet Feil, King Arving's mother, took a liking to me or pitied me at the very least. She handed me off to the Crown Prince as a sort of special project. As with everything the king does, he put his full effort into training me as a gentleman, and a warrior. It seems only the latter stuck." Talus laughed.

Shadow smiled from under his hood. "I was twelve moons old when curiosity got the best of me one day. I snuck up from deep within the mountains to see the sun, which is prohibited in Ryzarin culture. It was the most amazing sight I'd ever laid my eyes upon. I stayed for a few moments, soaking up the unfamiliar warmth, and fell in love. Upon my return, my father caught me sneaking back down from Forbidden Pass and dragged me before the tribal council. The elders ruled I was to be cast out from the colony for being an unclean topsider. That night, my mother packed me a small bag, and my father sent me out into the world as she cried. I've never returned."

"It seems we aren't all that dissimilar, my friend," Talus said, flashing a shallow smile. "I have to tell you, your work in getting Moric Tilk to give you the information on Varina the Decayer, and your skills in battle against the coven were both most impressive. I could tell returning to the Hands of Time weighed heavily upon you."

"The situation was far more complex than I had anticipated, and my past far more difficult to face. There, however, are a few things in this world more important than my personal matters." Shadow shrugged.

"Well, thank you. I was unsure of you at first, and you proved me a poor judge of character."

Shadow accepted the confession with a nod and the two rode, side by side through the woods, as the sun sank in the west.

"Lake Warda lies just ahead," Laudin said, pointing into the woods in front of them. "I suggest the shoreline as a suitable place to camp for the night."

"Agreed," Umhra said, finding comfort in the ranger's knowledge of the path to be traveled.

Trees soon gave way to the boulder-strewn beaches and clear, lapis-colored waters of Lake Warda. The great Ilathril Mountains were now visible over the tree line in the distance, their imposing size more easily appreciated with the improved view. The party let their horses drink at the shore, as they busied themselves setting up camp. While the others started a fire and set up bedrolls for the night, Laudin disappeared back into the woods, with hardly any of the others noticing his departure. When he returned an hour or so later, he carried over his shoulder one of his arrows, upon which he had skewered several rabbits. Already skinned and field dressed, he handed them over to Gromley, who licked his lips in anticipation of this unexpected treat.

The party sat around the fire on the shore of the lake, while the rabbits roasted on the open flame, and the sky turned amber above them. They ate until dark, and when sated, prepared for bed.

"Nicholas and I will take first watch," Umhra said. "Laudin and Gromley, we will wake you in two hours. Shadow and Talus will be next, and then Balris and Naivara." The group agreed, and were fast asleep, leaving Nicholas and Umhra alone at the fire. For some time quiet prevailed as the friends sat together.

"Nicholas, we haven't had much time to talk lately. How are you?" Umhra asked, poking at the fire with a long, sturdy stick.

"I'm holding up well, Umhra. Thank you for asking. Is there a reason for your concern?" Nicholas asked.

"No, Nicholas. We've all been through a lot lately, and you

have just been uncharacteristically quiet, of late."

"I suppose I've just been contemplating what lies before us," Nicholas said. "I've been on many adventures, but rarely have I been witness to such peril as I have been during the last few months. I suppose one can't help but have these experiences change them."

"In my years, I've come to know two kinds of men," Umhra said. "There are those who let adversity change them for the worse and those who choose to have it change them for the better. You strike me as the latter, Nicholas. I need you to be the latter."

"We're cut from different cloth, Umhra," Nicholas said. "You are sure and steady in your emotions, while I search in vain for solace. How do you thrust yourself toward unknown danger with such confidence?"

"Confidence?" Umhra scoffed. "Have you not yet worked your way past that façade? I think you confuse confidence with resignation. I'm resigned to the fact we are Evelium's only chance at salvation. Outside of that, I have merely decided to have the perils I face change me for the better. I share your concerns. All of us do. What we head toward, most would rightfully turn from."

"It's not that I consider running, Umhra, although part of me says I should. What eats at me is the enormity of the ramifications should we fail. The very life of Evelium...of all Tyveriel...lay in our hands, and we fight against an enemy far beyond our comprehension. We're still so far away from Meriden, and no doubt the Brothers of Resurrection progress with their plan. We may not even get there in time to stop this. I apologize for my despair." Nicholas rubbed his eyes as the smoke from the fire caught him in its path.

"I worry about these things as well," Umhra said. "All we can do is keep going and put our best efforts forward. I don't understand politics, nor do I care to, as I would have handled this matter quite differently if I had the choice. You saw our path before I did, but I now understand we are the only ones who can stop the destruction of our land, our home, and I mean to succeed." He paused. "For now, however, I am going to take a look around."

Nicholas nodded and stared into the hypnotic fire that warmed him as Umhra stood and headed into the darkness to ensure the safety of the camp. Umhra patrolled the edge of the woods, Forsetae emanating a soft blue light in his strong, capable hand. Circling the camp, he walked the water's edge of Lake Warda.

His keen eyes caught a disturbance on the lake's otherwise still surface. He held his ground as the perturbation surged in his direction. He raised Forsetae and strengthened his stance in anticipation.

A god approaches. Forsetae resonated in his mind. *Sheath me. I am not the proper tool for this moment*.

Umhra complied as a wall of water welled up in the shallows before him. In the soft moonlight, a large blue dragon emerged from the lake's waters. The beast unfurled its wings, throwing a shower across the shoreline.

"Brinthor," Umhra said, bowing, "I am humbled by your presence."

The god, in its imposing form, thundered closer and lowered its head to Umhra's level. Brinthor's immense eyes flashed with vibrant blue energy as he inspected the Paladin. The ancient dragon snorted, releasing a plume of steam into the air.

Umhra looked back over his shoulder to see Nicholas standing before the fire squinting into the darkness. Brinthor snorted again, and Nicholas ran for the beach, stones shifting and scattering under his feet.

"There's nothing to fear, Nicholas. This is Brinthor, God of Water."

Nicholas arrested himself, his chest heaving. Brinthor's gaze shifted to him, his long neck extending away from Umhra to better assess the intruder. He sniffed at Nicholas, drawing him closer by a couple of steps. Not determining any threat, he huffed, leaving Nicholas in another cloud of steam.

Brinthor lashed his tail in the dark water. He curled his head beneath his massive body and dislodged something from between the scales on his chest with his teeth. He returned to Umhra and dropped a gleaming chunk of metal on the beach. The gobbet clattered amongst the stones before settling at Umhra's feet.

Umhra knelt and retrieved the gift, clearing it of sand with his thumbs. The rhodium flashed in the moonlight.

"Thank you, mighty Brinthor. I am humbled by this gift and your presence. I will do my best to not disappoint you."

The dragon released a deafening roar into the night sky and then threw his head back toward the depths of Lake Warda. With a thrust of his wings, he burst into the air, inverted himself, and dove back into the waters from which he had emerged.

The rest of the party, startled awake by Brinthor's bellow, rushed to the beach with weapons drawn. The waters of Lake Warda were quelled and Umhra and Nicholas greeted them.

"All is fine," Nicholas said. "Umhra was visited by Brinthor, who appeared to us as a great blue dragon. The gods favor our friend."

Gromley fell to his knees upon the beach and grasped his holy symbol in prayer. Umhra revealed the second nugget of rhodium in his hand.

Naivara gasped. "You almost have enough for your final Suffusion. I've only read of such a feat in my ancestral tomes. To achieve Mysticism would allow you to transcend the mortal plane."

"Well, I have to survive Naur first," Umhra said, "The gods likely see little risk in showing their support with the odds so stacked against us."

Naivara walked over to Umhra and grabbed his hands in hers.

"No matter. They place you closer to divinity than any since before the Rescission. Their gifts pay you the highest of honors."

"For now, we must stay focused on getting to Meriden, otherwise nothing else matters. Let's get some rest so we can travel in earnest tomorrow," Umhra said, steering the conversation from the night's events.

They welcomed the warmth of the campfire upon their return. Gromley and Laudin assumed their turn at keeping watch while the others turned in. Umhra lay for some time, rolling the two pieces of precious rhodium in his hands. Eventually, he drifted off to sleep.

"Never in my days, did I ever expect to be a part of something so profound," Gromley whispered to Laudin, the campfire crackling.

"I have a feeling we haven't been amazed by Umhra for the last time," Laudin said.

CHAPTER 29

Neither king viewed the Fracture as a victory, but rather as the only means by which to avoid war.
—The Gatekeepers' Abridged History of Tyveriel

Vol. 3, Chapter 36 – Discovered in the Private Library of Solana Marwyn, the month of Vasa, 889 AT

—▲—

The pool of blood bubbled and burped as fifty men encircled it in prayer. The smell of iron hung pungently in the stale air. Now over half full, the pit offered the brothers hope they would soon take their rightful place at the side of the god they worshiped so faithfully.

Grand Master Evron Alabaster stood behind the glowing rune of Naur, his head bowed and eyes closed. He muttered words of prayer in unison with his brethren. The prayer ended and Evron extended his hands out to either side and held the brotherhood's undivided attention. "Our commitment has been steadfast, and yet, our progress has slowed," he said, his frown exaggerated by the stone's radiance. "First, we lost our supply from Anaris, and more recently from Vanyareign as well. I have been unsuccessful in my attempts to make contact with Manteis or the Morion Coven. We must assume both have been thwarted. While this may be an unfortunate coincidence, there is likely an effort underway to upend our movement or, at the very least, our disparate activities across Evelium are garnering unwanted attention. As such, we must double our efforts if we are to succeed in amassing the souls necessary to resurrect the Fire God in time for the Reaping Moon."

Evron's speech was met with murmurs from the crowd. "I realize your instructions were to keep a distance from the procurement of lifeblood for this ritual, but with the loss of Manteis and Varina the Decayer, two of our most prolific soul harvesters, we must make adjustments if we are to open the portal on the eve of the Reaping Moon. I now call upon you, the acolytes of Naur, to gather sacrifices at our altar. We no longer have the advantage of anonymity nor the luxury of time. Naur demands our direct involvement."

"Yes, Grand Master," the gathering said in unison, the reply echoing off the stone walls of the inner sanctum.

"Then go forth, and return with your offerings," Evron said. He placed his hand upon Naur's Rune, which glowed brighter with each contribution to the pit, and prayed. Then he lifted his hood over his head, covering his face in shadow. The others followed and then filed out of the room.

Evron remained in front of the rune as the others left. "Now I prove my commitment to you, Naur, my god. My faith is undying, but I know your patience is not and failure to provide you access to Tyveriel will find my soul forfeit in the afterlife." A door opened and two robed men entered the room. Between them, a woman bound with ropes struggled to free herself. Silently, they tied her hands above her head and her feet together against the stone-backed pedestal standing upon the altar opposite the Grand Master.

The woman was Evenese, with light-brown hair in a tight bun. She wore an elegant red day dress befitting of a lady of her station. Her delicate skin and refined features suggested she hadn't worked a day in her life. Her large brown eyes were wide with terror as Evron stepped out from behind the glowing rune.

"Leave us," Evron said.

The men bowed and left the room through the door from which they had arrived. Evron maundered over to the woman, drawing from within his robes an ornate dagger with a thin curved blade and ruby-encrusted hilt. His face covered, he cut the woman's dress from her body, she tensed in futile resistance.

"My love," he whispered, removing his hood, "years ago, I made you a promise. A promise to have and to hold you until death parted us. That day is today."

The woman gasped. "Evron, what is the meaning of this?"

"My dear wife. You see, long ago, I made another promise. A promise made by my forefathers. A promise that supersedes the one I made to you. This promise will reshape the world in which we live. Unfortunately, fulfilling this promise now requires you to pay the ultimate price. Naur is very grateful for your sacrifice." He plunged the blade deep into her abdomen.

Cassandra Alabaster's eyes widened in disbelief and then winced. She strained against the chains binding her, found them secure. Evron dragged the blade across her stomach. "I am sorry, Cassandra. It pains me to hurt you this way but I simply have no other choice."

Unable to speak, deep crimson blood poured from the wound, running down Cassandra's legs and onto the sloped platform upon which she stood. The blood ran over the edge into a narrow channel and slowly traveled to the pit, joining that of so many thousands of others. Cassandra's body fell limp, Evron grabbed her by the chin and looked into her fading eyes. "Of the twelve thousand, you alone will haunt me." Evron released her, turned his back, and walked the trail left by his wife's blood.

"We are one closer to our goal," Evron said with a grin while looming over the edge of the pit.

Evron stared into the pool of blood below, his hands folded behind his back. He then peered over his shoulder at Cassandra, her lifeless eyes fixed on the floor behind him, and shed a single tear. If not for the strength of his conviction, he would have wept for her loss. He wiped his face on the sleeve of his robe and straightened his posture, the door to the sanctum swinging open and a brother entering.

"Grand Master," the brother said, glaring at the naked body of Cassandra Alabaster, "Lore Keeper Scarth is demanding an audience with you. He's most disturbed and keeps going on about knowing you are up to something. He said he'd be waiting for you in your office. I couldn't assuage his concerns."

"I always worried the fool would eventually get some sense of our activities. We've been working under his nose for so long. I'll return with you to the lodge and try to put his mind at ease."

"Very well, Grand Master," the brother said.

The men left the sanctum, closing the door behind them.

▲

Evron removed his robe and wiped the sweat from his brow, his stomach churning.

"Grand Master, are you all right?" the brother who accompanied him on the ride back from the sanctum asked.

"I'll be fine. Thank you, brother. We've all had to make sacrifices for the greater good."

"Yes, I'm sorry for the loss of your wife."

Evron nodded, entering the basement of the Gatekeepers' lodge. "Yes, unfortunate." He walked to the base of the stairs and looked in the mirror. His face was pale, his clothes twisted. He straightened his shirt, smoothed his hair back, and ascended the stairs.

The lodge was empty, quiet. He made his way across the parlor and up the stairs. At the top of the stairs, he could see the door to his office was open, and Lore Keeper Scarth stood at the window looking out over Meriden. Scarth wore a light tan jacket and matching pants. The morning sun lit him from behind.

"Kier, my brother," Evron said as he bounded down the hall with a forced smile on his face, "to what do I owe the honor of you visiting me this fine morning? I was told you were quite beside yourself."

"Do you take me for a fool, Evron?" Scarth asked, still looking out the window. "I've known for some time you have been working on some grand deception. I believe it's time you come clean."

"I assure you, Kier. I have no idea what you're talking about."

"Please. Don't patronize me," Scarth said, turning to face Evron. "I see you and your men coming and going from the basement. Something is afoot. Tell me, does this deceit have something to do with the coming Reaping Moon festivities? I know my tenth anniversary as lore keeper is not lost on you. I'd been expecting some modest recognition, but I can't stand the thought of you surprising me with some lavish ruse."

Evron couldn't suppress a laugh. "Kier. I know you are wont to be the center of attention but allow me my little pleasures. After all, I don't often get to celebrate such a significant milestone with a long-standing friend."

"Very well, but please keep the engagement limited to the lodge. We don't need all of Meriden turning out for this event."

"I assure you, what I have prepared will be most intimate. The Gatekeepers alone shall witness my little surprise for you."

"Much appreciated, Evron. I felt as though I needed to express myself on this. Now, I must be off to see the magistrate. I expect to be at the lodge later this week. Hopefully, we can spend some more time together then."

"That would be most welcomed," Evron said.

"Until then, my dear friend," Scarth said, offering his hand.

Evron took Scarth's hand in both of his and smiled. "Until then."

"Dullard," Evron said under his breath as Lore Keeper Scarth walked down the hallway and descended the staircase until he was out of sight. "What an interruption to an otherwise productive day." Evron ran his index finger along the full length of his desk as he walked to the window in thought. Time was fleeting and the brotherhood was falling behind on its goal. Drastic times would call for drastic measures.

CHAPTER 30

I have accomplished all that Evelium needs of me.
The time has come for me to explore the outer
continents in search of new adventure.
—Telsidor's Missives

Diary entry dated 3rd of Anar, 55 AF. Unearthed from the Ruins of Anaris, month of Emin, 1156 AT

—▲—

The Barrow's Pact exited the forest at Whitewood Knoll, the small community bustling with Iminti and Farestere, living sustainably off the forest to the east and grasslands to the west and south.

At the center of the commune, was a large communal grass-thatch hut surrounded by several smaller family dwellings of similar construction. The simplicity of the village spoke to its inhabitants' disdain for the industrial progress of the rest of Evelium, in favor of the simpler lifestyles of old.

As they entered the community, the late-morning sun warming their faces, an old Farestere man, wearing simple leather pants and a natural linen shirt, was the first to notice them. "Outsiders," he said at the top of his lungs. In response, a group of young Iminti men and women wearing fur armor and bearing pikes emerged from the woods behind them, while others could be seen in the trees, with bows drawn and ready.

Umhra raised his hands over his head. "We mean no harm. We're merely travelers passing through and shall be on our way presently."

"And where, may I ask, are you heading?" the old man asked, his voice gravelly and nervous.

"We head to Lindamere from Vanyareign," Umhra said. "We've been traveling for nearly twelve days."

"Then you make good time," the old man said, keeping his distance. "But I'm afraid your way forward shall throw you off your pace. We've heard the giants of the Spire Rift have a roadblock in place about a few days' travel between here and Lindamere. The filthy beasts are levying tolls, or worse. If Lindamere is your destination, I suggest you head either south across the plains, or north to the Stoneheart Pass, and avoid the Spire Rift altogether."

The Spire Rift was a deep canyon filled with stone spires which gave it the aura of a great petrified forest. Just south of the Ilathril Mountains, the rift divided a goodly portion of western Windswept—traversing it was the most direct path to travel. Circumventing it to the south would cost too much time; being forced north, inopportune.

"Your advice is most appreciated, and we shall adjust our plans in accordance," Umhra said.

The young warriors stood down, keeping a watchful eye over the travelers. "Will you join us for lunch before you move on?" the old man asked, stepping forward, his stern expression cracking into a grin. "And perhaps share some news from outside Whitewood Knoll? We rarely have the opportunity to communicate with conformers."

"I suppose we have to eat," Balris said, his tone friendly. "But then we must be off shortly after, as time is of the essence."

"Of course, of course," the old man said. "Welcome to Whitewood Knoll, I am Themis Grainne, Magistrate of the

Cornucopians." He held his hands out wide as if to unveil the splendor of the Cornucopian village.

"The pleasure is ours Magistrate Grainne. We are the Barrow's Pact, a group of adventuring travelers," Balris said as the others dismounted from their horses and tethered them under a small grove of trees.

"Adventurers. How exciting," Themis said, "Please tell me, what adventure sends you west to Lindamere?"

"We're yet to be sure," Talus said. "We've yet to explore the western regions of Evelium, and hope they offer much in the way of intrigue."

"I see. I see. Well, best of luck to you. Please follow me to the communal hall, where we can sit and enjoy an early lunch, and get you back to your travels without much delay." Themis turned toward the large thatch roof hut and noticed Nicholas for the first time. "Where do you hail from, young brother of the Farestere?" he asked in their ancestral tongue.

"Anaris, far to the south," Nicholas said, rusty and unsure of his Farestese. "My name is Nicholas Barnswallow, and it's a pleasure making your acquaintance."

"Always lovely having one of my own kind visit us. We see so few Farestere these days. Not many folks venture from Festbury. Please, come."

Themis led the group into the communal hut. The hut consisted of a single large room, the floor covered in hide and fur rugs surrounding a large fire pit that burned brightly at the center. The smoke escaped through a hole in the thatched ceiling which domed upward above them. A group of men and women sat around the fire, cooking meats, unleavened bread, and foraged root vegetables. Themis walked around to the back of the hut and took a seat upon a large brown bear hide that lay upon the floor.

"We are an egalitarian community, where no matter what your responsibility, you are viewed as an equal member of society. You earn your status through your contribution to the whole, rather than your accumulated wealth and power as seen in the rest of modern Evelium. We ascribe to the ancient ways of life," Themis said, a bit of derision in his tone. He patted the ground next to him as an invitation to his visitors to sit.

"A wonderful community you seem to have here," Balris said as the others each took a seat around Themis on the bear hide. "What may we tell you of the Evelium you and yours have left behind?"

A half-dozen young children, no older than ten years old, entered the hut, and scurried directly toward the fire. They each picked up a couple of wooden plates, the last grabbing a hollowed gourd fashioned into a jug of water, and carried them over. They passed the food and drink around to Themis and the outsiders. Cautiously eyeing their visitors, they took particular interest in Umhra.

"What are you?" one of the children asked. "Your teeth are scary."

"Child, that's no way to treat our guest," Themis said, his brow furrowed, "You must excuse the boy. He has likely never seen any of your kind."

"No, no, it's fine," Umhra said. "He's just curious. My father was an Orc, and my mother a human. I get my teeth, my skin color, and my size from my father's lineage. I like to think my mind and temperament are from my mother's."

"Well, you are very handsome," one of the girls in the group said. "I've never seen anyone like you, ever."

"Thank you. Have you seen a Ryzarin, like my friend Shadow?" Umhra asked gesturing to the other side of Themis where Shadow sat, keeping to himself.

"Once. A bad one came here from the mountains, and the Village Keepers needed to scare him off. His eyes were not nice like your friend's, though," the little girl said.

"On your way now, children," Themis said, dismissing the intrusion. The children respectfully ran off to serve other members of the commune that had arrived for lunch.

"My apologies. Children will be children. Now, back to our conversation. Please tell me what you know about the tensions between the two houses of Forene. We, who walk the line of neutrality, would like nothing more than to see the Fracture behind us and Evelium united once more."

"Unfortunately, we cannot share with you the news you wish to hear," Talus said, "The king has made several sincere efforts to engage those at Ohteira in diplomatic conversation, but they refuse to come to the table. There is currently no open dialogue or progress being made to move beyond the Fracture. There have been several incursions from the north into sovereign territory which some on the Elders Syndicate thought should have been answered with a show of force. The king, in his wisdom, resisted, thinking his forbearance would be taken as a sign of willingness to work toward a future better than the present. The incursions continue."

"Most unfortunate, I agree. I will assert, however, there are two sides to every story. I suspect those in Ohteira would offer a different point of view," Themis said.

Talus flushed, his eyes narrowing, but then he bit his tongue and nodded. "I suppose they would." He looked down at his plate and grabbed a piece of bread, tore it in half.

Nicholas jumped in, filling the void Talus's silence left. "I believe we would all like to see the two factions come to the table in the name of unity. We are all one people, after all, and are stronger together than we are divided."

"Well said." Themis smiled.

The conversation continued, maintaining a cordial tone until lunch was finished. "Unfortunately, we must be moving on." Balris stood. "Thank you so very much, Magistrate Grainne, for welcoming us into your village, and providing us with such fine food. As promised, we shall leave Whitewood Knoll in peace, and make our way toward Lindamere while circumventing the Spire Rift."

"And I wish you all well on your journey. May you find great adventure in the west. Please feel free to join us again on your successful return," Themis said, remaining seated. Talus stood, bowed, and rushed from the hut. The rest of the Barrow's Pact said their goodbyes and found their way back to their horses.

They started west, with several of the Village Keepers watching them depart. "Do we challenge the giants' roadblock or head north to the Stoneheart Pass? I'm fine with either," Gromley asked, once they were out of earshot.

"I suggest we head north, and try to avoid the giants, although that seems to be a matter worthy of attention, were we not already pursuing a matter so urgent," Laudin said. "The Stoneheart Pass may prove to be no less harrowing, however. The trail is narrow and dangers are lurking in those mountains."

"We should take our chances with possible confrontation, rather than certain confrontation if I am to have a say," Nicholas said.

"Very well. If there are no objections, we head north into the Stoneheart Pass, and then west through southern Winterashe, and on to Meriden." Laudin looked around for opposition to his proposal. Seeing none, he spurred Ansel into a trot. The rest followed, the afternoon sun hanging high in the cloudless sky, and Whitewood Knoll fell out of sight behind them.

▲

The open northern foothills of Windswept teemed with wildlife, but little else. The grasses and shrubs climbed halfway up the horses' legs as they progressed across the rolling landscape, Taivaron gliding overhead on the persistent tailwind. The party rode for several hours with the wind at their backs and ventured upon a large polished stone set flush with the terrain, around which no grass grew. Laudin dropped from his saddle and walked over to inspect the enormous marker.

"A Waystone," he said, rubbing his hand over the stone's smooth surface.

"I thought such a relic would be inert after all this time,"

Talus said, "and yet its glyphs still glow."

"I suppose a modicum of the energy it possessed during the Age of Grace remains. Regardless, it marks the entrance to the Stoneheart Pass to the north." Laudin pointed to a narrow break in the ubiquity of the Ilathril Mountains. "A day or two of travel from here should put us in Winterashe if the pass is unobstructed."

"In that case, we should continue forward." Talus nudged Maelstrom up the path and toward the gap in the mountains ahead. Laudin leaped back up upon his saddle and followed quickly after. The rest, their horses balking as they urged them forward, fell in line behind them.

CHAPTER 31

During the Age of Grace, the Waystones were powerful enough to transport entire legions of men to the other side of Tyveriel in an instant.
—The Tome of Mystics

Unknown Origin. Unearthed from the Ruins of Oda Norde, month of Bracken, 1320 AT

—▲—

Umhra stood before the yawning mouth of the Stoneheart Pass, dusk creeping through the sky. Diffused sunlight still painted the western horizon, but the pass itself was already as dark as the night of the Reaping Moon. The sheer stone walls rose upward into the heavens, their peaks obscured by clouds. The path was wide enough to allow the party to ride three-wide into the abyss, but a persistent breeze buffeted their faces and sought to extinguish their torchlight.

The rocky path undulated through the mountains, providing little scenery other than the dusty, rubble-strewn footing immediately ahead. Every so often, the ground would tremble beneath them as they rode.

Laudin dismounted and halted the party. He knelt, and placed his hand upon the earth, hushing his companions with the other.

"I suggest we pick up our pace through this section," he said, standing and turning back toward Ansel. "I fear we're being hunted."

He climbed back upon his saddle and the ground caved in before him, an enormous armored creature emerging from within. The beast's razor-sharp mandibles snapped at Ansel. The horse reared high to retreat, throwing Laudin, who was not quite settled, from his back. The beast's immense maw slammed shut, just shy of tearing Ansel in half, spraying venom across the narrow path as it thrashed.

Rock showered down around the party, with one large boulder crashing to the ground next to Talus and Maelstrom with a deafening thud. A cloud of dirt billowed into the air, and the party scrambled backward to avoid the massive beast's onslaught. Laudin hit the ground and rolled to his knees, letting two arrows fly. The first ricocheted off the creature's thick, armored hide, the other embedded itself in the suture between the first two stone-like plates of its long, segmented body. Leg after leg, the beast emerged from the tunnel, rubble cascading from its back. It released a displeased roar, having not consumed anything on its initial advance.

Shadow threw two daggers as the dense cloud of dust settled to the ground. Both struck true, drawing bright crimson blood from the creature's chest. The daggers returned to Shadow's hands and he dove behind a large rock; a rust-colored leg piercing the ground where he had stood as the creature continued its assault. Nicholas held his right hand out toward the beast. The ruby inset upon the silver ring on his index finger flashed, emanating a vibrant red light. He thrust his fist farther still in the creature's direction, the ring releasing a beam of energy that, upon making contact with the myriapede's body, burst into flames, engulfing the creature's face in an inferno.

The myriapede screeched, thrashing its head violently among the flames. One eye singed, and seeping a dark ichor, the monstrosity bounded forward in pursuit of its quarry, the ground trembling with each step. Now emerged from its burrow, the creature exposed its full body, covered in plates nearly identical to the stone of the mountains themselves. Each segment that crawled from the hole boasted a set of legs terminating in a razor-sharp point, the rear two of which were elongated with hooks at their ends. Again, it released a shrill roar of defiance.

The myriapede reared into the air and spun toward Gromley, Talus, and Umhra, sending another cloud of dust pluming upward and an immense tremor through the earth. Umhra and Talus dove beneath its barbed mandibles, placing themselves under its trunk. Gromley, who had been flanking Umhra to the left, was met with the full force of the creature's mass.

He crashed into the wall of the pass, blood spraying from his mouth, and slumped over, motionless. The creature turned to him, and opened its cavernous mouth, expecting its first meal of the night. Umhra and Talus plunged their swords upward into its underbelly, eliciting a shriek and calling its attention away from the unconscious cleric.

The beast staggered back with several uneven steps. Balris ran to Gromley's side and wrenched at his cuirass, but his armor made him far too heavy to drag. Instead, he knelt beside him and placed one hand on his holy symbol and the other on Gromley's forehead. There was a warm glow in the darkness and Gromley's eyes opened. "We must get you to safe cover," Balris said. He helped Gromley to his feet and they retreated from the fray.

The myriapede lunged at Gromley and Balris as they retreated, its mandibles opening wide. Naivara focused on the stone wall of the pass and thrust her hands toward the beast as it bore down upon them. The stone bent to her will and shot toward the myriapede, forming a honed spike that punctured the creature's body and ran it through.

Laudin, Shadow, and Nicholas continued their ranged attacks, while Umhra and Talus held fast to their blades still embedded within the creature's torso. Mangled, the beast's focus shifted toward self-preservation, and it convulsed, trying to dislodge the swords from its abdomen. It spun toward its burrow and threw Umhra—Forsetae in hand—to the ground, shattering the stone spike lodged in its side.

The beast labored to escape, Talus trying to wrest Aquila from its torso to avoid being trampled. Naivara turned her attention to a small shrub growing from a crevice between two rocks along the wall of the pass. Under her focus, the shrub swelled, and then lashed out several vines, each wrapping around one of the beast's great legs. One of them snapped under the force of the myriapede's momentum, but three held true, allowing Talus to tear his sword from the behemoth's body, and thrust it again, this time just below its head.

The myriapede attempted a final roar but could muster only a choked gurgle. It tensed against its restraints one more time, and collapsed, dead. Talus hung by his sword over the chasm the creature's burrow had left in the floor of the pass. He scaled the myriapede's side, freed his sword, and jumped down to safety.

The party gathered themselves in the darkness, the crisp air of the narrow pass burning their lungs as they heaved with exhaustion. "This may be as good a location as any to camp for the night," Laudin said, as Nicholas and Balris tended to Gromley's injuries.

"My thoughts exactly," Nicholas said. "I don't feel Gromley is in any shape to travel."

"That's nonsense, Nicholas." Gromley struggled to his feet. "I won't be the cause of any delay."

"No matter," Talus said. "We might as well make camp."

In the pocket of space between the felled creature and the wall of the pass, Laudin made a small fire while the others made preparations for the night. The air was colder than expected, given the time of the year, and they gathered around the fire as dinner cooked. All but Umhra, who sat upon the enormous carcass maintaining a lookout, and studying the small pieces of rhodium he had been given by Kemyn and Brinthor. When the party finished eating, Laudin climbed up to him upon the myriapede.

"Is it enough?" he asked, passing Umhra a bowl of stew.

"What?" Umhra asked, his focus on the rare metal broken.

"The rhodium? Is it enough for your final Suffusion?"

"I dare think not but it's more than I would have ever imagined attaining. Mind you, none of this matters unless we succeed in Meriden."

"For something that doesn't matter, you seem distracted by it."

"Wouldn't you be?" Umhra said. "If the gods saw fit to have you join them. I can't imagine ascension would be a decision you would make lightly."

Laudin sat beside him, the carcass cold and unyielding.

"No doubt. I'm not advocating you rush. I'm just so far from such a path I find myself intrigued by what I'm witnessing."

"It's all new to me as well. I didn't seek the attention of the Great Creators, but now I find myself their implement in a war they foolishly assumed was over. Just like so many have bought my services in the past, they offer the prospect of ascension should we succeed. I have no such aspirations."

"That is why they chose you," Laudin said. "I've never met a man so selfless. Your sole motivation—at least that I can surmise—is seeing justice done. For that reason alone, we will fight until the end of Tyveriel with you."

"I'm not yet convinced your vow will long be put to the test." Umhra smiled, placing the rhodium back in a pouch on his belt. "Let's head back down to the fire. I'd like to try and get some sleep tonight."

"Go ahead. I'll keep watch. I've noticed you seem restless at night."

"What little sleep I get has been riddled with strange dreams and premonitions. The further we progress, the more intense, and regular they become. For all the years I hid from what I am...denying my god...she is making up for lost time."

"I cannot say I can empathize, my friend, but I can imagine the pressure you must be feeling."

"You don't have to worry about me, Laudin. I have come to understand I was made for this very moment. Everything that has ever happened in my life, every twist and turn along my path, has prepared me for the mission at hand. I won't fail you. I won't fail Evelium. I won't hesitate," Umhra said in between bites of stew.

"Never for a moment since we met, have I thought you were one to hesitate when it matters most. Our faith is squarely with you. I hope you know that."

"I do. Thank you."

"Before you leave, any thoughts on Talus?"

"A skilled warrior, and a seemingly honest man. Maybe a little full of himself, but he is still young, and looks at himself as invincible," Umhra said. "He was quite reckless with this beast."

"You have an amazing ability to assess people. I dare say you're better at it than I am at reading terrain. I would hate to think how you would describe me to someone who asked." Laudin laughed.

"The man who saved my life as a stranger, and then offered to gather his friends, and travel all over the continent with me to save civilization? I am sure I'd have nothing nice to say."

"That decision was one of the easiest I've ever made. It was plain to see this was going to be one of the greatest adventures of our time. I'm a moth to the flame." Laudin paused. "But I've kept you too long. You ate your meal, and now you deserve your rest. Shadow knows I will wake him in a couple of hours."

"Good night, Laudin." Umhra stood and gathered his things. He slid down one of the myriapede's legs, and made his way over to the fire, unfurling his bedroll in an unclaimed space between Nicholas and Shadow, who were both fast asleep.

CHAPTER 32

I have created a governing body of respected figures from each region and race of Evelium. It is to be called the Elder's Syndicate.
—The Collected Letters of Modig Forene

Letter to Haakon Forene dated 9th of Jai, 11 AF. Unearthed from the Ruins of Vanyareign, month of Ocken, 1301 AT

—▲—

As morning broke, such dense fog hung in the chasm that the walls on each side dripped with water, as though after a steady rain. Several rivulets formed along the sides of the pass, carving their way through the rocky soil on their way back toward Windswept. The party was sluggish and stiff when they woke. Naivara prepared a large pot of herbal tea, of which everyone partook. The pink aromatic beverage had a somewhat bitter taste but proved to be exactly what the group needed to get their day started after the fierce battle of the night before.

They ate a light breakfast, and then packed up camp and worked their way around the monstrosity they had felled, careful to avoid the periphery of its burrow, which was now collapsing in upon itself. Another full day on horseback, with little more to see than stone walls and the occasional glimpse of Taivaron as he darted between the stray trees growing out of small cracks in the otherwise monolithic walls of the pass.

They plodded on until coming to the end of the pass just before sunset. Here, the passage opened up into a field of heather speckled with juniper trees. Umhra took a deep breath, welcoming the fragrance after two days in the stale air of the pass.

"Welcome to Winterashe," Talus said. "We've now left the kingdom and are in territory under the control of Vred Ulest, estranged cousin of the king. Going forward, there will be no safety in the king's name. In fact, quite the contrary. As unknown travelers in Winterashe, we will be vetted about any loyalties to King Arving. We can trust no one and must hide our true identities and our directive.

Umhra nodded. "I spent some time in Winterashe. What Talus says is true. There is a visceral contempt for all things south of the Ilathril."

Naivara shrugged off the warning and stretched her arms to the heavens, walking out into the field. She smiled, surveying the open vistas and took in the fresh air after the claustrophobic pass they traversed the last two days. An emerald-green praying mantis fluttered clumsily to her arm. She cupped it in her hand, the thrush that had been chasing it flying into her to complete his hunt. The bird hovered for a moment, and Naivara offered her finger as a perch. The bird accepted, and bobbed its head up and down, still looking for the mantis. "Not today, little friend," Naivara said. "He got to me first." The thrush tilted his head to the left and then flew off into a stand of junipers. Naivara uncovered the mantis and nestled it into a vibrant pink mound of heather at her feet.

"We must turn west here and try to stay south of the mirrored cities of Amnesty and Retribution, for they will be teeming with those loyal to Vred Ulest, and we'd undoubtedly be followed or questioned upon arrival," Talus said. "A southern route should put us at Pyra's Travail—due south of Meriden—in three to four days. There should be little more than a few minor villages along the way, remote enough where even if we drew concern, it would take days for the news to reach anyone of relative import."

"Then we head west in the morning," Laudin said, turning Ansel toward the setting sun which had turned the entire sky of the western horizon a deep orange, and cast a purple cover over the landscape.

▲

"That was delicious," Shadow said, tossing a grouse carcass into the darkness. "Gromley, you outdid yourself."

"Yes," Umhra said. "Thank you, Laudin, for scaring them up. I don't know about anyone else, but I'm exhausted. If it's all right with everyone, I think I'll turn in."

"I'll take first watch," Shadow said. "Nicholas, you up for some cards?" He flashed a well-worn deck and smiled.

"Sure." Nicholas cracked his knuckles. "I'm always game to lose a little pocket change."

The rest of the party turned in, leaving Shadow and Nicholas to their game. They were kept company by a small pack of wolves that continued to probe the campsite throughout the night, some daring to come close enough to grab the discarded remnants of their meal.

"That one troubles me," Nicholas said, pointing into the darkness at one of the wolves, whose eyes glowed chartreuse, standing out from the rest of the pack. "The reflection in its eyes isn't natural, as the others seem to be."

"I see what you mean. Do you think it has somehow been enchanted?" Shadow asked.

"Yes. I think it's a scout for someone of significant power. Otherwise, I can't explain the odd glow in its eyes. I've seen this kind of enchantment before."

"Let's wake Balris and Naivara," Shadow said. "It's time for their shift on watch anyway. They might be more useful in dealing with this creature than you and me."

Nicholas woke Balris and Naivara and pointed the creature out. Both agreed it was an enchantment of some sort.

"I can go out there and talk with them...see what I can learn," Naivara said.

"All right," Balris said. "You two get some rest. Naivara and I can handle this."

▲

Naivara took on the form of a wolf somewhat larger than those in the pack and howled to announce her presence.

The pack replied with many scattered howls that resonated in the darkness. She trotted out to meet with the pack's alpha.

"Why do you bother our camp?" she asked abruptly, as she approached a dark gray male, two-thirds her size.

"You have food. We saw your hunters with their grouse. We smell their charred flesh and your waste," the wolf said.

"We took only what we needed," Naivara said. "What of the one with the green eyes? She is different than the rest of you." She nodded her head toward a pair of glowing eyes staring at them from a distance.

"One of ours. She was trapped by the humans and returned to us like that. It is a hindrance, as she is easily spotted at night."

"What humans? Where were you when she was taken?"

The rest of the pack circled Naivara and the alpha, weaving in and out of her range of vision.

"Just southeast of the mirrored cities. We roam between here and there but have been staying more to the east since. I've seen this in other beasts as well. There are birds, deer, fox, and more with the same eyes. They are equally easy to hunt at night," the alpha said.

"I'd call off your pack now. A confrontation wouldn't end well for you. We mean no harm and will be traveling west in the morning, undoubtedly leaving some scraps in our departure."

"You are free to do what you want," the alpha said. "As are we."

"Then I'll return to my camp for the night, and we'll leave your territory tomorrow. Until then, I offer you my word we will not give you any trouble but expect not to have any in return," Naivara said.

"As you wish, deceiver. We have no need for humans that pose as wolves here."

Naivara turned from the alpha and made her way back to camp. She was trailed by a few members of the pack at a safe distance until she returned to the light of their fire and assumed her Reshinta form. "The one with the chartreuse eyes has been enchanted. Outside of the mirrored cities. The pack's leader told me of other animals with the same effect. Someone may be watching us."

"I feared as much," Balris said. "We'll let the others know in the morning. We must be very careful in discussing our journey going forward."

Rotating shifts throughout the night, the party monitored the wolves, who played their game until the sun broke in the east. "What did you learn of the green-eyed one?" asked Nicholas, rising from his slumber and noting the pack trotting off into the woods.

"An enchantment, no doubt," Naivara said. "I was told other animals have been enchanted in a similar manner, as well. We must be very guarded going forward, as I believe these creatures are scouts of some sort."

"That's what Shadow and I thought last night when we spotted it."

"We should destroy any such creatures we encounter," Talus said.

"Agreed, if the enchantment can't be dispelled," Balris said.

CHAPTER 33

It is believed that Kemyn, Brinthor, and some of the lesser gods still walk this land. It is unknown whether they may still impart rhodium upon mortals.
—The Tome of Mystics

Unknown Origin. Unearthed from the Ruins of Oda Norde, month of Bracken, 1320 AT

—▲—

The Gatekeepers' lodge burst with activity as all of the society's members gathered in celebration of the onset of the Reaping Moon festival and the tenth anniversary of Kier Scarth's tenure as Lore Keeper. He had risen to prominence two short years after Evron Alabaster, despite not having any of his forefathers involved in the group. A self-made man, he was popular around Meriden—a symbol that the average man could rise beyond his station. Over the years he had held political office and other positions of import and stood in good favor with Vred Ulest's court. Evron hated him for all of it.

But Evron's job was one of great calling and the true focus and responsibility of the Gatekeepers Society. *One to keep history, and one to make it,* his father had always said. His ancestors had worked toward the resurrection of Naur since they uncovered his rune in the middle of the Lazarus Woods after Naur spoke to one of his forefathers in a vision during the Age of Chaos. One after the next, his bloodline cared for the rune, constructed the sanctuary, and dedicated themselves to deciphering its ancient dialect. And one after the next they had failed.

Evron himself found *The Tome of Mystics* buried amidst the Forenian Archives in Vanyareign. Written in Old Evenese with interspersed samples of several ancestral languages, the book was the only surviving account of the Age of Grace, when god and man walked Tyveriel together. Evron was able to use the codex to decipher Naur's long-mysterious rune and set the wheels of his resurrection in motion. *How proud father would be.*

Inside the lodge, the Gatekeepers gathered around a large banquet table. Lore Keeper Scarth was seated at one head of the grand table and Grand Master Alabaster at the other. Scarth's closest friends within the society sat between them, twenty per side, with the rest of the Gatekeepers seated around the perimeter of the room.

"Today we gather to begin our traditional celebration welcoming the season of the Reaping Moon," Evron said, standing from his seat. "Five generations of my bloodline have had the pleasure of being Grand Master of the Gatekeepers. Since our founding, this has always been at the side of another who was deemed worthy by the great men of our society and elected as lore keeper. Today we don't welcome only the Reaping Moon, but also recognize the tenth year of service by our beloved lore keeper Kier Scarth."

The room applauded. Scarth smiled—pride flushing his face—and nodded respectfully from his seat. Evron allowed the applause, and then held up his hands and quieted the room.

"Our society plays a critical role in not only the history but in the future of Evelium and Tyveriel in its entirety. We are not merely stewards of the past, but rather harbingers of the future.

As my forefathers always told me—One to keep history, and one to make it," Evron said.

Those seated around the table, Kier Scarth among them, took an awkward glance at Evron and started whispering amongst themselves. The men around the perimeter of the room stepped up to the table, each standing directly behind the chair of a brother Gatekeeper.

"In honor of Lore Keeper Scarth, I had a small group of our brothers undertake the commissioning of a gift for him and his closest friends, those of you responsible for his rise to prominence in our fine society, and who sit with him at our banquet table this evening. Consider it a token of gratitude for the support you have given him over the years."

The brothers standing behind the chairs each placed an oversized silver bowl on the table in front of the men who were seated. Each bowl was engraved with the symbol of the Gatekeepers—a book and chalice. Beneath the symbol was written the society's motto in Old Evenese, *Through Only our History do we Forge our Future*.

"You've outdone yourself, Grand Master Alabaster," Scarth said, the recipients applauding once more.

"Think nothing of it. They are but a small gesture to commemorate all of the excellent work you have done in curating the history of our fine land. I must admit to having an ulterior motive, however. The coming of this Reaping Moon is one of unique significance. I begin with a story, so please humor me.

"At the end of the War of Rescission, Evelium lay in near-total destruction having witnessed the full power of the gods as they waged war upon one another to decide the future of Tyveriel. Vaila, Kemyn, and Brinthor chased Naur into what is now the Lazarus Wood where he made his valiant last stand. Ultimately, Naur was banished to Pragarus for what was perceived as his attempt to usurp mankind and rule over Tyveriel in perpetuity."

"Yes, we all are well aware of this myth." Scarth sighed. "I'm quite ready to get on with the festivities."

Alabaster ignored the interruption and continued. "What is not told in this most famed story of our past, is that Naur had engineered his own banishment, knowing his sister would be too weak to destroy him outright. With a plan in place for his eventual return, he surrendered himself and was sentenced to spend eternity in Pragarus. Before his filthy sister and her lemming brothers cornered him just outside of Meriden's city gates, Naur summoned a rune made of pure rhodium which he buried deep within the Lazarus Wood. This rune would enable those who believe in his virtue to resurrect him so he may take his rightful place as supreme ruler of Tyveriel and remake the world according to his unfettered vision."

Those at the table now turned their full attention to Evron as he placed his hands on the table and leaned forward, supporting himself on his fingertips. This was indeed a part of the historical lore never before shared.

"Five generations ago, my forefather uncovered this rune and founded the Gatekeepers, which became recognized as Evelium's official historical society. He installed a lore keeper to see to the more mundane tasks required to grow the organization throughout the kingdom while he focused his efforts on decoding the rune which demanded his attention. Ever since that time, the sole imperative of my bloodline has been to decode the rune and resurrect Naur. After ages of tireless work, Naur's day is finally upon us."

The brothers at the table gasped. As they turned to one another in astonishment, the brothers behind them drew their daggers from beneath their robes and slit the unexpecting throats of the men before them. They held the men in place, allowing their lifeblood to spew forward and fill the silver bowls Evron had gifted each of them.

Scarth, having been left untouched, threw himself back from the table and gasped at the unexpected massacre. He rushed for the door, but the exit was blocked. He turned and affixed his gaze on Evron.

"Evron, how could you?"

"All too easily, Kier. For years, and right under your very nose. There were several times we thought you were closing in on us, particularly the other night when you came to me concerned about your anniversary party. That gave me a start, and then a hearty laugh, I will give you that much. But alas, I haven't finished my story."

Evron sauntered around the back side of the table, the Brothers of Resurrection draining the blood of their counterparts as he passed. Scarth backed away from him but was stopped by a wall of brothers blocking the exit. They held him by his shoulders.

"In order to return Naur to the material plane, Kier, we must collect the blood of twelve thousand souls. When combined in a pit upon our altar and in proximity to the rune during the Reaping Moon, a portal will open between Evelium and Pragarus, allowing the God of Fire to once again grace the mortal plane and assume his rightful place as our god-king."

"You've surely gone mad, Evron. Have all of you gone mad?" Scarth asked, staring wild-eyed over his shoulder at the brothers.

"I would have much preferred it hadn't come to this, Kier. As far as self-serving buffoons are concerned, I always held you in high regard. The problem is, we've fallen off pace in our gathering of souls and have had to resort to measures we hadn't originally contemplated. Even poor Cassandra, my beloved wife of so many years, was called upon as a sacrifice. Just as you are now called upon as well."

Evron turned his back to Scarth and observed the scene. Forty more souls to add to the portal. Success was within his grasp."Prepare him as I have instructed."

CHAPTER 34

There was no choice but to wage war on the land itself if we were to take Evelium back and achieve new heights of civilization.
—The Collected Letters of Modig Forene

Letter to Englen Penn dated 3rd of Mela, 999 AC. Unearthed from the Ruins of Vanyareign, month of Ocken, 1301 AT

—▲—

The group ate a quick, utilitarian breakfast, and readied their horses for a long day of travel. As soon as the steeds were loaded, and the remnants of their camp covered, Umhra mounted up. "Let's go, we still have a long way to travel if we are to be in Meriden by the Reaping Moon."

The party hurried to their horses and followed Umhra west along the northern base of the Ilathril Mountains.

Cresting over a ridge, the party looked down upon an expansive valley, at the center of which were two great walled cities, one the mirror image of the other. The Atalan River coursed between them, carving a deep chasm dividing the cities. On either side, rose a tower; one made of white marble and the other of black obsidian. As they ascended into the heavens, the two towers twisted around one another, until finally merging at the very peak of their form.

"The mirrored cities of Amnesty and Retribution," Talus said. "Home of The Three, nephew and nieces to Vred Ulest, and a place for us to avoid. We must stay south within the tree line and hope we don't attract any attention."

The party entered a stand of pines that ran west along the base of the Ilathril Mountains. Taivaron dove out of the sky into the woods, hitting a fox at full speed. Laudin ran over to the creature, who was still alive, with Taivaron digging his talons into its neck. The fox's eyes glowed green, like the wolf from the night before. Drawing his dagger, Laudin ended the creature's struggle.

"We're being watched," Laudin said.

"We best keep moving," Talus said. "We must pass the cities as quickly as possible."

They quickened their pace through the woods, all the time keeping an eye to the north, and the mirrored cities. Rising over another ridge, a phalanx of mounted black horses blocked their path, dispersed amongst the trees in the forest ahead of them. Their front stretched from the northern edge of the woods to a rocky outcrop to the south where the terrain was impassable. Shadow reined Ramoth to a halt and motioned to the rest of the party to follow suit. The horses stomped, testing their reins as another line of cavalry filled in behind them from the woods to the north.

Upon each horse, was mounted an armored soldier wearing a bright yellow cape. The image of a three-headed winter wolf, the center head black as night, was emblazoned on their white breastplates and shields, identifying them as soldiers of the mirrored cities.

"By order of The Three, you shall accompany us to the Towers of Amnesty and Retribution. Your fate shall be determined within," a soldier said.

"And what, may I ask, have we done to garner the attention of The Three?" Balris asked.

"Subversion," the soldier said. "Ride with us to the mirrored cities, or we shall end you here in the woods and leave you to be picked over by the wolves."

There was no show of force, there were no weapons drawn. Just the simple threat and assumed acquiescence. The party obliged, seeing no alternative other than trying to fight their way out, which would be difficult against so many. Even if they were to escape, they would undoubtedly be hunted down, putting the entire mission in jeopardy. Possibly, they could talk their way out of the current situation.

"We shall comply. Although we have done nothing wrong, I assure you," Balris said.

"That is not for me to decide. My orders are to escort you to the towers and before The Three," the lead soldier said, urging his horse forward.

Surrounded, they rode out of the woods, and across the rock-strewn plains, the mirrored cities appearing to grow as they approached. From this vantage, the architectural marvel of the intertwined towers was breathtaking as they rose into the cloudless sky. The guards continued through the gate to the city on the eastern bank of the Atalan River. This was Retribution.

Without delay, they rode to the tower, passing innumerable wooden and stone buildings with thatched roofs, and crossing beneath the white portcullis of the Tower of Retribution. Several soldiers waiting within gathered the myriad horses while the captives dismounted and were ushered into the main hall through large white stone doors polished to match the smooth façade of the great tower. The main hall was equally as stark as the exterior, without a fleck of color adorning its monotonous walls and floor. The guards led the party up a grand spiral staircase to the top floors of the tower.

Two doors opened on their approach, a white chamber with two thrones, also devoid of pigment, presenting itself. The absence of color dulled the details of the expansive room before them. Upon each throne sat a young lady, identical to the other, with long blonde hair, wearing a white flowing gown. Their skin was pale, as though they were made of fine porcelain. Behind them stood a young man, equally as beautiful as his sisters, but dressed entirely in black, with dark eyes and shoulder-length ebony hair. The starkness of his form amongst the sea of white called everyone's attention to him as they entered the room.

"My lord and ladies." The lead soldier bowed. "I've returned with the travelers you were keen on meeting."

"Welcome, travelers, to the mirrored cities," the man said with a clear, welcoming voice. "I'm Roen Anstand, and these are my sisters, Myka and Veien Lyst. We are the stewards of Amnesty and Retribution, but you may know us better as The Three. We apologize for the disruption to your travels, but one can never be too cautious these days, what with that deplorable Shale Arving persisting in his efforts to infiltrate our sovereign territory and usurp the rightful king of Evelium. Please, share with us the nature of your travels past the mirrored cities and to our presence?"

Talus rolled his eyes and then stepped forward from amongst the party to address the trio. "My fair lord and ladies of the mirrored cities. We're adventurers from Travesty, on a quest to cross the continent to Meriden, welcoming any just exploit that comes our way as we travel. If we offended by crossing into your purview, we apologize profusely." He bowed.

"Not at all," said Roen, his sisters staring up at him from their thrones. "You're welcome in our midst. There was some concern when you were camping near the Stoneheart Pass, you had come from Windswept, and were agents of Arving. I, personally, am placated by your explanation. My sisters, however, are not as trusting as me and ask you to prove who you say you are by completing a small goodwill task for us before you are on your way."

"That shouldn't be a problem. What do the ladies of the tower have in mind?" Talus asked.

Roen walked out from behind his sisters, who remained

seated. He was tall and thin, his leathers hugging his body snuggly. He folded his hands behind his back as he walked.

"We've received reports of people recently hearing an infant's cry emanating from the catacombs beneath Retribution. Most likely, we are dealing with an impoverished family that has taken shelter there, but we must be certain. We ask you to explore the catacombs, identify the source of this crying, and resolve the matter as you see fit," Roen said.

"We'd be happy to, my lord. Shall we get started immediately?" Talus asked.

"That would be most pleasing. Captain, would you please take these fine adventurers to the catacomb entrance closest to where the wailing has been heard? I'm sure they can handle the matter from there," Roen said, gesturing to a soldier standing over Shadow's right shoulder.

"As you wish, my lord."

"Then we shall be on our way to your catacombs, and report back as soon as we've satisfied your request," Talus said.

Roen nodded toward the party in acceptance. His sisters sat silently, a blank stare upon their faces.

"We follow your lead, Captain," Talus said, turning to the soldier.

The captain led them back through the white stained-wood doors and down the endless staircase to the ground level of the tower. They walked from the building, and out into the streets of Retribution.

The main road through the city was lined with small shops, modest in comparison to the average found in the cities in Windswept or Clearwell. Passing several peasants, some carrying heavy bundles, they turned left down a narrow side street and walked until they approached an iron grate door along the north side of the alley.

The captain stepped up to the door and removed a ring of keys from his belt. "I'll be locking the door behind you, to dissuade others from entering the catacombs and giving you any trouble. I'll leave you my key so you can exit easily upon your return."

The door creaked open, rusted at the hinges, and one by one, the party filed into the hallway on the other side. The door slammed behind them.

"Good luck," the captain said, relocking the door. He removed the key from his keyring and handed it through the bars to Balris. "Please be respectful of the dead."

CHAPTER 35

A great battle was fought at Antiikin. In the end, Naur's armies stood victoriously and the Evenese city lay in ruins, its population decimated.
—The Gatekeepers' Abridged History of Tyveriel

Vol. 1, Chapter 43 – Unearthed from the Ruins of Meriden, the month of Anar, 1217 AT

—▲—

Umhra peered down the narrow hallway, the relentless darkness choking off his vision. Gromley pulled a familiar orb from his pack, set it adrift, and willed it to life. "Shall we be on, then?" He hoisted his hammer onto his shoulder. "I'm eager to see what treachery awaits us."

"Yes, Gromley. Lead the way, if you like," Laudin said.

The party walked the length of the hallway until coming to a spiral staircase leading under the streets of Retribution. The air cooled as they crept down the staircase, which terminated at a long hallway with walls constructed of the very skulls and bones the those the catacombs interred. The skulls were aligned to form a centerline along the wall, for the full length of the hallway, interrupted only by the occasional recess, each filled with open tombs. Long-burned-out candles lined the way, piles of wax having accumulated on the forgotten walls and floors beneath their wrought-iron candelabras.

The Barrow's Pact proceeded along the hallway, clearing the recesses as they crept. They neared the end of the hallway, the faint, distant cry of an infant meeting their ears. "Whatever's down here must have delved deeper into the catacombs after the recent complaints," Naivara said.

The iron-bar door at the end of the hallway was ajar. Gromley prodded it open with the head of his war hammer, the squeal of the rusted hinges echoing throughout the corridor. Another long, dark, hallway similarly lined with the bones of those long since passed, their skulls again forming the centerline of the wall. "One thing is certain," Talus whispered, "this isn't a family with children we are pursuing."

Another iron-bar door awaited them at the end of the hallway. This one was already swung agape. The crying grew louder, coming from within the adjoining chamber. Umhra peered into the room from the edge of the doorway. There were fifty sarcophagi spaced uniformly throughout in five rows of ten. Each was covered with a thick layer of dust obscuring any identification of those within. On the far side of the room, he caught a glimpse of a form shifting slowly in the corner.

"Something is huddled on the far side of the room," he said. "It seems to be the source of the crying."

"Hello. You there," Gromley said, brazenly walking into the room. "You can't be down here."

There was no response other than the continued wailing of the infant. The party approached, spreading out across the room, checking between the sarcophagi as they progressed. Only when Gromley's orb shed light upon the figure, did the quivering pile of flesh become visible, its eight eyes haphazardly surrounding an open, screaming mouth.

Gromley gasped. "By the gods. What kind of abomination is this?"

The eyes affixed their glare upon Gromley, and the crying

intensified within his mind to a point he could not bear. He doubled over, gripping his head, and screamed out in terrible pain.

Laudin released an arrow, but the mass disappeared, the arrow clattering along the stone floor into the corner of the room. The monster appeared behind him, rising to his mid-thigh. It shrieked, looking up at him, an incensed stare from lidless eyes. The veins in Laudin's neck blackened and bulged. He grabbed his throat, white foam billowing from his mouth. He fell on the sarcophagus behind him and averted his gaze. Then, he rolled to his knees and struggled to the corner of the sarcophagus.

Shadow let his daggers fly. Both plunged into the creature's malformed body, its focus still on Laudin. It wailed in pain and anger and vanished again.

Balris raced to Gromley's side and laid his hands upon him to relieve his state of all-consuming hysteria. Gromley screamed in unrestrained terror, his gaze darting around the room looking for the fiend that tortured his mind.

Nicholas helped Laudin—who gasped for air, the blackened veins pulsing in his neck—guiding him behind one of the stone sarcophagi and out of the monstrosity's line of sight. He held Laudin close and tried to heal him.

The creature materialized behind Talus, who had anticipated as much and thrust Aquila backward into the creature's mouth, careful not to look at his target. The abomination affixed its glare upon him, a black tar-like fluid spewing from its maw. Talus's body stiffened and he fell to the floor.

Naivara focused her attention on the entity and raised her hand toward the ceiling of the catacombs while muttering an incantation under her breath. A wall of flame shot up from the floor, engulfing the creature in fire. It screamed in agony, its flesh consumed by the inferno. The flames dissipated—the creature was once again gone.

The abomination comes for you next. Forsetae warned

Umhra. *Behind you, now.*

Umhra swung around, his blade humming as it led the way. The monstrosity appeared behind him at the exact moment Forsetae entered its space. Before it could emit another spell, the great Evenese blade carved the creature in half, casting its gelatinous body to the floor in two misshapen, quivering chunks. The eyes on both halves of its body continued their search for another victim.

Naivara ran over, and laid her hands upon Talus's rigid body, while Nicholas and Balris helped Laudin and Gromley to their feet, their afflictions abating. She shut her eyes and whispered. The color rushed back to Talus's face, and his muscles relaxed.

"Is it dead?" he asked, rolling onto his side.

"Yes," Naivara said. "I've read of such creatures before. I believe what we just encountered was an Anathema—a corrupted aberration, occurring naturally only in the depths of Wethryn, much like the Dokktari. What it was doing here, I have no idea. Do you think there could be a connection?"

"That thing was here because it was a pet of The Three," Umhra said, wiping his blade of gore. "They well knew what we were coming down here to face, and they had no expectation of us returning victorious. I don't believe there is any connection between The Three and the Brothers of Resurrection, however. I don't see how they would benefit from raising Naur."

"I must say, I agree with Umhra," said Balris. "The Three are ardent supporters of their uncle and his right to the throne. I can't see them being involved in the brotherhood's plans. Regardless, we must take something back to them as proof of our success if we are to be granted our freedom."

Shadow walked over to the creature, which still twitched in the middle of the room as if trying to will its disparate parts back together. Unsheathing a dagger, he carved one of the eyes from the creature's carcass. "This should be proof enough," he said, wrapping the orb in a cloth and placing it in his satchel. The Anathema's convulsing ceased. "Let's return to the Tower of Retribution and be on our way."

▲

Making their way back to the entrance of the catacombs where the captain had left them, Balris retrieved the key he had been given from his robes. He slipped his arm through the bars of the iron door, inserted the key into the lock, and turned. The lock clicked, and the door swung open. The narrow street was quiet and in shadow, as it had been when they arrived a couple of hours earlier. Once everyone was out of the catacombs, Balris locked the door behind them.

They walked through the subdued streets of Retribution and returned to the tower, where two guards stood at the portcullis. They wore armor identical to the soldiers who had intercepted them in the woods earlier in the day. Their yellow capes flapped in the breeze, occasionally obscuring the Winter Wolf emblazoned upon their breastplates. They each held long white pikes, which they crossed upon the party's approach.

"My good men. Your captain asked us to meet him here this afternoon. Can you please send word of our arrival?" Talus asked.

"And who, may we tell the captain is asking for him?" the guard on the right asked.

"The travelers from Travesty," Talus said. "He'll know who we are."

"Very well, I'll send word. Wait here a moment." The guard entered the tower through an iron-reinforced wood door off to the right.

He emerged a few moments later. "All right, you are free to enter the tower. The captain will meet you in the entry hall."

"Thank you, sir," Talus said.

Once again through the great white doors, the Barrow's Pact entered the Tower of Retribution. The captain entered the room from the spiral staircase leading to Myka and Veien's throne room.

"I trust by your swift return, the family in the catacombs gave you no trouble. Were you able to locate them?" the captain asked, extending a hand to Balris.

"There was no family," Balris said, handing the captain his key to the catacombs. "We request an audience with The Three."

"Yes, of course, they will see you. Follow me."

For a second time, they ascended the spiral staircase to the top floor where the throne room resided. The captain led them through the great doors and into the chamber where The Three were waiting, seemingly having not moved since the party had left them earlier in the day.

"We're glad to see you have returned. Do you offer proof the infiltrators have been dealt with?" Roen asked, hovering over his sisters, as the party approached the thrones.

"There was no family," Shadow said, grabbing the eye of the Anathema from his satchel, and tossing it on the table before The Three. "Instead, we met face to face with an Anathema. Despite being a little more than we bargained for based on our earlier conversation, we dispatched the fiend, nonetheless. I suggest you not look directly at the eye, as they seemed to be the source of the creature's power when alive, and this one still functions despite being detached from its owner."

The eye twitched on the table, shifting its gaze between those present.

"How did such a monstrosity get into the catacombs?" Roen asked. He ambled out from behind the thrones and wrapped the eye in the cloth where it could do no harm. After a contemplative moment, he turned to his sisters. "Do either of you have anything to say about this?"

Myka and Veien remained silent but showed their hand, an impish smile coming over each of their faces upon making eye contact with their brother. "I thought as much." Roen shook his head. "I must apologize for my sisters. They lean toward the mischievous. I'm certain no harm was meant."

"Of course," Laudin said. "I hope this puts us in good stead and we may now be on our way."

"You're welcome to come and go as you please, travelers from Travesty. I do hope you find your way safely to Meriden, and find the adventure you seek," Roen said. "You are welcome to stay in the mirrored cities on your return trip, should you find the need."

"Thank you, Lord Anstand. We are still uncertain where our travels take us after Meriden, but we will keep that in mind."

"Very well. We bid you farewell, travelers. May the gods look over you," Roen said, returning to his sisters.

The captain bowed and ushered the party out of the throne room. They returned to the great hall and walked outside.

"Ready our visitors' horses and meet us in the courtyard at once," the captain said to one of the guards manning the main door. The guard ran off toward the stables.

"Your horses will be here shortly. They will be provisioned for your remaining travel west. The ride to Meriden from here should be fairly mundane, but I suggest you stay south for as long as possible. It's a far safer path," the captain said.

"Thank you, captain," Balris said, "you've been most helpful during our short stay in the mirrored cities."

"Well, I hope to see you again, without the formality of our original meeting in the woods."

"We'd very much like that. May you be well in our parting," Balris said.

"And you as well." The captain saluted the party.

The horses arrived, led by a few stable hands. They were laden with food and water for the remainder of the trip and had themselves been fed and watered. "Again, thank you for the provisions. We shall be on our way," Balris said, taking the reins of his steed. The captain nodded and returned to the tower, leaving the party to mount their horses and make for the southern gate of the mirrored cities.

CHAPTER 36

The deeper I ventured, the more unique and treacherous were the creatures I encountered.
—Telsidor's Missives

Diary entry dated 24th of Riet, 58 AF. Unearthed: Ruins of Anaris, month of Emin, 1156 AT

—▲—

The Barrow's Pact returned to the open vistas of Winterashe, traveling southwest away from the mirrored cities. "I have to say, that went better than I had expected," Shadow said, interrupting the silence.

Laudin laughed, looking over his shoulder. "Do you mean before or after we were poisoned and paralyzed?"

"That was the low point, no doubt. I meant the treatment we received from Roen and his men. I had expected The Three to be outright sinister."

"In that regard, I must agree," Talus said. "Other than their slander against the king, which tested my resolve, they were surprisingly hospitable."

"All that matters, is we are back on our path toward Meriden," Umhra said. "I'm grateful the delay in Retribution cost us only the better part of a day. I feared we would be required to stay longer or be imprisoned."

They rode until night consumed the terrain before them and their bodies ached from the trials of the day. Gromley, Laudin, and Talus slumped in their saddles when Umhra tugged Splinter to a halt.

"I believe we've all had enough for the day," he said. "This outcrop looks like as good a place as any to make camp. It should serve as a decent break against these winds."

"Agreed." Laudin yawned. "We're in for a cold night. Any protection we can get from the elements will help."

Camp was made and the party ate a quick dinner, leaving Umhra and Shadow to keep watch, while the others huddled together with the wall of stone at their backs.

▲

"We're two days or less from Meriden," Umhra said, greeting the rest of the party as they awoke the following morning, his icon displayed openly around his neck. He had stayed up all night and was now rustling through the bags the captain had loaded on Splinter the day before, removing whatever food items he found that could serve as breakfast. "If we ride all day today, we can be there by the afternoon tomorrow."

"Yes, and then we have the small task of identifying the Brothers of Resurrection, infiltrating their safe haven, and ruining whatever they're planning," Shadow said, rubbing his eyes as they met with the morning sun.

"I have some ideas on what to expect in that regard," Umhra said. "I'll share with you all what I've seen as we ride."

This created a sense of urgency in what had started as a morning rife with apathy. The party was tired, but Umhra had found something to get their minds refocused on the mission that still lay before them. The others packed up their bedrolls and quickly prepared for the day's journey. Within the hour, they were riding west along the northern foothills of the Ilathril Mountains, to approach Meriden from the south.

"Well, you got us moving. Now tell us what we're riding toward," Gromley said, after only a few moments into the day's ride.

"As you all know, the Brothers of Resurrection aims to return Naur to the material plane, enabling him to destroy Evelium and recreate the world to his will. The cult had at some point recovered Naur's Rune, and are using it to construct a portal, connecting Pragarus, where the Fire God is bound, to Tyveriel. This portal is fueled by the blood the brotherhood has been so methodically extracting through the network of fiends we've partially uncovered. When they have enough blood, the portal will open and release the devils of Pragarus upon us. The great Fire God, himself, will follow this plague and besiege Evelium.

"The brotherhood is based in Meriden, but my visions showed their temple to Naur somewhere deep beneath the woods to the south of the city. Here the trees and earth are petrified as the power of the portal grows. I don't know where or how we may gain access to their haven, but I anticipate the rest."

Ominous storm clouds gathered in the northwest. "The brotherhood seems to have made vast progress," Umhra said, pointing to the tempest on the horizon. "I'd imagine we will find what we're looking for at the center of that storm."

"Then, we ride to the storm." Talus charged ahead. "We near the end of our journey."

"For better, or worse," Gromley said.

Turning northward, the Barrow's Pact rode through the night, stopping only to rest their horses when necessary. The night was cold and offered little in the way of comfort with the confrontation with the Brothers of Resurrection looming over them. Umhra trailed behind, muttering to himself in a celestial tongue, praying for the inner strength to will himself onward. The others rode in a tight formation, their proximity a mote of solace as the night wore on.

A cool, dim sun rose in the east. In the subdued early-morning light, it was evident the storm over Meriden had grown, and now raked the sky above them like the claw of a great dragon. The group rode toward the storm, lightning dancing amongst the clouds as a reminder of the approaching danger. They slowed their progress to a cautious canter, all semblance of color fading from the landscape around them.

By midafternoon they neared the southern edge of the Lazarus Woods, the foreboding canopy of storm clouds obscuring any sign of daylight. The earth here was dry and cracked, the fissures burping noxious fumes from deep beneath the surface, molten rock glowing within. The trees in this section of the once-living, green woods were all petrified and had turned a deep gray from root to leaf. Ash hung in the air, reminiscent of a gentle, lazy snowfall.

The party halted at the edge of the woods.

"Whatever lies ahead," Nicholas said, "I want each of you to know that your friendship, regardless of how long or how short a time, has honored me beyond anything in my life. I've come to see each of you as extraordinary leaders, warriors, and people, and it's been a true privilege traveling and fighting at your sides."

"I couldn't agree more, Nicholas and the feeling is mutual," Umhra said. "Now we end this. We ride to Meriden for Evelium's salvation. Shall we fall, we fall in the name of valor and justice." He snapped Splinter's reins and rode into the petrified woods.

"For Evelium," the rest said together, urging their steeds forward on the same dark, narrow path down which Umhra had started.

The creatures of the Lazarus Woods had turned to stone, frozen in their tracks, as the ritual to raise Naur from Pragarus took hold upon the landscape surrounding where he had placed his prophetic rune ages ago. They passed a deer caught stealing a drink from a now dried creek. The wolf stalking close behind, still in a crouch, eternally ready to pounce on its prey.

A blur of red against the ubiquitous gray of the forest caught

Laudin's eye. He drew his bow, Talus following suit, and tracked the streak of color darting through the woods to the party's right. They halted their progress amongst the flurries of ash floating in the air around them. Another flash and Laudin released his arrow, which found an uninterrupted path through the dense stand of trees, whistling as it flew.

An unearthly screech in the woods prompted Umhra and Shadow off their horses and into the morass of brittle undergrowth. The once supple brush now shattered like glass as they rushed forward. Not far from the trail, they found the creature, lying prone across the monochromatic forest floor. It was still breathing, laying in a pool of inky purple blood, seemingly rendered unconscious. Umhra and Shadow approached, weapons drawn. As they neared, the creature made an unexpected lunge at Shadow, its razor-sharp claws slashing at his throat. Shadow dodged the attack and sunk one of his daggers into the creature's chest. In an instant the imp fell to the ground, dead.

Umhra turned it over with a nudge from his boot. "The end of days is upon us. There is no doubt this is a lesser devil from the hells of Pragarus. The portal must already be capable of transporting creatures through from the other side." He picked the imp up by the base of its ragged wings. "We must get to Meriden."

Together, they made their way back to the others. Umhra threw the imp upon the ground at Maelstrom's feet when they arrived. "We must hurry. The portal has opened. To what extent I am unsure, but no doubt this imp is from the fire plane." He and Shadow climbed back upon their horses.

"If there are others like this beast here, or things worse ahead, we must maintain some element of caution so we are not caught off guard," Laudin said. "We'll have little chance of success if we don't make it to the portal."

"I understand." Umhra furrowed his brow. "We proceed with purpose, but not recklessly." He urged Splinter on toward

Meriden.

The Barrow's Pact continued through the forest, eliminating several lesser devils along the way. When they arrived at the clearing outside the southern gate of Meriden, smoke billowed from the center of town. Alien screeches and all-too-familiar cries for help emanated from within the fortified walls.

CHAPTER 37

Those few that successfully suffused rhodium
walked among the gods.
—The Tome of Mystics

Unknown Origin. Unearthed from the Ruins of Oda Norde,
month of Bracken, 1320 AT

—▲—

Umhra led the charge into Meriden, passing through the main gates that laid asunder, little more now than a smoldering pile of wreckage. The town was in a hopeless state of disarray, with many buildings toppled and aflame. Groups of townsfolk scrambled through the streets looking for some semblance of protection. Two large, winged fiends hovered within sight, their sinewy purple forms looming over a group of locals that held them at bay while others escaped. Several other devils and innumerable townsfolk lay strewn across the rubble.

The townsfolk were grossly unprepared for battle with the devils. Seeing their despair, Nicholas instinctively released a fireball from his ring. The blast lit up the sky, casting the devils as silhouettes against the smoke-filled air. The attack drew the devils' attention. The fiends spun to face the more powerful adversary, flying with amazing speed in the party's direction.

On approach, they released a hail of razor-sharp spines at their quarry.

Shield at the ready, Umhra deflected several of the spines. He clutched his icon and summoned his armor which grew around his body plate by plate. Several of the spines passed by Umhra and impaled Balris. The barrage sent Balris flying off the back of his horse, and into the remnants of a small stone home. Gromley turned to his fallen friend, but the devils bore down on the group, and he ran toward the fight.

Laudin loosed an arrow and Talus a bolt, both finding purchase in the chest of one of the devils. Undeterred, the fiends continued their assault. A few of the townspeople who had been engaging the devils attacked them from the rear, some wielded swords or axes, but most with little more than shovels, sharpened sticks, and rocks. Despite their inferiority, they attacked with vigor in defense of their neighbors and kin.

Naivara jumped down from the back of her horse and raised her staff into the sky while reciting an incantation. A green sigil manifested before her in the air. As it dissipated, a whirlwind grew in its stead, engulfing both of the devils in a frenzy of gales. She honed her focus and the storm intensified, collecting everything in its path. The devils were obscured in a cyclone of dirt and debris, but for the stray arm or wing.

The devils struggled with feverish intensity to escape the whirlwind, but they were overcome by its strength and thrown from the vortex, the expulsion sending them careening into a immense marble statue of Mela, the goddess of peace and love. The effigy shattered into several substantial chunks upon impact, casting a shower of polished stone across the ground. The party closed in and encircled the fiends who staggered from the rubble. Shadow threw two daggers at one of the devils, severing one of the wings from its back. The creature hissed.

"Keep them on the ground," Shadow said. "We can take them."

Umhra rushed up to the other, swinging Forsetae down

upon the creature's back. He cut through a wing, cleaving a good portion of it from the devil's body. Spinning, he plunged the sword into the fiend's abdomen, eliciting a howl of rage and pain. The two locked in combat, Laudin rushing up beside them and thrusting his scimitar through the back of the devil's head, blackened brain matter covering his blade.

The remaining devil let out a shrill screech, and then climbed the moss-covered wall of a nearby tavern. Talus slashed Aquila across the back of its legs, amputating one at the knee, and leaving a gaping laceration in the other. The fiend's escape thwarted, blood poured from the wounds and it fell back to the ground, writhing in pain.

Talus stood over the devil and plunged his faithful blade into its heaving chest. Another of its kind, its flesh rotted and infested with maggots, swooped over the rooftop, answering its wounded brethren's call. The rancid devil dove at Gromley, its shadow enveloping the cleric as it bore down.

Gromley looked up and staggered backward. He stumbled over the corpse of one of the townsfolk and fell to the cobblestone, his war hammer clattering from his hand. The fiend screamed in Gromley's face, spitting acid from a mouth filled with countless serrated teeth running in rows down the back of a cerulean throat.

Gromley raised his throwing axes. The putrid devil attacked, snapping its jaws down on the head of one ax and ripping it from his hand. Gromley buried the other in the side of the fiend's head. Rearing back, the devil tore the other ax free from Gromley's grip and raised a claw overhead. Sparks flew, the devil slashing downward and raking against Gromley's armor, sending him scrambling backward. The fiend licked its lips and then buckled, a ball of fire blasting into its side. The devil slid across the street, crashing into the corner of a building, sending rocks and mortar tumbling. It turned and screeched at Naivara, who was now encased in flame and blocking Gromley from harm.

Naivara and the devil met one another in the middle of the street, exchanging blows of claw and flame. Two smaller black devils, wingless and covered in needle-like spines joined the fray, snickering as they approached Naivara from behind. Shadow spun, releasing two daggers in rapid succession, both bursting through one of the smaller devil's chests.

Gromley clambered to his feet, the devil falling to the ground lifeless, and retrieved his war hammer. He rushed to Naivara's side and swung the hammer upward as the second smaller devil leaped for her back. With a crushing blow, he sent the devil arching through the air and careening into a pile of nearby rubble.

Intent on ravaging her, the putrid devil snapped at Naivara. She dodged, the devil's razor-sharp teeth finding no purchase, and grabbed it around the neck in a choke hold, its momentum carrying it too far. The devil bucked, trying to throw her elemental fire form from its back, but she gritted her teeth and bore down. The intensity of the flames engulfing her was stoked by her fury, and she burned through the devil's throat and severed its head.

The devil's body slumped to the ground, Naivara discarding the head and turning to her friends, all of whom stood awaiting another barrage. All except Nicholas and Balris.

"Gromley. Hurry," Nicholas said from across the corpse-strewn road.

Nicholas held Balris's head in his lap, caressing his hair and crying. The immediate threat vanquished; the others ran to his side. "I tried to heal him, but to no avail," he said, "You must save him, Gromley."

Gromley knelt before the limp body of the priest. Several large jagged purple spines protruded from his chest, his vestments soaked in blood, his eyes dull. He placed a hand on his talisman and another on Balris's forehead and prayed. A familiar white glow emanated from beneath his hands and then dissipated. Gromley dropped his head. He tried again. Nothing. "I'm afraid it's too late," he said, looking up at the rest of the group. “He has fallen.”

“No,” Nicholas said, “there must be something you can do.”

“Nicholas, he is lost,” Gromley said, tears welling in his eyes. “I was too late. I’m sorry.”

Nicholas wept, touching his forehead to Balris’s. Tears streaming down his face, the silver medallion around Balris’s neck turned black and crumbled into dust.

Umhra fell to his knees, an intense anger building within. He prayed to Vaila to give him the strength to avenge his fallen friend, holding Balris’s hand as he did.

“If you should seek blame for Balris’s death, place it squarely with me,” he said, his tone a near snarl. “He ventured with us only because of my inadequacies.”

“Umhra, there’s no blame to be placed,” Laudin said, Naivara’s arm around his shoulders. He looked at Nicholas, whose face was pale with grief. “Isn’t that right, Nicholas?”

Nicholas lifted his stare away from Gromley to meet Laudin’s eyes. “Yes,” he said. “We all did our best under terrible circumstances.” He swallowed, looking back to Gromley with a shallow smile.

“Umhra,” Shadow said, “Balris wanted to be here, just like the rest of us. To see this through with you to the very end. I mourn his loss, but he was here of his own free will.”

A group of villagers gathered around the group of strangers who had saved them. They were bloodied and covered in soot and grime, their faces marred with fear. “Where did they come from?” Talus asked. The others fixated on their grief. “We’re here to vanquish this scourge.”

“They poured over the wall from the woods, along with the others of their kind. We suspect this all has something to do with the Gatekeepers, however. There have been rumors of strange happenings going on in their lodge, and they have all gone into hiding since the woods turned to stone,” said a young man with long, greasy blond hair. He had a ragged beard and a scar running the length of the right side of his neck. “Who are the lot of you? I fear we would have met our end if not for your arrival."

"Who we are is not important. Lead your group in getting as many of these people as you can to a safe place. We'll head to the Gatekeepers' lodge if you'll point us in their direction, and hopefully root out what's behind this nightmare, the gods willing."

"Of course," the young man said, "the lodge is along the main street through the northwest district of town. The Gatekeepers fly a green banner with a gilded chalice and writing tablet." He motioned to the others in his group and instructed them to aid in getting the other civilians to safety as he ran to see to a young mother and her child.

"I've seen this emblem in my visions," Umhra said, "We must get to the Gatekeepers' lodge at once."

"What are we to do with Balris?" Naivara asked. "We can't just leave him here in the streets."

"We can have the townspeople care for him until we return," Laudin said.

Talus waved to the young man he spoke with earlier. Noticing the gesture among the chaos of the moment, he ran over. "Is there something else I can do for you, sir?" The young man asked.

"Yes, our friend was felled by the devils earlier. Will you see he is kept safe until our return?" Talus asked.

"Of course, sir. It's the very least we can do for you. My condolences as well," the young man said.

"Appreciated. Unfortunately, we all suffered a tremendous loss today."

"Indeed, sir. We have."

The young man called a couple of members of his group over. "How can we help, sir?"

"These people are going after the Gatekeepers while we hold any more fiends at bay. Their friend, the priest, fell in battle and we are to keep him safe until they return."

"Understood. We are gathering the fallen at the Bastion. You can claim him there when this is over. We'll see he is well taken care of."

Two of the men gathered Balris. The party stood in shock, as they carried him off to a stone building closer to the center of town.

"Thank you," Talus said, shaking the young man's hand. "We shall find you as soon as practicable."

"Good luck, my lord. I'll be awaiting your return."

Umhra stepped up and put his hand on Laudin's shoulder. "We must find the brotherhood at once, or our losses will be much greater."

"I know," the ranger said, hanging his head. "They will pay for this."

"Yes, they will. Even if their end means my own life," Umhra said.

Shadow helped Gromley and Nicholas to their feet and the party took a brief moment to bury their emotions. Refocused, they made their way along the main road through Meriden, past the center of town, and into its northwest quadrant with fire and destruction guiding them along their path.

CHAPTER 38

Meriden was the only city in Winterashe not ravaged by the plague. It was also the only city to keep its name.
—The Gatekeepers' Abridged History of Tyveriel

Vol. 2, Chapter 17 – Unearthed from the Ruins of Meriden, the month of Ocken, 1240 AT

—▲—

The Barrow's Pact rode at full pace into the northwest quadrant of Meriden, coming to a neighborhood untouched by the destruction seen in other areas of the town. On the left side of the road, there was a great lodge made of stone and wood that towered over the surrounding buildings. Out front there flew two large emerald-green banners, each with a gilded chalice and writing tablet. The streets were empty and the building was quiet and had been secured.

They crept up the front stairs, Shadow leading the group to the door, which was obscured by a dense shadow cast by the immense overhang projecting from the building's façade. The door was made of heavy wood, stained a deep wine color, and had intricate carvings resembling the chalice and writing tablets on the banners flapping above.

"Do any of you know what language is scrawled upon those

tablets?" Umhra asked, his question met with silence.

"The Gatekeepers are an exclusive guild, having kept the written history of Evelium since the end of the Age of Grace," Talus whispered as Shadow picked the door's lock without effort. The tumblers clicked, and the door cracked open. "They claim this responsibility was handed to them by the gods themselves. It would be far too fitting for such an organization to be involved in this insipid plot."

Shadow swung the door wide open so the party could peer inside. They crossed the threshold into the darkened foyer.

"Is it me, or is this place kind of eerie?" Nicholas shuddered.

"Definitely not just you," Naivara said. "Something terrible happened here."

The dark-wood walls and heavy tapestries took on an oppressive feel with the drawn shudders blocking any natural light from the interior. The group inched their way into the main parlor, which was off to the right of the foyer. Everything, at first, seemed undisturbed and in perfect order. Toward the back of the room, however, a sallow-faced man hung from a rafter high above. He wore the remnants of a lore keeper's green vestments, the garment having been riven lengthwise, the gold chalice embroidered on its chest torn asunder. A small pool of blood coagulated on the floor beneath him, the rest taken by design, judging by the gaping laceration running from his sternum to his lower abdomen. Beside his entrails, was carved by blade the phrase, *We are Sated by the Chalice of Knowledge.*

They slipped around the body and into an adjoining meeting room, which had a large wood table surrounded by chairs which took up the vast majority of the space within. Upon the table lay another forty bodies, each wearing similar green vestments, albeit less ornate than those of the man hanging in the parlor. The bodies had all been exsanguinated, having had their throats slit so deeply they were nearly decapitated. Upon the wall, painted in blood was written, *But the Rune shall Deliver Us Immortality.*

"This is terrible," Nicholas whispered, unable to keep his horror to himself.

On the other side of the room, there was a doorway leading out to a hall. Shadow rushed to the doorway, ignoring the pile of corpses.

"There is a dim light emanating from one of the doors over here," he said, waving the others over.

Laudin inched up behind him and put a hand on Shadow's left shoulder. "See the light coming from beneath that door?" Shadow said, pointing down the hallway. "I would wager that is a staircase into the cellar."

"Then, we shall follow the light," Laudin said.

Shadow crept ahead, surveying the hallway with every careful step. Just before the door they intended to breach, he knelt and dismantled a tripwire rigged as an alarm. The rest caught up as he cracked the door open and peered within to find a staircase leading to the cellar.

"Empty," he said turning back to the party. "Shall we proceed?"

"Yes," Umhra said, "we proceed."

Shadow opened the door and led the party down the wooden stairs. At the landing, there was a wooden door off to the right. He pressed his ear against the door to listen for any sign of activity in the adjacent room. As he listened, a crossbow bolt pierced the door with a thud, just missing his face. "I guess that's our answer," he said, jumping back with a start.

Gromley swung the door open, revealing two men dressed in red armor, both brandishing crossbows with longswords at their hips. Shield at the ready, Gromley blocked a volley of bolts, allowing the party to enter the room. They charged the cultists who dropped their crossbows and drew swords. Readied for battle, the swords glowed red from the etchings upon their blades.

Suffused evil. Forsetae said to Umhra. *We must shatter these blades.*

The onset of the scuffle attracted five more men, three of which were armored, into the room from a doorway along the far wall. Those in armor released crossbow bolts into the crowd of intruders, sending Gromley staggering backward with a blow to the right shoulder, and the other two sending Laudin and Talus diving to the floor.

Undeterred, the Barrow's Pact careened into the five armored cultists with a crash of metal on metal as their weapons collided. The two remaining cultists wore garnet-colored robes with silver inverted cross pendants around their necks. They kept their distance, shielding themselves behind their armored allies, while simultaneously grabbing their pendants and setting forth two streaks of electrical energy. Naivara and Nicholas were struck and thrown from their feet.

Regaining her composure, Naivara stared across the room, her eyes narrowing, and thrust her hands upward in response. A stone pillar shot up from the floor, crushing one of the mages against the ceiling, his body bursting across the room. Nicholas laid his hands upon her soot-smeared face, smoke still rising from her leather armor, closed his eyes, and healed her burns.

The other mage, seeing his counterpart pulverized, slid sideways across the room, putting the frenzied battle between him and Naivara. Nicholas opened his eyes, Naivara's face flush with energy.

"We have to take care of the other mage," she said. "Let's circle the room in opposite directions to run him down." Nicholas nodded and the two separated.

The rest of the group had paired off throughout the room and were engaged in ardent battle, Gromley tearing the bolt form his shoulder and joining Laudin.

They were well-matched and could have fought a prolonged battle until Shadow parried his combatant's sword, giving him a second to throw one of his daggers at the armored cultist Umhra was entangled with. The blade sunk into the base of his neck just beneath his helm and killed him instantly. The blade returned to Shadow's hand in just enough time to parry the next slash from his counterpart.

Freed from battle, Umhra rushed over, and impaled another of the cultists from behind, releasing Talus from combat. "Help Shadow," Talus said.

Talus ran at the two armored cultists fighting Gromley and Laudin. They hesitated and opened their stances to counter his advance. He crashed into them, sending them off-balance into one another. Gromley took advantage of the distraction and slammed his war hammer into the chest of one, while Laudin plunged his scimitar into a gap in the other's armor.

Naivara closing in, the remaining mage grabbed his amulet, turned toward her, and prepared another spell. Nicholas edged up behind him, not half his height, and made a fist with his ringed hand. His eyes turned solid black as he touched the mages back. The mage fell to his knees, his arms limp, his eyes locked in a dead stare. Naivara approached him and slammed her staff on the floor. A portal opened beneath the mage and swallowed him whole.

In two large bounds, Umhra was upon Shadow's foe who, in defending himself from the Paladin, took one of Shadow's daggers under the shoulder. He fell to the ground, dropping his sword, and crawled to put his back against the nearest wall.

Shadow swept in to finish the job.

"Wait," Umhra said.

Shadow stopped, the point of his dagger inches away from the man's throat. Umhra walked over to the prone cultist, growling like an angry dog as he approached. "Where is the portal? Tell us, and I shall grant you a swift death."

The cultist spit in Umhra's face, his saliva stained with blood. "You are too late, fools. The gate has been opened. You can't stop the Fire God's return to Evelium. He will raze all of Tyveriel to the ground."

Umhra thrust Forsetae deep into the man's right shoulder, causing him to twist and scream in pain. The cultist grabbed the blade, his gaze darting but for a moment to the door through which he had entered the room.

Shadow and Laudin rushed to the door and cracked it open. "Looks to be a subterranean stable," Laudin said, turning to Umhra, "Empty, but there's a large tunnel bored through the stone wall on the far side."

"No matter," the cultist said. "The resurrection is upon us. You rush to your doom."

Umhra slipped Forsetae from the cultist's shoulder and reinserted the blade through his throat. The man's eyes widened, blood pouring from his mouth. "You've rushed to yours as well," Umhra said, the man's body going limp. He tore his blade from the body and the cultist slumped over at his feet.

Umhra turned to the party, not thinking twice about what he had just done. "We must destroy these blades, and continue onward," he said, nearing the door where Shadow and Laudin stood.

Gromley gathered the five suffused swords and placed them upon a crate Shadow and Talus dragged into the center of the room. He held them down by their hilts, their blades extending out toward Umhra, still pulsing with energy. Umhra raised Forsetae over his head, his armor and blade glowing a vibrant blue. He crashed Forsetae down upon the cultists' blades, sending shards exploding across the room. Gromley and the rest shielded themselves from the shrapnel as best they could.

"I'd imagine the brotherhood and their horses are on the other side of that tunnel, as they strive to complete their ritual," Shadow said, pointing down the dark underpass that was before them.

Umhra inspected his blade as if expecting there to be some sign of damage, but Forsetae was as perfectly honed as the day it was forged in the depths of Antiikin. "Let's go," he said. "We end this now."

Together, they entered the stable, which was lit by several torches around the perimeter of the room. The smell of fresh manure hung in the air. They hurried past the empty stalls, and toward the passage, down which torches continued to light the way.

CHAPTER 39

I wish you well on the path you have chosen. Your accomplishments shall forever be celebrated in the annals of history.
—The Collected Letters of Modig Forene

Letter to Artemis Telsidor dated 6th of Emin, 55 AF.
Unearthed from the Ruins of Vanyareign, month of Ocken, 1301 AT

—▲—

The ominous warning of their detainee still ringing in their ears, the Barrow's Pact quickened their pace at the expense of caution. The passage seemed endless, sloping downward as they ran. The air was cool but stale as they descended for more than an hour until the passage leveled out. As they met level footing, the party passed several small openings along the wall of the passage. Each of the openings flashed with a bright green light as they crossed their path.

"We must have set off some kind of alarm," Shadow said, stopping to inspect the recesses.

"Never mind that," Umhra said, "Let them know we are coming."

Shadow ran after the group to catch up. He breached a turn

in the hallway and narrowed the gap, the party having slowed its pace, wary of a heavy scraping sound emanating from the passage ahead of them, just out of sight.

"What is that?" Nicholas asked, the torchlight dancing off a hulking figure blocking the path before them.

"I don't know," Laudin said, squinting. "Some sort of construct."

Made of a dull alloy the exact color of the stone around them. The golem stood twelve feet tall and took up no less than half the tunnel with its width. Its face was unadorned but for two glowing red eyes. In each hand, the machine held a proportionately large mace, its immense arms rested rigidly at its waist. The party took what small liberties the tunnel gave them to spread out. The golem charged.

They braced for impact, the golem rearing its maces overhead, scraping the weapons across the ceiling of the passage. The golem barreled forward, undeterred by the storm of rock which sent most of the party scattering for cover. The thunderous steps of the stampeding construct and the grinding weapons merged into a deafening clamor.

Umhra stepped forward and met the first mace with his shield, partially deflecting the blow. The sheer force of the golem's attack sent him staggering backward but he refused to back down, staring into the golem's red eyes with defiance as they raged with arcane fury.

Gromley joined Umhra, ducking beneath the arc of the second mace and countering with a wild swing of his war hammer. He landed a crushing blow upon the construct's armor, leaving a dent in its torso. The golem turned its head, its empty glare shifting to the Zeristar. Its joints grinding to ready its maces for another attack, Nicholas released a fireball that burst across the golem's back with a reverberating echo but having only a superficial impact upon the resilient armor.

One of the construct's great maces crashed into the floor of the passageway, embedding itself into the stone, Gromley barely managing to roll out of the way in time. The other swung wide of Shadow who leaped upon the golem's back and stuck his two daggers into its neck where the armor showed signs of weakness. The golem took three large steps backward, Talus diving from its lumbering path. It crashed into the stone wall, sending Shadow falling to the ground.

Naivara commanded the stone wall to grow outward around the golem's feet and hands. The golem strained against the stone, managing to free one hand, and sending another shower of rock across the passage. Talus and Laudin advanced, swords drawn, and penetrated the golem's body at the waist in a joint between its plated armor.

The construct thrashed at Naivara's stonework shackles, but they held fast, giving Shadow time to climb back up on its shoulders from behind and sink both his daggers into its neck once more. With all of the force he could muster, he dragged the blades laterally across the breadth of the automaton's back. The golem's eyes flickered erratically and then dimmed as the arcane energy driving it dissipated. The massive metal shell slumped forward, still hanging from one arm.

Shadow jumped down from the golem's shoulders, waiving off Gromley's offer of assistance. "We must be getting close if we are running into this kind of opposition," he said. "I know we're winded, but we must get to the brotherhood before they can do more harm."

"Unfortunately, I agree with the sentiment." Talus nodded, his chest heaving.

The party lumbered forward, exhausted, but driven on by sheer will. The passage took a smooth, arching turn, at the end of which a second iron golem emerged from a recess in the stone wall, its maces taking a chunk of stone from the wall as they streaked over Nicholas's head, forcing Laudin to slide on his knees to avoid the attack. With another swing, one of the maces found Naivara. To the sound of cracking ribs, she crashed into the stone of the tunnel wall.

Nicholas turned and ran back for her, diving between the golem's legs in the process. As he slipped beneath the construct, he brushed its leg with the tips of his fingers. Ice grew up the golem's leg and across its body until it was nearly encased. Only by brute strength was the entity able to break free, sending shards of ice flying through the tight quarters. The glass-like shards cut into the party. Gromley and Umhra deflected the bulk of the barrage with their shields, but one shard sliced through Talus's thigh, sending him down on one knee.

With the golem slowed and Naivara unconscious against the wall, Laudin used Gromley's shoulder to leap into the golem's face. He released a flurry of blows with his scimitar and dagger directly into the golem's eyes. The construct swatted furiously at the air, trying to rid itself of the aggressor, the blades digging deep into its head, inflicting massive damage.

"Finish it now," Laudin said to his friends below.

Already in motion, Umhra, Gromley, Talus, and Shadow attacked the golem from each side at its waist. The golem fell to its knees as their blows found the gap in its armor, dislodging some of the mechanics within its torso. Laudin leaped from the golem's chest and flipped just out of range as the golem fell forward, crashing face-first onto the tunnel floor.

Nicholas dropped to his knees beside Naivara, her breathing labored and shallow. She was barely holding on. Gromley rushed to meet him, and both laid their hands upon her head. A blinding radiance emanated from their combined effort, as they refused to lose a second member of their party. There was no response.

Laudin loomed over them. "Gromley. Fix this," he said, his desperation palpable.

Gromley and Nicholas again willed her back to consciousness. This time Naivara spit up some blood and her eyes blinked open. Gromley helped her to a seated position, allowing her to catch her breath.

"Are you all right?" Laudin asked kneeling beside Naivara.

"I'll be fine," she said, her voice weak. "Thank you, Nicholas, Gromley."

Nicholas nodded and smiled, Gromley stroked his beard and sighed. He turned and walked over to Umhra who stood beside the golem, staring into the darkness of the tunnel ahead.

"That was close," Gromley said. "How far do you think we are from the sanctum?"

"Hard to tell. We must be somewhere below the Lazarus Woods at this point. The brotherhood can't be much farther."

Laudin helped Naivara to her feet. "I'm fine, Laudin," she said, wiping her bloodied chin on her sleeve.

"Then we move on," Laudin said. "We can't afford to lose any more time."

Umhra led the party farther down the passage, their pace slowed by injury and exhaustion. They traveled several more taxing miles, until the passage widened into another stable, as Shadow had predicted. The horses in each stall whinnied and snorted as the party approached, otherwise, all was quiet. They hurried across the room, passing stall after stall, to a set of iron doors on the far side of the room. Forged into the doors was the face of a terrible horned beast with a furious and vengeful expression upon its face. They paused.

"Naur, I presume," Shadow said, eyeing the doors cautiously.

"The moment before us is that for which we have traveled so long," Umhra said, caressing the image with the tips of his fingers. "Together, we have prevailed over trial and tribulation, with everything building to this point. No matter what lies on the other side of these doors, may we prove ourselves worthy of the tomes of history, should our story be told, or not. For Balris, for the gods, for all of mankind, but most of all for each other."

CHAPTER 40

There are at least two dozen known gods that grace Tyveriel. This does not include the Ascended Ones.
—The Tome of Mystics

Unknown Origin. Unearthed from the Ruins of Oda Norde, month of Bracken, 1320 AT

—▲—

Laudin took a step back as Umhra pried the doors open. With a resonant scrape of metal against stone, the doors swung wide and the party peered inside. A large oval room, constructed of a light tan sandstone and well lit by oil sconces, met their eyes. At the very center of the room was a statue of a ancient demon-god, baring great, asymmetrical curved horns and jagged, tattered wings. He was posed as though in flight, looming over his dominion, pointing downward as if casting scorn upon his opposition.

In two separate phalanxes on either side of the statue were groups of cultists, each dressed identically to the armored foes the group had fought in the basement of the Gatekeepers' lodge. Each carried a long sword etched with glyphs, their ruby glow the same as those Umhra had shattered earlier.

"Intruders," one of the cultists said, "stop them." The guards swung their weapons forward and charged, shouting warnings to whoever may have been within earshot.

The Barrow's Pact rushed into the room and spread out to meet the mass of attackers hurrying toward them in a frenzy.

"Naivara, we will buy you as much time as possible, but we need you to come up with something fast," Laudin said, glancing over his shoulder as the guards neared. Taking the left flank of the perimeter Umhra, Gromley, Shadow, and Talus formed around Nicholas and Naivara, he met the first strike with a parry from his scimitar. Outnumbered four to one, they held the aggressors at bay as best they could while Nicholas stood behind them next to Naivara, whispering in her ear as she sat on the floor and closed her eyes.

A couple of guards fell upon the blades of Umhra and Talus, but their line was breaking. Laudin was stabbed in the shoulder as one of the cultist's blades breached the line, while Shadow was knocked to the ground by the sheer force of the attack. He scrambled from the scrum, a cultist stepping over him, sword overhead. A vile roar and the cultist stepped back and regrouped with his retreating brethren.

"How can this be?" one of them asked, a look of terror on his face.

"How dare you not bow before me," Naivara roared, having taken the form of Naur, the God of Fire. She charged forward, forcing the group of guards back with a cloud of black smoke billowing from her mouth. Her demon form was sinuous and amethyst in color. She beat her immense wings, the lanterns lighting the room blown out.

The forward cultists choked as the cloud of smoke she spewed forth enveloped them. They foamed from the mouth, grabbing their throats, and then fell to the ground, writhing with blackened veins swelling in their necks. Those not within range of Naivara's attack prostrated themselves before the living avatar of the god they both worshiped and feared.

With the momentum of the battle shifted, Umhra led his

friends forward, Shadow scrambling to his feet. They cut their way through the remaining guards and made for another set of iron doors across the room from them, avoiding Naivara's noxious cloud. The black cloud dissipated as the last of the cultists were released from life. Naivara dropped her demonic form, coming to rest on her hands and knees, her breath labored.

In his haste to bring the brotherhood's scheme to ruin, Umhra grabbed the doors and, in a flash of purple light, was jettisoned backward across the room, crashing into the base of Naur's statue. Nicholas ran to him and helped him stagger to his feet, Shadow running to inspect the door.

"Nothing I can do about this one," Shadow said. "Nicholas, any ideas?"

"Yes. Let me take a look," Nicholas said, assured Umhra was sturdy enough to continue.

Nicholas approached the door, and held his hands close to its surface, all the while careful not to make direct contact. The door reverberated at his proximity. He closed his eyes and rubbed a small sachet of dried herbs between his hands. There was a pulse of pure white energy from the ring on his right index finger, after which, he grabbed one of the door's handles.

"The magic sealing this door has been dispelled. We may enter."

Talus strained against the weight of the doors, exposing the sanctum within. Darker than the outer sanctuary, the inner sanctum was square and plain. At the center of the room was a large, raised altar containing a circular pit now filled to the rim with the blood of nearly twelve thousand souls. The surface of the pit's contents pulsed with a garnet-colored glow, causing the remaining cultists of the Brothers of Resurrection surrounding it to be lit from below as if standing upon a funeral pyre.

The men were dressed in black robes, their heads shrouded by oversized hoods. They were holding hands and chanting in prayer, undeterred by the interruption. Leading the ceremony was a man dressed similarly to the others, but for his robe being red. He stood behind a stone pedestal etched with a scene of a great demon-god laying waste to the city of Vanyareign and its paltry army of mortals.

He looked up from his prayer, making eye contact with Umhra as he entered the room. He held up his hands and took a step back from the pedestal. "You are too late. Our most recent offering has accomplished our goals. All there is for you to do now is to sit back, witness the coming forth of Naur, and accept your reckoning," Evron said, gesturing to the now empty barrel of blood being held over the pit by two of the brothers.

"I must give credit where it's due," he said, staring at the Paladin in the doorway. "I assume it was you who undid Manteis and Varina the Decayer. You almost succeeded in slowing our progress enough to make a difference. Don't despair. We have been preparing for this inevitability for generations. Those before you are but the lucky few to witness the Fire God's triumphant return to Evelium. You had no chance of victory."

He averted his gaze toward the pool of blood, which continued to pulse, its garnet hue unchanged. A transient look of dismay crossed his face, and then he walked from behind the pedestal and behind the circle of brothers who remained in prayer. From beneath his robe, he drew a dagger and slit the throat of one of the brothers in the circle and shoved him into the pit. The brothers on either side of him joined hands and continued their prayer, unphased.

"He's buying time," Shadow said. "The ritual has not yet been completed. This is the opportunity we were hoping for."

The party charged toward the brothers, the pit shifting in color to pale violet. The portal released a gust of preternatural wind, forcing them backward momentarily. As the gust abated, the brothers unlocked their hands and consolidated in front of the pit, each slipping a blade from beneath their robes.

"The portal is open, protect it until our god shows himself," Evron said, wiping his dagger on his robes.

The brothers formed a phalanx, four men deep, at the top

of the altar stairs between the Barrow's Pact and the Portal of Pragarus. Evron walked back and resumed his position behind the pedestal, which now cast across his form the same violet glow as the pit. A broad, wicked smile grew upon his face.

"Make me a path to the portal," Umhra said. "I know what must be done if we're to spoil the brotherhood's plans."

"You heard him," Talus said, as though commanding the Raptor's Grasp, "clear Umhra a path to the portal."

Talus led the charge directly into the heart of the phalanx. The others followed, but for Laudin, who stood at Umhra's side, firing arrow after arrow into the cloaked mass, weakening the cultists' formation.

"What are you planning, Umhra?" Laudin asked, continuing his barrage.

"I saw this all play out in a dream. In that dream, Naur succeeded in returning to Tyveriel and, despite our most heroic efforts, was invincible. He defeated us with little effort and had his way with our world. The only chance we have is if I go to Pragarus and face him there, so the rest of you have a chance to destroy the rune."

"Umhra, there will be no coming back, despite the outcome."

"I understand, Laudin, but it must be done. This is my fate, and I'm prepared to face it."

Laudin nodded, grimaced. He looked one more time upon his friend. "I shall never forget you, brother. May you bring the God of Fire to his knees."

"Nor I you," Umhra said, Forsetae in hand, preparing himself for the one opportunity he might have to change the fortunes of the day.

Talus crashed into the first line of defense at the base of the three steps leading up to the altar and the glowing pit, Aquila cutting through several cultists as the rest of the party joined his assault.

They concentrated their efforts on the center of the phalanx, causing the brothers, who were far greater in number but lacking in skill, to spread out around them under the pressure. Umhra waited, the purple glow of the portal penetrating the wall of black cloaks like dappled sunlight through a lush grove of trees. With a fleeting glance at Laudin, who shouldered his bow and drew his scimitar, he ran for the nascent opening, his speed unmatched. Taking a few brothers down with Forsetae as he raced to the altar, he bounded up the stairs and leaped out over the portal.

The whole room paused as time hung for a moment. The Paladin, in his shining armor, flew through the air, his knees bent. Forsetae pointed down at the portal as he held the sword overhead with a reversed grip. Evron threw his dagger with speed and accuracy into Umhra's torso as he careened through the air. The blade pierced his platinum armor just below his rib cage, sinking deep into his abdomen.

Umhra's momentum carried him to the center of the pit, where he landed on one knee and thrust the tip of Forsetae into the portal as he landed. As a stream of his blood hit the portal, its color intensified to a vibrant heliotrope. With a burst of energy, he vanished.

His selfless act was met with a derisive laugh from behind the podium. "The fool. He would rather meet his end in Pragarus and forfeit his soul than salvage a chance at absolution under Naur's rule. He has abandoned you, and now you shall die upon our altar."

"We won't give up on him," Laudin said, tearing his scimitar from the chest of a cultist.

Shadow and Gromley met amongst the chaos. "I'm going to make a move on the ringleader," Shadow said. "Follow me and destroy the rune."

"I'm with you. Lead the way."

Shadow navigated the morass, danced between his robed adversaries, deftly dropping them with his daggers as he passed. He made his way to the top of the stairs, a trail of bodies in his wake, and Gromley a step behind him hammering his way through the severely thinned out crowd. Shadow's glare locked on Evron, who staggered back from the rune, putting a modicum of space between him and the Ryzarin.

Shadow dashed toward the Grand Master, Evron fumbling for a second dagger from his belt and stabbing at the air. Shadow was upon him in a matter of heartbeats and slashed at him with the dagger in his right hand. Evron parried the attack, but Shadow spun and plunged the dagger in his left hand under Evron's chin, through his mouth, and into his skull cavity.

The Grand Master of the Brothers of Resurrection stared at his killer, and then at the gateway from Pragarus which maintained its glow but showed no sign of the god he had dedicated his life to pleasing. Blood spilled from his mouth, and he collapsed in Shadow's hands.

CHAPTER 41

The outer continents are a beautifully wild frontier. I believe Shent is, so far, my favorite.
—Telsidor's Missives

Diary entry dated 25th of Prien, 58 AF. Unearthed from the Ruins of Anaris, month of Emin, 1156 AT

—▲—

Umhra awoke to the searing heat of the bleak Pragarus landscape. In the distance, an endless range of impossibly tall mountains loomed in every direction. The sky was scorched, and as red as the earth upon which he lay.

A sharp pain pulsed in his stomach. He sought out the source and found Evron's dagger lodged under his ribs. Rolling to his back, he grasped its jeweled hilt and slipped the thin, curved blade from his body. The spray of blood from the wound boiled as it hit the earth. He groaned and cringed, but fought through the pain. There was still work to be done.

He labored to his knees, the portal throbbing behind him having ruptured through the barren terrain—a jagged, misshapen likeness of the one he had leaped into. Encircling him and the portal was a blue-white cloud that raced in a counter-clockwise formation. It was as if he were within the eye of a cyclone. He grabbed Forsetae and got to his feet.

He walked to the edge of the cloud, the unmistakable sounds of battle calling to him from the other side.

He placed an outstretched hand into the cloud—a preternatural cold numbed his arm. From within the cloud, he could now make out the twisted faces and tangled arms of thousands of souls, circling the portal, somehow shrouding it from the evils of Pragarus. Hesitating for a moment, Umhra entered the cloud and was overcome by the tormented screams of the spirits within, frost growing on his armor. His head rang with the pain of the many thousands of souls offered by the Brothers of Resurrection in their ritual to return Naur to his material form.

"Umhra, Champion of Vaila," a familiar voice said over the unquenched wails of the cloud of souls.

Umhra turned to see the ethereal form of Balris hovering amongst so many others the brotherhood had damned. "I found my way here with the others," the specter said with the same paternal tone Balris had favored in life. "Naur and his devils fight this collection of the untimely chosen in their bid for the portal. It is only a matter of time until they break through."

"Then together, we will stop them," Umhra said. "I look forward to fighting at your side one last time, my friend."

His pyramid icon, displayed with pride around his neck, glowed with unmatched intensity, a beacon to his god, and the souls he walked amongst. He emerged from the cloud, spirits wafting over his form like smoke, his shield covering his right arm, and Forsetae in his left hand, prepared for battle.

Innumerable devils of many shapes and sizes, buzzed about the area, squawking and screeching as they picked at the transcendent wall holding them at bay. Looming behind them was the vast form of Naur, the winged God of Fire, summoned by the intense violet glow of the gate. Any sane man would have shuddered at the sight, but Umhra steeled himself as the god's shadow blackened the red sky. This was the moment all other moments in his life had led to—he was ready to meet his fate.

Naur released a deafening roar, scattering the mass of souls obstructing his path only for them to regather. "I will not be delayed any further in my return to Tyveriel." He smashed a nearby mountain with his enormous arm, sending an avalanche of near-molten rock down upon the area, crushing many of his own minions in the process.

Umhra rolled out of the way of a boulder that crashed down in his proximity. His movement drew Naur's eye. "And what do we have here? A mortal in the plane of Pragarus? I shall consider your soul forfeit." Naur roared again, this time expelling a shower of black plasma in Umhra's direction.

Umhra stood his ground, Forsetae at the ready. Just before the plasma rained down upon him, he thrust his shield overhead to protect him from its effects. The collision sent a huge plume of black smoke into the burning sky. As the smoke cleared, the formerly red earth turned into a bilious black sludge in a large radius around the intended target, but Umhra's shield and armor shined as if they were new.

The lack of satisfaction sent Naur into a rage, the Paladin standing before him still. The seething god lashed out at Umhra, and with little more than a flick of his immense arm, sent Umhra hurtling through the air. Expecting to hit hard, torrid earth, Umhra braced for impact. Instead, he landed gently upon a soft, welcoming surface.

He looked behind him, eyes wide with surprise, to see what had broken his fall. He was in a hand, an enormous, pale, blue-white hand, with gold and platinum bracelets lining its forearm. He craned his neck and was met by the welcoming face of the god with which his entire life had been intertwined. Vaila placed Umhra on the ground.

"My champion, Umhra the Peacebreaker," she said, her long, black hair hanging over her shoulders as she stooped down to assure his safe placement, "I had once told you I could not interfere with life in the material world. You see, my child,

I needed you to get here to Pragarus, where angels dare not venture. Here I may still be of purpose."

The aura around Umhra's form was blinding in the presence of his god. He said nothing. Vaila rose to face her greatest adversary, intent on ensuring the future of the world she so loved. Her feet were bare, but she was otherwise covered in a shimmering gown, reminiscent of the late afternoon sun dancing across the ripples of a lazy river. On her back were strapped two great swords with hilts fashioned into the form of angels with outstretched wings.

"Naur," she said, "I cannot let you leave Pragarus, brother."

"Sister," Naur said, "after all these years, you finally join me in hell. I'm sorry I can't stay longer and get reacquainted."

"I don't want to have to kill you, brother."

"You and our brothers banished me here so many ages ago. Oh, how you must regret being too weak to do what was necessary that day in the woods and smite me. And now you stand before me, without Kemyn and Brinthor at your side, and think you have the strength to stop me again? I will destroy you and Tyveriel will be mine." He growled.

"Do you not see?" Vaila said. "Tyveriel is not yours to take, nor mine. It advances of its own accord. Imperfect, yes, but free, and beautiful."

Naur clenched his fists before him, and two fire-born battle axes materialized within his grasp. "You have always lacked vision, sister. I shall claim Tyveriel and bestow upon it perfection under my rule." He ran at Vaila, his eyes glowing white with indignation, the ground thundering under every footfall.

Vaila unsheathed her blades, which hummed as they were drawn forth. She ran to meet her brother face to face in battle. Umhra snapped out of the trance this encounter had placed on him and ran toward the portal, laying waste to any of Naur's minions in his path. Each one to fall was one less to beget further terror upon Evelium and his friends.

The shock wave caused by the two gods colliding leveled

most of the mountains in view and destroyed a great deal of the devils swarming the skies overhead. Umhra scrambled over the piles of rubble strewn across the landscape. Nearing the cloud of souls, a black devil landed and blocked his path.

"The Fire God commanded your soul forfeit. I will take pleasure in tearing it from your mortal form," the devil said.

The devil was three times Umhra's size, its muscular form bound in hooked chains that pierced its flesh. With a sinister hiss, it lunged at him, razor-sharp talons screeching across his armor before Umhra could defend himself. He rolled away from the assault and slashed into the devil's form at its shoulder. The fiend turned to him and whipped out its tail, wrapping it around Umhra's neck. Like a constrictor, the devil squeezed, the veins bulging in Umhra's neck. It bore down, a glint of delight in its yellow eyes as Umhra struggled to free himself.

The devil lifted Umhra off the ground, snickering as the Paladin fought for air while his god was distracted with her own battle. "Your flesh shall be my first of many from your world," it said.

Umhra dropped Forsetae, the sword clattering upon a pile of rocks. He shut his eyes and stopped struggling. The devil drew him closer, licked its disfigured lips. It opened its mouth, its jaw dislocating to accommodate a large meal, but the light emanating from Umhra coalesced around the tail strangling him and burned the fiend's unctuous skin. What at first began as a snarl, escalated into a piercing scream. The devil shook violently, trying to escape the pain, which only intensified until it released its grip and dropped Umhra to the ground.

The fiend leaped upon Umhra, who rolled, exposing Forsetae, which he had grabbed from the debris. He thrust the ancient sword into the devil's chest. The sword burst through the devil's back, and Umhra wrenched it sideways, exacerbating the wound. The devil's acrid blood spilled onto Umhra, as its life force escaped.

Umhra cast the devil aside, got to his feet, and continued

toward the portal. Naur released a deafening scream. Umhra spun to see him impaled upon one of Vaila's swords. The sword, embedded in the right side of the Fire God's chest coruscated, throwing sparks from the edges of the wound, and fusing itself in place within his massive body. The wound sent Naur into a rage. He crashed his flaming axes together and besieged Vaila with a flurry of blows. She parried a number of the furious strikes before one got through her defenses, and Naur buried an ax into her stomach. She doubled over, engulfed in flames. Naur stepped over her and lifted his other ax over his horned head with both hands. As he slammed it down upon her, she looked up and thrust her other sword into his lower abdomen. Again, the sword fused in place, Naur's ax cleaving into the base of her neck.

Vaila fell to her knees, Naur standing over her triumphantly. He turned as she fell to the ground, and made his way to the portal. His size diminished as he approached the rift, preparing himself for his journey to Tyveriel. Umhra crossed into the cloud of souls first and walked among them.

Naur entered the cloud, the spirits screaming in agony as his form passed through them. Emerging from the other side, the portal's welcoming purple glow garnered his gaze. As he stared into the light that would return him to Tyveriel, Umhra emerged from the cloud beside him and plunged Forsetae into the upper left portion of his chest. Forsetae, along with the swords Vaila had bonded to him, formed the perfect symmetry of an inverted triangle.

"No," Naur said as the triangle on his torso illuminated. Umhra threw his weight against him, and forced him out of the circle, despite his protests.

"Naur, God of Fire, by Vaila's will, I bind you to Pragarus. I forbid you to enter Tyveriel. You shall remain here for all time," the Paladin said, continuing to force the god backward. He drove Naur back into a wall of stone that had not crumbled. The three blades pierced the stone as easily as flesh, and in a flash of brilliant white light, bound Naur in place.

Naur struggled to free himself, straining at the base of Forsetae's blade. "No. How can this be? My plans will not be undone by a mere mortal." He let out a roar, glaring into Umhra's determined eyes, but could muster no venom.

The ritual is complete, we have succeeded in binding this fiend to Pragarus for all time. I have been redeemed. Thank you, Peacebreaker, it has been a privilege to fight at your side. Forsetae said.

Umhra's gaze shifted from Naur's contorted face to Forsetae's hilt protruding from his chest, which he still grasped in his left hand. "It's you I should be thanking," Umhra said aloud.

You still have a chance at salvation. Go to your fallen god.

Umhra released his grip and ran to Vaila's side. Having been drained of her godly powers, Vaila's form was now the size of a human woman. She lay face down in the red earth, her gown dancing in the persistent, arid breeze. Umhra dropped to his knees and rolled her over, resting her head on his lap. Moving the sweat-soaked hair from her face, he lifted the icon from around his neck. He placed it on Vaila's still chest, the pyramid's sapphire light flickering. His armor retracted.

Umhra closed his eyes, placed his hands on her forehead, and prayed. For several moments, there was no response, but then the pulsing of the pyramid became regular as if it were itself a beating heart. Vaila's eyes fluttered awake, the glow of the icon growing brighter, and her wounds healed. A tear streaked down Umhra's face.

"I knew you were my champion," Vaila said, sitting up and handing the icon back to Umhra. "I believe this is yours." She smiled.

Seeing Naur bound to the stone wall, she sighed. "It is done. My brother shall remain in Pragarus until the end of days. How I wish things would have been different."

"My deepest sympathies, my lady," Umhra said.

"He chose his path long ago. It is best this way. Tyveriel is safe."

"My lady, there is still the matter of the guardian souls. Is there anything you can do for them? Among them is a dear friend."

"And what of yourself?" Vaila asked, tilting her head and gazing into Umhra's eyes. She stood and extended to him her radiant hand. He accepted it and stood beside her, taller than her current form. "Is there no reward you seek for your efforts here today?"

"I would happily come with you and walk at your side. If you should want," Umhra said.

She looked up at him, her lonely black eyes wanting of such company. Without a word, she led Umhra over to the cloud of souls which continued to circle the portal, its pace slowed, calm. The spirits were no longer screaming, but weaving about one another in silence.

"I will take them with me. They passed before their time and will find peace among the gardens of Kalmindon," Vaila said. "But you I cannot take, as you ventured here of your own free will."

"I understand, my lady. It has been my honor to serve you," Umhra said, hanging his head.

"Your journey is not yet over, Umhra the Peacebreaker, Champion of Vaila, and all of Tyveriel. There is more to be written in your story. Alas, I must leave you here as I have been weakened and Kalmindon alone can restore me. Thank you for all you have sacrificed, and for your faith." Vaila said, taking Umhra's hand in both of hers and smiling.

She turned to the now pacified mass of souls, keeping hold of Umhra's hand. "My children, follow me, and I shall show you the meaning of tranquility." Vaila and the twelve thousand unfortunate souls vanished.

Umhra was left standing alone in Pragarus, another nugget of pure rhodium in his palm and a small group of devils flying toward him at a harrowing pace. He had no weapon with which to defend himself. His only chance was the portal which pulsed before him, its pattern now a haphazard convulsion of color.

CHAPTER 42

I shall send the Raptor's Grasp. They are the only ones I trust with a matter so delicate.
—The Collected Letters of Modig Forene

Letter to Stryke Modig dated 19th of Jai, 15 AF. Unearthed: Ruins of Vanyareign, month of Ocken, 1301 AT

—▲—

Gromley hoisted his war hammer over his head and swung it down upon Naur's Rune with a thunderous crash. He heaved the hammer back over his shoulder, revealing a crack spidering out across the entirety of the rune's metallic surface. The rune's glow intensified, the fissure growing in concert. He took a second stroke downward and shattered the rune, casting shards of rhodium across the sanctum. He scrambled to gather as many of the shards as possible to ensure such power would not again fall into evil hands, but the pure rhodium—enough for one hundred Suffusions—disintegrated into useless dust.

The cultists of the Brothers of Resurrection lay strewn across the room, their leader dead at Shadow's feet, his eyes still fixed on the portal he had labored for so long to construct. The rest of the Barrow's Pact tended to one another's wounds while Talus stood, peering into the portal, Aquila resting on his shoulder.

"Do you think he did it?" he asked.

"Not sure," Laudin said, Naivara wrapping his shoulder, "but I think we would know by now if he failed."

Talus nodded and turned away from the portal which crackled and hummed, holding Pragarus and Tyveriel together. To a thunderous roar, a beam of white light the full circumference of the portal shot into the air. Talus dove away from the surge, tumbling down the altar stairs. The energy slammed into the sandstone ceiling, which gave way under the tremendous force.

"We have to get out of here," Laudin said, the ceiling crumbling around them. "The entire complex is going to collapse." He helped Talus to his feet and they, along with Naivara and Nicholas, made for the exit of the inner sanctum, holding the door for Shadow and Gromley, who were still upon the altar.

Shadow and Gromley hurried down the stairs, a silhouette amidst the blinding light of the portal catching Gromley's eye. "It's Umhra," Gromley said to Shadow, shielding his eyes against the light, "I'm sure of it. We must get him out of there."

Shadow nodded, and both men jumped into the pit. The intensity of the portal destabilizing was barely endurable: the power tearing at their skin, the sound deafening, and the light blinding. Shadow and Gromley forced their way to the very center of the pit, where they found Umhra lying unconscious, Forsetae in its scabbard at his hip. They labored to drag him to the side of the pit. Together, they lifted him over its edge onto the altar floor. Shadow boosted Gromley up after him and then climbed out himself.

The power of the Portal of Pragarus, having riven the ceiling and the earth above, shot out into the heavens in release. The inner sanctum was collapsing around Shadow and Gromley who labored for the doorway, carrying Umhra between them. The smooth sandstone floor fractured, thrusting upwards, the upheaval causing a breach in the ground between them and their exit.

"Jump across and I'll throw him to you," Gromley said, the sanctum quaking.

Seeing their friends struggling to catch up, Laudin left the doorway and ran for Shadow. "Nicholas, we might need one of your miracles," he said over the din of the portal.

Nicholas reentered the room to Gromley throwing Umhra's unconscious body across a chasm in the ground to Shadow and Laudin. They dragged Umhra by his leathers toward the sanctuary door amidst the chaos. Gromley gauged the distance of the jump and shook his head, staring down into the abyss. The breach in the floor widened and the rest of the ceiling buckled overhead.

Nicholas held out his ringed hand and spoke inaudibly beneath the thunder of the imploding room. A black vortex grew before him as he spoke. Nicholas leaped into the hole, disappearing, and appeared in another vortex beside Gromley.

"Quickly now," he said, grabbing for his cleric friend. He grasped Gromley's hand and pulled him into the gateway which transported them both back to the doorway of the sanctuary.

"Thank you, mate. That was about to end very poorly," Gromley said, Laudin and Shadow catching up, carrying Umhra between them.

"We must get back to the horses," Talus said from the other side of the sanctuary.

The great statue of Naur shattered, its upper half crashing down upon the group as they ran across the sanctuary to Talus and Naivara. The entire subterranean temple, having stood since shortly after the discovery of Naur's Rune, was caving in on itself. The party dodged the falling debris and toppling pillars and dashed for the stables.

The horses were anxious, rearing in their stalls as the ground shook around them. The Barrow's Pact opened all of the stall doors, Gromley and Shadow hoisting Umhra's unconscious body up onto a sturdy chestnut stallion. Gromley climbed into the saddle behind him and cracked his reins. The others each mounted a horse of their own and urged the rest in the stable to run free.

Taking one look back at the imploding sanctuary of the Brothers of Resurrection, they raced to the tunnel leading back to the Gatekeepers' lodge. Never had they rode so fast, galloping through the passage as the ground gave in behind them, swallowing the remains of the second golem they had dispatched.

They outran the collapse, which quieted as the distance wore on, first diminishing to a minor quake, and then to an imperceptible tremor. Returning to the stable at the basement of the Gatekeepers' lodge, Gromley jumped down from his horse.

"A little help with our friend here?" he asked, struggling to drag Umhra down from the saddle.

Talus rushed to his aide and together, they lumbered through the basement of the lodge and up the stairs after their friends.

They burst out of the lodge into the cool night air of Meriden. The smell of smoke still hung in the air, although the storm had abated and the sky had cleared. Their horses were still gathered on the front lawn. The band of heroes collapsed on the dirt road in front of the lodge, exhausted from their feat. In the distance, in the direction of the forest, the great beam of radiant energy shot up to the star-filled heavens.

Several townspeople now gathered outside of their homes, staring up at the sky in disbelief.

"The end of days is upon us," said a young man from within the crowd as he pointed at the anomaly.

"No. It's over," a middle-aged mother said, clutching the two young children at her side. "The storm has cleared. Somehow, we've all been spared."

Indeed, they had.

CHAPTER 43

Vaila overruled her brothers and banished Naur to Pragarus. She returned, alone, to Kalmindon.
—The Tome of Mystics

Unknown Origin. Unearthed from the Ruins of Oda Norde, month of Bracken, 1320 AT

—▲—

Months passed, and life in Anaris carried onward, none the wiser as to what had happened north in Meriden. There were local accounts of an unprecedented occurrence and, for a while, talk of devils and sinister cults spread through the countryside. Some even reported seeing a streak of light tearing through the heavens from as far away as Lindamere and Ohteira. All of this eventually fell into lore, as nothing ever came of these matters. They were ultimately dismissed as an earthquake in Meriden that sunk the better part of the Lazarus Woods.

The Barrow's Pact kept close, as they waited for Umhra to awaken, but he remained unresponsive, in a comatose state. Nicholas had taken over primary responsibility for his half-Orc friend who only a few seasons ago had saved his life in the bowels of Telsidor's Keep.

Umhra was given quarters at the temple dorter by Lord

Morrow so Nicholas could be certain the man who saved Evelium from total annihilation would be looked after properly for the rest of his days, which everyone feared were few. Nicholas had requested he be given the room that used to belong to their friend, Balris Silentread. Despite being no different than the other rooms within the temple complex, Nicholas felt maybe, in some way, Balris would be present and help Umhra heal.

Nicholas visited several times per day, tending to Umhra's general upkeep, healing him, and singing and reading to him with the hope Umhra could hear him, and his voice would draw him to consciousness. He had arranged the room in a manner Umhra would find pleasing, placing his pyramid icon to Vaila beside his bed on a small table, the chain Nicholas had given him in a neat coil beside it, his leather armor displayed proudly on a stand in the corner next to the window, and Forsetae and his shield prominent on the wall above his bed.

As time passed, Umhra's physical body atrophied, the process slowed by some inner life force that kept him in much better condition than would otherwise be possible. His once strapping form was now gaunt, worrying Nicholas his time was running out. Nicholas sat beside his friend, pondering what was keeping him here, and for how long.

"Well, it's time for me to head downstairs. Today they are dedicating a statue to Balris above his grave in the courtyard of the temple, amongst the cloisters. The ceremony should prove to be a beautiful affair. Everyone will be here remembering him and celebrating his life," Nicholas said, standing from his chair and slinging his satchel over his shoulder.

The other members of the Barrow's Pact had remained in the proximity of Anaris as well, checking in on Nicholas and Umhra regularly, recovering from their journey to Meriden. Only Talus had left, returning to Vanyareign and King Shale Arving's side. This morning, however, he had come to Anaris in honor of Balris, who he often said he had grown to greatly admire and respect during their brief time together.

Laudin, Naivara, Gromley, and Shadow had all joined Talus, along with several members of the clergy, when Nicholas entered the courtyard. They exchanged pleasantries and caught up with each other while they awaited the beginning of the ceremony, Taivaron hopping to Nicholas's shoulder. Shortly after, Lord Espen Morrow arrived, arms linked with Lady Jenta Avrette. The members of Anaris's council followed them closely in procession. The last to arrive was Xavier Pell, who was dressed smartly, in a copper-colored velvet jacket and emerald-green pants.

"How is he today?" Pell asked Nicholas as he greeted him with a friendly handshake.

"The same, I am afraid. I won't give up on him, though."

"I know you won't Nicholas. He would never give up on any of us, and deserves the same in return," Pell said.

They all gathered around the statue at the center of the courtyard, currently covered in an oversized blue silk throw. Lord Morrow raised his hand, and the crowd grew silent. "We gather here today, to remember a hero, a trusted advisor, a man of faith, and a friend. Balris Silentread lived life as he preached, appreciating every day of his more than three hundred years, and surrounding himself with people of virtue. When I asked him to journey with the Barrow's Pact and Sir Umhra the Peacebreaker on, what at the time seemed a hopeless quest, he looked into my eyes, put his steady hands upon my shoulders, and simply said he would be honored. His selfless acts, unrivaled bravery, and endless kindness shall never be forgotten in Anaris, or throughout Evelium and the outer continents of Tyveriel. May he rest in peace, knowing he saved us all through his love and his actions."

Two guards stepped forward and removed the throw from over the statue, the silken material fluttering to the ground, revealing a perfect likeness of Balris made of pure white marble. "To Balris Silentread, long live his memory," Lord Morrow said.

"To Balris Silentread, long live his memory," the crowd said.

As Lord Morrow led the crowd in a round of applause, Nicholas stared up into the temple dorter and was greeted by the broad, yet weak smile of a familiar half-Orc, sitting at the window, enjoying the ceremony from the safe distance of the room he had slept silently in for months. Nicholas tugged on Laudin's vest and pointed up to the window where Umhra sat.

"The work of Balris, no doubt," Laudin said, calling everyone's attention to Umhra, who recoiled from the sudden attention. The Barrow's Pact held back, not wanting to offend the other guests by swiftly departing the ceremony for Balris, despite their excitement of seeing Umhra awake.

"Go to him," Lady Avrette said. "Balris would want you to be together."

Without further hesitation, they ran into the temple and up the dark wooden staircase to the living quarters above. They burst into the room, Nicholas leading the way, throwing himself at Umhra, embracing him.

"We've been waiting for you to awaken. What took you so long?"

"It would seem jumping between planes of existence leaves one quite lost upon return," Umhra said, his voice hoarse. He leaned over and hugged Nicholas from the chair where he sat.

The others gathered close, expressing their gratefulness for Umhra's return. The group, now reunited, remained together for some time, in the modest room Balris once called his own, content to be within each other's company. After an hour, there was a knock at the door. Laudin opened it and peered out into the hallway, blocking the visitor from seeing within the room. Then taking a step back, he opened the door wide, revealing the friendly face of Xavier Pell.

"Not to interrupt your reunion, but I thought Sir Peacebreaker would welcome some food and drink after his long sleep. Sir Peacebreaker, how do you fare? Seeing you awake warms my heart," he said, stepping into the room, followed by several platters of food carried by monks of the temple.

"I'm weak but pleased to be back amongst the living," Umhra said. "Thank you so much for thinking of me, Lord Pell. Would you care to join us?"

"I better not," Pell said. "I must be getting back to the orchard, but please come and visit me when you have the strength. I look forward to hearing your account of the journey to Meriden."

"It would be my pleasure, Lord Pell. Thank you again for your thoughtfulness."

Lord Pell excused himself from the room, bowing to each of the Barrow's Pact. "True heroes," he said, and then backed out of the doorway.

Again, they were alone. Umhra picked from the platters on the table. Nicholas, sitting by his side, continued to dote upon him as he did while he was incapacitated. "You were here every day. I owe you much in the way of thanks, Nicholas," Umhra said.

"Not all that long ago, you saved my life from a terrible end. Then you proceeded to jump into a portal to hell and saved us all from certain doom. It was the least I could do for you. Now, get some rest. There will be plenty of time to spend together. Lord Morrow, of course, will want to hear your story. We told him ours, but your side of the final battle is, of course, much sought after by us all. I'll hold him at bay as long as I can, to give you time to heal. I just want you to be prepared for his insistence."

"Please assure him I'll be happy to tell all, in time," Umhra said.

"We'll check in on you later, then. Allow yourself time to rest," Laudin said.

The group said their goodbyes and filed out of the room, leaving Umhra to rest.

▲

Umhra picked a small piece of roasted boar off one of the platters and hobbled over to the washbasin Nicholas kept fresh beside his bed. He disrobed, inspecting his emaciated, scarred body, and shook his head with a frown. He washed and, not without effort, put on a new set of clothes that had been neatly folded for him in the chest at the foot of his bed. From the chest, he also grabbed a small, blue velvet pouch nestled amongst his other belongings. He climbed upon his bed, emptying the contents of the pouch onto his lap.

He stared at the three sizable nuggets of pure rhodium, sighed. He closed them within the palm of his left hand, the glow of his icon on the table beside him intensifying.

"Thank you," he said. "I wish I could have returned with you. How wonderful I imagine life would be at your side. But I see you have more in store for me, and I accept your charge willingly. Maybe someday we shall be together again."

He laid back against his pillows and closed his eyes in prayer, a nascent blue light emanating from his closed fist. An unfamiliar sense of peace rushed over him, as though he wasn't alone, and never would be again. He focused on the rhodium—as well as his growing hunger would allow—and began the long process of his final Suffusion.

He sat for several hours, gently tumbling the smooth pieces of precious metal in his hand, their subtle clinking guiding his meditation. Thoughts rushed through his mind, passing as quickly as they arose. First, the image of his parents, their visage having faded with the years, and then of Ivory Lapping and his childhood at the temple in Travesty. His mind next jumped to the Bloodbound and the Barrow's Pact. Finally, his mind wandered to Pragarus where he held his god in his arms and resurrected her so she was able to return to Kalmindon with the souls the brotherhood had taken.

Grow your strength, my champion. Vaila's voice resonated in his head. *There will be ample time for us to commune as we heal. Only now does my light shine bright enough to awaken you as you did for me in the hells of Pragarus. How brave and selfless you were to meet me there among the devils. Go now, return to the living, be selfish, and recover.*

Umhra's eyes snapped open, returning to his room. He stood and lifted Forsetae from its mount on the wall. A familiar surge of warmth flooded his body—their connection renewed. In his compromised state, the blade was heavier than he remembered, but comfortable nonetheless.

"What a pleasant surprise to see you, my friend. It would seem we have both been given a second chance at life."

Yes. There is more for us yet to accomplish, Peacebreaker.

ACKNOWLEDGMENTS

When I set out to write Paladin Unbound, I had no idea the journey upon which I was embarking. I had no intentions of being a published author, just merely wanted to see if I could get a story that had been building in my mind for years out onto paper. The project was driven more by personal therapy than aspiration. As such, I am especially grateful to my amazing wife, Missy, for supporting me throughout the process, dealing with me only half listening to our conversations while I was lost in Tyveriel, and being my first editor, and the last person I see every night.

Every adventurer needs an adventuring party, and my sons, Wyatt, Owen, and Henry, are all that and more. I would particularly like to thank Wyatt, as I can attribute much of what became Shadow and Talus to characters he designed for our D&D campaign.

Paladin Unbound may have never seen the light of day if it weren't for my dear friend Kevin Fanning. I can't tell you how much I respect Kevin as a writer and, more importantly, as a wonderful human being. Kevin was the first person to read Paladin Unbound and, to my surprise at the time, encouraged me to pursue getting it published. I had no idea he would have had such a positive response to my little story, and can never thank him enough for being so selfless with his input and guidance.

The support that I have received from my mother, Madeline, and my sisters, Joyce and Jessica, has been overwhelming. They have always been my biggest fans and supporters, and their early reading of Paladin Unbound, constant enthusiasm for the book, and unbridled optimism for its future have fueled me through the most challenging times of this process...of which there were many.

I would be remiss to not acknowledge the wonderful people at Literary Wanderlust who have taken a big chance on an unproven author in a genre they have not historically published. Susan Brooks, my editor, has made Paladin Unbound a stronger novel than I ever could have on my own. Throughout the editing process, she pushed me to achieve more with my writing than I thought possible, and has become a close friend along the way. And she runs a great small press, the likes of which any writer would be lucky to work with.

Have you seen the cover of this book? Thank you to Ömer Burak Önal for bringing a pivotal moment in Umhra's journey to life. A special thanks also to Thomas Rey for creating a stunning map of Evelium. These two fantastic artists stepped in late in the process and put together two pieces of work that far surpassed anything I could have asked for. You both hold a special place in my heart.

Many other people deserve mention for their help and support in getting Paladin Unbound across the finish line. A special thanks to Kaitlyn Johnson for editing the query package that caught Literary Wanderlust's eye. The others (you know who you are) are the friends that regularly asked how things were going with the book without giving me strange looks when I began ranting about my half-Orc paladin and his adventures.

Finally, I would like to thank my father, Jeffrey L. Speight, Sr. While ALS claimed him before Paladin Unbound was contracted for publication, his advice and support throughout my life and up until his very last days sculpted the man that wrote it. I'd like to think that, somewhere, he is as proud of this accomplishment as I am.

ABOUT THE AUTHOR

Jeffrey Speight's love of fantasy goes back to an early childhood viewing of the cartoon version of *The Hobbit*, when he first met an unsuspecting halfling that would change Middle Earth forever. Finding his own adventuring party in middle school, Jeff became an avid Dungeons & Dragons player and found a passion for worldbuilding and character creation. While he went on to a successful career as an investor, stories grew in his mind until he could no longer keep them inside. So began his passion for writing. Today, he lives in Connecticut with his wife, three boys (his current adventuring party), three dogs, and a bearded dragon. He has a firmly held belief that elves are cool, but half-Orcs are cooler. While he once preferred rangers, he nearly always plays a paladin at the gaming table.

CPSIA information can be obtained
at www.ICGtesting.com
Printed in the USA
BVHW081343150721
612041BV00002B/125

9 781942 856764